Cry Ohana

Adventure and Suspense

in Hawaii

By

Rosemary & Larry Mild

Magic Island Literary Works • Honolulu, Hawaii • 2014

Cry Ohana

Copyright © **2010 by Rosemary and Larry Mild**
All rights reserved. No part of this book may be reproduced in any manner whatsoever without written permission except in the case of brief quotations embodied in critical articles and reviews. For further information please contact the publishers at:
roselarry@magicile.com

Second Edition 2014 Magic Island Literary Works.
Paperback   ISBN 978-0-9838597-8-9

First Edition—2001, Publish America
     Hardcover ISBN 978-1-4512-1270-9
     Softcover   ISBN 978-1-4512-1371-3
     Paperback ISBN 978-1-4512-4478-6
     Hardback ISBN 978-1-4512-6090-8

Printed in the United States of America by
Magic Island Literary Works.

Interior book design by Larry Mild.
Original Cover Design by Publish America
Reprint Cover alterations by Marilyn Drea, Mac-In-Town, Annapolis, MD.

Library of Congress Cataloging-in-Publication Data
Mild, Rosemary P. ; Mild, Larry M.

Mild, Rosemary P. ; Mild, Larry M.
ISBN 978-0-9838597-8-9

10 9 8 7 6 5 4 3 2 1

For our precious grandchildren—
Alena, Craig, Ben, Leah, and Emily, who
chase their own rainbows with gusto and courage

For our wonderful children—
Jackie and Myrna

For our marriage—soul mates, partners, lovers

Acknowledgments

We have so many people to thank, so many who took an interest in this enterprise. Our deep appreciation to:

Judith A. O'Neill. She did a masterful line-by-line final edit of the manuscript. But even more important, she gave us astute recommendations on how to sharpen the plot and deepen our characters.

Dr. M. Lee Goff, certified forensic entomologist.

Members of our former Honolulu critique group. **Al Izen, Martha Noyes, Susan Crystal**, and **Cathy Lee,** who gave us shrewd, yet encouraging wake-up calls on an early draft.

Alena Grace Lau, our granddaughter who generously read the manuscript at age fifteen and advised us on teenagers' behavior.

John and Ann Pollack, who dished out a stinging but loving assessment of the second draft. We took it sincerely to heart.

Millie and Ron Darby. They read the *Murdah is Foevah* draft and cheered us on. They corrected some of our environmental and local mistakes.

Myrna Sen, our close friend and Rosemary's Smith College classmate. She accompanied us to a Filipino restaurant in Honolulu to sample exotic dishes. She also fed us a steady diet of reference material on native Hawaiian flora and fauna and encouraged us to participate in the Great Backyard Bird Count (which we did at Magic Island).

The Honolulu Police Department, where we received patient answers to our very uninformed questions.

Professor Jonathan Osorio, Director, University of Hawaii at Manoa's Kamakakuokalani Center for Hawaiian Studies. His translation of the Lord's Prayer into the Hawaiian language proved most valuable, even though diacriticals and accents were omitted for this publication.

The University of Hawaii at Manoa Athletic Department that gave us information on the basketball teams.

Disclaimer

Cry Ohana is a work of fiction. Its characters, their names, and the events in which they are embroiled are entirely the products of the authors' imaginations. Any resemblance to actual events, businesses, or persons living or dead is purely coincidental. Most sightseeing venues, however, are the real thing and reflect our connection to and love of Hawaii as our adopted home. Please tolerate our literary license in loosely moving a few things about, creating some sites, and adjusting the layout of others purely for the convenience of our story.

The authors do recognize that many Hawaiian words contain diacritical marks and character accents, but have chosen to anglicize or otherwise simplify them for the ease of publishing and printing. The authors also acknowledge the many dialects and pidgin found in the islands, but, for the most part, have avoided them in the interest of smooth reading.

Table of Contents

* * *

Chapter 1
Death of a Rainbow
Honolulu, Hawaii, April 1972

HANK PUALOA leaped in the air and spiked the volleyball into a waiting two-hand block. He watched it spin out of bounds toward the picnic tables.

"Side out! Over here, hon!" Hank called from the makeshift court staked out with towels and sneakers in the grass.

Malia stopped the ball with her bare foot, and her husband loped over to retrieve it. But as he reached for it, she pressed down harder to get his attention. He snatched the ball out from under her foot and defiantly stood eye to eye with her, his craggy face brick-red from playing hard under the afternoon sun.

She scowled. "Hank, we gotta go."

"Your timing's lousy, Malia." He tucked the ball under one arm. "We're only behind by one point."

"It's never a good time for you. If you're not winning big you're desperate to get even. Believe me, it's time to quit."

Hank shrugged apologetically at the other players and sent the ball back to them with the impact of his fist. "What's your problem?" he muttered as they returned to the picnic table to get their belongings. The words slurred and his muscular bulk wobbled from a whole afternoon of drinking beer.

She grabbed his arm. "Look at that sky. We need to get going before we all get soaked." Turning her face away from his sour breath, her dark eyes glittered with controlled anger.

Mynah birds squawked overhead in the monkeypod trees like a quarreling family. Not that peace and quiet didn't exist in the Pualoa family. But Malia's mother, stubbornly tied to the old ways, lived with them. She believed that her side of the family descended from the *alii*, Hawaiian royalty. The mother interfered a lot and thought her daughter

1

could have made a better marriage for herself.

The Pualoa family had spent the day picnicking with three other families at Kakaako Waterfront Park. While infants and toddlers napped, older children roller-skated and biked along the promenade. Or, shrieking and giggling, slid down grassy knolls on flattened cardboard boxes.

The Pualoas were *kamaaina*, children of the land. They called the island of Oahu home, and on their island they felt protected. The Koolau and Waianae mountains watched over the locals, while the Pacific Ocean gushed up to embrace and nurture them. Hank and Malia were still sweethearts—most of the time. Only the boozing brought heated flare-ups between them. The more successful Hank's construction business became, the more he wanted to relax with a drink in his hand.

Malia shifted their eighteen-month-old son to her other hip and kissed his forehead. They called him Kekoa, "courageous one." With her free hand, she brushed back her bronze shoulder-length hair, revealing an oval face with wide-set eyes and sensual lips.

"Where's Leilani?" Hank asked.

Malia tilted her head seaward to where their four-year-old daughter sat on the low lava-rock wall, idly kicking her bare heels. Hank and Malia had named her Leilani, "heavenly child." She sat alone, daydreaming, taking refuge from her parents' argument.

By the time Malia had turned back toward the table, Hank had already hefted another paper cup to his lips. He drained the beer from the cup, crumpled it, and tossed it in the trash.

"That's enough, Hank. Don't you care about us?"

"You better believe I care about my *ohana*, my family. I bust my *okole* to make a living and keep us together."

"You do," she said. "You do, and I love you for it. But it's not getting any easier for me. Honey, your boozing's getting in the way."

"Don't be naive. When you work harder you gotta relax more. That's all. I work six days a week. Can't I have a day off and do what I want?"

Malia anxiously scanned the sky. A nearly full but oddly misshapen moon continued its ascent over the Koolaus. Was it her imagination or had she caught its pocked face leering at her?

Without warning, the clouds thickened, murky and threatening, as a squall rolled in from over the mountains. A rainbow appeared, a huge arm fighting its way through a hole in the clouds—but only a fragment of it, still deciding where, or if, to touch down. Another omen, she thought. But of what? Hope or doom? The first drops fell, catching them out in the open.

"Hank, get everything to the car!"

Malia reached down and bundled Kekoa to her shoulder. He squirmed a little, but dropped off again quickly. Leilani scrambled down from the wall and ran to help. She carried the straw beach mats and her mother's purse to the car.

The '62 Chevy Caprice wagon had seen better times. Patches of mustard-yellow primer bled through the maroon paint, and rust grew like an unforgiving weed along its seams, but no actual holes had appeared yet. The ceiling cloth over the front passenger seat sagged onto Malia's hair like a spider's web. She held the annoying veil up with one hand while facing the children in the back seat. Leilani whined.

"Shush, Leilani, you'll wake Kekoa."

"But he nap all the time. I got no one to play with."

"Sweetheart, that's what *keiki* do."

Hank arrived at the rear of the wagon, where he slammed the second ice chest up against the rear seat.

"Easy, Hank, you'll wake the baby."

"So?" he grunted from the way-back. He followed with a loud beery belch and an innocent grin.

"So! You want to hear *da kine* all the way home?"

Hank came around to the side, stuck his head in the driver's window, and rested it on his crossed arms. "Was one nice party, eh, sweetie?"

"Yeah, sure, nice party. You gettin' in? It's late. I wanna put the *keiki* t' bed."

"They one great bunch of *bruddahs*, eh? We talked story for hours. Went through one whole mess of brew. Sheesh, plenty strong stuff." His arms slipped off the window well, and he sat down hard on the paved parking lot. He swore.

"Hank Pualoa, that's no kind of talk for your daughter t' hear." Still sitting, he reached up and opened the driver's side door. "Hey, Malia, about time she know about the real world, eh?"

"I don't like that. You stop this right now."

"Gawd, you're beautiful when you're mad." He tried to get up using the car door as a prop, but it swung away, dropping him on his backside once more. He swore again and pulled himself up into the driver's seat. With a sheepish grin, he met her angry glare. "What now?"

"You gonna be able to drive us home?"

"Course! Drive better with a few belts under m' belt. Besides, you never learned to drive." He laughed, fiddling with the key until he found the ignition, and started the engine.

Malia reached over and turned off the ignition switch. The engine knocked and hissed to a halt. "We could wait here awhile. Maybe I should get you some coffee. You're in no shape to drive us anywhere."

"I thought you were in this great big hurry t' get home. Make up your mind."

"I am. I mean I was, but I want us to get there in one piece."

"Don't you worry none. Relax, I'm in good shape."

Hank restarted the car and revved the engine simply because he loved to hear it roar, and without waiting for the motor to warm, shot out of the parking lot onto Koula Street, burning rubber and scattering pebbles.

"Look out!" Malia yelled, but he continued to increase speed in the two blocks to Ala Moana Boulevard. She screamed, "Hank, the light, the light, it's red!"

He heard brakes screeching all around him in disaster's chorus. Thunks and crashing sounds came from everywhere. Metal crunched and bunched. The Chevy wove crazy-like, sideswiping a taxi and escaping the tangle in the eastbound lane. Somehow the station wagon entered the westbound lane toward home free of impact, but … a truck barreled toward them, toward her side, like a tank.

Leilani screamed, "Mommy-y-y!"

Chapter 2
Banished
Oahu, Hawaii, April 1972

PLAGUING HIM NIGHTLY and often during the day, the nightmare always ended with his daughter's piercing scream, "Mommy!" Once more, the prisoner's eyes exploded open to reveal the gray cement ceiling. His hair, face, and neck swam in sweat. Callused fingers slowly uncurled their grip on the steel rails of the prison bed.

Hank Pualoa lay flat on his back in the lower bunk of a cell in B block of Halawa prison, a space barely larger than a pickup truck. He wouldn't have minded the six-month sentence so much if he'd known Malia and the children would be there to greet him upon his release. But Hank had killed his *ui wahine*, his beautiful young wife, the mother of his two children. No, not murder, but he had killed Malia nevertheless and had to live with that knowledge for the rest of his life. Surely, guilt and remorse would punish him far more than any amount of jail time. By some miracle, Kekoa and Leilani had survived the car crash with only a few minor cuts and bruises. For now, they were safe with their widowed grandmother, *Tutu* Eme Waiwaiole. Malia had been Eme's only child.

Though the catastrophe had left Hank physically intact, his aching soul would not free him from that afternoon's calamity. He had destroyed his *ohana*, his family, and readily accepted all the blame. He could still hear the judge's voice reproaching him.

"Let this monster stand as an example for those who think they can get drunk and raise havoc on our roads. It is not enough that he be fined and set free. Simply not enough. Hank Pualoa killed his wife and recklessly endangered his children, leaving them without a mother. He also injured nine innocent strangers and wreaked thousands upon thousands of dollars in damages. He shall financially compensate the victims of this drunken rampage according to the schedule agreed upon

5

by the participating attorneys. It is also my judgment that this wretch sit in jail and contemplate the pain he has caused. Since his children are well cared for by their grandmother, I have no compunction about imposing the following sentence. Six months! And I'm probably being too lenient at that." The gavel slammed home to punctuate his decree.

Incarceration had not softened the muscular tone of Hank's six-foot, 210-pound build. Sure, a few more gray hairs now framed his wide, sun-browned face, weathered from two decades of construction work, but he still looked his thirty-seven years.

Hank drew up his legs as acid thoughts ate at his insides. His appeal for early release had been denied. Even worse, the children's grandmother refused to bring them to visit him, despite his repeated pleadings. Today was his eighth week in prison and still no word from her. Last Sunday's visitor, his brother, had promised to intercede for him. He prayed that Eme would relent. It was hard for anyone to deny Big John anything. They called him Big John as much for his tremendous heart as for his six-foot-six height and 300 pounds.

A voice outside the cell jarred Hank from his thoughts. He looked up to find a uniformed corrections officer standing at the steel bars outside his cell.

"Hey, Hank Pualoa! Get up! You got visitors." The guard waited for the master solenoid to release the cell group lock. The steel rammed against the stops, and a clanging metallic echo returned from some distant chamber. Hank swung his feet to the floor and sat upright as the guard slid away the steel bars between them.

The guard and another uniformed officer ushered him to the visitor control room. Short, squat windows just below the ceiling provid-ed the only natural light. A dozen wood and steel picnic tables filled the large, yellow-walled room. Before the officer could say table five, Hank spotted Eme seated there, holding his toddler son on her lap.

A shock wave hit him when he saw his children. It had been only eight weeks, but already they looked older and more serious. Kekoa's face was freshly scrubbed, his black hair combed in a fringe across his forehead. Dimpled fingers busily plucked at the ruffled sleeve of Eme's muumuu. Leilani sat on the bench beside Eme. Her fists were jammed into the pockets of her favorite dress, the blue one with white plumerias that Malia had bought for her last birthday. She buried her face in her grandmother's heavy arm. The child's dark, soulful eyes, so like her mother's, peeked out at him.

The guard stood with his back to the wall fifteen feet away, his body relaxed, his gaze benign. Hank knew the rules: he had to stay on his side of the table and keep his hands in view.

"Papa!" Kekoa squealed. "Papa, Papa, Papa!" He kicked his bare feet, squirming to climb down from his grandmother's lap. Eme held him loosely about the waist. Kekoa stiffened his chubby body and slipped to the floor. Hank knelt beside the bench on his side and stretched out his arms. Kekoa lurched forward and threw himself into his father's huge embrace. They rocked from side to side as they hugged. Then Kekoa wriggled away and climbed up on the bench on Hank's side. His father slid in beside him and encircled him with one arm. Kekoa nuzzled against his father's chest, settling in for a lifetime.

Reluctantly, Hank glanced over his shoulder at the guard and detected a flickering smile, a sympathetic nod. Meeting his gaze, the guard held out upturned palms and shrugged as if to say "Sorry, man, it's not my rule." Hank got the message—the guard wanted the boy back on the other side of the table.

"Go sit with *Tutu*, sweetheart," Hank whispered. He kissed the baby's forehead, then gently nudged him off the bench. *Tutu* scooped him up as thrashing little legs protested.

Hank felt triumphant. His son remembered him, and his mother-inlaw somehow hadn't denied him. Her creviced, nut-brown face looked polite, even pleasant.

Leilani straightened up and stared at her father. Hank gave her a loving smile and leaned over the narrow table to kiss his four-year-old daughter. But she shrank back and again buried her face in Eme's *muumuu*.

Hank slumped to the hard bench. Seeing the precious moments slip away, he tried hard to start a conversation. "You guys are shooting up like bamboo. I hardly recognized you." But even the simplest question he asked wound up with one-word answers or silence. Still, Hank wasn't discouraged; what was left of his family had come together again. He turned to Eme. "I'm sure grateful to you for bringing the kids." He looked into her ancient eyes and saw no animosity there. *It's going to be all right,* he thought.

"Hanale Kalahanohano Pualoa." Eme called him by his full Hawaiian name. His fingertips turned cold. The passive, tolerant

7

expression remained fixed, but her voice bore a jagged edge. "You take one *nui* look at your two innocent *keiki* without a mother—a big, long look at these two angels, 'cuz you're never gonna see 'em again." She paused to scrutinize Hank's face; to see if she had inflicted all the pain she intended. The hint of a cruel smile reflected the measure of her success.

"Papa!" Kekoa sobbed, sensing the menace in Eme's sudden outburst.

Eme hefted the baby to her shoulder and stepped over the bench. The orange and blue birds of paradise on her *muumuu* swallowed him up. She waited only long enough for Leilani to slide out, grabbed her by the hand, and marched them straight through the outside visitors' door. Eme's harsh voice had silenced Kekoa, but now that he was being carried away, he began sobbing again, his wails reverberating down the outer hall.

Hank had to consciously close his hanging jaw. The guard tapped him softly on the shoulder and led him back to his cell, where he dropped down on the hard bed. With elbows on knees, he held his head in his hands, knowing he could never hold it high again.

Eme's words continued to dig deep into his gut. *Could she be right? I don't deserve to be their father. What I wouldn't do for a drink right now.*

* * *

On a Thursday morning late in November, Hank Pualoa became a so-called free man. His mind made up and his purpose clear, he would sever all ties to the island. He dared not disrupt the continuity and loving relationships his children had established with their *Tutu* Eme. He wanted what was best for them. They didn't seem to need him or any more conflict in their lives. He would spend only four more hours on Oahu, just long enough to pay a visit to a lawyer friend and sign off on a trust fund he'd created for his children. His destination was Seattle, but even that would be only temporary.

Chapter 3
Kekoa's Nightmare
November 1982...Ten Years Later

KEKOA PUALOA sat high up in the cab of the Caterpillar bulldozer, jiggling all the locked-down levers protruding through the floorboards. His legs couldn't quite reach the pedals, so he just went through the motions of clutching, revving up, and stomping down on the brakes. Not that he was short. Kekoa had actually grown quite tall, lean, and agile for his twelve years. His dark brown hair tickled his neck and one cheek, and he frequently brushed it back with one hand. Very much a loner among his young male peers, the boy preferred to pal around with his father's brother and business partner who lived next door. Uncle Big John willingly filled the role of father figure in Hank's absence. Their weekends together were made for boating, fishing, and boogie boarding.

Kekoa often played in this construction shed with its corrugated steel roof, dirt floor, and no doors. The huge yellow Cat had become his secret plaything—big guys' fun. Kekoa imagined the Cat's powerful, thrusting movements and his masterful control over tremendous mounds of earth that lay waiting before him. He'd become one with the machine and had even improvised a chorus of noises to accompany every mechanical juncture.

Proud of himself, Kekoa played until his stomach growled—he'd overstayed the supper hour. His impatient grandmother wouldn't know where to find him. With the arrival of the damp evening air, he'd gladly trade this high adventure for some of *Tutu* Eme's pork *lau-laus* and steaming white rice.

From the equipment shed in the backyard, Kekoa looked out at a long gravel driveway that separated two single-walled wooden houses. He lived in the forest green one to his right. His uncle, Big John Pualoa, owned the gray one on the other side. Both homes were in Ewa on the southwest shore of Oahu, only a quarter mile from the massive sugarcane fields.

A pounding of unexpected footsteps broke the silence. Kekoa shrank down to hide as Uncle John strolled into the shed and began collecting tools. The boy remained motionless. If discovered, he'd be disciplined for playing on the dangerous equipment.

He peered down at Big John. Kekoa didn't remember his real father, only an image and a hatred; one burned into his mind by his sister and grandmother. He guessed his uncle's kindness and their closeness had something to do with John being lonely himself. His wife had run off with a rich Mainlander two years earlier. Big John saw to it that *Tutu* and her charges never wanted for anything.

The clinking and clanking of tools muffled the footsteps of a second figure entering the shed behind Big John. In the dusky light of the interior, Kekoa couldn't see who it was. The silhouette loomed large and carried what appeared to be a garden shovel. The shovel clunked against the frame of the open shed.

Big John spun around and shouted, "What the devil are you sneaking up on me for? Haven't you caused enough damage already?"

"Hey! I got your memo about the cash I withdrew, and it ain't what you think, John. It was only a loan. If you weren't so generous, giving all our profits to the old lady and Hank's brats, there'd be a lot more draw from the business for the two of us, and I wouldn't have to keep borrowing all the time. After all, he doesn't contribute anything anymore. It ain't like he's a full partner or anything."

"We owe my brother, man. Without Hank's initial cash, there wouldn't be any business or profit to divvy up. Besides, they're *ohana*."

"Your family, Big John, not mine. If you want to be so good to them, do it out of your share."

"You're an ungrateful son-of-a-bitch and you've crossed the line this time. Why don't you sell that damned airplane you're always puttering around with?"

"Flying is my relaxation, and it's my business what I do with my free time."

"Not when it sucks the blood out of our business."

"All right, all right! It's only a loan. I'll pay it back. I'm good for it."

"Ten thousand dollars? That's some loan. Don't bullshit me. I know what's been going on. All the other times you messed around with the books—five thousand here, three thousand there. Funny, I don't remember your paying back those loans."

"Why, you overstuffed bag of horse crap. You accusing me of cooking the books?"

Big John rose to his full height and threw his huge shoulders back. "You could say that. I got news for you. The game's over. I had the books audited last week. Maybe you'd like to talk to the cops and explain all those phony entries to them. And to think I trusted you all these years. I shoulda…"

John was still talking, his arms full of tools. The burly man facing him suddenly lunged forward and swung the shovel like a samurai's sword.

Kekoa heard a great thud. A bellow of pain. A second and third thud. Big John's tools clattered and clanged to the floor. The boy watched in stunned horror as his uncle swayed forward and collapsed in a heap on top of the sledge, pry bar, level, and rake. Afterward—silence. The dark figure slipped out of sight for several seconds and then reappeared in the doorway. Kekoa saw the shovel raised high to strike once more, but didn't. The figure disappeared again.

Kekoa heard digging sounds outside the wall of the shed, where the wooden forms for a new walkway had been staked into the ground. He wanted to scream, but held his hands over his mouth to squelch any sound. Two distinct noises emerged, making it easy to distinguish the scraping and rasping of the shovel from the pinging of the pick just beyond the wall. The digging lasted a long time. Then the attacker returned and slowly dragged Big John out of the shed. More shovel sounds erupted, closer together now.

The boy watched the dark figure return to put away the pick and shovel. Kekoa tried again to hold his breath and conceal his presence. He closed his eyes tight as if that would make all the horror go away.

Just at that moment he heard his sister calling him in for supper. "Kay-koh-ah!" The voice, elongating the syllables, came from the front lanai. "Kekoa!" This time it cracked out like a bullwhip.

Her loud and angry tone surprised him, causing an involuntary "Oh-oh" to escape from under his breath. The silence that followed seemed cavernous, so full of his echoing presence, and finally, he had to

11

breathe once more. His stomach gurgled aloud. Surely that would give him away. The boy cowered, hoping he had imagined his own telltale sounds and that the large lurking figure had not heard him.

The Cat's right-side door rattled. Its lock held. Then a hairy arm thrust itself into the cab above the half-door. A large hand with sausage fingers grabbed at the space only inches from him. Two fierce gray eyes zeroed in on the boy. Kekoa slid to the floor of the cab and cringed in the opposite corner, leaning hard against the left-side door, trying to make himself invisible. Once more the hairy arm swiped across the cab to grab him. Kekoa pressed harder against the side door, causing it to pop its catch. He tumbled backward five feet to the dirt floor of the shed, and landed on his backside. Without hesitating to see if he'd hurt himself, the boy scrambled to find his legs and bolted out of the shed. Pivoting around the corner, he dashed to the rear of the shed, climbed up the adjacent chain link fence, and leaped onto the corrugated steel roof. He scooted noisily along the edge until the roof ran out.

He looked down. Jumping to the ground would put him in the next yard behind the shed. But it was a ten-foot drop. A shuffling of shoes on the roof close behind warned him not to stop and look back. He jumped.

In the distance, Leilani still called, more urgently now.

The pursuer dropped to the grass and groaned. Rubbing his ankle, he swore.

Kekoa dashed through the neighboring yard, up the sloped driveway to the street beyond, up another driveway on the opposite side, and around the basement of a house that stood on concrete block pillars. Lattice-work with screening covered the dark basement around the four sides of the house. Kekoa darted into the open basement door at the rear and ran to the front screen to catch a view of his pursuer. The boy didn't need to see the man's face to know him. The gravel-voiced shouts and accusing eyes that Kekoa had feared so much in the bulldozer cab belonged to Red Murphy, his father's other partner in the construction business.

From his hiding place, Kekoa saw Red lurch to a stop and scan the deserted street. Then he limped away. As soon as Murphy disappeared around the corner, the boy retraced his own steps to the yard behind their shed and climbed a heavy-limbed winter mango tree. Through its bushy cover, he had a clear view of the yard beyond. The overripe fruit on the ground gave off a rotting, sweet odor.

Perched in his leafy treetop vantage point, Kekoa watched Red hobble into Big John's yard. Red picked up a short section of a four-by-eight post and began to tamp the ground where he'd buried Big John. After ten minutes of continual pounding, Red left and returned with a garden rake. He smoothed over a long bulge in the dirt between the one-by-eight wooden forms alongside the building. Concrete for a new walk was to be poured into the forms the next morning. Once again, Red picked up the post and pounded the remaining mounds level with the ground, leaving a totally smooth surface with only a few slight post marks. He put away the tools and hobbled toward the street, where he'd left his red and white Buick Regal.

Kekoa waited in the tree to be sure Red wouldn't return. Then, dropping to the ground, the boy scaled the chain link fence into Big John's yard. He crossed the expanse and counted the four cement foundation blocks from the shed front to his uncle's burial site. Not noticing that he'd left footprints between the walkway forms, Kekoa continued cautiously to the street to check that Red had really gone. Satisfied, he walked around to the rear of his own house, where he climbed in through the window of his first floor bedroom.

He'd barely set foot on the floor when a hand grabbed him by the ear, twisted it, and yanked him painfully across the room to the light switch. Blinding white light suddenly filled the room.

"Where you been?" *Tutu* Eme cried. "You think I run some fine hotel fo' rich *haole* tourists here? Your rice and *lau-lau* got cold and went dried out. I make special dinner fo' you and you no like come home. Just you get t' bed, and I no want t' hear 'nother word outtah you, boy." With that, she let go of Kekoa's throbbing ear and stormed out of his room, slamming the door behind her.

Kekoa started for the door, wanting to follow and tell her the truth, but she was so angry, he doubted she'd believe him. He couldn't go to the cops by himself. He knew Red had lots of buddies on the police force. He'd seen them hanging out and drinking together a number of times. The cops liked Red, especially when he entertained them with those sleight-of-hand card tricks. He was slick. They'd never take his word over Murphy's. Red might even convince the cops that Kekoa had killed his own uncle. And what would Red do if he thought Leilani and *Tutu* knew the truth?

The boy dropped onto the bed and slept an uneasy night, still in his shorts and T-shirt, turning over and over like *Huli Huli* chicken on a spit. Hunger clawed at his stomach.

He awoke to a strong morning sun and the grinding, whirring sounds of heavy machinery. The cement truck! Cautiously peering out the window, he could see the huge rotating cylinder in Big John's yard. A long chute spewed out gray cement, filling the space between the wood forms. He saw three of Big John's men hunched over the site, one pushing the mix with a shovel and two more working the concrete smooth as they slid a board back and forth across the top of the forms.

Kekoa watched, transfixed. Suddenly a shadow rounded the corner of the house. He backed uneasily away from the window, but not quickly enough. Red's face appeared, fierce and full, and Kekoa fell backward, his feet churning under him as he tried to regain his balance. He scrambled through the house and out the front door.

He reached the street about ten steps ahead of Red, when one of the three workmen yelled, "Hey, Red Ed! Where's Big John? He's got to sign for all this cement."

Red stopped and turned to respond.

Kekoa took advantage of Red's moment of distraction and ran and ran—out of the neighborhood. But where to? He could think of only one sure place to hide: the acres and acres of tall cane fields a few blocks away. Now that he had a goal, he picked up speed and sprinted, every so often snapping his head around to see whether Red was following. He wasn't. Kekoa's legs felt heavy now. He panted, struggling for distance, fighting for breath in the sultry morning heat. Almost there.

Darting into the cover of the yellowing cane stalks, he sat down hard and buried his face in his knees. The rough, spiky stalks of sugarcane irritated the backs of his thighs—leaving his limbs full of tiny scratches. He shuddered as he felt something crawl up his bare leg. A black, fat, hairy centipede crept along the skin of his calf. A flick with the back of his hand sent the eight-inch, poisonous creature tumbling through the air before it could bite him.

* * *

Wanting to remain close to those he loved, but far enough away to guarantee his safety from Red Murphy, Kekoa endured two nights in the cane fields. He had never spent much time away from *Tutu* Eme and

14

Leilani. When he had, it had been a pleasant experience—a camping or fishing trip with Big John, or even spending the night at his place.

Kekoa's whole body vibrated with anger. Life just couldn't exist without his uncle. He fought a strong temptation to return home, and a few times he actually came close, creeping back to the neighborhood. Maybe the whole thing hadn't happened, he tried to tell himself. But each time he spotted the old Buick, reality returned. He observed that now Red sometimes stayed overnight in Big John's house. He might even be lying in Big John's bed, waiting for Kekoa to show up.

Late on the third afternoon, Red's car had gone, and Kekoa managed to climb inside his bedroom window as he'd done so many times before. *Tutu* Eme and Leilani weren't home. He raided the refrigerator, wolfing down large quantities of leftovers: sweet potatoes, poi, a chunk of roast pork—and gulping a half-quart of cold milk.

After stuffing a plastic bag with bread, Spam, and cereal, Kekoa grabbed a piece of paper to write them a note, but he pressed so hard, the pencil point broke. While shaving another point with a paring knife, he heard a car in the gravel driveway between the houses. The pencil and paper fell to the floor. Grabbing his plastic bag, he climbed out the bedroom window and fled.

* * *

The cane field made a lousy bed, cold and damp. Kekoa found that bunching the dry cane leaf and rubble in close about him created a half-decent blanket of insulation and cushioning. But the third night it drizzled, and he felt a crushing despair in the complete darkness. He did not want to run away. It sickened him to think of breaking ties with the only family he had. More than once he'd heard Leilani's voice calling to him. And he liked the idea of raiding the kitchen at will. But he knew he couldn't live in the cane fields forever like a hunted animal. Just yesterday, he had had to avoid two policemen walking the ditches, searching for him. And he was reminded constantly that the plants were infested with centipedes, spiders, and mice.

Besides, the fields were about ready for burning. The field hands would soon come to burn off the excess dry rubble, leaving the moist, sturdy stalks behind for harvesting by the cane haul trucks. It would be only a matter of days before this field would be ablaze. By his calculation, he had another three or four days at most and then he'd have to clear out for sure. But it could happen sooner, much sooner.

On the fourth night, sleep eluded him for many hours, and he awoke late in the gray morning. Lying amid the cane stalks, he lazily stretched out his limbs and yawned. His nose felt itchy and irritated. Then he smelled smoke. He found this no cause for immediate alarm; he knew that the odor of fire borne on the gentle trade winds carried for miles.

Kekoa first sensed real danger when he heard the whip-like crackling flames consuming the rubble—reaching, bridging, and claiming more and more with their insatiable appetites. Ducking his head to escape the drifting smoke, he ran away from the likely source of the flames. Some of the stalks towered two to three feet above him, and he realized that he had mistakenly moved toward certain peril. The smoke thickened. Kekoa stopped to cough, and suddenly the brittle crackling sounds grew ominously louder, the heat more intense. He even heard men's voices, but not what they said or the traditional ditty they sang. Other noises loomed louder, more dangerous.

He tried to check his bearings, but every direction looked the same—no way to be sure that he'd been running in a straight line. Which direction led to the road? His whole body broke into a cold sweat, and his eyes stung with the thickness of smoke mixing with salty tears.

Looking up, the boy found an answer in the smoke itself. He remembered that cane field fires were intentionally set to take advantage of a downwind burn. Barely a hundred yards away, a small army of field hands tended the flames, first coaxing, then skillfully containing them. The smoke streamed toward him, so he turned and ran away from the burn along with both wind and smoke. He found it tough going, hardly able to see in any direction but up, and his feet kept tripping in the tangle of fallen and bent cane stalks.

Kekoa hadn't figured on reaching the irrigation ditch nearly so fast. He fell headlong into it with a splat. Standing in waist-high tepid water, the boy saw a fifteen-foot firebreak on the opposite side of the ditch. He knew exactly where he was: the ditch and firebreak ran perpendicular to the state road. Gasping for breath, he waded his way to the main road.

The sound of rushing water grew louder and louder as he approached safety. At last he saw the pipes filling the ditch with sparkling liquid straight from the water mains. He immersed his whole body. Standing again to feel the full force of the cooler water, he let it beat against him. Then he drank.

When the water had sufficiently purged the black smoke from his body and clothes, and his breath felt cleansed of soot, he dragged himself out of the ditch, across the main road, and into another cane field a couple hundred yards away, a field he knew was not yet ready to be burned. There, in the privacy of the tall stalks, Kekoa shed his T-shirt and shorts, spreading them out to dry while he lay down to rest and breathe deeply the cleaner windward air. He slept.

His growling stomach woke him, and he scowled, remembering the food stash from *Tutu* Eme's kitchen that he'd carelessly dropped in the burning field. The blistering sun had dried his clothes and the paper cash in his pocket. He counted $12.63 total. Hurriedly, he dressed and made his way back to the road. Now he would try his hand at hitching a ride to Pearl City along the road rimming the Pearl Harbor Lochs. He put out a thumb, and after a few cars had ignored him, a Dodge Dart pulled off the road onto the red clay shoulder. He ran to it. Twenty minutes later his ride dropped him off on Kam Highway. He saw commercial activity there—a dry goods store, a gas station, fast food joints, law offices, a dentist, car dealers, a grocer—and farther down the block, maybe an opportunity for work.

Sizing up his new surroundings, Kekoa decided to try a fast-food restaurant. The manager gave him a sour look. "What're you doing here, kid? They expel you from school?" Kekoa wheeled about and left. Next, he tried a gas station. The mechanic on duty snarled, "Get outta here," and threw a greasy rag after him.

The boy approached a used car showroom down the block. Just beyond the glass door, he found a middle-aged *haole* woman sitting behind a large wooden desk. She wore granny glasses and her matted blonde hair looked like shredded wheat.

"Good morning, hon. What can I do for you?"

"I, uh..." Kekoa hadn't expected such a warm greeting. "I...I look for work," he blurted out. He managed to produce an appealing smile.

"Well, now, young man, I suppose you want to become the youngest used car salesman in the islands?"

"No, ma'am, but I can sweep, clean up, empty trash, even wash cars."

She pressed a button on the intercom box. "Hey, Oscar, ya got a minute?"

"What's up, Edie?" the box answered.

"Come on out. I'd like you to meet someone." The box made a thud as her finger slipped from the button.

"What's your name, hon?"

"Kekoa."

"Kekoa what?"

"Just Kekoa," he replied. The door behind Edie swung open and a heavy man strode toward the desk.

"Oscar," said Edie, "this is Kekoa. He wants a job doing anything."

"Yes, sir, I can sweep, empty trash, and wash cars, too."

"Hmm." Oscar's hand went to his chin. "Wash cars, huh?"

"I'll do a good job, too, even windows."

"He does windows?" cracked Edie. "I sure could use you at home, hon."

"Hmm," Oscar repeated. "You're too young to put on the regular payroll, but if you'll give me three hours every day after school, I'll give you twelve dollars a day cash to wash the cars out front. There's seventeen of them out there now. Sometimes more, sometimes less. What do you say to that, Kekoa?"

"I can start right now, Mr. Oscar. *Mahalo*! You not be sorry. *Mahalo*, you too, miss."

"Oscar, you skinflint," she said, half under her breath.

Oscar walked to the open key rack on the wall and reached up for a key. "This is for the utility shed out back. You'll find everything you need there, son."

Kekoa took the key and went out the glass door. This time he noticed the sign, USED CARS TO DA MAX, and under it, HAPPY OSCAR FRUNKE, PROPRIETOR.

So Kekoa went to work for Happy Oscar's Used Cars, showing up at three each afternoon and quitting anywhere from 6:30 to eight in the evening, depending on the number of cars out front. The first night he slept in the utility shed, but the acrid detergent smells made him sick to his stomach. So the next night he left a rear door to an Olds Delta 88 unlocked and returned to it after closing time. The velvety upholstery welcomed his tired young body.

For the next three months, no one discovered his sleeping accommodations. He picked up a series of odd jobs from nearby merchants to occupy his mornings and settled into a routine. He ate heartily at any number of saimin soup places in the strip malls along Kam Highway. He even acquired a new blanket and a few clothes— underwear, shorts, T-shirts. Above all, he avoided strangers, lest one of them be a police officer; or worse, someone who'd report his whereabouts to Red. He thought often about going home. Kekoa tried phoning his grandmother, but her phone was only an extension of the business number in Big John's office. Each time Kekoa tried, Red picked up first.

* * *

The luminous clock face in the showroom window displayed the time as 10:15 p.m. Slipping into the Olds, Kekoa set his new gym bag on the rear floor and lay down on the seat, pulling his blanket around him. He closed his eyes and had slept no more than a couple of hours when he awoke. He wasn't sure why until he heard voices.

"Gimme da slim-jim, *bruddah.*"

"Okay, but keep quiet, fer crissake," a second voice whispered.

Kekoa continued to lie there, unnoticed and trembling. He saw a long, flat shaft of metal with a mess of grooves in its edges slide down the outside of the driver's side window into the door itself. It squeaked against the glass and clacked as its grooves were fitted to the task of lifting the door latch. Kekoa silently prayed for the would-be thieves to fail and leave, but he knew better. He hastily gathered his few things and stuffed them into the gym bag. No room for his new blanket. As the front door sprang open, Kekoa released the opposite rear door and took off, running as fast as he could. He had surprised the car thieves. The bolder of the two started to pursue him until the other called out, "Hey, bruddah, give it up. Let's get the hell outta here."

Kekoa had traveled so far out of earshot that he didn't know the thieves had left. He spent the rest of the night sleeping behind the shed out back and left at the usual time the next morning. That afternoon when he returned to work, he looked for the key to the shed. It was gone. He entered the showroom and checked the key rack for a spare. Again, there was none. He heard a voice behind him.

"Are you looking for this, son?"

Kekoa turned to face a somber boss who held out the shed key. He nodded. "Musta lost it, Mistah Oscar."

His huge boss loomed over him "I'm very disappointed in you,

19

son. I had to call the cops in. They found the key in the back seat with a blanket. They also found the slim-jim you used to break into the car. I thought I could trust you. You seemed to be a hard worker. I even thought of giving you a raise."

"But I didn't break in, Mistah Oscar," Kekoa protested. "Was *moke* guys, two tough guys."

"What two guys? Don't start lying now on top of everything." Oscar grabbed Kekoa's arm and forced him into Edie's chair. She had been standing behind the boss. Kekoa charged toward the door, but Oscar blocked his path.

"Have a heart, he's only a kid," Edie pleaded. "Let 'im go."

Oscar frowned, picked up the phone, and started to dial the police.

"Please stop him, Miss Edie. I never broke in. I left it unlocked from earlier. I didn't need to break in. I been sackin' out in one of the cars ever since I been here. Please, Miss Edie. I never hurt nothin'. Two guys broke in while I was sleepin'. Honest!"

Oscar Frunke continued to dial. "Don't give me that crap. You're a delinquent, a thief, and you belong in jail."

Chapter 4
Out of the Frying Pan?

EDIE SIDLED to the front of the desk, slowly pulling her secretarial swivel chair behind her. As Oscar's finger savagely dialed the numbers, she whispered to Kekoa: "Make a move for the door when I tell you." She placed her hands on the back of the swivel chair and, inch by inch, pushed it between her boss and the boy.

Oscar gruffed into the phone. "I want to report an attempted robbery."

Edie slammed the chair into Oscar's knees.

"Now!" she cried. Kekoa raced for the door.

"What the hell!" Oscar bellowed. He dropped the phone and turned to chase Kekoa. Edie stood there ready to ram his knees again. They eyed one another, and then, in self-defense, he slumped down into the attacking chair.

Edie picked up the dropped receiver and said, "Sorry, Officer, it's all been a mistake." She hung up.

From the safer side of Kam Highway, Kekoa looked back and saw that he wasn't being followed. He stood there for a moment and waved at Edie. Then, gripping his precious gym bag tightly, he hurried eastward, turned left at the corner, and disappeared from their sight.

"Oscar Frunke, you know damn well that angel-faced boy did you no harm. All he wanted was a place to lay his head at night. You've had cars broken into before. Did they ever leave their tools behind? No. I figure they found the kid in the back seat and ran scared. Kekoa must've got frightened off, too."

Oscar ran a hand through his greasy hair. "I guess you're right, woman. Damn it, you always are. Now I gotta find someone else to wash cars."

"You're all heart, Frunke. You ever think about anybody but yourself?" she reproached, shaking her head. "What about the boy?

21

What about him?"

* * *

Panting, his heart still pounding like a sledgehammer, Kekoa slowed his pace. He walked with his head down, wondering where to go from here. Everything he had tried had led to a dead end or worse. The early afternoon sun stung his eyes and beat its punishing rays down on the back of his neck. He walked for an hour until he found the next eastbound ramp to the H-1 freeway.

It was hard to stand on the ramp without getting run over. He positioned himself among the weedy grasses and a litter of fast food wrappers. A McDonald's soda cup reminded him of how thirsty he was. He extended his thumb until he felt his arm could hold it up no longer. Finally, a panel truck pulled up on the shoulder. The young Asian driver offered him a ride to Chinatown and hummed to himself the whole trip without speaking a word. But as he dropped Kekoa off, he said, "You should go home, kid."

At the corner of Hotel and Maunakea streets, neither the near-gridlocked traffic nor the lunchtime crowds milling about took any notice of the forlorn newcomer. The sweet scent of plumerias floated from lei shops. He walked on until the pungent smell of steaming dim-sum overtook him. Stepping into an alley, he glanced right and left to make sure he was alone and cautiously pulled out his wallet to check his funds. He had $143.12 left. At the Noodle Cafe carry-out window, he counted out $4 for a Styrofoam container of saimin and three steamed dumplings filled with pork, fish, or beef. He leaned against an old Ford sedan parked at the curb and ate the soft noodles with wooden chopsticks. Upending the container, he drained the savory chicken, onion, and egg broth. Tucking two of the dim-sum into his bag for later, he nibbled on the remaining beef dumpling as he strolled aimlessly through Honolulu's Chinatown.

When he came to the Chinese Cultural Plaza, he sat down on the low rock wall that ran along the Nuuanu Stream. He'd been here before. The plaza in front of him conjured up memories of lions, dragons, and fireworks. Its shops always smelled of steamed dough, shoyu, and Chinese spices—he could still hear the clang of gongs in his mind's ear. Staring at the mountains, he discovered a huge double rainbow, one spectrum arching above the other. The two rainbows reminded him of something Big John had once said. They had been out walking after

22

supper when a rainbow touched down across the cane fields.

"How far can a rainbow reach?" Kekoa had asked. Big John had put his arm around him and answered, "If a rainbow comes down to touch you, it'll take you anywhere you want to go—as far as your dreams, boy. And you can be anything you want to be."

As he sat on the rock wall, nostalgia filled the boy's mind, and he swallowed hard. How far, he asked himself, how far would he have to run to get away? But he already knew Big John's answer—as far as the rainbow reaches.

An ambulance careening around the corner, siren blaring, returned him to the problem at hand: getting work. A now-familiar mix of dread and despair spasmed through his body as he approached the doorway of each shop. Several Asian shopkeepers simply didn't understand what he wanted; a few ignored him; but most said they had sons, daughters, or other relatives who did chores for them. One motherly proprietor eyed him shrewdly from behind the cash register.

"Why you not in school, boy?" Kekoa quickly retreated and decided to try a different block the next day.

Now the sun had begun disappearing behind the buildings, and it occurred to him that he needed a place to sleep that night. He found a grassy park on the other side of King Street and wandered about until he found an empty bench. He sat there a couple of hours, people-watching. A feeling of dejection overtook him. Everyone in the whole world appeared to have someplace to go, someplace to be, someplace where they fitted in. Except him. Darkness settled over the park, and he stretched out on the bench, his head on his gym bag. Sleep enveloped him without warning.

Shortly after midnight, he felt the gym bag slipping from under his head. He reached out to retrieve it only to have his arm slammed away. He opened his eyes to find a grimy face with an evil-looking grin perched above him. A young tough—barely older than he, but certainly stronger—threw him off the bench onto the ground and rolled him over onto his stomach. A second tough, whose face he could not see, sat on his legs. He felt fingers going through his pockets and removing his new wallet. Kekoa lifted his head in protest, but a hand slapped it down again and pushed his nose into the muddy grass. Kekoa couldn't move the lower half of his body, but he managed to free his right hand to clear away the mud from his eyes.

23

The assailant abruptly stopped searching through his pockets. Kekoa tried turning his head again. He saw a man whipping and slashing at his attacker's face with a long stick. The tough dropped Kekoa's wallet under the bench and yelled out as he tried to protect himself from the beating. The pressure eased from Kekoa's legs as the tough's accomplice leaped to one side to dodge the blows of the flailing stick.

Kekoa rolled over and sprang up with every intention of running, but once on his feet, he saw his first attacker hobble off with a bloodied face. A large black dog snarled and snapped at the heels of the second hoodlum, who was now the newest victim of the whipping stick. He too bolted away, out of the park.

Kekoa observed the man who'd wielded his bamboo cane as a weapon. He was Chinese and quite old, but wiry with lean, muscled arms. The man moved slowly to the bench where Kekoa had slept and collapsed onto it. Sensing no threat from the man who'd saved him, Kekoa retrieved his wallet and gym bag from under the bench. The old man clutched at his heaving chest. Kekoa waited for him to recover.

Their eyes met. "*Mahalo*, mistah," said Kekoa. "You saved my life."

"I don't know that it was your life they were after as much as your possessions. I am known as Chou, Li Tien Chou. Ol' Chou to most. How are you called, young man?"

"I am Kekoa Pua…"

"Kekoa Pua?" asked Chou.

"No, mistah, just Kekoa."

Kekoa kept an eye on the dog curled up in front of them. This Black Lab mix seemed naturally friendly.

"I think that I shall call you Master Kay. Is that all right with you?" Chou asked.

"No mattah. That one nice dog, Mistah Chou." Kekoa sat down beside him. "Your dog?"

"Dog belongs to no one, but he chooses me for company," said Chou.

"Dog? What da kine name that?" asked Kekoa.

"I call him Dog because we've never met formally."

"I think I call him Ilio—'dog' in Hawaiian," said Kekoa.

Chou smiled. "I believe that Dog will adapt to his bilingual status quite easily."

The boy scanned the trees through the darkness, and a chill came over him. "You stay near here?"

"All of Chinatown is my realm, but I no longer call anyplace home. I suppose some would call me a man of the streets."

"But where do you sleep? How do you eat?"

"Come! You will share with me tonight, and tomorrow will take care of itself." Ol' Chou led the boy through a series of dark streets. Finally, they squeezed past a dumpster blocking the entrance to a narrow alley. Kekoa saw a corrugated metal lean-to at the end.

"Most nights Dog and I rest our bones here." Chou rearranged a hoard of ragged blankets and towels into a broader pile to accommodate Kekoa. The exhausted boy instantly dropped down and curled up among the blankets. He fell into a deep, dreamless sleep next to his two new friends.

With Chou's help, Kekoa found odd jobs: loading and unloading trucks, window washing, and delivering parcels. Even Ilio worked, for no one could ever take them by surprise while the Lab stood watch. Kekoa especially enjoyed Ol' Chou talking story and sharing his lore. Other homeless often joined them, and shopkeepers' children sneaked off from their chores to listen to him. Once, Kekoa heard Raggs, a forty-ish homeless woman, address Ol' Chou as "Purfessah," but he didn't know what to make of this.

Frequently, they were drawn to sit on the rock wall in front of the Chinese Cultural Plaza. With Chou and Ilio, Kekoa felt less troubled than when he'd randomly wandered there alone his first hours in Chinatown. Ornamental palms lined the promenade, and a life-sized bronze of Dr. Sun Yat-sen seemed to welcome him.

The Nuuanu Stream normally ran quite shallow, with rubble and trash penetrating the surface. Its walls of coarse gray block rose sheer and steep. Ol' Chou explained that during the heavy seasonal rains, water runoff from the mountains filled this streambed with deep swirling torrents before they emptied into Honolulu Harbor.

Today a large crowd had gathered to watch the filming of a *Magnum P.I.* TV segment. Back home in Ewa, it had been one of Kekoa's favorite shows. A huge tan and white RV belonging to the show's star sat in the parking lot across the river. Two towing rigs were parked adjacent to it. The scene, rehearsed several times before the actual video shooting, featured a black Cadillac in a chase. The Caddy, with live driver, drove rapidly up to a vendor's vegetable stand at the water's edge and screeched to a stop, just short of inflicting damage and crashing into the stream. For the live action, a dummy replaced the driver. This time the powerful Caddy roared forward and plunged straight into the water, obliterating the vegetable stand. Produce scattered into the stream, over rocks and rubble, and across the hood and roof of the crunched, nose-down Caddy.

"It's a wrap!" the director shouted. The wreckers moved into place to haul up the mashed car, while workers in a small floating punt tended to the remaining cleanup.

"I got one great idea, Ol' Chou," Kekoa said as they watched. He slipped over the edge of the wall, fitted his feet to the laddered iron rungs embedded in it, and lowered himself to the streambed. Avoiding the workers and wading to the middle, he began to toss vegetables up and over the wall to his friend. Bok choy, turnips, purple Okinawa sweet potatoes, eggplants, ginger root, and Maui onions flew through the air. Chou loaded the booty into his scavenging gunnysack as fast as the produce landed.

The police arrived quickly to chase them, and Chou was just as quick to disappear down the first convenient alley. Kekoa escaped under the King Street bridge and emerged a block downstream, near the Nimitz Highway bridge.

Kekoa trotted wearily back to their personal alley behind the green dumpster. Chou already had a fire going and water heating in a four-quart tin pot he'd retrieved from the dumpster only weeks before. The flames' shadows flickered on the sooty brick walls. The cunning Chou had made the fire from a stash of charcoal he had scavenged from live-coal receptacles in Ala Moana Beach Park. With a penknife, Kekoa cleaned, pared, and chopped their feast.

Chou pulled a pint bottle from his sack. Drawing a lengthy swig, he launched into one of his windy yarns that became wilder and wilder as he drank. Chou's speech turned sluggish and slurred, his train of thought wandered. Kekoa challenged him on occasion, but Chou merely grinned and said, "Some things are not easily unnerstood by the inesperienced." Kekoa's fireside stories were usually about family and considerably more honest. Chou avoided most questions dealing with his own family. But tonight the word "daughter" slipped out several times. Seeing the softer face of Chou by the light of the hot coals, Kekoa pressed him, asking where she lived.

"Nearby," he hiccuped in a squeak of a voice, "and yet so far away. I searched for her for two years and now I know where. No more, thass it."

Every so often Chou leaned forward, stirred their dinner with a large wooden spoon, and tasted the soup's progress. By the time it had finished simmering, Kekoa had told the tale of his exodus from Ewa and Happy Oscar's. Ol' Chou listened intently with head cocked.

"But why don't you go to the poleesh?"

Kekoa started to explain, but stopped mid-sentence. Chou had fallen asleep sitting upright, without having eaten a single bite. The boy turned his friend sideways and laid him down for the night. He took the pot off the fire. Patiently stirring to cool the stew, he shared his lonely meal with Ilio.

* * *

On a Monday afternoon late in May, they were out walking, when the old man suddenly stopped and leaned against a utility pole. A white carry-all van marked COMMUNITY SERVICES pulled over to the sidewalk. A man and a woman emerged, rushed past Kekoa straight to Chou, and grabbed his arms. They led him, struggling, toward the van while Ilio barked and nipped at the man's pants. The couple stopped long enough for the man to plant a sharp kick on Ilio's neck. The dog's front paws left the ground and he rolled into the street, howling. He recovered quickly and scrambled up, whimpering.

With blind fright for his friend and his dog, Kekoa cried, "No! Noooo!"

Chou turned to him. "Run, boy, run, or they'll take you, too. Get out of here, don't worry about me. Dog! Go to him." With that, Ol' Chou collapsed on the sidewalk. Kekoa took a step toward him, before it occurred to him that Chou might have collapsed on purpose to provide his friends time to escape.

"Come, Ilio, we gotta go!" Kekoa shouted and zig-zagged across Beretania Street, weaving through traffic, the dog loping behind. The youngster made it to the other side, but to his horror, he heard brakes screech and then a loud, dull thud. He forced himself to look back.

"Ilio!" he screamed. The dog lay motionless in the street. Kekoa lurched forward to help his canine friend when he saw the woman who'd seized Chou sprinting down the sidewalk toward him. He stumbled back to the curb, then broke into a wild run.

Chapter 5
Kaimuki

THE STURDY KOREAN woman from Community Services closed in on Kekoa. Shocked by her speed, he charged hard through the Chinatown alleys and narrow streets. Past old men playing mah-jongg and checkers on concrete tables. Past the cobblestoned mini-mall with its heavy odors of incense and fresh fish. Darting into a curio shop, he ducked behind the carved owls and jade elephants and spotted her halted at the curb, scowling and panting. The woman's bulk had caught up with her. A massive birthmark glowed purple across her neck and right cheek. She trudged back toward the van, picking her sweat-soaked blouse away from her skin.

Seeing the woman disappear into the official vehicle, Kekoa hurriedly retraced his steps. He reached the street where Ilio had been struck and wounded. But the spot was empty—no dog, no blood, and no one to ask. Locals and tourists filled the surrounding stores as though nothing at all of importance had just occurred.

A dispirited Kekoa dragged himself toward the makeshift lean-to at the end of their alley. Once so friendly, so familiar with Ol' Chou and Ilio there, it now struck him as foreign and even scary. He stopped in his tracks when he saw a human form at the sheltered end of the alley. Hardly more than a shadow, the form sat facing the other way. Had some stranger moved in already? Coming closer, he recognized the massive head of unkempt hair and the faded, soiled *muumuu* with its garish pineapple pattern.

"Mrs. Raggs?" he said. "What are you doing here?"

"I brought ya somethin', kid," the homeless woman replied with a wide grin exposing her missing tooth. "Besides, it's just Raggs, kid. I ain't never been hitched to no one." She shifted her body around, and he realized she cradled a bundle of rags in her lap close to her bosom. The bundle moved on its own, and a moist black nose poked its way out of one end. She pulled the flap away. *Ilio* wriggled out and crawled toward Kekoa—struggling and whimpering with each tender step, a bandage high on his right foreleg to mark where he'd been hit.

"Ilio!" Kekoa shrieked. He rushed forward, knelt, grabbed the dog's head in both hands, and kissed his face. "How are you, Dog? Are you hurt? I thought I'd lost you for sure."

A wide-eyed Ilio slurped Kekoa's cheek. The dog rolled over on his back and rocked his hind leg back and forth as Kekoa scratched his belly. His tail thumped the ground rapidly.

"Doc Lee, at the acupuncture and herb place, sez he didn't know any bones got broke, but his leg gotta be pretty damn bruised. Figures a couple of weeks, and yer dog ought to be good like new." Raggs rearranged the towels and raggedy blanket. She picked the dog up and laid him in the improvised bed. "Keep 'm quiet any way ya kin."

Raggs stood to leave and Kekoa hugged her around her sizable midsection. "Thanks, Raggs. I'll never forget you. You're welcome to come around here anytime."

Kekoa sat beside the prone dog and scratched him affectionately behind the ears as he watched Raggs walk the length of the alley and disappear.

Somehow, boy and dog managed to survive without Ol' Chou, and within a week Ilio could hobble everywhere—well, not exactly everywhere. Kekoa had sighted and dodged the same white Community Services van several times and knew that Chinatown could no longer hide them. They had to move on. Kekoa had helped Young's Wholesale Grocery Supplies load their trucks on several occasions. Kim, the dock foreman, said he had a flour, rice, and sugar delivery to a bakery in Kaimuki. If Kekoa would help with the loading and unloading, he'd take him there for free in the back of his pickup.

So, with $23.20 left in his pocket, Kekoa and Ilio accepted the ride to the blue collar suburb of Kaimuki, situated just behind the commanding hulk of Diamond Head crater. There were stores all along Waialae Avenue and odd jobs to be had. At least they wouldn't starve. Prowling the streets, he searched for a place to lay their heads at night, but Kaimuki's straightforward streets and tightly knit neighborhoods yielded few places to hide. At last, in a wide alley behind a furniture store, he discovered a cache of large cardboard boxes. These cast-offs from cabinets, chairs, and tables he fashioned into a series of lean-tos.

But only for one or two nights at a time. Efficient garbage collectors carted away his make-do shelters every few days. Kekoa wondered how long he could go on like this. Sure, the place was fairly clean for an alley, and he'd seen only one rat. He shivered at the thought of it. How he missed Ol' Chou's company, but he still could curl up to sleep against the safe and furry Ilio.

A few doors away, enticing aromas floated out of the Osaka Family Bakery, where he'd helped make the delivery on his first day in Kaimuki. Down the block, the pungent scent of ginger from the Taste of Asia Cafe so tantalized him that one night he could bear it no longer. He shelled out the enormous sum of $4.75 and treated himself to the Vietnamese house special, pho—noodle soup heaped with bean sprouts, mint, basil, chili pepper, lemon, beef, and chicken—all simmered for days on end. Afterward, fully satisfied, he scavenged for scraps in the bins out back for Ilio. The dog had progressed to foraging on his own with only a little help from his master.

* * *

Early in September, when work became scarce, Kekoa gathered up his courage and knocked on the rear door of the Osaka Family Bakery. Sam Osaka opened the door and found a tall, underfed local boy who looked to be in his early teens. The youngster's sorrowful larger-than-*haole* eyes pleaded to be noticed. He stood a head taller than Sam and had black hair that flopped in uneven lengths over his ears. One hand, covered with calluses, brushed the hair away from his dirty sun-reddened face. His T-shirt and shorts were torn and too small, barely covering his skinny frame. Both arms and legs bore fresh scrapes and bruises.

"Hey, mistah, I can do chores for you. I'll work good and hard for some food. Please, mistah? Maybe?"

Sam hesitated only a second or two. "Okay," he said. "I try you out. Day-to-day, we see how it go. But I start plenty early. Come tomorrow, four o'clock, morning. You can, *nei*?"

"I'll be here real early, yah? Thanks, mistah."

Kekoa showed up at exactly four the next morning and every day thereafter. A real job again, a place to go that needed him. And though it was only $3 a day and meals, he was being paid. He gobbled up the routines and procedures with an insatiable hunger that matched the cravings in his belly and the wonder in his eyes. Without Sam or Sam's wife knowing, there was always something extra for the dog at night.

Never had he known that a small shop could produce so many treats: *yamagata*, breads shaped like animals; *anpan*, buns stuffed with bean paste, whole limas, melon, or corned beef; mini-*anpan* filled with macadamia nuts or curry.

At first, Sam assigned Kekoa to the clean-up chores when all the major baking was done and again at night when the shop doors closed. The more tasks Sam piled on, the faster and better his new helper completed them. But Sam soon ran out of lowly tasks for the boy. So he began teaching him to measure out the mixing ingredients for doughnuts, twists, and dinner rolls. Then came the instructions on how to make *mizu yokan*, small crisp triangles of buttered toast, and how to pack them into Cellophane bags.

Several months went by. Late one afternoon, when the boy's chores were done, Sam went to the storeroom at the rear of the bakery and found Kekoa fast asleep atop a fifty-pound sack of flour. Sam tiptoed out, but when he returned an hour later to question him, Kekoa had left, unaware that he'd been discovered.

"Son," Sam asked him the next day, "why you so tired?" He learned the few facts that Kekoa doled out: that he had been homeless for nearly a year and had been sleeping in a cardboard box in the alley for four months. There was no mention of Ilio or the life he had lived earlier. Sam's wife, Mauro, stood silently as Kekoa spoke. A single tear rolled down her cheek.

"That no good," she said. "We make you bed here." They fixed up a corner of the storeroom just for him. He happily shared his "room" with the mountainous sacks, boxes, and jars of supplies, along with two massive refrigerators. It was sheer luxury compared to the cane fields and alleys. Under the stairs that led to the family apartment on the floor above, there was a bathroom. Kekoa crept slowly into the Osakas' lives, becoming more a family member and less a hired hand. He asked for so little and gave so much in return. Sam and Mauro's lives became filled with him.

The shop fronted on Waialae Avenue, with the letters OSAKA FAMILY BAKERY arched across both windows in gold paint. A gilded antique-looking cash register stood on the counter where Mauro ran the retail end of the business. A bony little woman of fifty-seven, she stood less than five feet tall. Kind but weary eyes peered out of her deeply lined face.

Sam was half a head taller than Mauro, four years older, and as tanned as she was pale. He appeared long in the torso and short in his bowed but sturdy legs. His fine muscle tone, acquired through years of manipulating heavy sacks of flour and sugar, had begun to diminish of late. The fitness of their business, their very survival, depended on Sam's health. Kekoa's physical strength, as well as his eagerness to learn, proved a double blessing.

The Osakas saw to it that Kekoa had plenty to eat. Occasionally, they rewarded him with extra cash. Their lives embodied simplicity and trust. Sam and Mauro assumed that Kekoa went to school when he left them at nine each morning after the chores. During his supposed "school day" Kekoa would pick up odd jobs: loading groceries into cars for tips at the Times Supermarket, sweeping up at a beauty parlor, and uncrating furniture at the rattan store. All the while, he watched anxiously in case Sam should pass by on some errand. Sam and Mauro had no idea that Kekoa's formal education had stopped more than two years ago. He could read and write well enough, but his math skills had all but disappeared. He could make change at the cash register when they needed him to, and that was all.

Kekoa wanted desperately to attend school, but he couldn't figure out how to go about it. If he enrolled officially, Red Murphy would be able to find him easily. So Kekoa left the bakery each weekday morning to keep the Osakas from becoming suspicious and returned about 3:30 to help out in the store until closing.

"How school today?" Mauro would ask ritually upon his return.

He'd smile and avoid responding with his own inquiry. "Busy day, eh, Mauro?"

Kekoa liked talking with the customers and he felt proud that the Osakas trusted him at the cash register, but he loved the baking best. This was his time with Sam. His routine satisfied him. Except for the worry that the Osakas would discover his secrets, he could live with it.

Ilio soon learned Kekoa's schedule. He slept out back of the bakery at night and wandered the streets of Kaimuki by day—content to show up near the back door when he knew the boy would be free.

But the nights were a different story for the new baker's help. He wished he didn't need to sleep at all. That was when his nightmare

33

bedeviled him. It was always the same: the night of Big John's murder. The shovel descending—thud, thud, thud. The killing sounds muffled against the shed walls. The scraping and scratching afterward. Uncle John's punished body being dragged across the gravel. Red's cutting eyes, his cruel grin.

Kekoa would explode awake in a pool of perspiration, soaking his pillow and the sheet beneath him. He'd never risk going home again. What would happen if he did? Would Red be there waiting for him?

* * *

The next morning started out quite ordinary. Kekoa added the eggs and milk to the electric mixer for the lemon Danish. Sam went to preheat the two ovens, one a modern stainless unit with electronic pilot and automatic controls, and the older cast iron unit next to it with its gas flame pilot and spring valve regulator.

Sam first opened the gas jet and hit the pilot button on the cast iron unit. Without warning, the door blew off its cracked hinges, knocked Sam off his feet, and pinned him to the floor. A faulty gas regulator spring had allowed the cooking gas to fill the oven's chamber to a dangerous mix. Instead of a modest heating flame, the pilot ignited an explosion. The door, on its way to striking Sam, also struck the pipe that housed the regulator, jarring it to its full-flow opening. Gas poured into the chamber unrestricted until the pilot ignited it for a second time, and a roaring, leaping flame erupted from the mouth of the cast-iron dragon.

Kekoa ran for the fire extinguisher, but Sam was trying to tell him something else. He pointed to the wall. "Hit cutoff! Stop gas! Turn off!" he shouted. Sam used the door as a shield to deflect the flames, but he dared not move out in any direction. It was only a matter of seconds before the door would heat up and burn him.

Kekoa grabbed one of the heavy black rubber aprons from its peg on the wall and slung it over his neck to protect his body. He draped a second apron over his head. Diving under the flames, he rolled to the wall, banging to an abrupt stop. Holding the apron as his own shield, he stood and reached up for the cutoff lever on the wall, pulling it straight down. The flame collapsed, protesting its demise with a mighty "wooumph!"

Dense brown smoke and the nauseating taste of raw gas filled the room. Kekoa threw open the double doors to the alley and took a deep

34

breath. He turned on the overhead exhaust fans and they roared up to speed. Mauro screamed from the front of the shop. She came running, then stopped short and stared in horror and disbelief.

There lay her husband, trapped beneath the heavy iron door. Only inches from his feet, the base of the door glowed cherry red.

Sam called to Kekoa, "Son! Help me!"

Slowly, Kekoa leveraged a long mop handle against the door. The heavy iron weight lifted from Sam's body. Sam crawled out from beneath it and a safe few feet away before Kekoa let go, allowing the door to crash to the floor.

Sam pulled himself up and sat with his back against the wall, panting and gasping. Mauro fell on her knees beside him. Kekoa filled a bucket with cold water, soaked some rags in it, and handed them to Sam. Rejecting the rags, Sam picked up the pail and dumped the water over his head. A self-satisfied grin crept over his face. Mauro and the boy broke into uninhibited laughter, a laughter borne of tested nerves.

Mauro hugged her husband, kissing his wet head and chattering in a flow of Japanese. Embarrassed by the show of affection for him, Sam gently pushed his wife to one side and rose to his feet, testing his limbs for mobility and strength. He'd escaped serious harm with only a few bruises and a slightly burned forearm.

Mauro turned to Kekoa. "*Arigato*. Thank you, son. You save my Sam for me." She stood on tiptoe and smothered Kekoa in a tight embrace.

Sam looked happy. "You do good job, Kekoa. I thank you, too. Today, close bakery and clean mess I make. Mauro, you put sign in window: we closed. Kekoa, you call gas company to come fix problem."

This day more than any other provided the glue, the bond to truly make them a family. But grateful as he was, Kekoa missed his own family more than ever. His house with the overflowing mango tree, Leilani's teasing, his Uncle John's big arms hugging him. He missed *Tutu* Eme's *loco-moco* breakfasts and her stories of ancient Hawaii. As he washed up at the sink, the reality hit him. "I can't go home. Evah," he whispered. "It's *pau*, all done."

But through his misery a stubborn determination jacked him up. *I'm gonna find Lani. Somehow. No matter what.*

Chapter 6
Leilani's World

CLUMPS OF EARTH slid from the shovel, landing on the coffin below with a hollow sound. Two strokes within a week had spelled the end for Eme Waiwaiole. Her three-pack-a-day cigarette habit had finally caught up with her.

The few mourners began walking toward their cars. Leilani Pualoa stared at the awful hole in the ground, then forced her gaze to the nearby spot where they had buried her mother twelve years ago. The graves of her mother and grandmother now lay head to head. Leilani lingered, a tall solitary figure, beside the open grave. Her severe black dress, bought hastily for the funeral, gave her a dignity unusual in an adolescent and somehow enhanced the natural beauty she'd inherited from both women. She had the pleasing curves of a healthy island girl, a substantial rather than slender body, and long legs with strong thighs and rounded calves.

But she didn't feel beautiful. She felt completely alone, orphaned. Kekoa had run off and even Uncle Big John had disappeared. How could that have happened? It didn't make sense. It just wasn't like her uncle, or her little brother, either. She had scant memory of the father who had abandoned them twelve years earlier. A vague image recalled an adoring daddy, all smiles and hugs, holding her on his lap at bedtime as he sang her a Hawaiian lullaby. But *Tutu* Eme's hatred had pretty well smothered those tender fragments. She had repeatedly painted Hank Pualoa as an unregenerate villain. Leilani's father had killed her mother, and that was that.

Eme had had another dimension to her—one that Leilani found intriguing but a little scary. Her grandmother often spoke affectionately of a spirit world, a realm that communicated with her mostly in dreams and symbols, but sometimes through visions and voices of her departed relatives. Until last night, Leilani never knew whether *Tutu* was taking advantage of her youthful vulnerability or whether she truly believed in these things. But last night Leilani saw her wise grandmother wave goodbye from the back of a horse-drawn wagon atop a cloud. She was so far off in the distance that speaking, even shouting, was out of the question. Leilani wanted to ask her about Kekoa and Uncle Big John. Were they on the Other Side, too? Tears soaked her cheeks.

A heavy arm fell across the girl's shoulders. "Come on, dear, it's time to go." Red Murphy nudged her toward his car. "I know how hard this is for you, but you'll get over it, everybody does." He leaned over to kiss her cheek, but she turned her head away.

This is not what she wanted to hear at all. They had just buried her grandmother. Leilani wanted him to shut up and leave her to grieve. Uncle Red's new attitude toward her made her uncomfortable. Before her grandmother died, he'd paid her no attention, and she wondered about his motives now. She couldn't quite put her finger on it. Perhaps he was a shade too slick. Eme's death left her with little choice but to accept Uncle Red's guidance. But she knew Red wasn't really her uncle—only her father's business partner. She called him "Uncle" at his insistence.

While driving out of Diamond Head Memorial Park, Red declared that, whether she liked it or not, he was her new guardian. A wave of nausea overtook her. She rolled down the window and gulped in a cleansing breath. Her chestnut hair, with just a touch of auburn running through it, rippled in the breeze. Then an unexpected question exploded upon her.

"How would you like to finish high school at a private school?"

"No!"

Red kept talking. "And...I've been making some inquiries... about a place for you to live, too."

He turned at the next corner, and she suddenly realized that they weren't heading toward her house in Ewa.

"Why can't I keep going to Campbell High? I like it there. And why do I have to live somewhere else, in a strange place?"

"Because, my dear, you're too young to live alone."

She lapsed angrily into pidgin. "I not too young, I ovah sixteen and almost as tall as you are, yah? You think I can't take care of myself?" Her voice broke as she struggled to keep her cool and not fall apart in front of him. "I got no family, and now you want me leave my house, and all my frien' too. It not fair."

"I'm your family, now, dear," he said, in his well-oiled voice.

"You not family and you nevah will be," she said. "Kekoa's the only family I got now. And heaven knows where he is." She drew in a deep breath to vent more protests, but hesitated. She knew Red's temper. "What school?" she asked cautiously. She began to sense that she faced a done deal anyway.

"Oahu Preparatory Academy! Got a great reputation, very prestigious," Red said. He'd already enrolled her.

She raised one sandaled foot and kicked the dashboard. "I know 'bout Oahu Prep," she shrieked. "It all rich kids, I no like fit in."

"Calm down, hon. It's not all rich kids. Plenty of 'em are just like you. I spoke with the dean of students and the principal." Red let this much sink in before continuing. "They told me some of the faculty take students into their homes as boarders to earn extra money. I've made some arrangements with a Mr. and Mrs. Paul Wong. They both teach at Oahu Prep and they have a daughter your age who goes there."

"I no have a say in this, Uncle Red? I mean, it my life."

"Hell, Leilani, you're still a child in the eyes of the law. I know what's best for you, you're gonna hafta take my word for it." Red suddenly heard the impatience and temper rising in his own voice. He decided he'd better put a lid on it. "Dear, these are nice people, you'll like them. In fact, we're on our way there right now. Would you like to meet them, the Wongs, I mean?"

"Like I have a choice," she replied, her eyes downcast. She wished he wouldn't call her "dear." Ugh! She wasn't his dear. She wasn't anyone's dear anymore.

"Dear, you won't be sorry," he said. "But if you want to make a good impression on the family, you'd be smart to drop the pidgin. I told you they're both teachers."

"Give me a break, Uncle Red. You think I don't know how to speak *haole* English?"

"I know they taught you properly in school, but somehow you kids never want to use it."

"You turn my whole life upside down and expect me to be happy about it? Do I want to meet my foster parents?" She spat the word out. "Oh, sure, I can't wait to be put in a foster home."

Red thought it better to keep his mouth shut as he picked his way down University Avenue, clogged with buses, plate lunch wagons, and University of Hawaii students. He made a quick succession of lefts and rights.

Leilani saw the landscape transform into a tropical neighborhood of ancient gnarled monkeypod trees and towering royal palms with smooth gray trunks. She craned her neck to take in the large houses. They all looked freshly painted and lovingly landscaped, some almost smothered in fuchsia and purple bougainvillea. Each house looks so well-tended, she thought, like their owners have nothing else to do.

Red noted her reaction with cynical pleasure. "Manoa Valley," he said. "The Oahu Prep campus is pretty close by." He pulled up in front of a two-story wood-frame house, pristine white. Large square pillars stood at each corner of a lanai that wrapped around the house on three sides. The small front lawn exploded with color: tall stalks of red and pink ginger and low hedges of yellow hibiscus.

Paul and Masako Wong awaited them on the lanai. A girl who looked to Leilani about seventeen stood coyly behind them. Leilani stepped out of the car, but straggled behind Red as he approached the Wongs. Seeing her hesitation, the girl ran down the steps and threw her arms about her, taking her totally by surprise.

"Welcome to our home, I'm Numi Wong." Her white teeth flashed a genuine smile. Numi took her by the hand and led her up the steps. "Leilani, these are my parents, Masako and Paul Wong, and they welcome you, too."

"We are pleased that you want to come live with us." Paul extended his hand to her, and she shook it tentatively.

Masako bowed politely and said, "I am very glad to know you. I hope you will be happy here. Numi will show you around. Meanwhile, we have some things to discuss with Mr. Murphy."

The two girls hurried inside, letting the screen door slam behind them. At the base of the stairs, Numi said, "We planned to have you sleep in the guest room, but now that I've met you, I want to share my room with you. Is that okay?"

"I guess so, I mean, sure, if that's what you want. Is Numi your nickname?"

"Everybody asks me that. No, that's all there is to it. I wish my parents had given me a more exotic name, like Cleopatra or Liliuokalani!" She giggled. "But I guess it wouldn't make any difference. My friends would prob'ly call me Cleo or Lil. And maybe being a queen is overrated anyway. I mean, one killed herself with a snake and the other one was deposed and imprisoned."

Leilani released a small smile, the first in many days. She wondered what kind of kook she'd be living with. The two girls started up the stairs. "Hey, Leilani. It's going to be wonderful to have a sister to confide in."

Leilani turned away and rolled her eyes. A sister? Oh, sure. She changed the subject. "Um...your parents seem very nice."

"They're the best," said Numi. "Dad's a hundred percent Chinese and Mom's totally Japanese. It's supposed to be kind of weird for Chinese and Japanese to marry. I'm glad they did, though."

In the upstairs hall, Leilani surveyed her new roommate. She stood half a head taller than Numi and felt large and klutzy next to her. Numi looked like a porcelain doll, with her petite round face and cropped black hair. She exuded a mix of innocence and confidence and seemed completely kind and generous. Only a quarter-hour after meeting her, Leilani reluctantly admitted that she both admired and envied Numi, even if she did sort of babble on. But it was all too much for the newcomer. The soul-wrenching emotions of the funeral and the abrupt uprooting from her home tugged so hard that she lost control. Without warning, glistening tears spilled down her olive-toned cheeks.

Numi looked alarmed. "What's the matter? Did I say something wrong?"

Leilani shook her head. "Oh, no, only...I'm so down in the dumps and kinda glad all at the same time and I feel guilty about being happy."

"But why? Why should you feel guilty?"

"I just came from my poor *Tutu*'s funeral. But I'm glad about finding you guys. You're really nice. I had no idea what to expect." She lowered her head, and her shoulder-length hair fell forward, covering her oval island face. "Oh, I'm so screwed up. I'm scared about going to a new school, and I already miss my friends."

"You'll make new ones at Oahu Prep. See? You've made one already!" Numi gave her a tremendous hug and handed her a box of tissues from the hall table. "Come on in, let's go see my...no, our room."

The bedroom had lavender walls, a purple shag rug, and a bookcase jammed with stuffed animals, photo albums, and music boxes. A rolypoly wooden doll's head sat on a shelf, like a Red Delicious apple with a gaping bite taken out of it. Its fierce face was painted black, red, and gold, and it stared out at Leilani with a single large eye.

"What is that?" Leilani blurted out. "Some kine stink eye?"

Numi laughed. "That's a daruma doll. In Japan, when you're going to start some important project in your life, you buy one. It comes without eyes. When you take the first step, you color in just one eye. When you reach your goal, you paint in the other eye for everyone to see."

"Uh-huh. So what's your goal, Numi?"

"Well, it's not exactly mine. My mother bought it. The daruma is supposed to inspire me to get a B in geometry." She burst out, "I hate math. I have the worst time in it!"

A stern voice answered: "Then I suggest you start spending more time on your homework." Masako stood in the doorway, arms crossed over her chest.

"Mom! You scared me. Do you have to embarrass me in front of my new sister?" Numi turned to Leilani with a deep frown. "That's what happens when your parents are on the faculty of your school. You're under a microscope every minute."

Having had no parents since she was four, Leilani thought that sounded pretty good. She couldn't figure out whether Numi was serious or not. *Tutu* Eme wasn't one to make jokes or deal in confusing subtleties; life was simply black or white.

"Okay, girls," Masako said, smiling, "I'd better not let Leilani see what an ogre I am at heart. You can wash up. Dinner will be in fifteen minutes."

"But where's Uncle Red?" Leilani asked.

"Your uncle went to Ewa to bring back your things. He'll return in a couple of hours. And please call me Masako." She stopped. "I do answer to 'Mom' if you prefer."

"Thank you, Masako. Maybe I can in a while."

"I understand, my dear." She left the room.

Numi sat silent but alert, waiting for her mother's footsteps to reach the bottom stair. "My parents get annoyed because I don't have a serious career goal," she whispered. "So, Leilani, what about you?"

"I want to be an artist—oils and watercolors. I want to paint

41

large canvases, spectacular scenes of Hawaii and our people. Right now I mostly sketch."

"That's great. You'll have to show me your drawings." At the top of the stairs, Leilani peeked into another bedroom. University of Hawaii banners studded the walls.

"Whose room is that?" she asked.

"My brother Alex's. He lives in town now, close to work. He's got two roommates. He'd rather have an apartment of his own, but it's too expensive. Sometimes he sleeps here weekends."

"What does he do?"

"Do? Oh, he's an accountant, works for a CPA firm downtown. He wants to make junior partner, but he's only twenty-four."

"You must be proud of him."

Numi nodded.

That first night, Leilani shared the story of her dwindling family.

"I'm not an orphan, at least I don't think so. But…" She managed to suppress fresh tears. "I feel like one."

"My God, Leilani, you've had such a tough life." Numi hugged her once more.

* * *

Over the next weeks and months, Leilani grew more comfortable in her role as a member of the Wong family. At least, she made a huge effort to appear comfortable. But a sense of apprehension and anxiety lurked inside her, fed by the gnawing sense of loss for her brother, Uncle Big John, and her grandmother. And that wasn't all. She'd been content in her Ewa surroundings, with her old friends, being the smart one in class, and not having to watch what she said all the time. The strictness of the strange new school, the piled-on homework, and the outsider treatment from most of her classmates had led her into a sullen mood.

One particular afternoon, when her school day had gone badly, Leilani dropped her loaded book bag on Numi's twin bed and flopped down on her own, stretching out on her back to sulk. Numi came up the stairs several minutes later. Quickly taking in this little scene, she slid her own book bag off her shoulders and pointedly dropped it on the floor. With a dramatic sweep, she hefted Leilani's and let it fall with a thunk on her foster sister's stomach.

Leilani pushed the bag to the floor, bounded up to face Numi, and shoved her backward. Numi stumbled, caught her balance, and stared at her roommate's crazed expression. "What did you do that for?"

"Cuz I felt like it."

"All I did was give you back your book bag."

"Yeah, you just happened to drop it on top of me. All you had to do was ask. Like I'm taking up too much room now. Maybe you're sorry you're sharing with me. Maybe you're just like all the other uppity bunch at school."

Leilani didn't expect the sharp slap across her cheek. She pushed Numi backward again, harder this time. Numi grabbed a handful of Leilani's thick hair and hung on as both bounced onto the bed, then wrestled onto the floor. The struggle raged amid the sounds of furniture sliding and bumping, voices grunting and straining. The clock radio fell from the nightstand in a loud crash, and a local rock station blared out the Beatles' "A Hard Day's Night" at top volume.

"Keep it down up there," Masako yelled from the foot of the stairs. "I'm on the phone."

Leilani dove for the radio and squelched its awesome beat.

"Okay, Mom," Numi yelled back. "Sorreee!" Her breath came in short gasps.

Sprawled on the rug, the girls glared at one another in heavy silence. The longer they stared, the tamer their expressions became. Sheepish grins became giggles. The two girls got to their feet and embraced as though nothing had happened. But it had happened and would again. Together, they straightened the room. And so there were times when Leilani's unwilling transition to Manoa Valley girl was not always as smooth as the whipped cream on chocolate haupia pie. It would never be complete.

For the most part, Red Murphy stayed away from his charge, showing up twice monthly to deliver trust checks to Paul Wong. Sometimes papers needed to be signed. On all these occasions, he conducted his business politely and inquired on three subjects: Leilani's progress in school, her health, and if she had heard from her brother.

* * *

Six months later, Red Murphy pulled into the parking garage of the Hosokawa Building. Using the 3393 Kapiolani Boulevard entrance,

43

he found a space on the third level. Too early for his three o'clock appointment, he walked to a railing overlooking the street and lit up a cigarette. Mulling over what he was about to do, he considered the risks. The passing of nine weeks since Hank's last trust deposit had convinced him they'd never hear from Hank Pualoa again. The police had long since given up on finding Big John—or Kekoa. Eme had waited two weeks before reporting them missing. Red felt confident that he had literally gotten away with murder.

Except...the smile on Red's face disintegrated. Something had to be done about the boy. That is, if he could ever find him. The girl could become a problem, too. He hoped not. Red needed to get into Leilani's good graces, and he felt certain he'd made progress toward that end. She actually seemed happy living with the Wongs.

He checked his watch again. The time for his appointment had arrived. He walked to the elevator and pressed the UP button. Some day he would have a suite of offices on the twenty-second floor and maybe even an adjoining apartment. The penthouse would be his choice. His ego soared with the rapid ride up.

As the elevator doors opened, he found himself in the spacious waiting room of Fujita, Fujita & Moria. The plush emerald-green carpeting and oversized rich wood furnishings instantly seduced his senses. No matter how many times he'd been here, these offices never ceased to stir his acquisitive juices.

A smartly dressed Japanese woman stepped out from behind her desk and greeted him. Lori Yamashita served the Fujita firm efficiently as an administrative secretary and paralegal. She had high cheekbones and black hair with thick bangs cut straight across. Her face struck him as more interesting than beautiful.

"Won't you have a seat?" she said, motioning to a chair. "Mr. Fujita will be with you shortly."

As soon as he sat down, he felt uncomfortable. The upholstered chair was so deep his knees could not bend to the floor. If he moved forward to set his feet on the floor, he lost his backrest. Damn, he thought, these people do this on purpose just to make you squirm. His eyes followed the woman as she moved about the room, disappearing and reappearing from behind three oak doors. He noted the hem of her slim skirt barely reaching her knees, but he lost interest once he saw how bowed her legs were.

At last, Terumi Fujita's voice came over the intercom. "Lori, I'll see Mr. Murphy now."

Red followed her through the first door on the left into a corner room dominated by floor-to-ceiling windows. A koa credenza with brass fittings ran along one windowed wall. Terumi stood behind his desk, a bean-shaped glass slab sitting atop a koa base. He made a slight bowing gesture to Red and indicated a chair across from him. Red offered his hand, but the lawyer had begun seating himself. His visitor shrugged and sat down.

"Tea? Coffee? Water?" Lori offered in her most gracious tone. Both men shook their heads, and she left the room.

"I guess you know why I'm here," Red said.

"I presume you are here to complete the terms of our real estate agreement. My client's offer is a most generous one, don't you think?" Terumi settled deeper into his chair.

"Sure, of course," Red muttered. He had assumed Fujita's mystery client was a major Japanese developer interested in creating both residential and commercial improvements on the block of real estate he'd been acquiring. Red cleared his throat. "But there are a few problems. We have all the properties except for two, and we're making progress on them."

"We? You have a new partner?" Terumi asked.

"No, just figuratively speaking."

"My client insists that all twenty parcels be intact and clear in title before the agreed-upon price and bonus can be paid to you. Also, the terms of the agreement specify that you are to deliver the properties within six months. By tomorrow, in fact. Isn't that so?" Terumi said.

"Yeah." Red shifted in his chair. "I already have eighteen of the twenty lots."

"Which eighteen?"

"Let's see..." Red stalled. "My four lots. Plus six belonging to my former business associates that I acquired under the partnership survival agreement. And the eight adjacent lots, which I've shelled out a good deal of my own personal cash for."

"Yes, yes. And the two keystone lots?"

"The keystone lots are owned by my former partner, Hank Pualoa. Actually, his kids own the lots now, but this property is being held in trust for them since they're minors. I hate like hell to hold the deal up, but there are some complications there."

"I'm surprised to hear that, Mr. Murphy. What kind of complications?"

"Well, it seems that when your father set up the trust for Hank's kids, all assets were passed to the trust, including the principal and income from Hank's special bank account and the deeds to the two keystone lots."

Terumi put his hand to his chin and swung his swivel chair around to take in the view of the city below. Suddenly, something did click in his mind. And he instantly swung his chair back. "My father, you say. What's he got to do with this?"

"Everything. In setting up the trust, your father appointed a Mr. Coland Benfield-Rice at First Sugarman's Bank as a co-trustee. The problem is that Benfield-Rice won't sell me the lots without Hank's consent, but he hasn't been able to get in touch with him. Says he has no idea where the man is and needs more time to locate him. He's also concerned over Hank's four missed deposits to the account, something that hasn't happened in seven years."

"And you have no idea where he is?"

"Not a clue," Red said. "Looks like he's vanished into thin air on the Mainland. Could be dead, for all I know."

"My client also has a lot of cash riding on this investment," Terumi said slowly. "There are other properties involved as well. A project of this magnitude cannot wait forever."

"I'm not talking forever, just a few months, one even."

"I'll speak with my client, but I'll have to recommend some alternative plan to him. He'll insist on it. Now I suggest that this meeting be adjourned." Terumi came around the desk, putting his hand on Red's back as he ushered him hurriedly into the reception area. Red was about to object, but Terumi had already returned to his office, closing the door behind him.

* * *

The next afternoon, as Numi and Leilani strolled home from an after-school snack at Zippy's restaurant, Leilani walked with her head down, shoes scuffing the sidewalk. As the weeks had gone by, each of the girls had become more sensitive to the mood swings of the other.

"Did something happen today?" Numi asked.

"Yeah. The principal called me into her office this afternoon."

Numi's eyes widened. "Oh-oh! The principal? She can be a real dragon."

"She was pretty nice, actually," Leilani said. "There was a man sitting on the bench outside her door. She asked me if I knew him."

"Well, did you?"

"I peeked out and…"

"What'd he look like?" Numi interrupted.

"He was short, prob'ly Japanese, very formal looking, black suit and glasses, but I'd never seen him before. She said he's an attorney, and he was asking questions about me. She wanted to know if he had any legitimate business with me. I told her I didn't think so. The whole thing really creeped me out, Numi."

"I wonder what he wanted. Well, don't worry about it. Maybe it was a mistake."

"Then we had a pop quiz in American History," Leilani continued, "and I know I screwed it up. I just couldn't concentrate. Now if it'd been Hawaiian history, I'd have aced it." She paused to adjust the book bag on her shoulders. "You know, it really bugs me: the thirteen colonies and all that stuff sound so unreal to me. It's their history, not mines."

"Better not use mines in front of Mom and Dad. They'll freak out," Numi said.

Leilani ignored the remark, and her voice grew agitated. "Why do they treat Hawaii like it's some kind of foreign country?"

"Um, I don't know, Leilani. I've never thought about it before. Did you notice the new guy in math class today?" she asked with forced cheerfulness. "I thought he was cute. Didn't you?"

"Not really."

"You never seem to notice anyone except Alex. I bet you have a crush on him." Numi giggled.

Leilani blushed. "Aw, don't tease me. I kinda do like him, but he'll never notice me. He prob'ly thinks of me as a kid."

"Hey, he already pays you more attention than he does me, his own sister."

"Oh, he's just being nice." Before Leilani could say any more, a gray BMW pulled up to the curb beside them, and the tinted window on the driver's side retracted. Leilani's heart pounded. It was the man she'd seen at the principal's office.

"Miss Pualoa? Miss Leilani Pualoa? May I have a word with you?" He held out his business card. Numi ventured a few steps closer, took the card, and passed it to Leilani. As she was about to read it, the man opened his driver's side door and got out. "Is there somewhere we can talk?"

"No! No! Get away from us," gasped Leilani, shoving the card in her pocket. The two girls spun around to walk away.

"I have some papers for…" he called out, but they kept walking. He returned to the car and began to follow them slowly.

The girls quickened their steps, and when he matched their pace, they broke into a run. Taking advantage of the one-way traffic on Beretania, they dashed a few blocks in the direction of the oncoming cars and darted into a dress boutique. Pretending to shop, they flipped through the hangers one by one, hardly noticing the opulent array of party gowns. From behind a display rack, they fixed their attention on the front window as they scanned the traffic.

"May I help you young ladies? Something in a prom dress, perhaps?" Both girls jumped as the saleswoman suddenly appeared behind them. They looked at each other nervously.

"Um, no thank you," said Numi. "We're just looking right now. We'll need my mom's permission before we buy anything." With that, the saleswoman began to dial the phone on the counter, keeping her eyes fixed on the girls.

While Leilani continued to search for the gray BMW, Numi inspected a silk dress with a mandarin collar. As she fingered the embroidery, the rack of clothes began to sway. She leaped back. Two large eyes stared up at her—a toddler hiding from his mother. A split second later, the mother stormed out of a fitting room in her high heels and unzipped dress with its sales tags flying. She scooped up her errant child with one arm and a firm warning. "Now you stay wi' me, you behave, *nei?*"

The commotion had commandeered Leilani's attention away from the window, so she could not be sure if the BMW had passed the store. Now she took the time to read the man's card: Ronald Moria, Esq., Fujita, Fujita & Moria, Attorneys at Law. "What could he possibly want with me, Numi?"

"I don't know, but I wish the creep would leave you alone."

Under the increasingly suspicious gaze of the saleswoman, thirty

48

minutes passed before the girls felt secure enough to venture into the street again. Six lanes of traffic moved rapidly to their right. No sign of the BMW. They lost very little time getting home.

* * *

Paul Wong stepped through the front door that evening and the girls pounced on him, both jabbering at the same time. When he managed to calm them down, they related their afternoon encounter with the stranger.

"May I see that card?" Paul asked. "I know the Fujita law firm. Perhaps I should give them a call and see what the mystery is all about. It's 5:30 now. Maybe Mr. Moria is still in his office."

Paul tapped out the seven numbers, half expecting an answering machine. A mature woman's voice said, "Law offices, may I help you?"

"Yes, please. I'm Paul Wong. This afternoon a Mr. Moria made two attempts to contact a young lady named Leilani Pualoa, who lives with my family. In doing so, he frightened both her and my daughter. Can you tell me what this is all about?"

"Oh yes, Mr. Wong. I have instructions from Mr. Terumi Fujita that if you called, I'm to make an appointment for you to come in and see him as soon as it's convenient. He extends his profound apologies for this afternoon's debacle and will explain further at the meeting."

"Could you tell me the subject of this meeting?"

"I'm sorry, I can't. Would tomorrow afternoon at three be good?"

After checking with Leilani, he confirmed the appointment. "Yes. Thank you. Goodbye." He hung up, frowned, and ran a hand through his full head of gray hair. "I don't know any more now than before," he told the girls. "We'll meet with one of the other partners, Terumi Fujita, tomorrow afternoon and get some answers. The woman I spoke to did apologize for Mr. Moria's unacceptable behavior."

"Do you suppose it has anything to do with my brother?" Leilani asked.

"I don't think so," said Paul. "Why would a lawyer be the one to contact you? For that matter, why wouldn't he contact one of the trustees to make an appointment? This is very peculiar indeed."

Masako poked her head through the door. "I could use a little help, girls." They followed her into the kitchen. "Numi, you prepare the sushi."

Numi began chopping filets of cooked ahi, yellow-finned tuna, adding a paste that Masako had prepared earlier of cooked rice mixed with sugar, salt, and Japanese rice vinegar. Water boiled beneath a bamboo basket on the stove, steaming the seaweed wrappers. Numi laid a softened wrapper inside a special kitchen gadget, dished out a spoonful of the rice mixture, then a spoonful of ahi. As she folded the gadget shut, the mixture rolled into the wrapper, forming an individual portion of sushi. She garnished the top of each one with finely chopped red and green shrimp.

"Mom, can we tell you what happened to us today?"

"Dear, I want to hear all about it. Lani, would you dice this onion, please?" Masako said, swishing slices of ginger root around the hot oil in the wok. Using a pair of wooden chopsticks, she stir-fried cubes of tofu, mushrooms, and snap peas, then added chicken broth, oyster sauce, and white wine.

"I still wonder if this has something to do with Kekoa," Numi remarked after retelling their ordeal. When Leilani remained silent, Numi pressed on. "Didn't he say anything to you the night he left?"

"Not a word, nothing at all," Leilani murmured, chopping away at a half-cut onion. "After *Tutu* sent him to bed without supper, I brought him a Spam sandwich, but he'd already fallen asleep. The next morning the sandwich hadn't even been touched. The weird thing was, he ran right by me out the front door and kept going. I called him to breakfast, but we never saw him again—for breakfast or anything else."

Tears flooded her eyes. Numi finished her last sushi roll and came over to put her arm about her new sister's shoulders.

"I can't think of anything that could have frightened him so much that he ran away," Leilani said. "I keep wondering if it had something to do with Uncle John's disappearance."

"What happened to him?" Numi asked.

"That's just it. Nobody has seen my uncle since breakfast the day before Kekoa ran away. He left everything he owned. There's no explanation."

"Ooh! That's eerie," whispered Numi. "Your family is so full of mysteries."

"Maybe Kekoa couldn't come home. What if he was hurt? What if he's dead?" Leilani began to sob while she held her onion-soaked hands out in front of her, unable to wipe the tears away. "And if he does go back to our house, how will he ever find us?" Numi led her to the sink and helped her wash away both onion and sorrow.

Chapter 7
Alleys and Offices

ONLY THE PINPOINT glow of a lit cigarette signaled Red Murphy's presence in the dingy doorway, one of many dotting this stone and red clay alley. The lone street lamp half a block away cast long, faint shadows to stalk this passage. Broader than most alleys in the heart of Chinatown, had it been properly paved, it might have become a street with a name and a suitable signpost. Red couldn't be sure that the locals didn't have a name for it. By daylight a handful of tiny shops flourished along its two-block length, peddling the exotic: dried sea horses and snake skins, greasy hog heads, and roasted crisp duck. Now, close to midnight, the aromas lingered, but little else.

A homeless *Pake* turned into the alley and approached the doorway where Red stood, hidden. The old Chinese man stopped for a moment. Though it wasn't apparent to the onlooker, this exact spot was deliberately chosen and not merely a place to rest. He gazed up at the dark apartment across the alley before sensing the presence of another person behind him. Encountering Red, he slipped into his street character.

"Sir! Some odd change for Ol' Chou? Some hot soup to keep him warm?"

Red raised a fist and snapped, "Beat it!" He watched the bent old man with the bamboo cane hobble down the alley and around the corner.

Red fixed his attention on the flight of white wooden stairs across the alley that led to an unlit apartment on the second floor. He knew it well: kitchen, bedroom, bath, and parlor.

A light came on in the parlor. Red dropped his cigarette, stepped on it, and pulled deeper into the shadows. He could hear faint voices—louder and clearer now as the door opened to cast more light. Ducking down, he hid his face in his arms and knees like a sleeping derelict.

Raising his head just enough to observe, he saw a man and woman emerge. They stood together on the stoop, embracing for a few moments.

"Oh, I almost forgot," the man said, reaching into the suit jacket folded over his arm. "Here's a little something extra for you, my dear." His voice carried across the silent alley. She took the envelope, pulled down on both tails of his unmade tie, and kissed him hard on the lips.

"Next Tuesday?" she asked.

"Next Tuesday it is," he replied. He knotted his tie and slipped into the jacket. She closed the door when he reached the bottom step.

Red watched the well-dressed man walk briskly to the corner. Just as he arrived there, a cab appeared out of nowhere. When the cab pulled away, Red rose from his squatting position and stretched his aching legs.

He crossed the alley and started to climb the stairs, but changed his mind. It's just not my night, he thought. That bitch. I won't be second to anyone. As he strode to his car, he passed a blue and white Chevy parked down the street. The motor was idling, but he couldn't make out the driver's face. He didn't recognize the car, but something about it impelled him to make a mental note of the tag number. He hurried around the corner to his Buick. By the time he'd driven back for another look at the Chevy and its driver, it had gone.

* * *

Kekoa awoke the next morning with a new resolve. He meant for this day to be different: a time to be brave and finally do something about his aching conscience and scary dreams. He would go back to *Tutu* Eme and confess everything. The explanations wouldn't come easily. It had been over two years since he'd run away, but the intense fear and loss had clung to him like a cold sore that wouldn't heal. Red wouldn't expect him to return home now, not after two years. He slid the last loaves of fresh-baked bread carefully out of the oven and hung his apron on a hook. After washing up, he pulled a clean T-shirt over his head and combed his mop of black hair a little more carefully than usual, a gesture of gathering up his courage.

Mauro smiled at Sam when she saw a very tidy Kekoa leave the bakery. "Maybe Kekoa like girl at school, *nei*?"

"No, no, he too serious for girls…and he only fourteen," Sam replied.

Outside in the alley Kekoa stopped for a few minutes to pet the waiting Ilio. He put out a paper plate with some table scraps and rubbed his canine buddy affectionately behind the ears. "Got no time for you, today, fella. Got important things to do." With that, the boy walked up to the avenue to wait for the bus. The dog started to follow and then became distracted by another furry creature in the alley.

It took two buses and two hours for Kekoa to get from Kaimuki to Ewa. En route, he allowed his mind to wander, sadly recalling faces from the past as the second bus plodded its way through downtown Honolulu, Chinatown, and Pearl City. Now, as it swung south around the Pearl Harbor Lochs, the cane fields came into view; the street where he had attended school; the *manapua* stand where Leilani had taken him often. He could almost taste the soft steamed bun filled with *char siu*, a sweet, purple pork hash.

Only a few more stops now. Jumping off the bus, he broke into a trot, his *slippahs* slapping against his heels and the pavement as he approached his street and the house where he had once been so happy.

Stunned, he jerked to a stop. All the excitement bled from his whole being. He knew he was standing in front of his grandmother's house—the fourth one from the corner. But was it *Tutu's*? Hers had been the rich green of mango leaves. This house, with its new coat of tan paint, seemed to pop out of its surroundings like a fresh-hulled macadamia nut. And what did that SOLD sign mean in front of Uncle John's gray house next door? He sighed because he knew.

Cautiously, he approached the front door of the tan house and tried the knob. It didn't budge. He ran around to the back door, only to find that it too was locked. But *Tutu* wouldn't do that. He and Leilani had lost so many keys that Eme finally gave up locking the doors at all. Back at the front door, he found a doorbell, which hadn't been there before either. He pressed it.

"Someone's out front," he heard a man's voice say. "Get it, will ya, hon?"

The door opened to reveal a young woman Kekoa had never seen before. "Yes?" she asked.

The boy wanted to run, but he stood his ground and asked for Eme Waiwaiole and Leilani Pualoa.

She shook her head. "I don't know anyone by those names."

"Wait, hon. Wasn't that the old lady that died, the girl's grand-

54

mother?" the man asked as he appeared behind her. He studied the boy for a moment. "When we bought the house from the bank, they told us the owner had died. Was she anything special to you?"

"Oh, jeez, yeah! She my grandmother!" The shock hit, wiping out all the fear and joy he had conjured up for the reunion. His chin dropped to his chest. A sinking, nauseated feeling clamped down on his stomach, and anger collected under heavy breathing. He hadn't been prepared for this. *Tutu* wasn't that old. He'd just assumed she'd always be there. He could barely raise his eyes, and his voice broke as he asked:

"You know where she went, the girl? She's my sistah."

"I'm sorry, no, we don't."

"Thanks, mistah," Kekoa mumbled as he trudged down the steps to the street. He looked in the yard toward the open shed. Empty now, no bulldozer or tools there. He saw the new walkway to the rear of the shed, forcing him to think of Uncle John lying cold and helpless beneath it. Could he still be under there fighting to get out? Did it all really happen? It was as though that part of Kekoa's life had never existed. No one here had ever known him. He felt more dejected than ever as he boarded the bus back to Kaimuki.

The bus had driven a mile or two before Kekoa realized he was riding the wrong one. He hadn't bothered to check the number. It was an easily fixed mistake—he'd simply change buses on Kapiolani Boulevard opposite the Ala Moana Center.

* * *

At ten minutes to three, two days after meeting with the younger Fujita, Red Murphy stepped into the same law offices. This time he chose a no-nonsense, straight-backed chair and picked up a magazine, not to read, but to hide behind while he contemplated his next move. The last meeting had not gone well. His eyes scanned the waiting room, and he became aware of another person seated there, in a far corner. Actually, he saw only brown socks, slippahs, and a pair of dark pants legs extending below a newspaper. Two metal canes with straps attached to the handles leaned against the adjacent chair.

Twenty minutes later, the two large elevator doors opened and Paul Wong, with Leilani Pualoa, stepped into the room.

"Mr. Murphy! What are you doing here?" Paul asked.

"The same thing you are. Mr. Fujita called and asked that I be present at your meeting with him." Red smiled at his ability to come up with such a good answer on such short notice. "And how're you, Leilani?"

"Fine, Uncle Red," she said without enthusiasm. Her face bore an anxious look.

Lori emerged from the center office to greet the newcomers and offer refreshments. "Mr. Fujita will see you now," she said.

All three rose, unaware that the man seated in the far corner had lowered his newspaper to observe them entering Fujita's office. Lori ushered them to the chairs surrounding the bean-shaped glass desk. She brought green tea for Paul and water for the others.

Terumi rose from his red leather chair, smiled, and said, "I'm sure you're anxious to find out what all this is about." Addressing Leilani and Paul, the lawyer began. "First, I must humbly apologize for Gerald Moria's most unprofessional behavior yesterday afternoon. He's our new junior partner and his instructions were to deliver a package to you, Mr. Wong, at Oahu Prep. Learning that you were teaching a class, he took it upon himself to contact Leilani. Unfortunately, he pursued the matter most clumsily. We are truly sorry."

"Thank you, your apology is accepted. I assume it won't happen again," Paul said. "What exactly was in the package?"

Terumi turned to the girl. "Leilani, I have a client who is interested in some land that you and your brother own."

Leilani's dark eyes widened. "Land? We own land?"

"Yes, indeed. And very valuable land, I might add."

"But where?"

"On the windward side, not too far from Kaaawa," Terumi said. "My client plans to build a whole development that will provide housing, stores, a recreation center for young people, the works. It's a huge project that will create many jobs and other economic benefits, too; a marina, condos, offices, and community services in an area most deserving of such a boost. This land was given to you and your brother by your father. It is of prime importance to my client's project. I have brought you here to make you a most generous offer on behalf of my client."

He slid a large manila envelope toward Leilani and Paul. "I'm sure you will find this not only beneficial to you, but to all the people directly involved. In the envelope—it's all explained. You'll see my client's proposal, copies of the plats, and a brochure describing the project. There is only one thing that I must ask of you. As this is a project of considerable risk in time and money, please assure me that you will keep the information confidential."

Terumi paused to take a sip of ice water and continued cautiously. "I understand there is a family trust involved, and that several trustees must be consulted."

"As you know," said Paul, "Mr. Murphy here is one of those trustees."

"He is?" Terumi Fujita swiveled his chair around and studied Red's face intently. "You never told me this, Mr. Murphy."

"Didn't think it was important," claimed Red. "Thought you knew. After all, your father drew up the original papers."

Terumi scowled, annoyed with himself for missing such an obvious connection. Taking another sip of ice water to cool his irritation, he proceeded in a controlled voice. "Leilani, my client is willing to give you thirty days to consider his offer. I'm sure you'll have many questions, and of course, I'll be available whenever you need me to answer them."

Leilani looked stunned. Paul responded quickly.

"This is astonishing news. I believe we have a good deal of homework to do before we can ask any intelligent questions. Don't you think so, Leilani?"

"Oh, yes," she said.

"And of course," Paul continued, "there are also other trustees to consult. We'll be in touch with you soon, sir. By the way, may we know who your client is or something about him?"

"No, I'm afraid that information is privileged," Terumi replied as he stood. He bowed politely to Leilani and offered his hand to Paul. "I look forward to our next meeting." He turned to face Red. "Aloha! Goodbye, Mr. Murphy."

Red's beefy face flushed crimson, as though ready to explode. He could hardly contain his anger. To close the deal he had to deliver all twenty properties. Fujita was cutting him out of the promised bonus by dealing directly with the trust to acquire the kids' lots! *Double-cross me, will he?* He swore under his breath, turned his back on Fujita, and led the party through the office door. No one noticed the man behind the newspaper still waiting in the reception room. By the time they reached the elevator, Red had simmered down, congratulating himself for holding his temper.

They rode down in silence. Red excused himself at the third floor, where he retrieved his car from its parking place. The others emerged at the ground floor and proceeded through the revolving door to the street.

* * *

Up on the twenty-second floor, the elevator doors opened once again into the law offices. Yoshiro, the elder Fujita and the firm's most senior partner, stepped off. "Ah, my good friend," he said to the man seated in the corner. "Sorry to keep you waiting. I've been in court all day. Please come in."

The man grasped both canes. Leaning forward, he struggled to raise himself up and followed Yoshiro into his office.

* * *

Out on the street, as Paul and Leilani waited for a cab to hail, Red drove out of the garage and rolled down his window to offer a ride. They declined.

Just then, a public bus pulled in next to "TheBus" sign and several passengers got off, including a lanky young boy coming their way. Leilani looked up with a shock of recognition.

Kekoa took a few hesitant steps toward her, then stopped short.

"Kekoa!" she screamed. "Kekoa, wait! It's me, Lani!" Her heart hammered. Her brother was actually alive and well and, above all, here.

Kekoa had recognized the driver of the car behind them—that beet-red face, the calculating gray eyes. Red Murphy! As Kekoa heard the car shift into drive, he panicked, whirled about, and dashed across Kapiolani Boulevard toward the Ala Moana Center, easily dissolving into the mall crowds. Meanwhile, the traffic devoured a fuming Red.

Leilani stood helpless at the curb, straining to catch another glimpse of her brother. But he had vanished.

Chapter 8
New Year's Days

KEKOA DARTED into the mall, intending to race straight through to an ocean-front exit, but he realized he should've known better. These were the after-Christmas hordes: gridlocked cars looking for scarce parking spaces; window shoppers strolling; idle smokers puffing on their cigarettes; locals waiting in line to return unwanted gifts; and tourists hunting for last-minute bargains before returning home. There wasn't any room to run. But he couldn't afford to stop either. He had to get away from the man who wanted him dead.

Was he overreacting? Driving a car, Red couldn't possibly follow him in here. Or could he? Kekoa slowed his pace to make himself look less like a fugitive and more like an indigenous mall creature. Faces coming toward him, faces appearing behind him—could any of them be Red's? Afraid of being spooked further, Kekoa put his head down and kept going. He threaded his way past the shops on the ground floor—swim suits, T-shirts, books, diamonds—and encountered a throng around Center Stage, where a trio of slack-key guitarists performed Hawaiian melodies. He managed to reach the escalator and take it up one flight. He walked to the far end of the mall level and hopped onto the DOWN escalator behind Long's Drug Store. Dodging a rack of *muumuus* rolled into his path by a delivery boy, he broke into a run in the parking garage, less jammed at this end of the mall, and exited into the street.

Waiting at the curb, he saw an old Buick much like Red's approach from the left. This sight injected a fresh dose of panic into the fevered youth. Kekoa bounded across the six broad lanes of Ala Moana Boulevard, eliciting a chorus of angry horns. On the far curb, the boy sprinted full-out for the break in the rock wall and the foot bridge leading into the beach park. He had to make it there before that Buick could make a U-turn around the median strip. Down the bridge, across green lawns and patches of red clay, he plunged into the park. An over-the-shoulder glance yielded no sign of Red. Kekoa's throat and lungs burned raw. Charging across a broad lawn, he blundered into a cluster of Chinese couples playing croquet. They shook their fingers at him and chattered their reproaches. But the fleeing youngster—heading for the cover of the tennis courts beyond—heard none of it.

Exhausted, Kekoa pulled up short. He'd covered a lot of ground in the few minutes since he'd gotten off the bus on Kapiolani. He now had a brand-new image of Leilani, complete with tears streaming down her sweet cheeks. She'd called to him, literally screeching his name, and he'd wanted so much to go to her, but when he saw Red sitting in the car behind her, no way. Kekoa collapsed on the coarse green grass. Beside him loomed the chain-link fence edging the tennis courts. Damning Red silently, the boy punched and pounded the innocent earth beneath him until his knuckles and fist hurt.

Kekoa soon became aware of new sounds: the thwack of racquets swatting balls and the thwock of balls hitting the court. The *haole* couple playing there managed long volleys while they surrendered their fair complexions to the late afternoon sun. Kekoa looked through the fence beneath the black mesh wind screen and noticed a zebra dove basking in the sun in the doubles alley. A gusting breeze softly ruffled its gray body and tail feathers. Its legs were tucked out of sight; and neither the blue-ringed eyes nor the blue beak flinched from the balls zinging to the right and left of it.

The bird's blind courage fascinated Kekoa. He decided that birds must live most of their short lives in some kind of imminent, yet unknown danger. Maybe this was true of people, too, and he might as well get used to the idea. He needed a plan to find Leilani. If only he could find her in a safe place, where Red wasn't stalking him, she'd know what to do.

Kekoa picked himself up and walked to the restroom at the end of the courts. After pulling the T-shirt over his head, he bent under the faucet and let the cool water drizzle down his face and spine, slowly drawing the heat of exhaustion from his body and the angst from his head. Soaking wet, the boy crossed the street to the lava rock wall lining the beach. Following the wall until it broke for the parking lot to Magic Island, he looked seaward. Picnickers sat beneath umbrella-shaped monkeypod trees and poincianas bearing claw-like clusters of red blossoms. The joggers, the mothers pushing strollers, and the lovers cuddling on the sand all seemed so relaxed, so carefree. Kekoa needed to calm down, too. Sam had taught him how to relax and achieve a kind of inner peace. He searched for somewhere to sit, a spot to recover his cool.

The youngster spread out his shirt to dry on the low wall that began again on the other side of the parking lot. Then he hoisted himself up onto the wall. As the sun dried his sweaty clothes, he noticed several men weaving new seine nets. They had secured the central cord for each net to a low banyan branch, with the net fanning out toward the ground. One of the men looked so much like his Uncle Big John that Kekoa did a double-take. He watched the man weave a spindle of nylon cord in and out of the open links at the outer edges. The net grew slowly, and the youngster soon became bored. He dozed until a misty spray from a dark, heavy cloud startled him.

Kekoa swung his legs over the wall and faced the opposite direction. On the *makai* or seaward side he saw a fisherman wading knee-deep on a flat shoal lining the channel to the Ala Wai canal. The fisherman, gathering a neatly folded seine under one arm, twisted first to the left, then to the right, tossing the spinning, circular net out into the channel. Weights tied along the border caused the net to spread open and then sink about its prey. The line attached to the center of the seine brought the weights together as the fisherman hauled the net back in.

"One-two-three-four," coached an intruding voice from farther out in the water.

Kekoa looked up to see a flotilla of outrigger canoes rapidly approaching the shore. The counting he heard took place each time the six young oarsmen changed the sides they paddled on. Five canoes raced toward him until each passed the last marker. Then back-paddling, the canoes slowed, coasting shoreward, one-by-one, scraping to a halt on the short ramp traversing through a break in the wall. Once the canoes were beached, Kekoa saw the high school paddlers lift the canoes and carry them across the park road to waiting trailers.

"Hey, Pualoa! Where ya been, *brah?*" a voice called out.

With a jolt, Kekoa recognized a boy he'd known from school— older now and more muscular. He wanted to respond to his friend, but an innate sense of panic seized him. Questions would be asked. He waved sheepishly, snatched up his partially dried shirt, and quickly scanned the park for any sign of Red. Satisfied, Kekoa knew the time had come to grab a bus and return home to the bakery.

Kekoa caught the bus on Kapiolani, at least five safe blocks from where he had encountered Red and Leilani. He sat down in the rear of a nearly full bus. A heavy-set woman sat down next to him and smiled, but his mind still reflected on what he'd seen in the park. The man weaving nets could have been his uncle. And if it had been, Kekoa would have been there helping him instead of just watching. Many times he'd wished that Big John was his father. A lot of good that would do him now—Big John had been murdered.

Kekoa wanted a father and a life like those guys in the canoes. Lani had told him their father had run off and deserted them. No one had ever heard from him since. Was he dead, too? Or was it that the sonofabitch just didn't love them? How could he do that to his own *kei-ki*—not care what's happening to us? Kekoa rubbed his still-sore fists and swore under his breath at an unknown figure and relationship he couldn't understand.

The heavy-set woman turned toward him and gave him the stink eye. The boy flushed and sank down in his seat, wondering how much the woman had actually heard.

* * *

Weeks later, Kekoa awoke one morning to a scraping sound in the storage area that had become his bedroom. His bleary eyes watched Sam struggle to pull a huge stone bowl and wooden mallet from under a bottom shelf. He rolled out of bed and labored along with Sam until they had manipulated the bowl through the storeroom door into the workroom, a massive kitchen of sorts.

"What's this for?" Kekoa asked.

"Get dressed, I tell you," Sam replied, smiling. Kekoa hurried into his clothes and splashed water on his face. When he returned, Sam had poured steaming sweet rice from the rice cooker into the stone bowl. "Today Sam and Kekoa make *mochi* for Japanese New Year."

"But the New Year was two days ago," Kekoa protested. "My Uncle John used to take us to the park at the top of Alewa Heights. We could see the whole city from there, and the sky full of fire and smoke. By midnight, you couldn't see the city lights through the smoke and the noise never stopped."

Sam scrutinized the boy's face. "This first time you mention family beside sister. Uncle very special for you, *nei*?"

"Yeah," Kekoa sighed. "He's my father's brother and business partner. I don't remember my real father—too young when he went away. Uncle Big John treats me like a son. He lives next door. He always eats at our table and looks out for us. He keeps us a real family. I like it best when we go fishin' and talkin' story." With a start, Kekoa realized he'd spoken about his uncle as if he were still alive. His voice trailed off. "But he's dead now."

"That too bad, son," Sam said as he lowered himself to sit cross-legged in front of the bowl. He picked up the wooden mallet with its flattened soft surface and contemplated its tolling of the years. "This year, this day, just beginning. Plenty time to talk story."

Kekoa imitated Sam's cross-legged position on the opposite side of the bowl to listen and watch.

"January first, that *haole* New Year," Sam said. "Hawaii is state of many New Years and many different peoples celebrate them. Only days later is Japanese New Year, a sacred time. We pray for good health and good year. We say *Shinen Omedetto Gozaimasu!* Also, time to bring food and drink to graves of ancestors." He began to pound the rice at the bottom of the bowl in a methodical beat, transforming it into a gooey, near-clear liquid. "There are other New Years. Next month we see Chinese New Year bring in Year of Dog. Chinese say *Kung Hee Fat Choy!*"

Testing the consistency of the *mochi* with a fingertip to his tongue, Sam poured the mixture into a large jar. He began again; more rice, water, sweeteners, pounding. "Vietnamese have Tet New Year, and Thais have theirs, too, in April."

Kekoa took his turns at the pounding. Sam supervised. He explained that most modern bakeries used electric *mochi* pounders, but he preferred the generations-old ritual pounding by hand. They were interrupted when Mauro entered the room with a lovely stranger who looked a year or two older than Kekoa.

"Kekoa, this my sister's girl, Yasuko Mitsui. She come help make *mochi*."

The boy stood and slowly nodded his head. Yasuko bowed in return. She carried an arrangement of fresh pine sprigs and green bamboo stalks. The three thick stalks, held upright, were cut on the bias at three progressive lengths and bound together with many turns of rice-straw cording.

Mauro received this New Year's gift of *kadomatsu*—doorway pine—with a religious grace. The three elements of the *kadomatsu*, she explained to Kekoa, were long life, virtue, and constancy. Setting the gift in the window closest to the front door, she opened up for the day's business.

Yasuko slipped out of a warm-up jacket, carefully placing it on the back of a chair so that it would show the Kaimuki High School Girls' Volleyball logo across its back. She wore a playsuit that accentuated her sturdy legs. Yasuko bowed gracefully to her uncle.

Sam nodded back and said, "Kekoa, he learn to make *mochi*. You work together."

Turning toward Kekoa and smiling, her round face and dark eyes expressed her immediate acceptance of him. Kekoa could not take his eyes from this very feminine creature with beautiful long black hair tied in a pony tail. Her embarrassment finally registered with him, and he mumbled a short apology.

She nodded her approval.

Sam and Mauro took no notice of this exchange. Sam returned to the daily baking, and the two *mochi* makers pounded away diligently. Yasuko sang and hummed as she and Kekoa tapped in and out of the tunes. He was soon caught up in the happy atmosphere of family activity. It reminded him of Leilani and the activities they'd shared.

Kekoa kept looking up at her jacket on the chair. An idea formed in his head. Leilani should be in high school now, too. He would get a list of the high schools from the phone book and hang around on each campus, waiting until they let out in the afternoon. He'd go by each school until he found her. He felt proud of this plan. For the first time he could do something about his predicament besides just running away. And Leilani would be looking for him too, now that she'd recognized him getting off the bus.

"Is there a girl at your school…" he blurted his question out, not knowing how to say it subtly, "named Leilani Pualoa?"

"Don't know the name. What grade is she in?"

"Junior maybe, or senior," he replied.

"I'm a senior, she's not in my class. Is she a friend? A relative?"

Kekoa looked over toward the oven where Sam worked and decided not to say too much in front of him and Mauro. "No, just a friend. I'm not even sure she goes there."

Yasuko sensed she shouldn't press him. "I'll ask around," she murmured.

They added food coloring and continued pounding until the *mochi* was smooth. After a time it had congealed into mounds, which they carried to a table dusted with *mochiko*, a dry sweet rice flour. Soon the mounds were flattened, cut into pink, white, and green shapes, and packed in bakery boxes for delivery to ice cream parlors and ethnic food centers in midtown Honolulu. Kekoa and Yasuko divided up the orders and set out to deliver them. They agreed to meet afterward at the Honolulu Academy of Arts for the Japanese New Year Festival.

* * *

Finished with his last delivery, Kekoa bounded up the Academy steps and joined the crowds flowing through the museum to the medieval stone promenades and courtyards where the festival flourished. Yasuko was nowhere to be seen.

The boy's eyes widened to a world of crafts and traditions unknown to him. Origami artists magically transformed paper into animals, flowers, and toys. He saw an immense rice-straw rope strung across an arch. "These sacred *shimenawa* ropes," the placard said, "symbolize eternal life and sometimes reached a weight of seven tons." He wondered who could handle such a thing.

He threaded his way among tables of gold Buddhas, porcelain good-luck cats, and Japanese dolls in kimonos and exotic headdresses, smiling out at him from their glass boxes. *Wow, he thought, a hundred dollars for a doll!* Backing away, he almost bumped into an aproned gentleman carving flowers out of *daikon*, long white turnips. At the next table, a bony old man bent over a bare tree limb. With a razor-sharp knife, he pared paper-thin shavings down to the branch base until a graceful bouquet emerged. Soon he had surrounded himself with a forest of these delicate ferns of wood.

The thunder of *taiko* drums propelled Kekoa to a courtyard, where a stage rose in the midst of a garden. Eight men and women were striking multiple drums of all sizes with pairs of heavily padded sticks. The lead drummer, bare to his waist, worked up a frenzy, his muscles bulging and gleaming with sweat. In the finale, the players continuously rotated among the drums, creating an unbroken hypnotic rhythm.

65

Kekoa felt their power. So transfixed was he that at first he didn't feel the brawny hand gripping his arm. He turned his head to see a woman standing too close to him. She had an ugly red birthmark splayed across her cheek and neck. The Community Services pursuer!

She yanked him around to face her. "Aren't you the homeless squirt that kept dodging me last summer?" Her blotch moved contrary to her mouth as if it had a life of its own.

"Let go of me. I'm not him. Don't know what you're talkin' about. Let me go." He tried to shake loose, but couldn't.

"Yeah, it's you all right," she boomed. "Got some new clothes too, I see."

"Hey! Take your hands off him!" The voice came from behind Kekoa. It belonged to Yasuko.

The woman's eyes narrowed into reptilian slits. Her body bent, coiled, inclined to strike. But her words carried the real venom.

"Butt out, girl, he's a homeless street brat that's better off in the Community Services juvenile system."

"You'd better let go of him before I call the cops," Yasuko screeched.

"I'm only doin' my job, little girl," she retorted. "We can't have him running wild in the streets, can we? And you better watch your mouth, or I'll take you in, too."

"He's my cousin," lied Yasuko. "He lives with my Uncle Sam and my Auntie Mauro. You better believe he's not homeless. If you hurt him, we'll sue you—and the agency, too."

The woman released her grip, but backed Kekoa against the wall while she asked, "Where do you go to school?"

"Kaimuki High, same as me," Yasuko spat back before Kekoa had a chance to reply. She stepped in front of the woman, grabbed Kekoa by the hand, and led him away.

* * *

By mid-February, a month had passed since the nasty encounter with the Community Services lady. Kekoa knew she could pop up anywhere. But nothing would keep him from enjoying Chinese New Year, despite his apprehensions about returning to Chinatown alone. As a small boy, Uncle John had always taken him and Leilani to the festivities as a special treat. Big John would heft him onto his broad shoulders and ramble through the crowd, pulling Lani by her hand. He could see everything and feel both immense power and security from his high roost.

Kekoa got off the bus at Maunakea Street and walked toward the Nuuanu Stream promenade. At once he heard the rat-a-tat-tat of fireworks popping, snapping on pavement, barking in the Year of the Dog. As each firecracker string spent itself, another, three to four feet long, took its place. Strings of fifty to a hundred firecrackers were gang-fused to fire in rapid succession. Spent black powder suffused the air with its acrid smell and taste.

Darkness had begun to shroud the crowded riverside promenade where the celebrants gathered. Tourists and locals drifted into the brightly lit restaurants of the Chinese Cultural Plaza. Drums and gongs beat a thunderous cadence. A huge paper maché lion's head, painted in dazzling colors, magically appeared. The lion's head was supported by long bamboo stilts that afforded it magnificent unpredictable lunges forward and upward in a frightening manner. Enormous eyes rolled with the head's motion. The lion's body and tail, draped in matching colors, bobbed obediently behind it.

The head was operated by an athletic young man leading two shorter boys in the body behind him. The head man fearlessly stomped into the exploding firecrackers. They danced the traditional Lion Dance, the youngsters conforming to their part of the feline anatomy. Others stood at the ready to replace the athletes in their strenuous dancing. Several musicians accompanied the charging lion, thumping drums and clanging cymbals. The grand lion entered an elegant Chinese restaurant and paraded among the tables. Parents handed dollar bills to their small children, who timidly fed the lion's gaping gold mouth. Before this night finished, as many as a dozen lions would snake through the streets. They would visit restaurants and shops to be "fed" along the way. A shopkeeper's donation would frighten off evil spirits and guarantee a prosperous business year.

Kekoa followed two lions down Maunakea Street. From a distance, he saw the face of a bearded old man in a doorway and immediately thought of Ol' Chou. Images of the kind man who'd mentored him through homeless months in the Chinatown streets stirred within him. What had happened to his friend? Could he be back on the streets again? When the boy looked a second time, the haunting face had disappeared. The surging throng carried him helplessly along as it pursued the lions.

As the evening lengthened, the explosions grew deafening, and many onlookers held their ears in pain. Voices became hoarse competing with the noise. Deep piles of red paper residue accumulated in the street. Smoke rose in billows, thickening in the throat. Shopkeepers and revelers alike threw the strings of firecrackers into the street to explode there. Others tied the strings to bamboo poles, ladders, and shop signs to raise the booming white flashes high above encircling crowds.

Not far in front of Kekoa, but partially hidden by the crush of the crowds, a spectator stood with his hairy hand on the rump of the flashy woman next to him. Occasionally, the man squeezed her bun, and the woman squealed and wiggled her hips coquettishly. Bet she's a prostitute, Kekoa thought. Fascinated by her tight dress and the delightful way the woman moved in it, his eyes completely ignored the man with her. Intrigued, his adolescent hormones stirring, he followed the couple at a safe distance.

Within a few minutes, he realized that he was not the only one following them. A man lurked close by, a local in a faded blue aloha shirt, black trousers, and slippahs. He was tall, but stooped over as if from age. Then Kekoa saw his metal canes, deftly manipulated as he kept himself hidden in the shadows of the shops. Something about the man, his bushy hair and craggy face, looked faintly familiar.

But Kekoa had more interest in the raunchy couple and moved closer to them. As the brawny man casually took in his surroundings, he noticed the boy. At the moment when Red Murphy and Kekoa spotted each other, neither could tell who was more stunned. Red lunged for him and grabbed at the sweatshirt tied around Kekoa's waist. The boy spun away, and his new UH sweatshirt slipped loose. Kekoa ducked into the crush of bodies and out along the storefronts. Red shoved his woman aside with such force that she fell to the pavement with a cry of pain and outrage. He charged toward Kekoa again, but abruptly stopped when a man in the shadows tossed a long string of sizzling firecrackers in his path.

"You sonofabitch bastard!" Red turned and shouted. But his anger withered in the din; the man had already hobbled out of sight. An unnerved Red edged back through the mob to find his fallen woman.

Kekoa disappeared easily into the crowd. He wanted to go home,

68

but he needed to get his UH Rainbows sweatshirt back without confronting Red again. It was a gift from Yasuko, and he couldn't bear to lose it. He hoped Murphy had discarded it somewhere. He slipped around the corner and skirted the block before returning to the spot where he'd last seen Red. Ducking into a noodle shop doorway, he spied Red's whore. She was a hot one all right, hotheaded, too, and it seemed she wasn't taking Murphy's abuse lying down. Surprisingly nimble in her spike heels, the woman leaped up and roundhoused Red with her large purse. Swinging it like an Olympic hammer-thrower, she caught him on the cheek and decked him. A wide-legged stance with both hands on her hips reflected the woman's triumphant revenge. The purse dangling from her right fist remained a threat—daring him to make something more of their fight.

"What the hell!" Red bellowed, holding the side of his face. "You got a brick in there, you bitch?" He took the dare, picked himself up off the street, and made a move in her direction.

She pivoted and plunged into the crowds. Red struggled to follow, but Chinatown was her territory, and the celebrating throng quickly closed in around her. She knew every street and alley here and easily lost him in the first block of pursuit.

Red returned to the corner where he'd dropped Kekoa's sweatshirt. As he recovered it from the road, he felt a sting below and behind his right knee. A stray spark from a firecracker was smoldering on his trouser leg. He bent over and slapped his calf to smother it, and at that moment caught sight of Kekoa, framed in the light from the noodle shop's open door. Red gave no sign he had seen the boy. He sauntered over to the curb, nonchalantly threw the sweatshirt in the sidewalk trash basket, and retreated into the milling masses. The sweatshirt remained visible through the basket's wire mesh.

Kekoa waited ten minutes to be sure that Red had gone. Then he slowly approached the prized sweatshirt. A few feet away, he heard a scuffle behind him and turned.

"Hey, watch who yer shovin'."

Red had bullied his way past a man carrying a baby and now bore down on Kekoa. The boy glanced back and realized Red's decoy tactic had closed the gap between them. Kekoa turned toward the river and saw, straight ahead, the sidewalk display of a kitchen supply store. As he ran by, he flung out his arm, pulling down two stacks of bamboo steamer baskets and toppling a cartful of wooden salad bowls. The enraged owner shook his fists in the air and screamed angry words in Chinese.

Red attempted to leap over the mess sprawled before him. Instead, he misstepped and fell, his bulk splayed out among the bowls and baskets. The owner whacked him with a broom as he fumbled for a footing. He yanked the broom from the angry shopkeeper, threatened the man, and tossed it in the street. The shopkeeper's tiny wife shuffled toward him with a baseball bat and a string of expletives he had no need to translate. He escaped her wrath by quickening his pace, but the kid had gotten away again.

Kekoa cornered the block, doubling back to Maunakea to retrieve his sweatshirt. He spotted it through the mesh sides of the trash receptacle in front of the noodle shop. But before he could get there, the stranger with the canes emerged from the shadows, scooped it out, and hobbled into the smoke-filled throng.

Kekoa followed him into the courtyard of the Chinese Cultural Plaza. With the two canes leaned against a steaming stall, the man bought a hot *jin dui*, a chewy Chinese doughnut. The rolled-up sweatshirt remained tucked under one arm. Stopping at another stall, the man offered several dollars to a young clerk to paint Chinese characters for "Prosperity, Health, and Serenity" in black and gold on a red ribbon. There were banners everywhere—Happy New Year, *Hauoli Makahiki Hou, Kung Hee Fat Choy, Shinen Omedetto Gozaimasu, Maligayang Bagong Taon,* and *Sae Hae Pock Mon Hi Pat U Ship Siyo.* The man disappeared.

Happy New Year? For Kekoa there was nothing to be happy about. It just marked another year without his real family. He bit his lip. It was all too much, the frustration, the sudden scare, the constant fear, and now his lost sweatshirt. Kicking firecracker rubbish out of his way, he headed for the bus home.

Chapter 9
Circle Island

"YOU REALLY don't have to do this, Alex Wong."

"Well, Leilani, I'd say that my parents didn't leave me much choice. I did have other plans, you know."

"I know. Seeing my trust land can wait, I s'pose—especially if you're going to be such an ogre about it."

"Even ogres have a right to a Sunday off, but this is a done deal—Mom and Dad have spoken." He tossed their beach bags on the back seat.

"You were in such a great mood when you came down to breakfast this morning."

"Yeah! Just get in the car." He held the passenger door open for her, and she slipped in obediently.

Masako stood on the lanai with her arms folded across her chest. She called to her son, "Drive carefully, dear. Don't be too late."

"Right, Mom. Don't worry about it." His voice carried his annoyance. He waved as he slid behind the wheel and started the engine.

He headed for the freeway entrance on University Avenue, then drove east along H-1 to Kalanianaole Highway, congested with Sunday traffic. They could see the sparkling ocean on their right, the *makai* side. On the *mauka* side, mountains ridged with deep valleys rose up like bundt cakes. The pastel homes perched on their crests resembled drizzled frosting.

"Are you gonna sulk like a little boy all day?" Leilani started. "Couldn't we call a truce?"

"That bad, huh?"

"Uh-huh!"

"I guess I've been a bit of a grouch," he admitted. "Sorry."

She gave him a sidelong hopeful glance. "It was only a casual

71

remark I made at the table. Well, not casual, actually. I do want to see the land for myself, but I didn't think I'd ever get the chance, and then your dad suggested we go today. Well, it's important to me, Alex. I mean, this land is the only real thing I own in the world. I'm glad you're going to be a good sport about it."

"Maybe we can stop for a swim and a plate lunch," he offered. Just past the community of Hawaii Kai, at the highest point on the road, Alex made a sharp turn into Hanauma Bay Beach Park. They walked down a steep path into a crater formed millions of years ago. Just off the narrow sandy beach, they swam with vibrantly colored fish in a crystal ocean that had washed through a rift in the crater.

Afterward, as Alex drove away from the park, Leilani playfully touched her head to his shoulder. "Now that was fun," she said.

The road wound its way downward and he pulled into a lookout. "It's pretty hazy today, but you can still see Molokai from here," he said.

Shading her eyes with one hand, she peered out at the horizon. "I can just make it out. I'd like to go there sometime. The other neighbor islands, too."

Pulling into the next scenic lookout, he called her attention to a spout of white sea spray shooting twenty feet into the air in front of them. Seconds later, a gusting cross-breeze wiped it away. The Halona Blow Hole, an old lava tube venting under the surface of the sea, pumped trapped water skyward on the force of succeeding waves.

At the right end of the lookout, jagged black lava cliffs formed a protected cove, and foamy green water lapped against a small patch of sandy shore below. Tourists leaned over the wall, taking snapshots of the brave swimmers who had climbed down the hill to swim in the cove.

"This is where they filmed the famous love scene in *From Here to Eternity*," Alex said.

She giggled. "Doesn't look like a whole lot of privacy for a love scene."

Leilani kept finding her eyes drawn to Alex. She tried hard not to stare at him. In his white polo shirt and khaki shorts he seemed so male today, much more so than in the house. She liked his trim, muscular body, all five-foot-ten of him. His profile reflected intelligence and self-confidence. Thick brows and a full head of straight black hair held generous highlights of silver—surprising in a man only twenty-four, but to her, they made him look interesting, not old. The wind ruffled his hair, but it always fell back perfectly into place.

Alex sensed the weight of her gaze and briefly allowed his eyes to wander over her. On impulse he took her hand as they strolled back to the car.

When the road, bordered by huge craggy rock formations, became level terrain, they came upon Sandy Beach Park. Squadrons of kites soared and dove above them. A complexity of cables and grips manipulated dragons and gull-winged birds as they contended with boxes, triangles, and planes.

"It's like a circus in the sky," Alex said.

"Swirling colors—more like an artist's palette," Leilani corrected.

"Lani, you say that as if you're visualizing your own personal painting."

"Thank you, Alex, that's nice. I feel that way. Sometimes I want to paint everything in sight."

She fell silent, reflecting for a moment. "You know what Mark Twain said about Hawaii? 'No other land could so lovingly and so beseechingly haunt me.'"

Alex listened to her with a new respect.

They leaned against the car, gazing out at the ocean's edge. Dozens of youngsters, face-down on boogie boards, rode the surf into shore, where the rough waves dumped them on the beach. The kids eagerly flopped back onto their boards and paddled out for additional punishment.

Could one of those boys be my Kekoa? Leilani wondered. Her mood shifted, a scowl intruded and seemed to dominate. Kekoa had looked so scared when he ran away from her that day on Kapiolani.

Alex intentionally interrupted her mood: "What about Michener? He wrote about Hawaii."

"I know," Leilani said. "He really understood how the *haoles* destroyed our civilization, from the day Captain Cook landed—the greed, the diseases they brought with them. Sometimes," she said slowly, "I feel that the only ones who really get the benefits here are the tourists and the rich *haoles*. The Hawaiian people—we got a raw deal."

"Maybe, but I don't see how we can change that now."

73

Leilani warmed up to her tirade. "We're the poorest in the state, the least educated. We have the lowest level jobs. The Americans overthrew our kingdom a hundred years ago, and it's been downhill for the Hawaiians ever since. We need to get it back."

This turn in the conversation made Alex edgy. "Get what back? We're the fiftieth state now. Don't you think Hawaii has an equal footing with the other states?"

"Only on paper, Alex. You know who runs this state? The Asians and the Caucasians. But the native Hawaiians—we're left out in the cold. Some people think the public schools just exist to churn out hotel workers. And things aren't going to change until we have sovereignty in our own state."

"But are the Hawaiians prepared to take over the state, to run the government? I mean, if they're disadvantaged?" Alex asked.

"That's a typical accountant's attitude," she snapped.

He needed to stop arguing with her. He disagreed vehemently, but knew he was coming on as the enemy. "Hungry yet?" He pointed to a lunch wagon with a side window and awning just down the road.

"Famished!" she said. "And I guess I'll get down off my soapbox now."

He put his arm around her shoulders and squeezed. "It's okay, Leilani, I want to know how you feel—even if I don't always agree. Now let's eat!"

He ordered a plate-lunch of barbecued beef ribs crosscut to the bone—Korean style; macaroni salad; and steamed rice. It all came on a crowded paper plate. Leilani chose two pork-filled manapuas. They took their plates and cans of guava-pineapple juice to the far end of the beach and sat on the sand.

Alex turned serious. "Leilani, Numi tells me you're doing great at Oahu Prep. Do you like it there?"

"I suppose so. I'm getting by. It's a great education, and I know I'm really lucky to be able to go to a private school. You probably think I'm whining a lot, Alex. I don't want to sound that way, but sometimes I feel like I'm from another planet."

"How come?"

"I'm not like the other kids. They have parents. They have sisters and brothers—even grandparents."

"You have us, we're your family now."

"It's not the same. Oh, I don't want to sound ungrateful. I love you all dearly. And Numi truly is a sister to me." Leilani absently ran the fingers of her right hand through her hair. Sunlight captured its auburn glints. "But sometimes...sometimes, after all that's happened, I feel like I'm a hundred years older than the other girls. I've got to find Kekoa. Once I find him, we'll be a family again. Oh, I know two isn't much of a family, but to me, it's the whole world."

Her confession came in such a burst that Alex reddened and nearly choked on his mouthful of rice. "I'm sorry, Leilani. I didn't mean to be so insensitive."

"You're not being insensitive. I'm glad you care enough about me to ask." She reached for his hand, and they smiled at one another.

Leilani cautiously continued. "I miss my brother so much. I wonder how he's surviving. Maybe one day I'll even find my father. I was so angry with him for my mother's death that I drove him away for good." She lowered her head and her thick hair fell around her face, almost as if she were trying to hide.

"You drove him away? If I've done my math right, you were too young to have so much power."

"Yeah, you're right, I was only four. I shouldn't blame myself. It was *Tutu* Eme who sent him away."

"Have you forgiven him yet?" Alex leaned onto his right hip so he could see her face.

"I'm not really sure, I don't think so." Leilani sank back to rest her elbows on the sand.

The packed sand finally felt too hard beneath her; she stood up, gathered their lunch litter, and dumped it in the nearest trash can. When she returned to him, she offered her hand, knowing full well she couldn't pull him up. He took her hand, but rose under his own power. The two came face-to-face, and the thought of kissing struck them both. Each regretted the opportunity lost.

They resumed their driving, and the road bent northerly, hugging the shape of Oahu. He sensed her silence and tried to jump-start the conversation again. "That's what you want to do? Be an artist?"

"Yes, but I want to teach Hawaiian history, too. I want to go to a Mainland college—Berkeley, maybe."

"Oh-oh, do I detect a budding radical here?"

She half-smiled. "I don't know, too early to tell. Actually, I want to major in art and paint big canvases of Hawaii, especially Hawaiian women, their strength and nobility."

His expression turned pensive. "Have you considered going to UH?"

She shrugged. "I guess I'll have to—if I don't get a scholarship to a Mainland school. Anyway, it's a year and a half off. Right now I've got to concentrate on my grades. And finding my brother."

They drove all the way to Kualoa Park before stopping for a rest station and a closeup view of Mokolii Island, Chinaman's Hat to the locals. Only 500 feet offshore, it looked close enough to swim to, but the deadly currents could quickly carry a swimmer out to sea. Leilani watched a park worker on a riding mower. White cattle egrets marched behind it in single file, pecking at the insects churned up in the fresh cuttings. As the mower doubled back to cut a new swath, the egrets turned in unison and followed. Leilani laughed, fixing the scene in her mind for a future sketch.

Before driving off, Alex checked the map for the exact location of Leilani's real estate. She sat tense and quiet in the car as they neared the spot where the narrow shore road bent in the shape of a horseshoe and left a low-lying marsh in its midst. He pulled onto the shoulder and unfolded the real estate plat his father had given him. They wandered several hundred paces in each direction. But even with the plat, they found it difficult to determine exactly which lots belonged to Leilani and Kekoa.

Inland, a flat stretch of marsh led into an unnamed valley, dense with brambled undergrowth and fallen trees. "It's not very scenic here," she said, her face crestfallen. "I expected so much more." Then her expression brightened. "But still, it's mine and my brother's—some of it, anyway. You know, Alex, we Hawaiians feel very attached to our land. It's something special—hard to describe. We owe our lives to the land. Everything comes from it." Her eyes sparkled with fresh tears.

Alex laid his hand on her shoulder. "I guess a good developer can turn any acreage into something spectacular. All it takes is..."

"Wait! Did you hear something?" Leilani interrupted. She'd heard a low growl or groan followed by another groan. "A hurt animal? No, it sounds human, or almost."

"It's coming from over there, where that set of tire tracks goes off the road!" he shouted, pointing.

He took her hand, and they picked their way through the thick brush. They followed the tire tracks until the rusted trunk of an old Pontiac Bonneville edged into view. The car's front end pitched down, as if the marsh were about to engulf it. The rear wheels, suspended above the mud, had left deep ruts where the driver had tried in vain to back up and out.

"Wait here," said Alex. "I want to see if anyone's in there."

He inched forward, measuring every slippery step before applying his weight. An old man sat in the driver's seat. His head lay askew against the window. Both eyes were shut, but the mouth gaped open. He moaned.

Alex pounded on the window without getting the old man's attention, then pounded again, this time clacking his class ring against the glass. Two eyes popped open like a time-worn cash register totaling a sale. The old man wet his lips with a gray tongue and tried to turn toward the sound, but the eyes rolled shut again.

"What's going on?" Leilani called.

"There's a guy in there. I think he's hurt." Alex tried the door. It sprang wide open. Only the still-secured seat belt kept the man from falling out. Alex felt a stab of distaste at the thought of touching this grubby slack body. Almost holding his breath, he pushed the man's left shoulder to set him upright, then unfastened the seat belt. But he slumped forward onto the steering wheel, blasting the horn nonstop. Alex reached for the freckled balding head with its white-haired fringes and pulled it gently back to the headrest. Blood ran from the man's nose. His eyes were fully open now—frightened red-lined eyes. Another moan escaped. His lips moved, but no words came out.

Leilani had worked her way down to the car. "We have to get him to a hospital. He needs help."

"Couldn't we just call an ambulance from somewhere?" Alex asked.

"Oh, sure, like there's a phone on the next tree," she replied. "It would take too much time to get an ambulance here. We can't leave him bleeding like this."

The two of them lifted the old man out and, half carrying, half dragging, managed to get him into the back of Alex's car. Leilani sat in back with him and held a tissue under his bleeding nose. He stank of alcohol. She turned her face away and hastily rolled down her window. "Let's hurry," she said. "He's disgusting."

Alex drove counterclockwise on the road around the island until they saw a blue 'H' highway marker leading them to the Kahuku Community Hospital. In a cluster of modular buildings they found an entrance marked EMERGENCY. Just inside, a nurse met them and arranged for a gurney. Alex and Leilani started to leave when an administrative nurse called out, "Sir! Ma'am! There's paperwork to be filled out."

"Oh, no," said Alex. "We don't even know the guy's name. We just found him in the marsh about eight miles down the road that way." He gestured with his thumb in the general direction they'd come from.

"His wallet says he's Horace Rodder," said the nurse. "Can't you tell us anything more?"

"Nope," said Alex with his hand resting on the front door handle. "Just that the police can find his car stuck in the mud back there." He pulled the door open and waved Leilani through.

"How about your names and addresses?" the nurse tried again. "How can we get in touch with you?"

"You can't," he replied, letting the door close behind him to make sure she got his message.

"Weren't you a little abrupt with her?" Leilani asked when they stood on the front steps.

"Naw. Well, yeah. But I don't want us to get involved." He guided her firmly to his car.

She looked puzzled as she climbed in. "Then what was the point of helping him if we're just going to abandon the man? How can we just forget about him?"

"We got him to the hospital, Leilani, that was the point. Most people wouldn't have done that much." He tried not to betray his irritation. "Besides, we haven't got any information to offer that would help him. Believe me, we did the right thing." He started the engine and pulled out onto Kam Highway.

"But what if he's all alone? What if there's nobody to care about him?"

"Leilani, you can't rescue the whole world, even though I know you'd like to."

Please God, she thought, *let somebody be doing more to help Kekoa.*

78

Alex recognized her silence and quickly changed the subject. "How about a little more great scenery, and later I'll get you the best hamburger on Oahu?"

She sighed. "Okay, I guess."

"I'll even throw in a super sunset."

On the *mauka* side, the fields were being irrigated with large pipe fixtures that looked like the frames of children's swing sets. On the higher ground, propeller blade windmills generated electricity. The Turtle Bay Hilton came into view on the *makai* side, surrounded by manicured hedges of yellow hibiscus.

She drew a deep breath. "Why couldn't my land look like this?"

He reached over and squeezed her hand. "I was thinking the same thing. But it will, baby, someday."

Dusk approached, and they stopped at a park bordering Sunset Beach. Hundreds of yards offshore, tiny surfers lay on their boards, waiting for just the right wave. Leilani and Alex took off their shoes and waded along the shoreline. A knee-high wave unexpectedly intercepted them; the deep, wet sand tugged at their feet as the receding surf tried to suck them out to sea. They hastily retreated back up the beach.

They stood on the grassy knoll at the sand's edge, waiting for the sun's final plunge, and turned and gazed into one another's eyes the instant before it did so. Their bodies touched electrically and pressed closer. Catching the red magic in the clouds and burning sky, they kissed and missed the sun's fiery exit. She hugged him afterward and rested her head on his shoulder for a moment. When he began to ease away, Leilani clung to him and lifted her chin. Once more their lips met, soft and cool. When their eyes finally opened, they saw each other in a new way.

His hand traced her cheek, neck, and shoulder. He felt goose bumps on her forearm, and he realized she was cold. He looked up. The beach was deserted. They kissed again, and this time she was less tentative, eagerly sliding her arms around his neck and pulling his head close to her. Their bodies pressed together.

When they finally parted, a slightly breathless Leilani said, "Maybe we'd better get that hamburger now."

The huge juicy burgers and trimmings in the little town of Haleiwa lived up to their reputation. At the Weed traffic circle Alex took the road south through the pineapple fields, perfect rows as far as the eye could see between Oahu's two major mountain ranges, the Koolau and the Waianae.

Leilani cuddled close with her head on his shoulder, napping here and there, making quiet nuzzling noises. They drove south past Schofield Barracks and the other military reservations, meeting the H-2 freeway and then H-1 toward home. The rest of the trip passed with little conversation, both of them wrapped in their own thoughts.

It was after eight when they arrived back in Manoa at the Wong house. The lanai light glowed in welcome. Masako greeted them at the door.

"It's late, I was beginning to worry," she said.

They selectively recounted the day's events: finding the stranger in the marsh, taking him to the hospital, and their disappointment with the trust land.

"It's just swamp, now," Alex said, "but a developer with big bucks will be able to do wonders with it."

Leilani nodded. Secretly, she wondered about turning her chunk of nature into bastions of concrete.

"You two want anything to eat?" Masako asked.

They both shook their heads. Leilani excused herself to tackle her homework. She gave Masako a hug and Alex something much more enthusiastic than the usual nighttime peck before climbing the stairs two at a time.

Alex anticipated his mother's raised eyebrows, and smiled back at her with a reddened face.

"Is there something I should know here?" Masako asked.

"Mother, can't we talk about this another time? I've got some office work to catch up on." Before she could answer, Alex disappeared into the den to turn on his father's computer.

Chapter 10
Persuasion

ON THE BOARDROOM wall of the First Sugarman's Bank, five dour faces, former directors, peered down from their gilded frames at the men seated around a mahogany table. The portraits appeared to be scowling in anticipation of the fight just begging to erupt.

Coland Benfield-Rice had convened the trustees of Hank Pualoa's revocable trust, created for the benefit of his children. He handed out bound copies of two land purchase proposals: one from Ocean Vail—Fujita's client—and the other from Rodminn Estates, submitted by a firm called Rodminn Reality. Both proposals needed to be considered at this meeting, as the sale proceeds would represent additional investment capital for the children's education.

Only Hank Pualoa himself, creator of the trust, was missing. He had not been heard from in months. As the first order of business, Paul Wong was confirmed as alternate trustee in Hank's absence.

Coland began: "The parcels of land we're concerned with today are the two lots belonging to Kekoa and Leilani Pualoa. The parcels are isolated marshland having little commercial value per se. Their importance is in their location, of course. The lots sit on the edge of an area targeted for a huge development project. It cannot proceed without acquisition of the two Pualoa lots."

Red Murphy shifted in his armchair, wondering how long this pompous ass was going to drone on about details everyone already knew.

Coland cleared his throat. "I have important news: a third player has entered the field. The state and county are jointly preparing a third proposal for the entire package, including the children's two lots. We don't know why they want it at this point. Are there any questions?"

Red broke the din of paper shuffling. "I think we should accept the offer from Rodminn Estates. It provides the most cash up front."

"What about the offer from Ocean Vail?" asked Paul. "The payment schedule is a little drawn out, but theirs is actually the higher bid. And the kids certainly aren't in any hurry for the money. What do you think, Coland?"

"I'd like to wait and look at the offer from the state. After all, it's the kids' interests we're looking out for here."

"The state will never match either offer," Red quickly interjected.

Paul agreed. But this was the last thing they agreed upon.

Coland cleared his throat. "Gentlemen! I feel quite uncomfortable acting without Hank Pualoa's input. This is not a life or death matter. And all the offers will probably be sweetened in time, or at the very least, renewed for another month."

"I'll be damned and gone to hell," cried Red. "What happens if they don't sweeten and the whole deal goes to pot?"

"It won't happen that way," snapped Coland. "We owe it to the children to be prudent with their property."

"That's idiotic," Red snorted, pounding his clenched fist on the table. "Having the cash up front means it goes to work for them sooner, the sooner the better."

Paul intervened. "Gentlemen, gentlemen, please! Lower your voices."

"I apologize," murmured Coland. "However," and his voice grew firm again, "we might even get a higher offer from the government group."

Red slapped both hands flat down on the table and shouted, "Bull! You know that's nothing but hogwash."

Paul lifted his hands, palms toward the group. "Gentlemen, gentlemen, please! I have a suggestion. Why don't we adjourn for one week to reexamine the facts? It'll give us all a chance to cool our tempers."

After some muttering the group nodded cool goodbyes and departed.

Paul walked around the corner to Auntie Annie's Cafe, where Alex waited for him in a booth. A teenage waitress strolled out from behind the counter and took their orders.

Alex asked, "What's up, Dad? You don't look too happy."

"The meeting went poorly this morning."

Cry Ohana

The waitress brought their platters, and while Paul picked at his food, his son chomped on a hefty burger. Alex reached for the ketchup, turned the bottle upside down, and smacked the bottom with his open palm. "Isn't it strange that Kekoa hasn't tried to contact Leilani?"

"Son, you're assuming he knows that she lives with us. I doubt that he does. He's obviously in hiding. The question is, why? Now it's up to the trustees to find him."

"Can't you check the school system, Dad?"

"I tried that, but the boy is not enrolled anywhere that we can determine. At least, not under his own name. I distributed his description to school principals as well. And that's what's so frustrating. They've all asked to see a photo of him, which is understandable. But we don't have a single one."

Paul raised a clump of sticky white rice on the end of his chopsticks, but midway to his mouth, changed his mind and returned it to the plate.

"I even encouraged Leilani to do a sketch of Kekoa for the police. I thought she did a fine drawing, but they weren't impressed. Said it looked like hundreds of other Hawaiian kids his age. I also ran a personal ad in both Honolulu daily papers without any response. Oh, by the way, your mother wanted me to talk to you about last night."

"What about last night?" Alex took a large swig of coffee and swallowed hard. He knew what was coming.

"Well, she sensed something new happening between Leilani and you. She told me the two of you looked awfully cozy when you got back from your circle island. I don't need to tell you that your mother and I feel a special responsibility for Leilani now that she's under the protection of our household." Paul's voice advanced to an authoritarian tone.

"Dad, wait! I would not do anything to harm or compromise Leilani in any way. I think you already know that."

"Yes I do, but I don't have to remind you, Alex, that you're seven years older—seven and a half, actually, and sometimes things can get out of hand."

Alex stopped eating, leaving most of the fries on his plate, and wiped his mouth with his paper napkin.

"You're done already?" Paul asked as his son rose to leave.

"Yeah, I really have to get back to work. I'll call you."

Paul finished his own lunch half-heartedly, paid the bill, and hastened to his car.

* * *

Darkness enveloped the cluttered alley in Chinatown. Red Murphy navigated the long wooden flight of stairs to the door at the top. He knocked softly at first, then banged three times with his fist. He was about to abandon his mission when he heard the door unlock and spread to the limits of its security chain.

"Who's there?" a sleepy female voice asked.

Before answering, Red snaked a $100 bill through the narrow opening. "Ben Franklin," he laughed.

When Cindy saw his face, she tried to close the door on him. "You!" she said. "You red-headed bastard. Get the hell out of here before I kill you."

"Hey, babe, see this?" He jabbed at a small red bump on his temple where her purse had landed a week earlier.

"You deserved it!"

With his free hand, he slid another $100 bill through the crack in the door. "I'm sorry about knocking you down," he said, "but I needed to catch that kid. It was important."

"Important? Why?"

"He cheated me out of some money, the little bastard."

She hardly heard him. "Nobody treats Cindy Chou that way," she said. But she calmed down while she studied the $200 she held in hand. Sliding the bills into the pocket of her peignoir, she unhooked the chain on the door, and he stepped inside.

"What's this money for?" she asked.

"Let's just say I have a proposition. There's a good deal of money in it for you, a lot more than two hundred. Are you interested?"

"There are some things even I don't do. I got my pride and I got my scruples. I'm a good girl and I don't make trouble. Um…how much money are we talking about?" She closed the door behind them, locked it, and slid the chain across.

"At least $3,000. I doubt you can make that for a night's work anywhere else. Or can you?"

Unfortunately, Cindy knew she couldn't. She led him into the bedroom.

It always startled him to enter this adult playpen. The wallpaper, bedspread, and matching drapes filled the senses with their hot pink.

84

The black lacquered dresser and nightstands gleamed. Mirrored tiles covered the wall behind the king-size bed.

Cindy seated herself delicately on the edge of the bed. Her white peignoir hung loosely around her full breasts. He sat in the velvet easy chair opposite her, taking it all in.

"Excuse the mess," she purred. "I wasn't expecting you, of course." She waved her hand at the clothes strewn about the rose-patterned carpet. A minidress, bikini panties, garter belt, and black mesh stockings lay where she'd slipped out of them. She turned thoughtful. "What do I have to do for that kind of money?"

"You have a Tuesday night regular, a john named Coland Benfield-Rice, don't you?"

"I do?" she asked.

"Don't play coy with me."

"Yeah, sure. He's a nice and generous gentleman, but what's he got to do with this?"

"Let's just say he could use a little friendly business persuasion. I need an explicit and compromising photo of him in the sack with you, and I need it by next Friday. He can't know the picture was taken. And I'd prefer that your face not appear in the picture. Can you arrange this for me?"

"If I do, I'll certainly lose his business."

"There's a good chance I might not have to use the photo," Red lied.

She hesitated.

"Would another $2,000 take care of finding a replacement?"

"Maybe. But wouldn't that be blackmail? I won't do anything illegal."

"Of course not, hon. No money will change hands, so it can't be blackmail. Like I said, it's persuasion. I wouldn't ask you to do anything illegal." He stood and stepped to the bed. Leaning over, Red kissed her lightly on the nose. She smiled up at him.

Cindy Chou's high cheekbones and darting eyes gave her a shrewd, wary expression, making her look older than her twenty-six years. But her deliciously ripe body and silky skin could turn any man's head.

"Shall we seal the deal?" he asked. He took her face in his hands and kissed her hard on the lips. She, in turn, grabbed firmly at the bulge in his fly, and the two fell backward, laughing, on the bed. She playfully pulled away, got to her feet, and stood over him. First propping two pillows under his head, she undressed him slowly and sensually. When there was nothing left but ruddy flesh and red hair, she pulled the satin tie on her peignoir, permitting her breasts to fall freely. She leaned over him, dragging her hard pink nipples over his body, and slid her robe off.

Their sexual feast was deliberately coarse and violent, he leaving minor bruises on her breasts and buttocks; she leaving scratches all over his back with her long polished nails. They rolled over only once to put Red on top, and she slid up the bed with each of his powerful lunges until there was no longer any place to move. The headboard pounded the wall in coxswain's cadence. They pushed to the finish line with one great groan of gratification and sank to their respective pillows. Cindy seldom felt sensual pleasure any more, only when she consciously allowed her mind and body to experience it. She knew it was unprofessional of her to "let go" with Red, but at that moment she didn't give a damn.

They lay on the rumpled bed for twenty minutes before getting dressed. Red smacked Cindy affectionately on the behind and gave her another $200 on the way out the door. It was not only a nice tip, but insurance that she would keep her part of the bargain.

* * *

The Benfield-Rices had been married nineteen years without ever knowing the excitement of real love. They were both British. Constance had inherited wealth and married Coland for his sophistication, his finely chiseled face, and dignified demeanor. He had carved out a minor niche for himself as a banker and basked in their social standing in the British colony in Honolulu. But one aspect of their marriage had severely disappointed him. The highly touted thrills of the sexual experience simply eluded Constance. And marital relations had become nonexistent since she'd caught him in bed with the maid two years ago. They cared for one another in a simple matter-of-fact way.

Constance held the majority of stock in First Sugarman's Bank. Through her inheritance and her bank stock, she controlled her husband, and in a loose sense, the bank as well. She tolerated Coland's taste for risky personal investments, and for the most part, they had proved highly profitable.

Husband and wife each had their own queen-sized bed and

adjoining bath off the white-satined bedroom. Coland found his wife already abed in a high-necked nightgown, the covers tucked about her waist. Bifocals perched on the end of her nose, an open book on her lap. Impeccable even in bed, she had not a hair out of place.

"Constance, my dear," he began. She kept reading her P.D. James mystery. "Constance!" he repeated.

"Don't shout, dear. It's so unbecoming of you," she scolded without looking up from her book.

"I'd like your undivided attention for just a moment."

She shut the mystery with a literary clap and smiled up at him.

"Now, what's so terribly important?"

"I received a call from my broker today. You know that Pacific Rim real estate venture stock I told you about? I bought it on margin to sell short at the end of the month. I'm embarrassed to tell you it didn't turn out that way."

Coland knew he'd made a risky investment. Selling short meant an investor actually borrowed the stock from the broker and counted on the price dropping by a certain date; then he could sell it, making enough money to pay the broker, and reap a profit for himself.

Coland continued with the bad news. "I can't understand it. The stock was wildly overpriced and due for a drop. But the bloody thing shot up $10 a share. Of course, now I'm forced to buy it high at a considerable personal loss. I would write the broker a check, but I need you to cover the funds for me. Right now I'm in a terrible bind."

"I see. How much is the bottom line this time?"

"I'm afraid it's $20,000, but don't worry."

"Don't worry? Coland, dear, that was rather reckless, wasn't it? We've been dipping into Daddy's money for some time now and there are limits to it."

"Constance, you know very well that everything we've taken from your daddy's account has been more than replaced in our personal portfolio. If it'll make you feel better, you can transfer funds back to your daddy's account later. Please! I think you know the consequences of passing a rubber check."

She gave a profound sigh. "Yes, dear. In the morning I'll authorize the transfer of funds to your brokerage account." She seemed disappointed that she couldn't taunt him a bit longer.

"Thank you, my dear Constance." As he bent down to kiss her

cheek, she waved him off and resumed her reading.

Coland settled into his own bed and turned out his lamp. With a sense of relief, he fell fast asleep, dreaming of his last visit to Cindy. He didn't hear his wife say, "Goodnight, dear."

Chapter 11

Into the Oven

"KEKOA! KEKOA!" In his deep sleep, someone called him. The boy awoke with a start and heard sounds of stumbling on the stairs. "Kekoa!" Sam's voice called urgently now. The alarm clock read 2:30 a.m., an hour-and-a-half before he normally got up.

"Coming, Sam!" he shouted. Reaching for his shorts, he pulled them on with a single tug.

A light was on in the front of the shop, where the two Osakas stood huddled at the door. "What's wrong?" Kekoa asked.

Mauro replied, "I feel great pain in night, Sam take me emergency room Straub Clinic."

Wow, thought Kekoa, *Mauro looks terrible. Sam, too.*

"I call you from clinic," Sam said, "but you do baking alone today, please. I know you do fine." A cab pulled up to the curb. Kekoa helped Mauro inside and set her overnight bag on the front seat.

"Don't worry, I'll take care of everything," Kekoa called after the departing taxi. Suddenly, he felt painfully alone again. Until he found Lani, Sam and Mauro were the only family he had. He loved and needed them both. What if Mauro died? He whispered a hasty, awkward prayer that nothing bad would happen to her.

Kekoa flopped back into bed and tried to sleep. He squirmed and tossed. Pulling his knees up to his chest, he wrapped his arms around them and stared into the shallow depths of the night.

He arose at four, washed quickly, and pulled a faded T-shirt over his head. In the great workroom of a kitchen, he assembled metal bowls and scoops. Then the baker's apprentice measured, mashed, combined, and stirred until he was sure the various blends would meet Sam's most critical standards. Three mixers churned—yeast and flour; butter and eggs; sugar, spices, flavorings; and crocks of chopped fruit. He rolled, pounded, shaped, and twisted mounds of dough onto baking sheets,

89

creating crescents, swirls, stars, tubes, and loafs. Many had fruit fillings. Some were dusted with seeds or delicate spices; some painted with glazes.

The first trays went immediately into the ovens, while others found their way onto shelved holding carts. Kekoa smiled when the oven's aromas eventually reached his nostrils—a sure sign that he had done well, despite his carelessly scorched thumb from touching the preheated oven rack. The clock never rested, so much more to do.

The phone rang. Kekoa tucked it under his chin and stretched out the cord so he could continue rolling dough. "Hello! Hi, Sam! How's Mauro?"

"They give her sedative and she rest now. The doctors do tests and poke her too much, but she good strong woman and don't complain. They not sure what wrong yet. I stay 'til they know. I call Mauro's niece, Yasuko. She come open shop to customers."

"Great, Sam." Kekoa grinned.

"How baking coming?"

"So far so good, but I need to start on the doughnuts now."

"Good boy! I talk you later and... *arigato!*"

"No need. Bye now." Kekoa hung up and ran to swap trays between the oven and the carts. He switched on the mixer for the first batch of doughnut batter, and so it went until he heard a banging at the front door some three hours after he had begun.

He recognized Yasuko, and fumbled in his pocket for the front door keys. Just inside the door she hugged him quickly.

"Have you heard anything yet?" she asked.

He shook his head. "The doctors will know more later."

"Have you eaten yet?"

Kekoa was about to answer when they both smelled something burning and ran to the ovens. "Oh, no!" he said as he pulled out the overdone, but not quite burnt apple Danish. Luckily, he had made an extra batch and all he had wasted was a little time.

"No harm done," Yasuko said. "Looks like there's Danish for our breakfast. I'll make some coffee while you finish up."

Another half hour passed before Kekoa completed his morning baking. Exhausted, he sat down with Yasuko at the tiny table behind the bread counter. They ate quietly, understanding each other's mood, a deep concern for the elderly Osakas.

Yasuko had planned to miss a few days of school to run the shop.

"When do you go to school?" she asked, trying to break the ice.

"I don't."

"It's against the law. How do you get away with it?"

Before he could reply, the front door bell jingled and Yasuko went to attend to the first customer of the day. When she returned, she asked, "How? Why?"

"How? Why? What?" he mimicked her.

"You know what I mean."

"I just don't go. I can't go. It's a long story. You don't want to hear it."

"I do want to hear it. I care a lot."

She stood to answer another jingle from the door. "Thank you, come again," she said upon completing the sale of a half-dozen *anpan*.

Returning to Kekoa, she said, "Please tell me."

In six breathless minutes, the boy spilled his whole story.

"That's scary," Yasuko said. Reluctantly, she responded to continuing door jingles and customer sales, but hurried back to hear more of the story. "Why didn't you go to the police?" she asked.

"Red's got too many police friends. He hangs out and drinks with them. Anyway, who'd believe a fourteen-year-old kid? I don't even know if the body is there anymore."

"What about your grandmother and sister?"

"*Tutu's* dead."

"How do you know?"

"I went back there when I thought it was safe, and I learned she had died and our house was sold. Other people live there now, only they don't know where Leilani went. Been trying to find her ever since. I've got a plan for finding her, though."

"A plan?" she asked.

"Yeah, I go to all the high schools and watch when they let out. Maybe I'll see her leave. No luck yet, but I think it's a darn good plan." Another thought struck him. "Hey, maybe she's at your school, yah?"

"I asked around like I promised you I would," said Yasuko. "But they've never heard of her there. It's a good plan, Kekoa. I sure hope it works for you. How'd you happen to come to Uncle Sam and Auntie Mauro and the bakery?"

"Oh… About two-and-a-half years ago, I slept in cardboard cartons in the alley out back and…" Kekoa continued relating the story of how he had earned a place for himself in the Osaka business and family.

"Don't they ever ask you why you don't go to school?"

"They think I do. I told them I'm in a "work and study" program at the high school, and every weekday I leave at noon and come home at six. They don't know the truth. I haven't even told 'em how old I am." With this admission, Kekoa felt new pangs of guilt.

The door jingled far too frequently now for Kekoa to continue, so he retreated to his room for a short nap. He awoke later to put several afternoon trays in the oven.

"Did Sam call?" he asked Yasuko.

"Not yet," she said. "I was wondering if you could go to Kaimuki High."

He was a little annoyed that she was still pressing him, but he did feel better that he had confided in her. He knew now he had acquired a much-needed friend.

"Schools need proof of who you are and all kinds of age and address records."

"So?"

"So, Red's no dummy. Once I enroll, he'll find me. Then I'll have to run away again. I wanna go to school, I wanna find Lani, have a life like other guys. I never thought I'd miss school, but I do, and my friends, too. You're the only friend I got." By now Kekoa had choked up. He swallowed hard.

"You know, Kekoa, I could help you with your schooling. You're smart. I can tutor you if you want."

His eyes flickered with uncertainty for a moment and then his entire face brightened. "Hey, Yasuko, that'd be great."

He had already confessed so much to Yasuko that he didn't tell her about his dog.

* * *

Later that evening Kekoa thought that he heard a scratching at the back door to the bake room, so he gathered as many day-old scraps as he could find and started out the back door to find Ilio. But the dog wasn't anywhere to be seen. This was nothing new. When they'd first arrived, Ilio never missed his meal times at the back door. They had shared plenty of time together until Kekoa became more and more involved in the operation of the bakery. After many lonely afternoons, the dog would miss an occasional meal—then a few more. The boy assumed that improved foraging had enticed him elsewhere. But now it had been more than a week since he had seen his furry friend, and he missed him sorely. Kekoa knew he needn't worry, though—Ilio understood how to survive in the streets.

* * *

Red sat in the construction site trailer going over the cost figures for the new school wing modifications ordered by the Department of Education. He lifted his eyes for a moment to mull over the last number when his phone rang. "Finast Construction, Murphy here. Can I help you?"

"Oooh, can you now," replied Cindy in her most kittenish voice. "I have that item you ordered here in my hands. Would you like to pick it up tonight?"

"Is it good quality? No mistaking the party?"

"Oh yes, good quality, sir, I'm sure you'll be pleased with it."

"Excellent! I'll be by to have a look tonight…The only reason for coming? We'll talk about that when I get there, my good woman."

He heard the smacking sound of a kiss as she hung up.

Red had a call to make. He started to dial, but immediately thought better of using his own phone. Instead, he locked up the trailer and drove to a public phone booth two blocks away in a mini-strip mall. He dialed anxiously.

After three rings, Coland Benfield-Rice answered. "Hello?"

"Red Murphy here. I have a business proposition I'd like to offer you. I'm sure you'll find it both lucrative and revealing." Red chuckled at his choice of words. "Are you free tomorrow morning?"

Silence. The pause lasted so long that Red wondered if they'd been disconnected.

Finally, Coland replied: "This is quite unexpected, Red. I believe I could make it for a few minutes tomorrow. My office at nine sharp."

"I'd prefer somewhere out of doors, say the top of Punchbowl at 10 a.m. Make it the memorial chapel."

"Isn't that an unusual place for a meeting?" Coland's voice grew apprehensive.

"Oh, no, it's the perfect place." *The perfect place to kill your career,* he thought.

"Well, then, if you insist, I'll be there."

"I do," Red said, and hung up before Coland could change his mind.

Chapter 12
Tranquility Broken

HIGH ABOVE the pulsing arteries of Honolulu, cradled in the embrace of an extinct volcano, lay 40,000 heroes. On a spring day in 1985, monkeypod blossoms blew like pink powder puffs across a small plaque bearing the inscription "CPL. William A. (Buddy) Yamashita [1924-1944]." Lori Yamashita knelt to arrange her own spray of red carnations.

Today Buddy would have been sixty-one. Lori came here to Punchbowl, the National Cemetery of the Pacific, every year on his birthday. Buddy rested in the section devoted to the 442nd Infantry. This World War II division comprised the *Nisei*, second-generation Americans of Japanese ancestry who fought in Italy. Buddy's death, when she was only seven, had been a terrible loss to her. Only one other loss had affected her as much: the death of her best friend.

Lori tilted her face toward the breeze. Baskets of fruit, and even a bottle of beer, graced many other graves—offerings to sustain loved ones in the Hereafter. Lori had come here to feel at peace and was in no hurry to leave this haven of the heavy-hearted. She walked along the path toward the edifice dedicated to all the United States's military actions in the Pacific from World War II on and sat down on a stone bench. It faced a huge semicircular wall of multicolored marble and mosaic panels, depicting major battles with maps, narratives, and illustrations.

Lori gave a start as an unexpected face passed between her and the wall. She recognized Edgar Murphy from his visits to the Fujita office. His muscled body moved through the colonnade as if he owned the world. She watched him enter the chapel and emerge several moments later with a silver-haired man in a finely tailored gray suit. This man she recognized from his pictures in the society pages: Coland Benfield-Rice, a local philanthropist and banker. The two men walked quickly, too deep in conversation to notice her, and selected a bench several columns to her left.

An overwhelming urge to eavesdrop enveloped Lori. She knew she shouldn't, but she just couldn't stop herself. Slipping quietly from her bench, she edged to one adjacent to theirs. The massive ionic columns between the benches easily hid her slight form. Lori strained to hear Benfield-Rice's irritated voice piercing the stillness.

"What kind of business proposition? Why couldn't you have come to my office to discuss it?"

"Let's just say we can both profit from a most creative little venture I have in mind. If you cooperate, there might be as much as $50,000 in it for you."

"Just how or why would any cooperation of mine be worth that much to you? That is, even supposing I would cooperate at all."

"It would be, and I'm sure you will."

"Oh? You've got a lot of nerve," Coland said. "This meeting is over, Mister Murphy."

"Wait, Coland, hear me out! This has to do with the Pualoa Trust."

"What about it?"

"All I'm asking for is your vote. You vote to accept the Rodminn Estates offer and we'll both profit. No one will ever know. You wouldn't throw away the opportunity for an easy fifty grand, would you?"

"But that's illegal. It's a conflict of interest. I won't have any part in it. This entire conversation is highly inappropriate."

"Inappropriate? You don't know the meaning of the word, pal," Murphy said. "Take a look at this photograph."

Lori heard Coland sputter in raging half-sentences. As she leaned forward, she saw him snatch a photo from Red's fingers.

"That shameless little tart betrayed me. And after all my generosity. How did you get this, and why was it taken?"

"Never mind how or why. And don't blame Cindy. She has nothing to do with this. Oh, don't bother destroying the photo, I've got several copies, and the negative, of course. So, Coland, how about your cooperation? Can I count on it?"

"You rotter, if you mess up my life, you will go down with me. That's something you can count on."

"You've heard of Murphy's Law, haven't you? Well, I'm Murphy and I'm making law here. If you cross me, you can be assured things will go wrong for you."

Lori gasped. She rushed her hand to her lips as though the unintended sound could be recaptured. But the men, oblivious, kept up their bitter argument. She continued to listen until she realized someone else was listening as well. A shadow appeared over her right shoulder, radiating from a spot adjacent to the column behind her. Seeing her turn to look at him, a man withdrew quickly, despite his reliance on two canes.

She stole away and broke into an awkward trot, not stopping until reaching the safety of her car. She threw herself into the driver's seat and slammed down the door lock.

Just as Lori's car cleared the entrance and pulled out onto Puowaina Drive, Red and Coland walked to the parking lot. They stopped at Coland's Lincoln Town Car long enough for Coland to say, "I will make no promises. I need time to think."

"You have until the Tuesday meeting to make up your mind."

"I will not give you an answer for at least another week."

"Listen carefully. Your $50,000 incentive will be reduced by $15,000 per week and on the third week, copies of this photo go to your wife and then to your friends." With that, Red turned on his heels and walked to his shabby Buick Regal.

Breathing hard, Coland sat for ten minutes before starting his engine. Red pulled out of his space and disappeared down the road. A moment later a second car pulled out. Coland hardly noticed. The pit of his stomach soured. He shuddered and began to sweat, something he never did. He backed the Lincoln out, and clutching the steering wheel as if it were a life ring, followed the winding road out of Punchbowl.

* * *

Late in the morning, when Kekoa woke up from his after-work nap, he heard a commotion out front in the shop. The boy washed his face to shake the sleepiness from his head and rushed to see what was going on. Yasuko had been minding the store for days now, while Kekoa handled nearly all of the baking, freeing Sam up to spend as much time as he could with Mauro at the hospital. Kekoa's surprise at seeing both Mauro and Sam out front put a smile on all their faces. Mauro had come home only two days after her gall bladder operation.

Sam helped her upstairs to their bed, where she closed her eyes almost immediately. He tiptoed out, and at the bottom of the stairs, he met Kekoa.

"Too late for you go school today, *nei*? I afraid you miss too much."

Kekoa looked at Yasuko and winked. "Uh…yeah, I guess I'd better get going if I'm going at all today."

The boy had already decided to use the afternoon to take flowers to his mother's grave. That part of his past had not been taken away from him. He knew the cemetery location and her marker. *Tutu* had brought him and Leilani there many times. As he went out the jingling door, he said to Sam, "I'm glad Mauro's home, glad for all of us."

Kekoa rode his rusted bicycle to a flower shop several blocks from the bakery and then a dozen more blocks to the *mauka* side of Diamond Head crater. He'd salvaged the bike from a dumpster a few months ago and tinkered with it until it became passable transportation. He laid the bike down on its side at the road's edge and walked slowly through the cemetery toward his mother's grave.

A bronze plaque marked his mother's place in the ground. Another marker startled him—the grave of his grandmother. He felt a stab of guilt about missing her funeral. But there had been no way of knowing. Kekoa gently parceled out his long-stemmed birds of paradise: two on each grave.

But now that I'm here, he wondered, *what am I supposed to do? Should I cry?* He tried forcing a tear, but it wouldn't come. He sat down cross-legged beside the elongated patch of grass where his mother lay.

Slowly the thoughts came, and he spoke to her in hesitating whispered tones. He began by telling her about Sam and Mauro and Yasuko. "I can't remember much about you, Mom, except for what Leilani and *Tutu* told me. But I know you loved me. I miss you and *Tutu*. I miss having a father, too. I miss Leilani. I miss going to school." Uncrossing his legs, Kekoa rolled over on top of the grave, stretching out his arms in the grass around her. He laid his head down where he imagined her breast to be. He remained there for several minutes until the last of these thoughts sifted through his mind.

Hearing steps, Kekoa slowly picked his head up and looked around. He wasn't alone! A woman was walking quickly toward the grave. Alarmed, Kekoa jumped to his feet and ran to his bicycle.

She waved her hands frantically. "Wait! Stop! Wait! Don't run away, I want to talk to you," she shouted.

Cry Ohana

Kekoa heard her, but he kept running until he reached his bike. He looked over his shoulder as he rode and realized that she showed no intention of following him. She had stopped at his mother's grave and knelt in the grass. He braked, dismounted, and walked his bike behind the long white chapel building at the cemetery entrance. There he had a perfect view of this woman he'd never seen before.

He watched her place a large bouquet of torch ginger there and move his offering to a more prominent position. She fussed about the grave, picking up dead leaves and cleaning bird droppings from the plaque with a tissue and spittle. Her actions were so caring, so loving. How odd after so many years. And who was she? Just as he made up his mind to approach her, she headed back to her car. As she walked past, he edged behind the chapel to remain hidden.

* * *

Crowds gathered in the lobby of the Neal S. Blaisdell Center for the Performing Arts to see Gounod's *Faust*. Many opera-goers dallied to view the peers and tiers of society. Attire varied greatly from tuxedos and gowns to aloha shirts and jeans. The lights blinked twice, and the lobby crowd moved into the vast concert hall.

Following the opening night tradition, the orchestra first played the national anthem, followed by the state anthem, *"Hawaii Pono'i"*— "Hawaii's Own." The strains of the overture began, and the curtain rose to the scene of a steamy laboratory. Here the Faustian contract was signed and sealed, and the story wound its musical way toward intermission.

Lori chose not to join her friends in the lobby. Instead, she rose in place to stretch her legs. Just two rows in front of her, she recognized Paul Wong coming up the aisle. She moved toward him.

"Mr. Wong! How nice to see you again," she said.

"Ms. Yamashita, may I present my wife, Masako, and my daughter, Numi. And you know Leilani, of course."

"Yes, my pleasure. You have a beautiful family," answered Lori.

"Your dress, it's absolutely stunning, my dear," said Masako.

"Thank you!" Lori paused, not quite sure how to continue. "Mr. Wong, and you too, Leilani, I need to talk to you. Very soon, if possible."

"We have a few minutes right now if you like."

"Oh, no," Lori murmured, "I can't speak freely here."

Masako scowled at her husband.

99

Paul caught her look and raised his bushy gray eyebrows. "Okay. I'm planning to take my three ladies to the Contemporary Museum tomorrow," he said. "Would you be our guest for lunch there, say, 11:30?"

"I'd be delighted. I'm sure Mr. Fujita won't mind."

As the lights dimmed and they returned to their seats, the orchestra began. The opera continued with large swaths of sin and retribution, heavenly forgiveness, and eternal damnation. *Faust* ended, and the applause lingered, then faded.

As Lori and her two friends walked to the car, she reflected aloud on the opera's moral dilemma. "Faust sells his soul for eternal youth, pleasure, and power. Then he loses his woman and is sent to eternal damnation. But forgiveness and salvation are granted to this woman who killed her own child. I don't get it." Lori stopped suddenly. "You know what, ladies? There was a man I knew, way back when—a Mr. Right I couldn't have. At this point in my life, I think I'd sell my soul for that man."

Chapter 13

Revealing

THE CONTEMPORARY Museum hides like a nesting bird in the rain forest off Makiki Heights Drive. Lush trees and flowering jungle shrubs conceal the museum from the road that leads to the top of Mount Tantalus.

In front of its patinaed bronze doors a mini-skirted girl paced back and forth, repeatedly checking her watch.

"Come away from there, Numi," Masako Wong reproached her daughter.

"But she's already fifteen minutes late."

"Fifteen minutes is not a big deal. You wouldn't want her to think we're ill-mannered, would you?"

"No, Mom, but I'm hungry. I didn't eat breakfast."

"And whose fault is that?" retorted Masako.

Numi strained to see any approaching cars, but couldn't. She resumed her pacing, despite her mother's reprimand. Having reached the end of the lanai, Numi whirled back toward the entryway and nearly bumped into a pearl-gray suit.

"Oops, I'm so sorry. Oh, Ms. Yamashita, it's you!"

"Yes, and very late, I'm afraid. It's nice to see you again, Numi."

"We're all dying to hear what you have to say. My parents and Leilani are over there." Numi pointed.

Lori greeted everyone, and Paul led them down the stone steps through a small sculpture garden to the tea room. She ordered black bean soup and a veggie plate; the others chose sandwiches.

"Lori," Paul began, "you have peaked all our curiosities. What did you have in mind?"

Lori addressed Leilani in particular. "Your mother and I grew up together. From the time I moved to Aiea in the third grade until she married your father, we were best friends. She grew into a stunningly

101

beautiful and loving human being. You remind me a lot of her. If we had been sisters, we could not have been closer. That's why I've asked to meet with you today."

Leilani's wide-set dark eyes gave Lori a searching look. Even her long, thick lashes could not conceal her anxiety. "Did…did you know my father, too?" Her full lips trembled. "Do you know where he is or even if he's alive?"

"Oh, of course I knew your father." Nibbling on a carrot stick, Lori added, "I haven't heard from him in years. I don't know if he's even alive, but I don't know why he wouldn't be. He loved life almost as much as he loved your mother."

Leilani slid to the edge of her chair and leaned forward. "Tell me about them!"

The waitress arrived with their lunches, giving Lori a moment's breathing space. She studied Leilani as subtly as she could without staring. "You have the same magnetic presence and unself-conscious beauty as your mother. I'd say Malia was a little shorter and slighter. You surely get your height and irrepressible energy from your father."

"What were they like?" Leilani prodded again.

"We double-dated more than a few times," Lori continued, "and I served as maid of honor at their wedding. And…she stood up for me at my wedding."

"I didn't know you were married," Leilani blurted out.

"I was, but it lasted only a few months. That, my dear, is a story best forgotten."

"I'm sorry," Leilani said, burning to know more about the friend-ship with her mother, but hesitating to put this nice woman on the spot. She took a large bite of her eggplant and roast pepper sandwich to occupy her mouth.

Lori needed no prodding. "Hank was a loving husband, a good father, too. You were his pet, Leilani. He'd take you on his lap and tell you stories, Hawaiian folk legends." She sipped a few spoonfuls of her soup. "For the most part I found your father ambitious, hardworking, and quite reserved, really. Except when he had a few beers in him. Then he turned sloppy, didn't know when to stop. In the end, it was his undoing."

Lori saw the pained look on Leilani's face and realized she'd probably said too much. "I liked him a lot, though," she added hastily, "and, frankly, I envied Malia. The truth is, I knew my ex was the wrong man for me. But I married him anyway, because I blindly wanted the kind of love your parents had found. I thought some of their happiness would rub off on us. How wrong I was!"

"But why did my father go away when we needed him most? Didn't he love Kekoa and me?"

"Some answers I just don't have," Lori said. "I'm sure he loved you both very much. Perhaps that has something to do with why he went away. You mentioned your brother. He should be twelve, maybe fourteen, by now."

"He's fourteen-and-a-half."

"Where is he today?" Lori asked.

"I have no idea," Leilani said. "He disappeared right around the same time Uncle Big John disappeared. Everyone assumed they'd gone off together. *Tutu* Eme didn't think so. Neither do I. Anyway, I haven't seen either one of them for over two years now. No, that's not true. I saw Kekoa get off a bus on Kapiolani Boulevard a couple months ago." She told Lori about her frustrating encounter.

"Have you tried the police?"

"Yes, when he first ran away, and then again when we sighted him at the bus stop. The police had no luck either time. He simply disappeared into nowhere. Why do you ask about Kekoa?"

"A very strange thing happened to me yesterday," said Lori. "I went to place flowers at your mother's grave and I interrupted a teenage boy there. He had left his own flowers and was lying on the grass with his head upon the grave. When he saw me coming toward him, he took off on his bike. I thought it might be Kekoa, but the last time I'd seen him, he was only two years old. The boy I saw was thin but healthy looking, and he seemed to be dressed well enough."

"Why would he be afraid of you?"

"I don't know, but it does give me an idea. Since the grave is a place you both frequent, why not leave a note for him so he can get in touch with you?"

"Oh, Lori, that's a terrific idea!" A sudden smile showing very white teeth transformed Leilani's mournful expression into a glimmer of sheer joy. She brushed her abundant hair behind one ear with fresh confidence.

"Way to go, Lori!" Numi burst out.

"That's the most solid suggestion we've had in a long time," said Paul. "Thank you for coming to us. We all appreciate what you have told us."

Lori smiled. "You're very welcome, but there's more." She took a hurried final spoonful of her soup. "It's most disturbing."

"About Kekoa?" Leilani asked.

"No. I'm not even sure I understand the full meaning of what I heard. First, Mr. Wong, do you know a man by the name of Coland Benfield-Rice?"

"Why, yes. He's a co-trustee in Leilani and Kekoa's trust."

"At Punchbowl yesterday I accidentally overheard a conversation between Mr. Benfield-Rice and a man named Murphy. I happened to be sitting on a bench up at the memorial. Mr. Murphy was a partner in Hank Pualoa's old construction firm. In fact, he runs it by himself now."

"Yes, I know," said Paul. "He's Leilani's 'Uncle Red,' the co-trustee who arranged for Leilani to live with us—her education, too. What did you hear?"

"I overheard Mr. Murphy attempting to bribe Mr. Benfield-Rice. Then he threatened to blackmail him if he didn't vote for something called Rodminn. I wanted to hear more, but I discovered another man eavesdropping on them. I've seen him before in Mr. Fujita's office, as a matter of fact, but I don't have any idea who he is. Then this other eavesdropper spotted me, and I got nervous and left."

"This information may turn out to be valuable to us," said Paul. "Have you told anyone else about it?"

"Uh, yes, Yoshiro Fujita. He's the elder partner in the law firm. He acknowledged the second man as a client, but, curiously, refused to say any more about the whole incident. But I could see he was disturbed. And when I saw you at the opera last night, I thought you ought to know, too."

Paul nodded slowly. "I'm beginning to understand what's going on here. The Rodminn firm is bidding to buy land from the trust. They're a real estate firm that I have been very wary of from the start. In fact, I have a sneaking suspicion that Red Murphy and Rodminn Estates are one and the same. If so, he has a conflict of interest there."

"I'm glad it makes sense to you, Mr. Wong," said Lori. "I wouldn't want the children to be cheated. I should think that Mr. Murphy could be prosecuted for extortion, or at the very least, censured for bribery and misconduct."

"There's been no crime committed yet, so we really can't go to the police," said Paul. "They'd just consider it hearsay. However, both men, and especially Mr. Murphy, will bear close watching. Lori, are you concerned about the other man at Punchbowl? Do you feel threatened in any way?"

"Maybe I overreacted. My boss thought so. The listener didn't seem to be interested in me, and now that I've thought about it, he seemed just as upset over being discovered as I was. At any rate, he didn't try to follow me."

"Please, Lori, don't put yourself in any danger. Amateur sleuthing is risky business."

"I won't. I'm not really that adventurous. Now I must get back to work."

Leilani kissed her warmly on the cheek and hugged her, saying, "Thank you very much." The woman had provided her with her first true ray of hope.

They watched her leave and brush past a young man as he entered the tea room.

"Alex! What a surprise!" Leilani cried, jumping up from the table. "We didn't think you'd be able to make it. You'll never guess what happened." A blush suffused her face and her eyes sparkled. "We're going to find Kekoa. Lori—Miss Yamashita—told us how to do it."

Alex bussed her lightly on the cheek and escorted her back to her chair. "Easy does it, little lady. Take your time and explain it to me."

He signaled the waitress for a cup of coffee and settled himself into Lori's empty chair while Leilani brought him up to date on both stories.

Alex listened intently. "It may be some time before you make contact with Kekoa," he told her. "You don't know how long it is between his visits to the cemetery, do you? And your message will have to be protected from the elements, won't it? Maybe you could put it in a sealed, clear plastic envelope."

"Don't you think it should contain some reassurance from Leilani that he need have no fear in coming to us?" Masako asked. "I do believe the boy must be extremely frightened of someone to stay away from her this long."

"Good point," Alex said. Then, turning to his father: "What can you do about this apparent conspiracy? Are you going to confront Mr. Benfield-Rice?"

"We can't do anything yet—not until there actually is wrongdoing. And Lori's information is pretty sketchy."

Alex nodded, then pushed his chair back and announced, "I'd like to take Leilani on a little stroll through the international gardens."

Without waiting for a reaction from his parents, he led her out the door.

"I think we have a romance in the making," said Paul.

Masako started to protest, but Numi laid her head on her mother's shoulder. "Isn't it wonderful?" she said. "They're in love. This way I get to keep both my brother and sister." Numi sprang out of her chair and pranced halfway across the courtyard before looking back. "Mom? Okay if I go inside to see the exhibits?" She hardly heard her mother say, "A half-hour, no more."

Masako scowled. "Such romantic enthusiasm scares the daylights out of me."

Her husband looked blank.

"Paul, I'm talking about Leilani and Alex, as if you didn't know."

"Of course, but…"

"We were nineteen once, going steady, and working toward our degrees at UH. Or have you already forgotten what it's like to be young and impetuous?"

"Oh, no," Paul said. "I'll always remember that terrible night— the night we told your parents you were pregnant. Your mother went from polite and soft-spoken to endless shrieks and tears. Your father simply went for my throat."

The parents had insisted on an immediate ceremony at City Hall, which was fine with Paul and Masako.

"Aren't we jumping to conclusions?" he asked. "After all, they're not sleeping together."

"And I suppose you think we should wait until they are," Masako retorted.

"No, of course not, dear."

"Well, what do you propose we do about it?"

"Do?" he repeated. "What is there to do? Forbid them to see

each other? Your father tried that. A lot of good it did, or have you forgotten?" Paul grinned with a mischievous glint in his gray eyes. Her father's determination to keep them apart had merely intensified their secret rendezvous and elaborate lies.

Masako shook her head. "The traditional ways were so much simpler. Parents ruled with an iron hand and children obeyed."

Paul looked earnestly at his wife. "And would we be here holding this discussion if we had followed the old ways?" He waited while the stern frown melted away and the curl of a smile took its place. He took her hand in both of his and held it tenderly.

* * *

In the Volcano House restaurant, Cindy Chou poured maple syrup on the last of her taro pancakes. Red Murphy had finished his breakfast and excused himself, promising to be right back. Last evening he'd flown the two of them in his own plane from Honolulu to Hilo. Cindy had never been to the Big Island before. Their night at Volcano House, the lodging atop Volcanoes National Park, had ended at 2 a.m. with rapturous lovemaking.

Cindy could never really love this barbaric man, who'd been just another trick less than a week ago. Her hard life had not permitted her the luxury of real love. But Red performed well in bed, and she hadn't known many men who could wildly arouse her. For her day-to-day professional encounters she relied on the delicate dramatic abilities that she had cleverly honed over the years. Red wasn't ashamed to be seen with her, either. On the down side, he did have a horrendous hair-trigger temper.

Popping the last bite of pancake in her mouth, she gazed out the window at the Kilauea Caldera. The stark lunar-like panorama stretched to the horizon.

"Well, here I am," a gruff voice said. Red slid into his chair and handed her a multicolored gift bag. "Enjoy." A schoolboy smirk covered his face.

"Something for me?" Cindy's hands unraveled the curled ends of the bag and withdrew a blue and white playsuit. "Oooh, I like it." She got up from her chair, walked around the table, and leaned over Red to kiss him. "I love it. I hope it fits. Thank you." She kissed him again.

"Go try it on. I'll wait here for you." He watched her move across the rustic wood and lava-rock dining room, and looked to see if others watched as well. He liked being seen with an attractive woman. Besides, she didn't ask too many questions and certainly didn't argue with everything he said like so many other women he'd known. He occupied himself with the morning paper until she returned fifteen minutes later.

The new outfit seemed a skosh tight, but he enjoyed the overall effect it produced. Her bountiful figure pressed from within. Cindy's eyes flashed with pleasure, convincing Red that his gift had been a hit. They made their way outdoors to start a day of sightseeing.

He maneuvered their rental Mercury around Crater Rim Drive to Halemaumau Crater—once a vast pit of fire, smoke, and molten lava. They took the path to the crater's edge. Striations in the wall revealed lava levels at different periods in time. Just inside the safety fence, an Asian couple knelt, offering their sacrifice to Buddha. The sacrifice included the head of a pig, along with assorted fruits, vegetables, and grains. The couple prayed in earnest even though they prayed in the cauldron of the mythical goddess, Pele.

A strong sulfur smell permeated the air. Red and Cindy picked their way back toward the car along a rocky field with curls of pungent steam emanating from crevices in the surface. Red stood defiantly upon one of the flat rocks about eighteen inches above the ground, and the sulfur-yellow steam nearly enveloped him.

"It fits you, Lord Satan," she chuckled.

Their tour took them to open rifts in the black lava, where bright metallic colors of the quickly cooled rock formations appeared in unlikely crags. Small patches of moss and tufts of grass dotted the rifts. Wind-blown dust and dirt trapped in the rifts provided a basis for life just as it had millions of years before, when the whole earth had begun its cooling.

Devastation Trail took them through a forest that had been consumed by the heat of molten lava. Trees burnt entirely to ash left ghostly imprints in the cooled lava. Gray tree trunks lay wasted—seared bones of the forest past.

They drove east, past the lodge, until they encountered a number of tourists facing a mountain crest just a few miles away. Smoke and a sporadic line of flames billowed from the crest. The erupting Mauna Loa held them spellbound for the better part of an hour.

A park ranger waved them back to their car. "Don't get any closer," he warned. "It's much too dangerous."

Along the edge of the crater in the other direction, well out of the ranger's line of vision, Cindy and Red noticed a series of small rifts and deep crevices with steam billowing forth. A tanned Nordic couple in bikinis immersed themselves in the steamy bath. The two tow-headed figures moved in and out of the hot mist to take pleasure in both the heating and cooling of their lithe bodies. They stood precariously on a smooth lip-like formation that had been shaped by molten erosion. It appeared to almost swallow them whole as they cautiously descended and then disappeared into the steep vent.

"What a perfect way to get rid of a body," Red said with a chuckle. "Down the ol' chute and nature finishes the job. Poof! No evidence."

Cindy stared at him. "Are you crazy?" she asked. Then she wished she'd kept her mouth shut. *What if he gets mad? He'll ruin the whole weekend.*

But to her surprise he laughed. "Just joking, baby. Not to worry."

As they drove back to the lodge, Cindy snuggled close to Red. The encroaching night sank to pitch-black as the vog—dusty volcanic ash and foggy mist borne of tropical humidity—settled over their last hours on the Big Island. Tonight they'd play. Tomorrow they'd return to Oahu, to business as usual.

Chapter 14
Confession Is Bad for the Head

THE CHINESE banyans lent their lacy shade as Leilani knelt at her mother's grave. She would shed no tears today; she harbored new hope for finding her brother. Numi had driven her to the cemetery to leave a message for Kekoa. The girls taped a plastic-covered note to a small stake and pushed the pointy end into the soft ground in front of Malia Pualoa's bronze marker.

In a voice barely above a whisper, Leilani communed with her mother's *uhane,* her spirit, explaining the message and all the events of the past few days. She had no doubt that her mother heard her and understood.

Her mission fulfilled, Leilani rose and brushed the grass off her shorts and bare knees. She blew a gentle kiss in the direction of her grandmother's grave where the bronze marker read *"Mea aloha kupuna wahine kuku* (Farewell my dearest grandmother of grandmothers), Eme Waiwaiole."

"Numi? Did you know my *Tutu* was a *kupuna* at our grade school? She came once a week to teach the old Hawaiian ways and customs. The kids adored her."

"We had a *kupuna,* too," said Numi, "a wrinkle-faced old Kauaian. He'd sit cross-legged on the front lawn and talk story about the demigod Maui and the *Menehune* people who lived over on Kauai centuries ago. I loved the legends, but I think he made a lot of them up. Those *Menehunes* sounded too much like leprechauns."

"Oh, no, Numi, they were real. Archaeologists found the bones of little people who came to the island long before the Polynesians, like a thousand years ago. The Menehunes built many of the ancient fishponds throughout the islands."

Numi's almond eyes flickered with amusement. "If you say so. Hey, it's getting dark. I'm not sure I want to meet up with any creatures or their ghosts in this place. And Mom will have kittens if we don't get home soon."

A brush of pink, amber, and purple stroked the sky. Leilani gazed pensively toward Diamond Head, looming dark and secretive over the cemetery. "I wonder..." she said, "I wonder if Kekoa lives somewhere near here." She folded her arms across her chest, rubbing them against a sudden chill. "I hope he sees the note soon. What if he doesn't come back here for weeks? Or months? Oh, I don't know how much longer I can go on like this, Numi. I felt so upbeat when we got here and now I'm full of doubts again."

Numi took her hand as they walked to the car. "Don't even think like that, Leilani. You're doing all the right things." Glad to get away from the cemetery, Numi guided the Ford Escort down Twenty-second Avenue and through Kaimuki on Harding Avenue within a block of the Osaka Family Bakery. "Besides," she added, "maybe Kekoa does live nearby."

* * *

The bakery had become Kekoa's classroom. From 5:00 to 6:30 each evening Yasuko brought out her old textbooks, and between customers, tutored him in math, English, and social studies. Kekoa hunched over an algebra book on the small table wedged behind the display case, his hair flopping over his forehead and one leg folded under him. Today he was learning to do time, rate, and distance problems, so the day wasn't a total loss. Earlier, he'd returned from a disappointing afternoon, observing yet another high school dismissal without seeing his sister. He'd be out of schools soon. What would he do then?

"Okay, kid," Yasuko said, "6:30, time for me to get home."

Kekoa snapped his book shut, hugged her, and grabbed his basketball. He trotted out the door and down the block to the rec center on Waialae between Tenth and Eleventh.

A youngster about his age, though slightly shorter, was shooting baskets by himself.

"Okay if I join ya, dude?" Kekoa asked.

The boy nodded. They played H-O-R-S-E in the half-court space for a few minutes. Then the boy stopped in his tracks, bounced the ball a few times, and said, "Hey, I've seen you here before. I'm Andy."

Andy Ballesteros had a round face with Filipino features, a thatch of black hair, and a natural talent for jump shots. He also talked story nonstop while working the court. When he double-dribbled and went in for a lay-up, the ball circled the rim and rolled out again. "Oh, man," he declared, "maybe I'd do better if I didn't talk so much." They both laughed.

Dusk fell, the court lights came on, and the two boys sat down on the stone wall along Waialae to cool off. Andy did most of the talking. "Maybe we can shoot some more tomorrow, yah?"

Kekoa nodded vigorously. His first guy friend in nearly three years. Maybe his luck was changing.

* * *

Coland Benfield-Rice stole into the marble foyer of his Kahala Avenue home and slipped the door keys into his pocket. His Rolex read 10:25. Dreading the inevitable showdown with his wife, he'd been inventing excuses for coming home late. For three nights straight his ruse had worked—she'd been asleep when he got in. But he knew he couldn't avoid her forever.

Strains of Tchaikovsky's *Violin Concerto in C Major* floated into the foyer—her favorite piece. He hoped it signaled a mellow mood. He moved quietly to the bar in the dining room. Pulling out the stopper on a decanter, he poured himself a fortissimo of Chivas Regal, downing it neat. Now he'd face the music. He stood for an instant in the arched doorway of their French Provincial living room. The artwork, the velvet sofa, the gilded mirror over the mantel spoke of elegance. All indicated success, yet seemed so trivial compared to the bloody mess he'd made of their lives.

He found Constance seated primly, ankles crossed, in an arm-chair near the stereo. Her silver hair was perfectly coiffed, as if she'd just emerged from the beauty salon. A half-finished square of needlepoint spread across the lap of her beige linen pants suit. His peck on her cheek elicited a small smile, and then she resumed her stitching. But he was not so easily put off. He purposely blocked her light.

Constance switched off the stereo, castrating the concerto in mid-note. She studied the determined figure before her. "I love your tie," she said. She really meant she loved him. "It has such subtle colors."

"Thank you, my dear. It's the one you gave me for my birthday. Can we talk about a serious matter now?" he asked. "Can I get you any-thing? A brandy perhaps?"

"No brandy just now, I'm fine. But what's so disturbing that you require an invitation to speak? You look like you're about to face an audience with the Queen."

He removed his suit jacket and laid it carefully over a brocade chair. "I don't quite know how to begin. Basically, I'm in serious trouble and I beg your help." He sat down on the tapestried ottoman in front of her and placed his hand firmly upon hers. "Please, darling!"

"Is it about money? I transferred the funds early last week as you wished."

"No, this time it isn't about money. I only wish it were. It's about me and my damned indiscretions. I never meant to hurt you. I still don't. In fact, I am as much in love with you today as the day we married." His voice choked. "Please forgive me."

"Just what kind of indiscretions are you talking about?" Furrows formed deep gullies in her forehead.

"Well, I remained celibate for about a year after you banished me from your bed."

"Ah, how noble, how stoic."

He ignored her sarcasm and continued. "And then I made a discreet arrangement with a…a call girl. I could hardly be expected to live forever like a Jesuit priest, Constance. We only met once a week. Tuesdays for sex and a light supper."

"On Tuesdays? Your so-called cribbage night at the club? How infinitely clever of you. Is this your confession?" She yanked her hand out from under his, the large emerald in her cocktail ring scratching his palm.

"Yes! I mean no! Believe me, my dear, this is not easy for me."

"So you've said. From my point of view, you've had it too easy. You'll get no clemency from me. You…you vile, devious…" He'd ambushed her so completely that the words clogged her throat.

"Constance, there's more. Please hear me out. I am truly desperate. The relationship meant nothing to me, except for the physical liaison and a little playful diversion that I couldn't enjoy with you. I had every reason to believe our rendezvous were both secure and discreet. I took every precaution and I impressed the need upon her as well. A few days ago…" He paused and inhaled a long breath as if he were about to plunge under water. "A few days ago, I learned that the little slut had sold me out to a business acquaintance of mine named Murphy. As it turns out, Murphy is an unscrupulous bully who will pull out all stops, even extortion, to gain what he wants."

"He tried to blackmail you?"

"Yes."

Constance mulled this over. "How can he blackmail you without some sort of proof?"

"He has proof. He collaborated with Cindy, plotted with her to..."

"Plotted? What the devil do you mean?"

"Murphy had us photographed together in compromising positions. The worst of it is that nothing is left to the imagination."

"Is your face actually recognizable?"

"Yes, I regret to say. Murphy has the photos and is using them to force my vote in a financial matter at the bank. He wants me to accept an improper bid from a bogus firm he's set up to purchase land from a guardian trust."

Behind her bifocals, her eyes narrowed. "This makes no sense, Coland. At least do me the courtesy of spelling it out."

He leaned forward and locked his eyes on hers. "The trust was created for two teenage kids who might even be orphaned at this point. Murphy and I, we're co-trustees with a fiduciary responsibility to the trust. The deal he's trying to force me into is definitely not in the children's best interest. Not to mention that it's illegal. He's also offered me a good deal of money as an incentive, a bribe..."

"Isn't this a matter for the police?"

"Yes, you're quite right. Don't I wish it were that easy. If I report him to the police he says he'll give the photos to the press and our friends. It would ruin our lives. I could handle the scandal if it were me alone, but it affects you, too." He slowly rose and stood before her.

Now Constance pulled the plug on her anger. "You should have thought of that before you went to that cheap, unfaithful bitch of yours."

"That's the point. She wasn't cheap and she's marvelous at what she does."

"You insolent bastard. You have the nerve to stand there and tell me that? And just how cheap wasn't she? How much of our money, my money, have you squandered on her?"

"Please, Constance, let's not get vicious, let's not destroy everything we have together. Believe me, I didn't know she'd do this," he pleaded.

"What?" Constance cried. "You expected faithfulness from your whore when you don't know the meaning of it yourself?"

She leaped up at him, pounding her fists on his chest, wanting to hurt him as he'd hurt her. But he stood there like a martyr, absorbing the blows, hoping to defuse her fury. Red blotches spread over her cheeks, blue veins protruded from her neck and forehead. When thrashing him failed, she pushed him hard. He fell backward over the ottoman, crashing first into the floor lamp and then to the floor itself. She looked for things to throw at him. She tossed the sewing basket by its handle, then pitched a silver-framed picture of Coland grinning, and then a weighty volume of art prints.

Coland could not regain his footing. Still, he managed to deflect every one of his wife's missiles, even a marble statuette. Venus de Milo sailed past him to collide with a bric-a-brac cabinet. The crash of glass only fueled the fire of his wife's anger.

"It's one thing when you trash your life, but it's another story when you bring ruin on the whole family," she shrieked. "There isn't a decent bone in your body."

She picked up a Waterford crystal ashtray, and this time took careful aim. Just as she let go, he struggled to get up, his hands pushing down against the floor. He saw the ashtray coming, but couldn't get his hands up in time to deflect it, nor did he have the agility to duck it. He instinctively turned his head aside and caught the brunt of the heavy cut-crystal at his left temple.

His arms buckled, and he collapsed backward onto the floor. A thick trail of red rolled slowly down his sideburn, but Coland knew no immediate pain, only the depths of darkness.

Constance stood poised to pitch her next missile, an Oriental lamp.

"Get up and take it like a man, you...you...philandering bastard." She tilted her head, waiting for his response, but met only dead silence.

And then she saw the stream of blood crossing his left cheek. Constance melted. The lamp slipped from her limp fingers. Porcelain chunks flew everywhere as the heirloom collided with the ceramic tile floor. Approaching Coland, she knelt over his still form. Lowering her head to his torso, she listened. She felt the slow rise and fall of his chest, heard the faint murmurs of his breathing.

Constance sat back and reached up for the princess phone on the end table. She caught the cord and pulled. The phone fell to the floor with a clang.

"Damn!" she cried, setting the phone upright. She dialed 911 and shivered as she waited for someone to answer.

"Honolulu Police Department. What is your emergency?"

"It was an accident," Constance blurted out. "My husband, he's lying here unconscious and bleeding. Hurry, for God sake!"

Chapter 15
Ball and Chain

"WOW! LOOKS like World War III in here," said one police officer viewing the carnage in the living room. He picked up a leather-bound edition of T.S. Eliot's poems, rescuing it from a pool of blood. Next, he retrieved *Treasures of the British Museum*. He probed the ruins with his nightstick, discovering the broken head and torso of Venus de Milo. *Not much of a loss,* he decided wryly, *the babe didn't have arms anyway.*

The EMTs had taken Coland away in an ambulance. The officer joined his partner to lead Constance down the front steps in handcuffs. The gas lamp on the lawn cast its harsh yellow light on the unlikely trio.

"Where are you taking me?" she cried. "What right do you have?"

Then she suddenly stopped protesting. If she made a scene...*Oh, God, what if my neighbors hear me? What if they actually see me like this? I'll never live it down.*

In the midnight air, a tremor shook her body. She leaned against the cruiser door to steady herself before the officers settled her inside. The cruiser pulled away, leaving only the sound of unsympathetic ocean waves lapping at the shore of the Kahala beachfront estate.

* * *

Coland awoke the following morning to find Constance in his dimly lit hospital room.

"You look like hell. How do you feel?" she asked timidly.

"Terrible!" Coland winced with headache pain as he spoke. He lay in bed with a bandage wrapped about his forehead. "You don't look so hot yourself."

Though her clothes were neat and pressed and not a hair was out of place, weariness lined her handsome face and reddened eyes.

"How would you expect me to look after spending most of the

117

night in jail?"

"Jail?"

"Yes, jail," she answered. "After the ambulance took you away, the 911 officers arrested me for 'abuse of a household member.' They even put those horrible manacles on my wrists. I was so embarrassed. I told them it was an accident, but they wouldn't listen. Coland, I had to post $25,000 bail!"

"I'm sorry," he said, "but I'm afraid we're not out of the woods on that score. A police officer dropped by here an hour ago. I told him I'd had a heated discussion with you, and that was all. He insisted that I press charges. When I refused, he said the department would file, anyway. Apparently, these cases go automatically to the city prosecutor's office."

"It's your fault that I lost my temper, Coland. You did give me good cause."

"I tried to be honest with you. I wanted to break it to you easily...I just didn't know how."

"Well, if you hadn't been out cheating on me, none of this would have happened."

Coland pressed both of his hands to the thick bandage, closed his eyes tight, and clenched his teeth.

"Painful?"

"Yes, enormously!"

Coland had been admitted to Queen's Medical Center with a concussion and was being kept under observation. The doctor had told him they were checking for subdural hematoma, internal bleeding, but there was no sign of it yet.

Coland watched his wife's fingers toy nervously with her pearl choker. She said nothing at all.

"The doctor tells me I'm probably no longer in danger," he said, trying desperately to reopen a conversation. "The swelling is on its way down. I should be out of here in a few days."

Constance nodded, but looked away quickly, lest she make eye contact and lose all control in front of him. Silence filled the room.

"I'm not proud of how I've behaved," he tried again. "At first, looking elsewhere for sex seemed justified. By the time I realized how selfish I was being, I didn't know how to put an end to it. I'm ashamed, darling, I truly am. I never meant to hurt you."

She continued to avoid his eyes and chewed on her lower lip

118

instead.

"I love you, Constance, and I hope you will find a way to forgive me. Please!"

Her composure crumbling, she lapsed into subdued sobs. Coland tossed a box of bedside tissues and it landed at her feet. She gratefully picked it up and plucked out a tissue or two, buying herself a few moments. He waited patiently. Then he told her again that he loved her.

At last she looked across at him—his open arms inviting her to come closer.

"I don't know if I can ever love you again," she said with a croaking, unsure voice. But her body betrayed her words. Cautiously, she approached the bed, took his hand, and squeezed it. She regarded his face, looking for some guarantee of future fidelity. What she saw there seemed enough; she held his hand and wept quietly. "I could have killed you," she murmured.

Coland asked, "Can we ever go back to the way we were?"

"Nothing can ever be as it was. I'm not sure that I'd even want it to be," she said softly.

* * *

Kekoa sat in the top row of a ball field bleacher between the middle school and the high school. His Timex, a gift from a grateful Mauro for saving Sam, read 1:45. He'd chosen this perch to give himself a clear view of the campus. Maybe this would be his lucky day, the day he'd find his sister at last.

He could hear the racket of construction equipment from the street side of the high school. He saw a two-story crane hauling materials up to and down from the roof. The boom swung laterally over the street and back again. A small cabled trolley ran a ball and hook the length of the boom and sometimes it just hovered.

The weather—windy, hot, and dry—felt as oppressive as the boy's mood. Reddish sand from the grassless ball field blew in a dust cloud that almost enveloped him. Squeezing his eyes shut for a moment, he didn't see the tall uniformed figure hurrying up the path past the dug-outs. But the authoritative voice was unmistakable.

"Hey, boy! Get down here, quickly and no nonsense."

Before Kekoa could open his eyes, he knew he'd been caught. He recognized the same police officer he'd escaped from nearly a week earlier. He slowly climbed down.

The officer clasped his hand on Kekoa's shoulder. "What's your name, boy? Why aren't you in school?" Kekoa remained silent and continued to wriggle and squirm. He couldn't escape this time.

"Settle down, son. I'm not gonna hurt ya. Is this your school?" Kekoa shook his head.

"What's your school, then?"

Still no response. His silence inflamed the officer, so he hauled Kekoa across the ball field to his cruiser. He'd hastily misparked at the curb in the orange-coned work area. "You're goin' downtown. They'll know just what to do with you. Call your folks, too."

Red Murphy watched them from the stairs of his firm's construction trailer. The officer's boisterous scolding had alerted him. Red also knew that the crane operator had gone to use the portable "Sanitoy" propped at the edge of the school yard. He'd left the diesel engine running and the equipment cab unattended.

Red slipped from the trailer into the empty cab of the idling crane. He'd recognized Kekoa and seized what he thought to be an excellent opportunity. Slowly, he positioned the boom in line with the officer's cruiser and ran the wheeled cable trolley with hook and ball directly over it. He watched the officer push Kekoa into the caged back seat of the police car.

With precision timing, Red pulled the crane's brake release and clutch on the winch drum, and the heavy wrecker's ball accelerated toward the police car with all the force of gravity. As the ball and hook fell, Red ducked out of the cab and ran back to the trailer.

The idling diesel engine masked the groan of the spinning winch unwinding. The falling load deflected forward, glanced off a protruding tree branch, and shattered the cruiser's windshield, demolishing the hood and front seat. All four cruiser doors sprang open, and the impact sent the officer into the street, where he landed stunned but unharmed, on his backside.

The force of the ball crashing on the hood flipped Kekoa to the floor of the cruiser. He lay there for a moment, confused, aware only that the doors had popped free. He crawled slowly out in a state of near-shock, but when he realized his stroke of good fortune, he took off running while looking over his shoulder to see if he was being followed. Dazed, the officer rose to his feet, shaking his head, his hands brushing his trousers. For the moment he forgot the wayward boy.

Kekoa crossed the street, and still looking over his shoulder, ran straight into the arms of a tall man standing on the curb. The man had dropped one of two canes he used to support his legs. Kekoa's first instinct was to struggle free, but when he looked up, he stopped.

"Hey, you're the guy from Chinatown, the guy that was following Red Ed."

The man relaxed his hold on Kekoa and knelt down to pick up the fallen cane. "Yeah, you're right about that. I'm Hal Perry." He offered his hand, and the boy shook it.

"Whew! You sure saved my life that night," Kekoa said. He looked over Hal's shoulder and saw the bewildered cop still looking around for him. "Can you get me outta here now?"

"Quick, get in my car before either of them figure out where you are. Keep your head down. I'll drop you anywhere you say."

Kekoa slid into the front seat and slouched down as far as he could. Hal Perry drove away from the curb and turned onto King Street.

"What's your name, son?"

"Ah...Keith."

"Keith what?"

"Just Keith."

"Oh." Hal decided not to probe.

"I was thinking..." Kekoa said. He could extend his trust only so far, but somehow he was drawn to this guy. Maybe because the man had helped him out of trouble twice. His voice quivered as he began again. "What happened back there, anyway?"

"The guy you called Red Ed? It was him in the crane cab. That bastard deliberately tried to drop the hook and ball on you. It was no accident, I can tell you that. I know him well. His name is Red Murphy. I saw him watching you from his trailer steps, but I didn't know what he was up to until he got in the cab. Say, Keith? How do you know him? Why would he want to hurt you?"

The boy could hold it in no longer. "He's a bad-ass murderer. I saw him kill my uncle, and he knows I saw him. I watched him bury the body, too."

"Where's that?" Perry asked. When the boy didn't answer, he repeated, "So where?"

Kekoa felt a sudden panic. This stranger asked too many ques-

121

tions. "I forget where," he said. "Lemme out at King and University. You said you'd drop me anywhere I wanted."

Perry slowed the car and pulled over to the first curb space past the University intersection.

"I have something that belongs to you in the trunk. You can fetch it when you get out." He pulled the trunk release.

There in the trunk sat Kekoa's Rainbows sweatshirt, the one he'd lost that night in Chinatown. Tucking it under his arm, he slammed the trunk shut and went to the open driver's window. "Thanks a lot! How'd you know it was mine? How'd you even recognize me?"

"Dumb luck, I guess." Hal wondered about that himself. "Here, son, take my business card. See the telephone number? Call me if you ever need help or even if you want to tell me more about Red. He's dangerous. I want to put him in jail where he belongs. I think I can do that with your help."

Kekoa scanned Hal Perry's business card, and the words Private Investigations jumped out at him. The boy hesitated a moment, then blurted out, "Mister Perry, you ever find missing girls?"

"Yeah, sometimes. Who's lost?"

"My sister, but I can't pay you anything."

"Let's talk about it. Get back in the car."

Kekoa was sorely tempted, but things were moving entirely too fast for him now. He needed time to think. He knew he would contact Hal Perry—but later, when he could sort everything out. "I'll call you," Kekoa promised and darted across King Street between honking horns and braking cars.

Hal Perry held his breath until Keith reached the curb, then watched the boy sprint down the King Street sidewalk back in the direction of University. Expertly dodging shoppers and the planters in front of the flower shops, the boy's long brown legs carried him past Puck's Alley and out of sight.

Shrewd kid, Hal thought, *he knows I can't follow him there.* Perry continued on King, swinging left onto the ramp for H-1.

* * *

The crane operator screamed at Red. "Who the hell's been in my damn cab? What crazy bastard moved the boom? Can't a man take a crap without some nut screwing around with his rig?"

"Your fault. You abandoned your cab without stowing the hook or locking up. Why didn't you send your hook tender to watch the cab? I'm gonna hafta report this to the union."

"You will, like hell!" the operator bellowed back.

"Hey, you two," cried the police officer, who had finally recovered from his initial shock. "What about my car? It's totaled. Who the hell's gonna pay for it?"

Red thought about that for a moment and decided he didn't need any more trouble, especially now. "Sorry, Officer. But hey, look where you parked. You'll be lucky if any insurance will cover it. After all, we're not liable." He winked at the crane operator, who was taken by surprise at the sudden turnaround in Red's attitude.

"Oh, man," the officer muttered, "the department's gonna love this." Fearing he'd be blamed for the damages, he asked to use the phone. His radio-phone hadn't survived the accident.

"Of course," Red replied. "On the desk at the end of the trailer." He lowered his voice and spoke to the crane operator, "You go along with the accident report, and I won't tell the union. There's an extra fifty bucks in it for you, too."

"Done."

Five o'clock came and went. The car had been towed off, the Police Department's claims inspector had come and gone. Red was finally alone with his thoughts. "That little brat lives a charmed life," he said half-aloud. "I'll get him yet." He wondered why the boy hadn't gone to the police. If he hadn't by this time, was he still a threat? If he couldn't finish Kekoa off, at least he could keep him scared.

Murphy picked up the phone and tapped out a number. He waited. On the fourth ring a woman's voice answered. "Benfield-Rice residence."

"Mr. Benfield-Rice, please."

"The Mister is in the hospital. May I take a message?"

"Do you expect him home soon?"

"I can't answer that."

"And who are you?"

"I'm the housekeeper."

"Would you tell him that Red is waiting for his answer?"

"Yes, sir, I'm writing it down. Red...is waiting...for his answer.

"Is there a last name?"

"Not necessary, he knows me." Red hung up. *Hospital?* That

puzzled him. *Could this be a ploy—Coland hiding out to avoid me?*

Chapter 16
Search for Rodminn

HAL PERRY'S CANES leaned against the wooden table where he sat in the Hawaiian Department of Commerce and Consumer Affairs. He jotted notes on a lined pad, ripped the top sheet off, and stuck it in his briefcase, then walked to the desk and turned the Rodminn Realty portfolio over to the clerk. The folio contained the incorporation papers for this real estate brokerage. He'd found the firm's Waimanalo address and phone number, a list of major assets, and a license to do business in the city and county of Honolulu. One Horace Rodder was listed as president and broker of record; a Wilma Minnet as vice president and secretary.

Rodder and Minnet...Rodminn? No mention of Murphy, but not a bad morning's work, Hal decided. He found a phone booth in the hall and retrieved the Rodminn number from his notes. The phone rang without answer—not even an answering machine. What a way to conduct a business. He wanted to have a look for himself.

* * *

Hal pulled his Chevy into the parking lot of the Waimanalo strip mall. A sandwich shop and tourist kiosk full of trinkets flanked three small storefronts. The first two, dark and obviously empty, had "For Lease" signs propped up in their display windows. The one on the far left had a tan shade pulled down behind its glass door. A crudely lettered cardboard sign hung on the shade. The phone number on the sign matched the one he had found for Rodminn Realty in the telephone book and had called without success.

Hal tried the door and found it locked. No surprise there. From the pay phone in the parking lot he dialed the listing, but didn't wait for it to ring. He let the receiver dangle from its wire cord and, working his two canes, hobbled quickly to the shaded storefront. Sure enough, he heard the phone ringing—still an active number. Returning to the

125

phone booth, he hung up the receiver and took himself inside the sandwich shop, Peke's Pantry, next door. Hal surveyed the sunlit interior of the tiny place. Seeing no one, he wondered who was minding the store. He slid into one of the two red vinyl booths and laid his canes beside him. The place had a scrubbed look.

"Got some great chili," bragged a husky voice from behind the counter. The stocky island woman had been bending over and now straightened up, placing fresh-filled salt and pepper shakers on the counter. She had a pink hibiscus blossom tucked behind one ear and gestured to the wall menu above the grill.

"Uh, let's see. A bowl of your chili and a Diet Coke, medium."

"Good choice," she said. "My specialty." She served it with crackers plus a healthy scoop of rice. After setting the plate down, the woman lingered at the table as if waiting for a compliment. Her floral muumuu filled his view; the ruffled sleeves seemed oddly out of place encircling such muscular arms.

"It is great chili," he said. She smiled, satisfied.

Swallowing a large mouthful, he decided to question her. "Say, uh…anyone ever go into the real estate office next door?"

"No, no one, except for Pop, maybe," she replied.

"Who's Pop?"

"Pop Rod!"

"Would that be Pop Rodder, by any chance?"

"Yeah. You know him?"

"Not really, but I would like to talk with him."

"Well, if you want to wait till I close at three, I'll take you. It's just up the road there." She pointed with the damp rag in her hand. "He's still asleep though, his afternoon nap, you know. He went through a whole gallon o' wine last night. I try to bring the old boy leftovers that I can't sell no more. If I didn't bring him nothing, he'd starve. All he wants to do is drink these days."

"You mean the place with the porch roof hanging down?"

"Yeah, that's it." She walked back behind the counter and swished the rag around. The counter didn't require any wiping, but she needed to look busy.

"Thanks, but I think I'll just take a little walk up there now. Are you related to him?"

"Naw, he's just my friend. Helped my family when we needed it a

126

buncha years ago. I just can't do no more for him. He won't listen to me or do what's good for him. He don't go to church no more, neither."

"And you are?"

"Peke Palaneke. I own this place."

"Miss Pala..."

"You can call me Peke." She pronounced it "Paykay."

"Peke...Thanks. Terrific chili. Now if you'll fill up a large coffee, I'll bring it on up to your friend."

"He ain't gonna like that."

"Don't worry, I'll pay for it."

"That ain't gonna make him like it any better."

Hal paid for his lunch, leaving her a large tip. She looked pleased. Pouring the coffee into a tall Styrofoam cup, she secured a lid on it and placed it in a brown paper bag. Hal twisted the top of the bag and gripped it deftly in his left hand, along with one cane handle, then worked his way up the short rise to the paint-peeled house with the corrugated tin roof and collapsing porch.

He knocked on the door, causing it to slap between a hook latch and the jamb. A weak voice groaned, but no one came to the door. Hal set the coffee down and removed a pencil from his pocket. Inserting it in the space between the door and jamb, he lifted the hook out of the eye. Picking up his paper bag he entered the house.

The moment Hal stepped through the door he wished he hadn't. Rotting food and dirty clothes lay strewn across the bare floor. The stench of urine and vomit permeated the room. A man in rumpled clothes sprawled on a couch that Goodwill would have rejected.

"Horace!" Hal said, leaning close to Rodder's ear. No response. "Mr. Rodder, it's Hal. Red sent me. I've got some money for you." At the word "money," Rodder began waking up from his drunken stupor.

"Who? Who the hell are you?"

Hal recoiled. Rodder's breath smelled even fouler than the room.

"Wadda ya want?"

"I'm Hal. Red sent me here with some money for you. Here, drink this. It'll wake you up."

"I don' wanna." But Hal pushed the coffee toward him. Rodder took it with trembling hands and sipped slowly, then gulped to satisfy a hangover thirst.

"Whew! Tha's hot. How mu'…much money did he send?"

"Enough for a few more bottles, anyway." Hal flashed a couple of twenties in front of Rodder's eyes.

"Wad's tha' for?" He sipped more of the coffee.

"He said you'd let me into the office to get some papers," Hal lied.

"On da wall by the door." Rodder sat up shakily.

"What's on the wall?"

"Da key, you dummy, da key to the office." His voice trailed off as he collapsed back onto the couch.

Hal left the money on the table, took the key hanging on a hook by the door, and retreated down the drive to the office.

The key worked. Letting himself in, he kept the lights off and carefully went through everything in the lone desk and file cabinet. The top middle drawer of the desk had been sprung previously, rendering the other drawer interlocks useless. His pick-lock set made short order of the file cabinet lock. Inside, he found Rodminn Estates brochures and accompanying pricing data. The other documents he scanned would have to be evaluated by a lawyer. He took notes and tried the photocopier. To his surprise, it worked. He copied the papers he thought necessary. Nowhere did he find the name Murphy. When he finished, he grabbed his canes and locked up.

Hal returned to the Rodder house, silently reached in the door, and hung up the key. Pop had lapsed back into a stupor. A few minutes later, Hal drove out of the parking lot in a cloud of red dust.

Chapter 17
Taking Stock

PEKE PALANEKE hummed softly as she scooped the last of the chili from the cast-iron pot into a carry-out container. The chili had dried out from continuous heating throughout the day, so she'd added a little water to make it palatable for Pop. Into a second container she poured the last of the Portuguese bean soup and put lids on the two containers. Both fit easily into a white paper tote bag, along with a handful of soda crackers. Peke finished her nightly scrub-down, lights-out, and lock-up ritual. She had started toward Pop's place when she heard Hal's car pull out of the lot. He waved to her. Nodding back, she continued up to the hovel on the hill, wondering how the man got Pop to talk all this time.

As soon as Peke entered, the rancid odor almost smothered her.

"Hey, Pop, wake up, it' me, Peke."

No response.

She tried again. "Who dat guy? Wad he want?"

But Pop couldn't be roused. Noticing the $20 bills crumbled in each hand, she pried one out of his fingers, flattened it, and slid it into a book from the shelf over his bed, saving something for him for later. She placed the book back on the shelf.

Peke cleared a space on the table between the litter of sandwich crusts, a half-empty coffee cup of floating mold, and two scurrying cockroaches. Setting her bag of food down, she threw open the windows. How many days of trade winds would it take to clear out the stench? She managed a hasty tidying of Pop's rooms and promised herself she'd do a better job next time.

Peke stuffed garbage into one trashcan liner and dirty clothes into another. Twenty minutes later, after shutting the windows again, she left with both bags in tow—dropping one at the dumpster behind the diner and carrying the second bag with her as she trudged down the highway toward her own place.

The Rodders had let Peke's family stay in their rental house free when times had been really tough eight years ago. Pop had also lent her family the cash to start the diner a year later. Pop's wife had been good to them, too. When she died, Peke had seen the man go to pieces and never come together again. As the bottle became all-important, his credibility as a real estate broker had ebbed.

Horace Rodder died later that night of liver complications. His waitress friend found him when she returned with his laundry the following evening. Peke Palaneke, the only person in the whole world who seemed to care, wept for her friend.

* * *

Alex arrived at the Wong home a little after six and found his family gathered around the dinner table. Bussing Leilani on the cheek, he pulled a spare chair up beside her. Masako looked a bit miffed. Leilani was the only one he kissed these days. Without a word, she passed him the rice pot, and he paddled a generous portion onto his plate.

Afterward, as Numi and Leilani cleared away the dishes, Masako called from the kitchen: "Anybody want ice cream?" Coming back into the dining room, she continued, "We have mocha almond and two new flavors, red bean and green tea, would you believe."

"I believe you, Mom, but I'll take the mocha almond," chuckled Numi.

Masako had no takers for the new flavors. Leilani and Alex took their dishes out to the lanai and chose the wrought iron glider with its puffy cushions to cuddle in. Kicking off her sandals, Leilani sat down and immediately laid her head on Alex's shoulder. A faint squeak accompanied their gentle swinging motion.

To his parent's chagrin, Alex rarely used his apartment anymore. He spoke of moving home for good. The closeness of the past few weeks had pressed Leilani and Alex to a plateau beyond infatuation.

"So, Leilani," he murmured, "what do you want for your seventeenth birthday?"

She raised her head with a slight tilt. "A cruise to Tahiti would be nice."

"Oh, yeah? Is that all?"

"No. That would be the first stop. Then on to Hong Kong, Bangkok, Singapore." She giggled.

"Singapore? That might stretch my wallet a bit. The rest would

130

be fine." He grinned.

She sat up straight and looked at him. "Alex, have you ever thought what it would be like to live anywhere but here on Oahu?"

"Why? Are you getting island fever? I thought only *haoles* got that when they'd spent too much time here."

"I want to expand my horizons," she said.

He turned to face her, surveying her openly from breasts to rounded hips and back again. "Your horizons don't need expanding. They're perfect just the way they are."

She laughed and blushed deeply. "You're silly. I just wonder what the rest of the world is like. Don't you ever think about those things?"

"Sure I do. I want to travel. Maybe on my honeymoon I will."

"Your honeymoon? Are you going alone?" she teased.

"Our honeymoon, then."

"Is that a proposal, Alex?"

"That's called entrapment, Leilani. You know what I mean."

"I don't care. I'd rather have a proposal."

"I'm trying to be cautious," he said, "so we don't get over-involved too soon."

"But I so want you to propose to me."

"Officially? That has to be a ways in the future."

"Why?" she pouted.

"Because my mother would have me arrested, that's why."

"Oh."

"You're disappointed?" he asked. "Aren't you the girl who told me she wants to go to a Mainland college? I distinctly remember Berkeley being mentioned."

"You're right," she said reluctantly, "and I still want to. I have only a year till graduation. But..." She fingered a button on her denim blouse, then gave him an anxious look. "It'll be five years before I finish college. What happens if you find somebody else?"

"And what happens if you find somebody else? Don't you think I haven't thought about that? You can solve the whole problem by going to UH instead. Then we can be together."

She rearranged herself on the glider, crossing her long, supple legs yoga style. "I know I can, Alex. But...Oh, I love you so much, but I can't stay here and go to UH. It's too easy. It's too cowardly. Then for the rest of my life I'd be wondering..." She shifted positions, stretching her legs out in front of her and wiggling her bare toes.

"Wondering what?" he asked. "You want to put a lock on me, but you want to make yourself available at the same time. You can't have it both ways, Leilani."

"I can and I will. You'll just have to trust me," she said. "Otherwise, I'll always feel I missed out on something."

He gathered her in his arms and they embraced tightly. The squeak of the glider slowed, then stopped, just as the lovers' protests had also ceased. The mocha almond puddled in its dishes on the wicker table beside the swing.

* * *

Kekoa took aim and tried a running lay-up shot at the basket, but it rolled around the rim and dropped out. Andy Ballesteros leaped high trying to snatch it from the rim, and came down on Kekoa's back. The two boys stumbled to the concrete court, and the ball rolled away.

"Hey, dude, quit your shoving," Kekoa protested.

"Gimme a break," cried Andy. "You woulda made that shot if you'd gotten your butt off the cee-ment."

"Bug off!"

Kekoa scrambled to his feet ahead of Andy and raced to retrieve the ball. He dribbled toward the basket. Andy leaped to prevent the shot, but he missed this time, and the high arcing shot swished through cleanly. The friends were playing a little one-on-one at the Kaimuki rec center. After running the court for an hour, they rested on the lava rock wall while Andy waited for his dad.

Mr. Ballesteros worked as an alterations tailor for the dry cleaner a few blocks down Waialae. After work, father and son would drive home to the northwest shore of Oahu. They lived in Mokuleia, a section inhabited largely by Hawaiian and Filipino families.

"There's a 'Bows game at UH tomorrow night," said Andy, still breathing hard. "My dad got hold of three freebies from some customer, but my brother's gotta work. You can have his ticket. You wanna go with us?"

"Hey, sounds cool." Kekoa's eyes lit up. He'd never been to a UH basketball game. Then a shadow crossed his face. "Gee, I don't know. How can I get there and home again?"

"We can pick you up at the bakery and go directly to the game. My mom says you can come home with us after and sleep at our place.

We've got plenty of room. And Dad can drop you off here in the morning."

"But the morning baking. I gotta ask Sam."

"Git off it, dude. Go ask him, then." Andy tucked the basketball under his arm, and the two of them trotted up the street to the bakery.

The boys darted in the doorway, clanging the customer entry bell to its limits. Behind the counter, Yasuko wrapped a box of pastry with several turns of fine string from a spinning white spool.

"What's up, you two?" she asked. She snapped the string, knotted both ends neatly, and pushed the box toward her customer. "Thank you, Mrs. Shinkawa," Yasuko said as she scooped the bills and coins from the counter and sorted them into the cash drawer.

"So, boys, what's up?" she repeated.

"Where's Sam?" Kekoa asked.

"In the back putting together an order for more supplies. Anything wrong?"

"Nope!" Andy blurted out, answering for Kekoa, who had already rushed past to the storeroom.

A breathless Kekoa placed his hand on Sam's back as he approached him. "Sam, I got a special favor to ask. Andy guys invited me to the basketball game at UH tomorrow night. His dad'll take us, he has an extra ticket. I'd like to go, but I gotta stay overnight at their place in Mokuleia. Do you think you could handle the morning alone?"

Sam turned on the tall stool and looked deep into the boy's eyes. "Kekoa," he said, smiling, "forty years Sam Osaka baking by self, and now you ask if I can bake one morning? I 'preciate what you do for Mauro and me, but you can pleasure sometimes, too. I not be selfish, so you go enjoy basketball game."

Kekoa felt so overjoyed that he hugged Sam, and Sam responded in kind. "Tomorrow," Kekoa said, "I leave everything all set up for you." His heart pounded with excitement.

Mauro padded slowly into the room, coming downstairs on her own for the first time since her surgery.

"You come down all alone?" Sam asked.

"Someone need to look after you two. I not stay in bed all time." She hugged them both.

* * *

Hal Perry walked into his efficiency apartment and threw his

133

windbreaker down on the sleeper sofa, still open from the night before. He shut the dusty blinds and opened the fridge. The top rack in the door held a lone can of Pabst beer. It had been there for months. In fact, it had come from the Mainland with him when he moved. It wasn't that he no longer liked beer—far from it. No, he kept the can as a bitter reminder of his drunken past. But more often these days, he thought of it as a symbol of his new self-control and abstinence.

He reached for a waxed carton of POG, a sweet drink of passion fruit, orange, and guava juices. After popping the folded top, he drew a long swig. He set the carton on the table and from the fridge helped himself to bread, mustard, bologna, and cheese. The sandwich proved filling enough, but definitely uninspired. A leaf of lettuce, a slice of tomato, a dill pickle, raw onion, just about anything would have been an improvement. He made a mental note to spend a little more time at the grocery store.

Hal had returned home famished after an entire evening at the library. His search through telephone books from eight major West Coast cities had produced two W. Minnets and one Wilma Minnet. He knew that Red Murphy had once been married for a short time to a Wilma something-or-other. Also, he remembered that when they divorced, she had taken back her maiden name and fled to the Coast. If he could find her and prove who she was, this could be the necessary connection between Red and Rodminn Estates. Hal fished around in the kitchen cabinet and discovered a package of stale Oreos. Polishing off two, he reached for the wall phone next to the table. He used a pencil stub to dial the Los Angeles number.

"Ms. Minnet? Ms. Wilma Minnet? I'm with the University of Hawaii, Sociology Department. My name is Dr. Ralph Friend, and I'm doing a follow-up survey on local divorces occurring in the last five years. I'd like to ask you a few questions, if you wouldn't mind. You wouldn't? Thank you. Now, what was the name of your former husband? That's Edgar A. Murphy? Were you employed at any time during your marriage? I see, two years as a secretary. You were employed in your husband's business? What was the name of that business?...I see. Were you ever an officer in the business? In what capacity? And you have your real estate license? I see. Are you employed now?...As a secretary and receptionist. Ms. Minnet, you've been most helpful. Of course your name will be kept confidential. One more thing. When our interviewer is in your area, would you consent to a personal interview? It's the department's way of verifying information. You would? Thank you! Thank you for your time. Goodbye now."

Ms. Minnet's willingness to talk without verifying his credentials took him by surprise. It never ceased to amaze him how trusting people were. He hung up the phone feeling pretty good.

Chapter 18
An Eye on the Ball

RAUCOUS BASKETBALL fans swarmed into the Blaisdell Arena, a cavernous cocoon filled with concrete steps and folding seats. But few seats were left to be had that night. The local rivalry between the University of Hawaii Rainbows and Brigham Young University Seasiders always filled the stands. Kekoa, Andy, and Papa Ballesteros climbed up to the section behind the visitors' basket. At the second row from the top, they stumbled over shoes and knees to get to their seats.

Kekoa had never been to a sports arena. A nervous anticipation hung over him as he waited for the game to start. Andy and his dad huddled together over the program, leaving their young guest with too much free time. And like a cat stuck with the choice of nothing to do but wash, he stood, pulled a comb from his rear jeans pocket, and drew it through his mop of brown hair. He felt better now.

A roar accompanied the starting jump-ball. The 'Bows drove hard to take an early lead, but the Seasiders picked up steam and grabbed six quick points. The first period left the 'Bows with a four-point deficit and BYU fans smelling success. But the Seasiders got greedy and drew several fouls. The 'Bows cashed in on the free throws and ended the half six points ahead.

At half-time, Andy's dad bought them chili dogs and Cokes. Kekoa hoped the greasy orange spot on his green and white Rainbows T-shirt would come out in the wash. He'd just bought it for tonight.

The jump-ball opening the second half ushered in a more defensive game. Any new score created a frenzy in the arena. But the Seasiders refused to fold and inched toward a tie deep into the third quarter. With the 'Bows one point ahead, Andy and Kekoa cheered themselves hoarse.

In the fourth quarter, as the UH team passed its way free from a full-court press, Kekoa caught sight of a face moving through the stands to the left. Meanwhile, the 'Bows' star forward tossed a dramatic one-hander from the corner. The fans roared. For a split second, Kekoa's eyes broke away from the familiar face in the stands to watch the ball swish through the hoop. He turned his gaze back to the stands on the left, but the faces all looked mixed up now. He couldn't find the spot again. A cry escaped his lips.

"What's wrong, K?" asked Andy.

"Oh, man, I thought I saw my sistah."

"Where, K? Show me, I'll look too."

Kekoa pointed and shook his head. "I can't find her now."

"Maybe you're wrong. Maybe it ain't her," said Andy. "Sorry, *bruddah.*" He gave Kekoa a friendly slap on the back, and turned his attention back to the court.

But the game was ruined for Kekoa. He scanned the seats in the section on his left, row by row, hardly aware of the crescendo of cheers. The 'Bows had stolen the ball and driven down-court. A desperation three-point shot in the final seconds clinched the game for UH.

As the fans began to file out, Kekoa kept his gaze fixed on the stands. And suddenly, there she was, heading for one of the exit portals.

"I see her! I see her! My sistah!" he shouted to Andy. "Meet you at the truck in fifteen minutes. If I'm not back by then, go on without me. Sorry, Mr. Ballesteros."

The boy vaulted over the seat in front of him, then another and another, descending row by row, and elbowed his way among the throngs bulging through exit portals too few and too narrow. He climbed atop the concrete railing and ran along it to the adjacent portal. There he caught another brief glimpse of Leilani before she exited into a portal still beyond him.

"Lani, Leilani," he called, his voice wobbling with frustration. "Wait up, it's me, Kekoa." He jumped down from the concrete railing. Crouching low, he pushed and bullied his way out. An inertially propelled crowd shoved back, kicked, and stepped on Kekoa's feet, leaving him hurting but determined. Finally outside, he climbed up on the first lamp post pedestal he could find. Holding on with one hand, he scanned the tops of hundreds of heads, but to no avail.

"Leilani! Leilani!" he shouted. A few faces, all cold and strange, looked up at him with curiosity. There was nothing more for him to do. He climbed down and ran through the massive, three-tier parking lot, dodging the cars and blinding headlights as they moved toward the street. The lot emptied quickly. Then, at the far end of a row near the grass, he spotted the Ballesteros truck with its motor running. He waved and ran. Andy flung open the door and Kekoa climbed in. Fighting back tears, Kekoa rested his head against the seat. He didn't say a single word during the long ride to the North Shore.

It was almost midnight when the truck pulled into the dirt driveway. The kitchen light was on, but Andy's mother and sisters had already gone to bed. His room on the second floor had a sloped corrugated tin roof with a small window that looked out into darkness at the rear of the house. The room had only two beds, one for Andy and the other for his brother, Enrico. Andy reached into a doorless closet covered by a thin curtain and pulled out a sleeping bag.

"Our guest room," he joked as he unrolled it. "I know it sucks."

"It's cool. Thanks for bringing me to the game. Sorry 'bout keeping you waiting."

"Hey, bruddah, it's okay." He rolled over to immediate sleep, but Kekoa lay awake a long time before drifting off. Then he succumbed to a dream.

He was walking on a deserted beach, several steps behind a tall girl with long chestnut hair. Whenever he quickened his step to get closer, a surging wave of sea and sand crashed over his bare feet, slowing him, bogging him down, widening the distance between him and the girl. He tried to run, but another wave forced him back. And then, abruptly, the girl turned to face him, smiling, arms wide, hair flying in the breeze. Leilani! She looked older and so much prettier than he remembered her.

* * *

Numi Wong awoke in the middle of the night. She thought she'd heard crying. Then she saw her foster sister standing at the window, her back to the room.

"Lani, what's wrong? It's 2:30."

Leilani whispered, "I have the strangest feeling. It might've even been a bad dream."

"What was it? Tell me."

"It's so weird, Numi. I have this feeling Kekoa is calling to me over and over. Oh, I know I don't actually hear him, but it's like he's looking for me and he wants me to wait for him."

"Wait for him where?" asked Numi.

138

Cry Ohana

"I don't know, but at the game tonight…Oh, this sounds sooo crazy. I had a feeling he was there, especially when we were leaving."

"That's creepy. Is that why you were hanging back?"

"Yeah. I kept looking for him in the crowd. It's been eight months since I spotted him at the bus stop on Kapiolani. Could he have changed so much I wouldn't recognize him now?"

"Not a chance." Numi tried to sound reassuring. "Come back to bed. Let's talk about it tomorrow." She yawned and slid under the covers. But Leilani remained at the window, staring out at the darkness.

Chapter 19
Feathers in the Night

A BLOOD-CURDLING screech jarred Kekoa awake. He tried to keep his eyes squeezed shut. But now he heard men's voices—shouting, laughing, arguing. He started to drift off again, but the screeching began anew, wrenching him from sleep. The night couldn't possibly be over. Up on one elbow, Kekoa struggled to clear the fuzz from his eyes. He sought out the big bell alarm perched on the dresser. The luminous green hands pointed to 1:15. The cries of intense pain and defiance startled him once more.

Eerie flashes of headlights intruded through the open window, then passed. Enrico snored; Andy's big brother must have come in while they slept. Jeez, Kekoa thought, those guys could sleep through anything. Burrowed in the sleeping bag against the raw night air, he wormed the bag over to the window and rested his elbows on the sill. The lights and the commotion came from a large barn on the property behind the house. The racket now sounded like crowing, but wilder, fiercer than any roosters he'd heard before. Hardly the friendly crowing he used to hear at 3 a.m. in Ewa. *Tutu* Eme had always joked, "Loco rooster need one alarm clock."

Squirming out of the sleeping bag, he stood over Andy's bed. His friend lay curled up, facing the wall.

"Andy, Andy," Kekoa whispered. "Wake up. Somethin's going on out there. Wake up, Andy." He grabbed his friend by the shoulder and shook hard.

"Wha? Wha? What's the matter?" Andy flipped to his other side, eyes still shut.

"Look what's going on outside. It's all lit up. And all that screaming, too."

Andy opened one eye briefly and closed it again. "Go back to sleep. It's only the cockfights. Be over soon."

140

"Cockfights? Can we go? I never seen a cockfight before." He shook Andy again.

His friend's eyes popped open. He sat straight up in bed, an impish smile on his face. "My dad'll beat my *okole* raw if he finds out. But... let's do it anyway."

They slipped into their jeans, pulled on their T-shirts, and opened the bedroom door to listen for anyone moving about the house. Hearing nothing, they sneaked down the stairs and out the screen door. Andy nursed it shut so there wouldn't be a bang. Kekoa trotted toward the fence.

"Hey!" Andy warned. "Wait up! We can't go bargin' in the front door."

"Then how're we gonna get in?"

"See that tree over there? The big branch hanging over the hayloft boom? That's how!"

They scaled the rail fence and headed for the stout monkeypod behind the barn.

Streaks of light oozed from seams in the barn sides. The boys zigzagged around tiny A-frame structures that littered the barnyard. They heard the rustle of feathers and the scratching of feet. Kekoa accidentally tripped over one of the tethers, yanking the unsuspecting bird into a foul mood. The fearless one flew at Kekoa with a threatening caw, which sent him dodging for safety. Andy chuckled.

The boys approached the monkeypod. Its lowest branches began about seven feet from the ground. Kekoa gazed upward. A square boom swung by its hinges above the large loft doorway. A pulley with ropes for hoisting bales of hay hung at the end of its five-foot length.

"Hey, Andy!" Kekoa whispered, grabbing for the ropes. "How 'bout this way up?" He knew he could hoist himself easily enough.

"Pulley's too noisy. It's the tree or nothin'. Hey, bruddah, no problem."

Andy gave Kekoa's butt a shove up the thick trunk. Kekoa grabbed hold of the first branch, pulling himself up and over the rough bark to a fork in the trunk. Andy followed.

"One at a time," Andy murmured, as he reached the base of the heavy branch overhanging the boom. Kekoa understood. The limb couldn't hold both boys crawling out at the same time. Andy edged out first, one knee inching in front of the other. He grabbed for the boom and swung himself down into the loft. Kekoa's heart hammered as he took his turn. On the second swing to the boom, he made it.

Kekoa crouched beside his friend. But even stock-still, his panting breath came too loud. Andy held a finger to his lips to quiet him. Kekoa wondered why; the barn shook with deafening noises anyway.

He coaxed his eyes to adjust to the light inside. Only thin rays seeped through cracks in the weathered floorboards. But brightness flooded in through the open square where the ladder hung from the loft to the barn floor. They crept toward the opening to see without being seen.

Several dozen men and a handful of women sat down below on benches, boxes, and rickety folding chairs lined up along the walls. Spectators swigged from whiskey pints or beer cans. Others milled about directly beneath the loft opening. The stench of tobacco floated up into the loft, and the sickening-sweet odor of pot, loco weed, and blood mingled with it. Fistfuls of folding money and white paper chits were exchanged, sorted, and filed between the callused fingers of dirty hands.

Two hulking men in sweat-stained tank tops stood in a round pit covered with bloody straw. Tattoos adorned their biceps and forearms. In gloved hands they held two raging-to-go gamecocks, beautiful jungle fowl with feathers of iridescent red, black, green, and yellow. The men jabbed their already frenzied birds at one another, goading, teasing, and menacing. The feathered furies—especially bred and sometimes drugged to make them more aggressive—screeched and strained at the hold. The betting subsided, then ceased, and the hushed crowd waited. To make the fowl even more angry, they were held upended just before release.

"Now!" yelled a third man behind the table, slapping his hand down hard on the surface. The two men dropped the gamecocks and jumped free of the arena.

The fighting jungle fowl came to battle. Tiny razor-sharp blades fitted around their necks and curved steel gaffs tied to their clipped spurs drew blood on contact. The spectators cheered and cursed. Feathers filled the air. The succession of assaults soon wore the weaker fowl down. It stumbled and fell—a wing broken, an eye gouged, a lung punctured.

Kekoa turned away, clamping his hand over his mouth. The acid contents of his stomach climbed and fell back again.

By the rules, only one of the combatants could emerge victorious, and sometimes neither did. All bets were off in that case. This fight ended with a crowing winner. His opponent lay twitching, near death. A tattooed man retrieved the victorious but bloodied winner and held him high for all to see. The loser was dispatched with the stained straw after a quick but final twist of his neck.

The men returned to the pit with fresh hay and new challengers. Chits-for-money, money-for-chits, the gamblers settled their prior wagers. And then they resumed new betting in earnest. Shouted offers, counteroffers, acceptances, and denials filled the air. Voices overlapped voices, cussing, boisterous laughing, and the maniacal screeching of the fowl reverberated in the smoke-filled loft.

"That's for Dirty-Birdy. Put two hundred on the beak!" a gravelly voice roared and laughed. The voice shocked Kekoa—he recognized it. The man attached to the voice stepped closer to the pit, nearer the loft ladder. Kekoa couldn't see his face, just a massive head of red hair and hairy freckled arms; on the left forearm, a Seabees tattoo. He had no doubt now: Red Murphy! And he had a woman with him, that whore from Chinese New Year. The chase down Maunakea Street. It all came back in a sickening rush.

Shaking, the boy pulled away from the loft hole altogether and touched Andy's arm. "This place sucks. I gotta get outta here," he whispered. His belly spasmed.

Andy nodded. Grabbing the boom, they swung out of the loft, into the tree, and climbed down to the ground. The moment Kekoa landed, he ran to a high stack of mulch behind the barn and dropped to his knees. He retched and vomited, then struggled to his feet. He knew they couldn't stay there; people were already leaving the barn and heading to their cars. Andy helped him over the fence and to the house.

In the bathroom Kekoa cleaned himself up. Stripping off his new T-shirt, he soaped, rinsed, and wrung it out twice before he satisfied himself that it had come clean again.

They crept upstairs without a word. Kekoa hung the wet shirt over a chair and crawled into his sleeping bag. Andy fell asleep instantly, but his eyes refused to close. He could still hear the ruckus from the barn. His thoughts swelled in self-pity and a sense of isolation. Would he ever have a family again? Go to school like other kids? Be free of Red's stalking? But through his misery, a stubborn determination jacked him up. *I'm gonna find Lani,* he thought. *Somehow. No matter what.*

* * *

"Hey, *bruddah,* get up, we'll be late, eh?" Andy stood over him, already dressed for school. "See ya downstairs."

Kekoa hurried into his clothes, rolled up the sleeping bag, and stuck it in the curtained closet. His T-shirt, still damp, felt clammy against his skin. He'd never met Andy's mother and wanted her to think of him as a well-mannered guest. He could hear Mama Ballesteros shouting orders to her daughter Maria and scolding her sons in a torrent of shrill words. Only when she noticed Andy's guest at the bottom of the stairs did she switch to a more kindly tone.

Mama greeted him with a rush of Tagalog words he couldn't recognize, wrapping both her arms around his body.

Assuming she'd asked how he'd slept, Kekoa smiled weakly and said, "Great, thank you."

Andy pressed his lips and shot him a warning look to keep his mouth shut.

Mama had shiny black hair pulled back into a single braid and a toothy smile. Releasing her grip, she slipped her hands to Kekoa's shoulders and held him at arm's length.

"Not much meat on your bones. We'll take care of that now." She led him to the table and very nearly pushed him down onto the chair.

The rest of the family took little notice of his late arrival. Except for Maria. She watched his every move as she collected silverware from a drawer to set a place for him.

Kekoa stole a glance at her, trying not to stare back. She looked to be about thirteen, with a bird-like body and two neat braids. She winked at him and smiled.

"Maria!" Mama barked. She smacked her daughter's backside with the flat of her hand. Forks, knives, and spoons flew across the room. Maria let out a whimper and her face went red as she scampered to retrieve the dropped utensils. Kekoa slid off his chair to help.

"No, please, I can do it," she said. But he was already on his knees. They nearly collided just below the end of the table. A solitary tear appeared on her left cheek. Kekoa helped her to her feet, never taking his eyes from hers.

"Maria!" Mama snapped. "Hurry up, and get to the table!" Mama

144

turned to the stove where no one could see her smile. "We'll have to keep an eye on that one," she mumbled in her native language to Papa, sitting closest to her. "Thirteen years old and she's already discovered boys."

Papa reminded her of Esmeralda, who'd be married in two short weeks. Their older daughter had been just as wild—in a hurry to grow up, too.

Kekoa faced a plateful of fried eggs, sausage, ham, peppers, and rice, and wondered whether he could eat it all without being sick again. He'd better, he thought, or Mama would have his head, too. Actually, the warm honey-crusted bread soothed his belly. But the milk tasted kind of thick and strange. He didn't really want to drink it.

Andy caught the funny look on his friend's face. "Straight from the cow. You get used to it."

"Uh, I think I like it this way," Kekoa lied. "You got cows?"

"One," Andy said. "Got 'er from a friend that moved away."

The family ate in comfortable conversations. Despite Mama's bluster, Kekoa envied them their family meal. At the bakery, the business ruled their lives, there was no time for togetherness. He understood completely, but a pang shot through him. How he missed the breakfasts with *Tutu* and Leilani—the taro pancakes and egg with rice, and Uncle Big John, with his jokes.

Mr. Ballesteros pushed his chair away from the table. "Eat up! We leave in five minutes. It's an hour drive."

Kekoa followed him to the pickup, still chewing a hunk of sweet bread. No time to even brush his teeth. He flipped his gym bag onto the seat.

"Just a minute, young man," cried Mama. "You got a milk mustache." She lunged at him with a napkin and wiped his mouth. Andy and Enrico guffawed. Maria giggled.

Kekoa jumped into the pickup beside Andy. "Thanks for everything," he called, waving as they backed out of the red clay driveway.

Before they were out of sight, Maria turned to her mother and asked,

"Mama, can Kekoa come to the wedding? Can he?"

"We'll see. Get ready for school now. You'll miss the bus."

The way back to Kaimuki took them down the two-lane roads of the pineapple fields and then over highways past Pearl Harbor toward Honolulu. Andy had once asked Kekoa where he went to school.

Kekoa had replied that he was home-schooled and quickly changed the subject. Somehow his friend got the message and never asked again. Andy had a "geographic exception" to attend Kaimuki High so he could help his father at the cleaners afterward. This had proved lucky for Kekoa or otherwise he would never have met Andy.

Papa Ballesteros dropped Kekoa off at the corner nearest the bakery. Entering the shop and squeezing past the crowd of customers, he found Sam mixing up the second of the morning batches.

"Eh, boy, good you back!" Sam regarded him with a broad smile. The deeply lined face seemed to visibly shed its fatigue at the sight of his "son."

* * *

Red awoke with a start, as he always did in an unfamiliar bed. Sunlight pressed its way through the miniblinds into the hot-pink and black-lacquered bedroom. He had spent the entire night with Cindy Chou, something he rarely did.

"Hell, 11:30 already!" He flipped the satin sheets to the end of the bed, leaving Cindy's ample behind exposed. As she groped for the missing covers, he slapped her round soft bottom with a loud splat.

Cindy's nakedness didn't inhibit her. She bolted upright and onto her knees, her large breasts quivering. "That hurt, you bastard." She clenched her right fist and aimed a punch at his chest, but he grabbed both her wrists, pulled her to him, and kissed her hard.

She stopped struggling long enough to return his kiss, then abruptly pulled her head back. "Ugh! Yeesh!" she said.

He smirked. "Glad you liked it, we should do it more often."

"You taste like the Manchu army just marched through, boots and all!" She frowned, then ran her tongue around her own mouth. "But so do I. It's that rotgut you call liquor. If you weren't so damn cheap, you'd buy some decent stuff with the hangover removed up front."

He let go of her, and she slipped into a satin lace-edged robe. "You won plenty of dough at the cockfights, didn't you?" she asked.

"Did I?"

"Well, didn't you?"

"Enough, babe." He wasn't about to tell her he'd won 1,700 bucks. He watched as she began brushing her silky black hair away from her face. He liked what he saw. Not too bad for the morning after.

Red pulled on his street clothes and asked, "Got anything to eat in this joint? Do you get a newspaper?"

"It's not a joint. It's my home. Anyway, the paper's outside the door. I've got coffee, toast, cheese, and jelly. Ain't that good enough for your royal gut?"

"Easy, babe, I'm not planning a war for today." He retrieved the paper from beyond the front door and sat down at the table to read. After scanning the front page, he pulled out the local section. His steely eyes caught one name in the obituaries, Horace Rodder.

"Damn it to hell! Probably drank himself to death."

The Rodder funeral was set for two that afternoon at the Windward Seas Funeral Parlor. The obit listed no survivors. *Why did that bastard have to go and die on me?* Red thought. *Great timing. Now what's gonna become of Rodminn Realty?*

Chapter 20
Damage Control

EXCEPT FOR the faded sign out front, the Windward Seas Funeral Parlor looked like an ordinary wood bungalow. Red Murphy parked on the gravel road and walked up the path to a lanai only two steps above ground. Inside he found himself in a small, tired reception room trying its best to look dignified. A potted split-philodendron dominated one corner, the tips of its leaves curled up and brown. A threadbare path in the carpet led him into the makeshift chapel. This room had folding chairs arranged in rows facing a single stained-glass window behind the wood lectern. A lay preacher sat beside the lectern. The man appeared to be running through his eulogy and marking highlights for the service he was about to render.

Red recognized no one among the handful of mourners. Anxious to get this over with, he retreated to the reception room. There he found an elderly man standing over an island woman seated in a wing chair. Red stared impatiently at his watch and waited.

The woman said, "I'll miss him, too. I saw him practically every day." She shook hands with the white-haired man, and he moved into the chapel.

Red took his cue. "Hello, I'm Ed, Edgar Murphy, one of Horace's business associates." He held out his hand to her. "Are you family? I thought Pop—uh, Horace— had none left."

She accepted his hand. "I'm the nearest thing to family Pop had. I'm Peke Palaneke, very dear friend of Pop's. He's been *ohana* over thirty years now."

Red looked over his shoulder to be sure no one else had entered the room. "Miss Palaneke, I know this isn't a good time to be asking questions, but could you possibly know who the estate executor or personal representative will be?"

"Mr. Murphy, you got *that* right. This isn't a good time for ques-

148

tions. But I'm his personal representative and only heir to his estate."

"I understand completely. I'm very sorry for your loss. But are you aware of what that estate might entail?"

"Yes, I think so. The clerk from the Registrar of Wills read me the details this morning at the courthouse. Um… let me see… the house, the five stores in the mini-mall, the land lease… some investment shares and a few savings bonds go to me. There weren't no cash. I have to send his next…" her voice stumbled, "Social Security check back." She eyed him suspiciously. "Besides, whatta you need to know all that for? It's none of your business. And now I gotta go inside."

"Of course. Thank you, Miss Palaneke. I appreciate your indulging me at this sad time, but I do have a business to keep running. Perhaps we could meet again in a few days to discuss our business?"

Peke gave him a strange look. She had no answer. A recording of mournful organ music beckoned, signaling the start of the service. Moving into the chapel, she took her seat and scanned the handful of other mourners—all her own friends.

The preacher began. "We are gathered here to pay our final respects to Horace Rodder. Pop was a kindly man, who…"

…*pissed his life away with booze*, Red mused. As the preacher's voice merged into the monotony of the moody background music, Red had his own thoughts. *I bet this Peke woman genuinely loves Pop and misses him already. She keeps looking over her left shoulder at me. Something in this woman's expression gives her away. Doesn't trust me and doesn't understand what I want from her. Maybe she's thinking about fixing up Pop's place and moving in there herself. Maybe she'll expand the luncheonette, too—the rent from the other stores could easily pay for the expansion. And maybe, just maybe, I'll sweeten the pot for her.*

He became aware of the preacher's final words, "… in everlasting peace and tranquility."

Red stood while six strapping men carried the casket out the door into the congregation cemetery that stretched for half an overgrown acre behind the bungalow. There, the wrecked remains of Pop Rodder found their final resting place.

Red seized on an impulse. Peeling rubber as he pulled away from the funeral home, he drove straight to Pop Rodder's house. His mission: to retrieve Pop's office key; he'd stupidly misplaced his own. He found the

Rodder door locked. Well, he'd just have to force it. A rusting screwdriver lying on the lanai served as a jimmy tool. The door lock popped immediately under only slight pressure. Red slipped inside and reached for the office key in its usual place, on the hook by the door. But his hand came away empty. *Where the hell is the key?* He frantically started searching the house—rummaging through rickety dresser drawers, throwing open the meager kitchen cabinets. Then he caught himself—he was acting like a crazy fool—and slowed down, making sure to put everything back in its place. He didn't want to leave any sign of his presence.

A quarter-mile away at the office, Red found that the door could not be jimmied; it had a new hasp and padlock as well as a built-in deadbolt lock. He would have to get the key from Peke. Any visible damage to the locks might look suspicious. Maybe he shouldn't panic, he didn't have to clean out the office just yet—nothing in there could tie him to Rodminn Realty. He knew he couldn't stick around. The funeral party would be coming by on the way to Peke's house for the wake.

He climbed into his car and slammed the door in annoyance. Driving back toward Honolulu, he formulated a plan. It would require help from the only other shareholder in Rodminn Realty, Wilma Minnet Murphy. Actually, "Willie" had dropped the Murphy part when they divorced two years ago. They had remained friends, acknowledging that they just couldn't live together for more than a week at a time. But the love-making during that week was always a doozy. He'd call her when he got back to his place. He knew his ex-wife would help him. She liked money as much as anyone. And he knew she would always have a thing for him.

A young boy on a bicycle shot out of a side street directly in front of Red and he had to swerve toward the center of the road. "Sonofabitch brat!" he swore. But the kid and his bike sparked an idea in Murphy's head, and a sneer replaced the anger. He thought of Kekoa and the danger the boy posed to him. If he moved Big John's body, it would be only Kekoa's word against his own. After two years, nobody would believe the kid anyway. But first things first. Rodminn Realty remained a priority right now.

Red pulled into a gas station to use the pay phone. That way he wouldn't leave an obvious telephone trail to Willie. He exchanged five dollars in bills for coins, and listened while the coins dropped through the metallic channel and came to rest in the cash box.

"Hello."

"Hi there, sweet stuff."

"Red! Where are you? It's been months. Are you in L.A.? I'd love to see you."

"Whoa, sweet stuff. I'm still in Honolulu. You can come see me, though. I'd want you to stay awhile. I'll even send you a ticket. How's that?"

"Sounds great, Red, but what about my job and my place?"

"I'll make it worth your while, and I'll pay your rent to boot."

"But I like my job."

"You'll get another one—or take leave if you can. I need you here."

"Oh, Red, you still care."

"Yeah! … ah … Not exactly, babe. You know… business, strictly business. But there's always the possibility of a little lovin' on the side. Can I count on you?" He had to admit the sound of her voice still set off tremors in his innards.

"Of course! When do you need me?"

"A-S-A-P, sweet stuff."

"I'll make all the arrangements and call you back tonight. Will you meet me at the airport?"

"Sure, just let me know the time."

"I'll call you."

"Thanks, Willie." He said it with such sincerity that she hung on his words. He hung up the phone, feeling pleased with himself.

* * *

Kekoa completed a bakery delivery to My Belle Taste, a gourmet shop in the Ala Moana mall, and walked across the boulevard to the beach park to catch the spectacular sunset. On the grass near the lagoon, a heavy-set woman was performing the ancient Tai Chi exercises. She wore a faded skirt of uneven lengths, a shabby red jacket, and badly scuffed unmatched shoes. Yet she moved each limb with meticulous care and grace. Approaching from behind her, Kekoa traced a loud Latin dance tune to a boom box nestled among piles of soiled, but neatly folded clothes in a grocery cart. A bulbous plastic bag filled with aluminum cans—to be exchanged for cash—hung over one side of the cart. Hanging from the other side were a threadbare purse and old vinyl briefcase. The tune ended, and the woman turned to her cart—her only property, her wardrobe, her possessions.

"Mrs. Raggs... er, Raggs?" He corrected himself as soon as he recognized the homeless woman.

"Master K! I thought it was you. Ol' Chou and me, we were talkin' about you just yesterday. He wanted to know if I'd seen you anywhere, and I told him I hadn't."

"Ol' Chou is on the street again?"

"Hah! They can't keep him locked up for long," Raggs boasted. "He and that old dog of his have been roaming Chinatown for months now."

"You mean *Ilio* is back with Ol' Chou?"

Raggs gave Kekoa a strange look. "I thought you took the dog with you when you ran away."

Kekoa reddened and felt a stab of shame. "I did, but I live in Kaimuki now. When I found work, I sort of neglected him and he wandered off. He came back from time to time and then not at all. I feel really bad about it."

"You can't forget your friends, big or small," she chided.

Kekoa saw newspapers bundled for recycling on the bottom shelf of the cart. He tore a corner off. Fumbling through his pockets, he found a pencil stub, wrote the bakery's name and address on the torn page, and handed it to Raggs. "Tell Ol' Chou I miss him and *Ilio*. Okay?" He surprised her with a spontaneous hug, partly borne of guilt. "Gotta go back to work now. I'll see you all soon."

Chapter 21
Passing in the Night

HAL PERRY HATED Los Angeles and what it had done to him. No, that wasn't quite right, he admitted—he'd done it to himself. But that was another time and place and he'd had a different agenda then. He tossed a few things into his soft-pack overnight bag and zipped it up. By going to Los Angeles he hoped to document a legal connection between Wilma Minnet and Red Murphy. A marriage license, a contract, or some joint property deeds would fill the bill nicely.

Hal knotted a striped tie over a short-sleeved white shirt. His suit jacket waited, draped across the shoulders of a nearby chair. In his blue-gray suit he might even pass for a mature businessman. But the depth of his tan revealed a man who spent a good deal of his time outdoors. Despite the long reddish scar on his neck and the two canes he used to maneuver about, he knew some women considered him attractive. A slight facial puff, some major graying at the temples, and noticeable waist handles on a once-athletic body gave away his age as fifty something. Most of the time he got by with only one cane, and perhaps in a few months, he could dump them both. In his own kitchen he could do that now.

Hal opened the refrigerator door for a short swallow of pulpy-thick orange juice straight from the carton. He hesitated a second to determine if it tasted rancid; satisfied that it didn't, he took a larger swig. He wiped his lips with his forearm and rubbed the bottle opening with the palm of his hand before replacing the cap and returning it to the fridge—a gesture he saw as a remnant of an adolescent habit rather than any stab at sanitizing the bottle. Besides, he lived alone. Who cared?

Hearing a car horn downstairs, he hit the light switch, grabbed his jacket and the overnighter from the kitchenette table, and slipped the luggage strap over his right shoulder. Holding both canes in his left fist,

153

he locked the door with his free hand and descended the hall stairs to the street. The waiting cab sped him to the airport.

At the Honolulu International Airport terminal he paid the cabby and sent his bag through agricultural inspection. Still forty-five minutes until his 11 p.m. flight, he decided to go straight to the departure gate anyway. At the newsstand Hal bought a copy of the Los Angeles Times and proceeded along the second-level open-air concourse to the satellite waiting rooms. He checked in at the desk and received his boarding pass before taking a seat in the closed area.

The loudspeaker blared "United Flight 3210 now arriving from Los Angeles at Gate 23."

Friends, relatives, and tour personnel began to gather around the gate as the first of the passengers came through it. Some flashed signs with names and others bestowed leis on new arrivals.

A handsome *haole* family of five moved out from among the arriving passengers. The father led two romping young boys, and the baby girl clung to her mother's shoulder. A pang shot through Hal at the sight of them. It lasted only a split-second, but seeing the family filled him with such loneliness that it hurt.

A leopard-print jacket over a black leather miniskirt appeared off the same flight. As the lone woman sauntered toward Hal, she made eye contact with him and smiled. It wasn't a come-on smile, more one of detached civility, but the sensuous pink mouth seemed to beckon. He nodded politely and smiled back.

Wilma Minnet smiled at the interesting-looking man again as she headed for the DOWN escalator to the baggage carousels, a flowered carry-on in one hand.

Red was waiting at the carousel for her. On cue, she jumped into his bear hug. He swung her around in a full circle before putting her down again. She left a smudge of lipstick on his thick neck. Long wisps fell over her eyes from a frenzied hairdo of honey-blonde curls. The bargain-basement jacket barely contained her large, upturned breasts, while black stockings neatly molded meaty thighs and calves.

They stood at the silent carousel, looking each other over, relishing what they saw, the physical closeness. *What a succulent morsel, this ex-wife of mine*, he thought.

Maybe this time will be different, she hoped.

The hidden machinery hummed, jerking stainless steel sections of

154

the conveyer belt into lateral motion. Bags pushed through the opening at the top and tumbled, then slid to the belt. Red loaded Wilma's three purple-flowered bags aboard a luggage cart, and they walked to the car in the multistoried parking garage across the road.

"What's this trip all about, lover?" she asked.

"Well, sweet stuff, the first thing I want is to buy back Big John's old house in Ewa. Then we have some wheeling and dealing to do. Do you remember that dummy real estate corporation we formed with Horace Rodder?"

"Yeah."

"Well, old Pop dropped dead on us and left his shares to a local woman who knows nothing about Rodminn Realty, Inc."

"My, how inconvenient," she said. "What's that to do with me?"

"Don't be so flippant. I want you to buy back those shares."

"So? That part's easy."

"Do you still have your real estate license?"

"It should be good for another two years as long as I pay this year's fee. I don't have to take refresher courses until the end of next year. In other words, yes."

"Take care of it. Now the next question: Do you want to bunk at my place temporarily, or would you rather I put you up at some inexpensive hotel?"

"Inexpensive? Don't you mean cheap, you four-flusher, you? Some choices you give me. I think I'll put up at your place, and you can go to the inexpensive hotel if you want."

"Okay, okay! It's only a temporary arrangement."

Wilma asked, "How long do you think it'll take to buy the house back from the new owners?"

"Don't know. But we can start on it first thing in the morning."

"Why Big John's house?"

"It's sentimental," he answered.

"You sentimental? That'll be the day. These people just bought the house. What if they don't want to sell?" she asked. "And what happened to Big John, anyway?"

"He just got fed up with the business and took off. Don't ask so damn many questions." This was one thing Willie didn't have to know anything about. He didn't want to implicate her in the murder for her sake as well as for his. That much feeling for her he did have. Besides, if she found out, she'd run on home as fast as she could. Maybe she'd even call the police. "Did they feed you on the plane?" he asked.

Wilma wrinkled up her nose and pursed her lips. "I got a bad piece of fish and left it—smelled terrible. Do you have anything in the apartment that's edible and still has its normal color?"

"I'll go one better and buy you a real meal."

"That'll be a novelty."

Red and Wilma sped east on the H-1 freeway until he pulled off the first exit toward Waikiki. He manipulated several streets, turning off Kalakaua Avenue onto Ena Street, and in the second block just before Ala Moana Boulevard, right into a driveway that led to basement parking. They climbed the stairs to the Wailana Coffee House on the first floor.

The elderly hostess led them to a table close to the front corner window. Red stopped short. Seated right next to it, Cindy Chou chatted with two of her friends. He couldn't change restaurants now. There would be no way to explain it to Wilma. He quickly tapped the hostess on the shoulder.

"Could we have a table in the rear instead, ma'am?" The hostess shrugged, made a forty-five-degree turn and steered them to a table in the back. She left menus, and for the moment, Red felt secure.

"I brought clothes enough for about two weeks," Wilma said. "If this takes longer, I'll have to pick up a few things. Is that okay?"

"Sure. You'll manage."

While they studied the tall, plastic-covered menus, Red lowered his just enough to see Cindy at the salad bar only ten feet from their table. He raised the menu to cover his face. The waitress appeared. "You two guys need more time?"

Red said in a barely audible voice, "Another few minutes. Why don't you bring two coffees now, one black and the other cream." The waitress left and Red peeked over the top of the menu in time to catch Cindy returning to her table. A sense of genuine relief poured over him.

* * *

Cindy polished off her second helping: pasta salad and striped squares of cherry, *haupia*—coconut cream, and green gelatin. She paid up the check, waved goodbye to her friends, and took a cab to Chinatown.

Cindy climbed the flight of wooden stairs in the dimly lit alley.

A cat snarled in the dark below, and some tin cans tumbled, filling the alley with signature sounds of the night. She slid her key into the lock, but the already-unlocked door swung inward with a spooky creak. She trembled and reached for the light switch. Even before the light flooded the room, she sensed another presence, but fear gave way to curiosity, and she stood her ground.

A somber-faced Coland Benfield-Rice sat on her sofa, looking as if he had every right to be in her apartment.

"What are you doing here? How did you get in and what do you want from me?" she shouted at him.

"Easy now! Aren't you glad to see me? It's Tuesday night, isn't it? Don't we have a standing date?"

"Huh? Oh, sure," she replied, recovering her professional composure and a more hospitable tone. "How are you? I, uh, just forgot what night it was. You know I look forward to your coming here. But how did you get in?"

"Your bedroom window. I went around your neighbor's lanai to the back and saw the window open, so I climbed in. It's not my usual style, I admit, but I'm quite proud of my resourcefulness. You should be more careful," he said slyly.

"Yeah. Give me a minute to change into something more appropriate for you."

"No need. I can't stay very long. The night is practically gone already. I just want to talk for a few minutes."

"That's a shame. Talk? What did you want to talk about?"

"Mostly about you and me." Coland reached into his pocket and pulled out a photograph. "What do you know about this?" he asked, holding it up.

A vise of fear now gripped her, but she kept a stony face. "Never seen it before—don't know anything about it."

"I found these in your top dresser drawer." Like a practiced card player, he fanned out a pile of photographs and negatives.

"You had no right to go in there."

"Perhaps not, but I did anyway. How much did he pay you? Just how much of this garbage does Red have?"

"None of your damn business."

"Do you know that being an accessory to the felony crime of extortion can get you a lengthy prison term?" He watched her face intently and saw tears flooding her eyes.

"Red made me do it. I didn't want to hurt you, but he would have hurt me instead."

"I'll ask you once more. How many prints and negatives did you give Red?"

"The photographer gave the whole package to me, and I gave two prints of the best shot to Red. I picked out the one where your face, not mine, was recognizable."

"Not the negative?"

"No, he forgot to ask me for it."

"How the devil did a photographer snap the pictures?"

"Through the bedroom window from the neighbor's lanai—you know the one. I left it open. He used some kind of high-speed nighttime film. A friend told me that this guy was reliable and honest, so I gave him the money up front and he delivered the package Wednesday morning."

"Reliable? Honest? Someone in his line of work? I'll bet. I want the truth now," Coland said sternly. "How many prints does Red have?"

"Only the two, I swear. I'm so sorry, Coland. You know I wouldn't want to hurt you. I had to go along with it, Red made me." Her silent weeping continued.

"He gave me one of the prints," Coland said. "I'll make you a deal. If you can bring me the remaining print, I won't prosecute and you can keep the money Red gave you. If he uses that photo against me and my wife, I guarantee you will go to prison and do hard time. Do you understand me?"

Without raising his voice, Coland lectured her in a monotone. "Do you?" He got up from the sofa and walked toward her.

A shudder ran through her whole body. "Yes," Cindy whimpered, having no idea how to retrieve the photo. "But Red hasn't been here in days. He just used me and now he's throwing me away."

"That's your problem," Coland said. He let himself out of the apartment quickly so as not to weaken the fearsome mood he had carefully constructed. He'd gone on the offense against the enemy.

* * *

Bone tired at nine p.m., Kekoa set about his last chore of the day, making the rounds of all the bakery doors. The front door he checked last. His thoughts drifted elsewhere as he set the deadbolt. Something white on the floor caught his eye: an envelope that had been slipped in from outside. The bakery had no need for a mailbox; the postman always came into the shop, handed the mail directly to Mauro, and left with a smile and a sweet roll or two.

Kekoa picked up the large square envelope and saw his name and address in neatly penned script. He turned it over. It came from Mr. and Mrs. Ballesteros. His heartbeat quickened. He ran his fingertips over the name and address and whistled softly. Tearing it open, he read the handwritten message, then hurried up the stairs to Mauro and Sam's rooms. Mauro answered his knock, and Kekoa shoved the envelope toward her. She read through it slowly as he peered over her shoulder.

"Is invitation to wedding, Esmeralda Ballesteros and Manuel Portfia. The fifteenth. That one week from Sunday, two o'clock in afternoon."

Kekoa beamed. He'd never been invited to a wedding. Now he'd get to see Maria again.

Mauro put her arm around him and winked at Sam across the room in his rocker. "We must buy new clothes for most important guest."

Kekoa hadn't felt so happy in a long time. He bounded down the stairs to his room, visualizing the sweet face of Maria with no effort at all.

Chapter 22
Every Nook and Grammy

THE LATE morning sun, fighting its way through the hotel room's flimsy drapes, warmed Hal's face. Checking his watch, he saw he'd overslept. The time change—it was already 9:30 here in L.A. After a quick shower and a shave, he donned the same suit and tie, but conceded to a fresh shirt. At the hotel's counter-only coffee shop, he made do with a packaged raisin bran muffin and black coffee. The apple pie looked three days old. He should start staying in better places, he decided. He could actually afford it, but he'd gotten used to living on the cheap.

Finding a Checkered Cab waiting outside the revolving lobby doors, he gave the driver Wilma Minnet's suburban address. He deliberately hadn't called her in advance. He hoped the surprise visit would yield him the advantage. She wouldn't have time to concoct canned answers.

The Latino driver jockeyed the cab to the outskirts of L.A., past million-dollar homes tucked precariously into the hills. Off the freeway, pastel suburbs popped up. Cluttered strip malls came next—White Tower hamburgers, Kwickie Car Wash, Baseball Cards Bought & Sold, Senora Rosita—Palm Reader.

How could the world need so many Mattress Warehouses and Waterbed Cities? Hal wondered. It all brought back memories, none of them nostalgic or endearing. He'd bunked in L.A. to make a living, and that was that. By force of habit, his hand went to his neck to scratch the long scar there.

Ten years earlier, Hal had spent twenty-two months in L.A. He hadn't had what he'd call "a life," but the money was good and he might never have left if it hadn't been for that night at Crazy Jake's Sports Bar.

The conversation had seemed innocent enough. Three hours and six double-scotches later, he and a stranger named Joe had left to hit yet

160

another joint around one a.m. Hal had passed out in his own pickup and woke up in time to find his wallet being lifted. His good old drinking buddy turned out to be a coke-head looking for cash. Hal struggled, but drunk, he was a patsy. Coke-head Joe gave him a present he'd never forget: a shiv cut across the neck. After taking Hal's wallet containing $600, Joe left him bleeding in the pickup. A storefront clinic had taken nineteen stitches to close the cut, and sent him to a neighborhood charity detox ward.

The mugging had left him with a six-inch red scar and enough self-disgust to pull himself out of the clutches of alcohol and degradation. Hal sighed; the humiliating memories remained vivid. Today's taxi ride ended $28.55 later in front of a tan stucco duplex with brown trim. The duplex looked almost comical to Hal; with its two entryways huddled together in the center of the structure, it seemed to stare at him with crossed eyes.

A balding man in a tank top was watering a flower bed with a garden hose in the tiny front yard. Hal yelled to him. "Wilma Minnet live here?"

"Yup."

A five-dollar tip sent the cab driver on his way. Hal stepped onto the sidewalk, propped himself up on the two canes, and approached the man. "Which doorway is hers?"

"One on the left, but she ain't there."

"Why didn't you say so before I let the cab go?"

"Didn't ask."

"You sure are a man of few words."

"Yup."

"Any idea where she went?"

"Nope."

"Mind if I use your phone to call another cab?"

"Nope." Keeping the hose stream on a clump of daisies, the man edged his way toward a screened-in window. "Gram, man's gonna use the phone." He motioned toward the door on the right.

Hal climbed the few steps and checked the name plaque on the door: "Minnet." *Same name as Wilma's*, he noted. Stepping through the doorway, Hal found himself in a small living room furnished with many old pieces still in decent repair. Cream-colored curtains filtered lacy light into the room.

"Good morning, young man." The voice came from behind, causing him to spin around. "Oh, I didn't mean to frighten you. I find it somewhat cooler here in this corner of the room."

Hal saw an old woman with bluish-white hair sitting on pillows in a wheelchair, a magazine and a plaid shawl strewn across her lap.

"That's no problem, ma'am." Hal scrutinized her friendly face and decided to take a chance at using the interview ruse on the woman he now believed to be Wilma's mother. He pulled out his UH adult education ID card and flashed it in her direction. "I'm Dr. Ralph Friend. I'm with the Sociology Department at the University of Hawaii at Manoa. That's Honolulu. I spoke with…"

"I'm called Grammy, and I don't get too many visitors any more. That's the truth." She flashed him a bright, uncomplicated grin, and he couldn't help smiling back.

He pulled up a straight-back chair just opposite her. "I hope you don't mind, but I want to hear everything you have to say."

"Of course not, silly, I'll take all the company I can get." She squared her frail shoulders, ready for any action that might come her way.

"I spoke with your daughter, Wilma, about a university study on divorces in Hawaii."

"Not my daughter, Wilma's my granddaughter. I brought her up as my own when her parents were killed in an accident thirty-some years ago."

His mistake had been minor. She would have all the information he'd need. "I spoke with your granddaughter about our study, and she agreed to an interview with me. Must have been something terribly important for her not to have kept her appointment with me."

"It's a shame you missed her. She went to Honolulu on business. You could have interviewed her there and saved the plane fare. You see, she got this phone call from her ex and took off. Business, she said, but she wouldn't tell me what it was about."

"Do you have an address for her there?" he asked.

"No. She promised to call in a few days and let me know where she'd be staying. As if I didn't know. I suppose I shouldn't be telling you this, but it really pisses me off when she gets secretive like that."

He nodded. "Know what you mean, Grammy. Would you mind answering a few questions instead?"

162

"Fire away, young man. I thought you'd never ask."

"Can you tell me where and when Wilma and Edgar Murphy were married?"

"The courthouse, on May... eighteenth... '73. She wore a pretty print dress and a crazy little pillbox hat. No one wears hats any more. A shame, too." Grammy paused, steeped in thought. "I remember now, a nasty day, rained from morning till night. We all got drenched before the ceremony. An omen that the marriage was definitely wrong—no doubt about it. Do you believe in omens, young man?"

"Uh... no, ma'am," Hal said, writing abbreviated notes in his spiral-bound pocket pad. "Would the license be recorded in Orange County?"

"Yes, I went with them to get it. In fact, I paid the two dollars. The clerk wouldn't accept Red's check. Can you imagine anyone going out in this day and age without two lousy dollars in their pocket? Another bad omen."

"Can you tell me where and when the divorce was granted?"

"In the same place, July of '81, I think. Oh, they were separated dozens of times, but they kept going back for more. They fought like cat and dog, real violently, too. Someone always got hurt—usually Wilma. The crazy thing is, they'd part as enemies, but—sure as shootin'—they'd return as lovers. Maybe there's more to this physical love thing than I ever found." Grammy sighed. "She's still nuts about him. I never could see why—such a wheeler-dealer and always busted. I have to admit he was a handsome dude. Had muscles that just wouldn't quit. I understand now he's doing pretty well in the real estate and construction business."

"Did they ever own any property together?" This was the answer Hal was waiting for. "No houses or nothing. They rented an apartment. But I think they had a real estate business in Honolulu."

"Would you know the name of the firm, by any chance?"

"I'm afraid not. Wilma never talks about her business affairs. I love her dearly, but she never takes my advice. She'd get in a lot less trouble if she did." Grammy eyed Hal apologetically. "But that's my problem, son. You don't want to hear it."

"It's okay, Grammy, I understand," Hal said, pleased that he'd ingratiated himself with her. "Did your granddaughter actively participate in that business?"

163

"Don't know. She does have a real estate license, though, if that will help."

"Yes. Well, I certainly do want to thank you, Grammy. You've been more help than you know." He leaned closer to shake her hand. She grabbed his arm instead and pulled him down to where she could buss him on the cheek with her withered lips. They exchanged smiles. Each had benefited immensely from the visit.

Hal called a cab. As it pulled away, Grammy waved to him from her chair in the open doorway. Hal waved back.

"Where to?" the cabby asked.

"Main courthouse in Orange County," he replied. Hal flipped through his notes and chuckled at one of the entries. He had used local divorces as the subject of his Honolulu "study," whereas the actual divorce had taken place in California. Wilma had not picked up on that fact during his phone interview with her.

Hal paid off the cabby in front of the courthouse and gazed up at an endless set of steps leading to massive doors. A young man in jeans and a faded shirt sauntered down the steps. He had manacled wrists. There didn't seem to be anyone with him. Hal thought it rather peculiar for a prisoner to be wandering around loose without an escort. He watched the man descend a third of the way down before two uniformed police officers burst out of the door after him. They turned him around and hurried him back up the stairs, all the while arguing about whose fault it had been.

The prisoner grinned. "Hey, man, I weren't tryin' t' escape. Just felt like takin' a walk. Hey, I planned t' come back."

Hal couldn't help but enjoy the incident, but he had work to do, and spent the next two hours on the third floor in the Bureau of Vital Statistics. Sitting before the microfiche projector, he clicked the small reel of film into place and scanned horizontally and then vertically for the document he sought. Having found it and adjusted the focus for clarity, he pressed the COPY button. An enlarged sepia copy emerged at the bottom of the projector, and the mechanical counter within the projector's key incremented by one. The process dragged out, as the clerk would allow him only one microfiche canister at a time.

Hal paid for the copies, and then paid again to have the clerk notarize each copy. Another cab ride returned him to his hotel.

Back in his room, he reconfirmed his flight to Honolulu for 8:50

that evening. Next he made a list of major local banks from the phone directory and began calling each one, using the guise of an estate assets locator. He explained that he was only verifying the existence of accounts in the name of Edgar Murphy or Wilma Minnet. Many replies were negative and some reluctant without a court order, but he did find a savings account and a checking account in Wilma's name alone. As expected, the bank would release no specific financial information.

His trip had been a qualified success. He had linked Wilma and Red together, at least marriage-wise, if not business-wise. He knew now that a business connection did exist. He needed to verify that connection somehow. It had to be proved that Red was indeed Rodminn Realty.

* * *

An ocean away, near midnight, Leilani lay stiffly on her bed, wondering why she couldn't fall asleep. Numi's bed was empty; she was taking a long shower.

Suddenly, Leilani saw an eerie stream of light hovering near the ceiling. Not a flash, but a tiny bright ball with an elongated tail the length of her forearm. Was she dreaming? Whatever it was, it made a shrill noise as it flitted all over the bedroom, alighting nowhere. It moved so quickly she couldn't determine if there was actually more than one.

Leilani wasn't the least bit frightened. These were the spirits of the unavenged dead. She knew all about them from *Tutu* Eme—story after story. They did no harm, nor were they evil. They came to warn, pester, and con you into righting a wrong. And if you scolded, swore, and shouted loud enough at them, the spirits would fade and go away. But Leilani didn't want that. She wanted to know whose spirit this was. Why was it here in her room? And why tonight?

She thought of her grandmother and the funeral. Then her mind wandered to her missing uncle. The ball of light halted in flight. Its tail shortened for an instant above her, then flitted on. She knew then that the spirit belonged to Big John Pualoa. Was it a warning? Again it hovered above her bed.

Leilani screamed out, "Tell me, is it a warning? Tell me now!" The ball of light faded and disappeared.

Chapter 23
Shapes in the Sand

ON SUNDAY Leilani turned seventeen. Alex drove them up the Pali Highway, passing consulates, Asian temples, and Queen Emma's Summer Palace. Leaving civilization behind, the Pali—"cliff" in Hawaiian—plunged through forest and climbed a gradual grade before boring into the Koolau mountain range. Emerging from the double tunnel near the top of the steamy ridge on the cliff side, the Pali unveiled a breathtaking panorama of Oahu's windward side.

Alex had chosen Kailua Beach Park as his surprise destination for Leilani's birthday. The UH architecture students were creating sand sculptures in an annual competition there today. Alex wedged the tiny Escort into a tight parking spot half on the road and half on the grass.

At the bathhouse they changed into swim suits. Their bare feet prickled from the coarse grass strewn with pokies, sharp round seed pods from the ironwood trees. With every plot of shade already claimed, they grabbed a meager place in the scorching sun and unrolled two tatami mats. From there, they could see the competition entries.

Alex and Leilani meandered toward the exhibit with their feet awash in the white foam surf. Leilani self-consciously tugged her one piece Lycra suit down over her partially exposed backside. Then she reached for his hand and gripped it tightly.

Crowds clustered around the sculptures, vying for better views of the Taj Mahal with its domes and spires; a sea turtle, its five-foot shell a pattern of precise hexagons; a monk seal on a rock.

"Alex, look!" Leilani stared down at a strange-looking amphibian from the sea. The sculpture had been cut in half by tire marks. "It's a protest piece—this is so cool!"

"Kind of obvious, if you ask me," Alex said. "Not very subtle."

"Well, what do you expect—*The Gates of Hell*? We're not talking Rodin here," she snapped. Frowning, she moved to the next sculpture: three fish heads gasping for clean air and water from a pond of sand. A partly submerged swimmer floated on his back, a shark's fin headed toward him. Leilani giggled. "Good show—maybe it's revenge for people ruining their environment. You've got to admit, it's pretty clever."

"Okay. At least that one's got some humor."

"These are so great!" she said.

When Alex didn't answer, Leilani took his silence to mean disapproval. "Look, Alex. Think about it, these students are trying to do something original, doing this work to make a strong statement— even though it's all going to be destroyed in a few hours."

"I know, and I get the messages, but isn't it okay to just entertain people? Do they have to preach? I mean, this is the beach, isn't it?"

"But it's also a competition, Alex. Anybody with artistic ability can create stuff like this." Her arm swept over war canoes, a clan of geckos, Garfield the cat, and the Roman Coliseum—each one constructed with sand. "They're nice and all, but the pieces about the environment— they go further. It's raising people's consciousness, for heaven's sake. Isn't that what real art is all about?"

Her face felt hot, and not from the sun. She enjoyed debating with him. She baited him, and he always bit. She wanted to get in the final dig, but decided to make it playful. Pulling him close to her, she asked under her breath, "Are young up-and-coming CPA's always so conservative and—predictable?"

Her closeness, her throaty voice, the sweet scent of the sunscreen on her cheek overpowered him. "Not always," he murmured in her ear. "But clients do get a little unnerved when we're too creative with their money."

Passing the farthest point in the exhibit, Leilani turned to him, her face glowing. "Thanks for bringing me. I loved it—even if you didn't."

"Hey, I liked it a lot, just not necessarily in the same intense way you did."

They strolled along the water's edge. Leilani let go of Alex's hand, bent down, and splashed his sun-heated backside with cool water. She knew better than to just stand there after such a rash move, and he took off down the beach after her. Catching her easily, he scooped her off her feet and deposited her in the surf amid her laughter and shrieks. They swam and when they'd had their fill, they retraced the ambling shoreline until their suits were dry.

She plunked herself down on her tatami mat and handed him the beach towel that had covered their things. One of her sneakers flipped over, and her wallet, thick with bills, fell out. While it failed to attract their attention, it didn't go unnoticed altogether.

Behind them, a young tough slouched on the ledge where the grass-topped dune stepped sharply to the sandy beach. A black braid tugged the upper portion of his hair severely away from his face. The greased-down lower portion forced an unusual hair part that encircled his head. He wore black shorts and a Grateful Dead tank top. Tattoos, signifying protection of an island gang, covered both iron-pumped biceps and shoulders. He drew deeply on a cigarette, feigning a casual look, but he watched and listened, a hawk stalking its prey.

Alex brushed the sand from his legs with the towel. When he looked over at Leilani again, he saw a lone tear rolling down her cheek. He took both her hands and pulled her to her feet, then wrapped his arms around her waist.

"What's wrong, hon?" he asked as he kissed away the tear.

She shivered and pointed. "See that kid over there digging in the sand?"

"Yeah, I see him."

"He reminds me so much of Kekoa. Younger, but—oh, Alex, I can't help wondering what kind of trouble my brother's in. I wish we could find him."

"You still think he lives in Kaimuki?"

"I'm sure of it," she said, her voice urgent. "Lori Yamashita saw him there with a bike."

"Hardly any guarantee. Look, you've done all you can to locate him. Lori told you he looked healthy enough. And now there's nothing we can do but wait for him to contact us. I wish I knew why he's running."

Alex bent over and picked up their things, including the wayward wallet. They headed back to the bath house, and Leilani stepped under the outside shower. She shuddered under the onslaught of icy water. Alex watched her wet hair cling to her back, streamlining her whole Lycra-covered body, a glistening green shoot springing up in the rain.

In the dressing rooms they changed to shorts and T-shirts for the drive home. Leilani stepped out of the bath house first, still brushing her hair. Her shirt blazoned the Oahu Prep emblem across front and back. Near the picnic tables, for the first time, she noticed the young tough with the weird hair and tattoos. She tried not to make eye contact.

With an insolent grin, he approached her. She backed away.

"You Lani?" he asked.

She cringed—didn't answer.

"You got a *bruddah*, Kekoa, yah?"

This time she said, "Yes!" Her heart pounded.

"You wanna see your *bruddah*?" he asked.

"Yesss," she stammered.

"I take you tomorrow night. You catch da bus t' Waialae and Sixth. Come at nine, alone, yah? Git off da bus and walk up Waialae. I'll meet ya. You'll see Kekoa. Say nuthin' t' nobody. Yah?"

"But where on Waialae?"

"You'll see me—dat's enough. Understand?"

She finally nodded, and he disappeared around the edge of the building just as Alex emerged from the men's bath house.

"Who's that?" he asked, seeing fear in her expression.

"No one," she replied loudly.

"Lani, what's wrong? I saw that sleazeball talking to you."

"Shhh," she said, and whispered, "I'll tell you in the car." Her eyes begged. "Please."

Their once-glowing mood dimmed as they drove off. The sun dropped. The ironwoods and coconut palms cast long, distorted shadows. The ocean waves licked the beach and tasted the sand as the tide crept in. Shapes in the sand began to erode, their sculpted messages faded, mostly forgotten.

Chapter 24
Two Kinds of Dreams

THE REAR SERVICE ALLEY seemed unnaturally quiet. Only the Osaka Bakery and Banyan Tree Barbershop were open. Even on Sunday, Kekoa had chores that ended with mopping the workroom floor. He wrung out the mop and stood it upside down on its wooden handle, outside next to the rear door of the bakery. Looking up, he discovered Ilio standing there. While he experienced a rush of joy, the dog made a moaning, whining sound and his tail hung motionless between his hind legs. If Kekoa hadn't known better, he would have judged Ilio to be crying. Ilio's head kept turning from his friend to down the alley as though he wanted the boy to go there.

Kekoa glanced in that direction and saw a mound of flattened cardboard boxes teetering next to the dumpster behind the furniture store. For a moment he thought he saw a dark rubber flip-flop moving between the layers of cardboard. The boy followed the dog. Approaching the pile cautiously he spied a second flip-flop, hairless spindly legs, tattered shorts, and a grayed T-shirt torn at the chest. Only then did he notice the unmistakable bearded face.

"Ol' Chou!" Kekoa looked down at the crumpled heap of skin and bones. Eyelids fluttered open. A road map of red veins stared up at the boy as the eyes filled with tears.

"Master K," he said feebly, struggling to a half-sitting position, leaning on one elbow.

Kekoa knelt next to him and laid his hand affectionately on Chou's shoulder. "Old man, you look very sick."

"I am sick. At seventy-nine my legs do not work well any more, so I do not find what my body needs to eat. I abuse it with alcohol, too. It helps with the pain."

"But what happened? The Community Services people, didn't they help you?"

Chou shook his head and smiled grimly. "They tried to sober me up, but I'd have none of it. Escaped from their clutches." He looked hazily at Kekoa. "But you—you, my friend, look fine. You must be living the good life."

"I got lucky. The Osakas took me in, I work for them now. I'm well and happy here. But you, Ol' Chou, you need help. I'll bring you a bite to eat."

Ignoring Chou's weak protest, Kekoa disappeared and returned a few minutes later with a white paper sack filled with pastries from the day-old sale rack. He also brought a metal measuring cup filled with cold milk.

"Thank you," Chou whispered. "Your life's dreams will be fulfilled because of your kindness to this sick and worthless man."

Kekoa stood by, watching Chou struggle to eat. He felt helpless, so he rearranged the cardboard to provide some shade from the sizzling sun. "What more can I do for you, Chou?"

Clearing his throat, the old man swallowed hard. "There is something urgent you can do for me," he said in a faint, cracking voice. "I no longer have anyone to turn to but you, my young friend."

"Of course, Ol' Chou." Kekoa took the gnarled hand in his own and squeezed it gently. "What can I do?"

The old man continued in a slightly stronger voice. "I have spent these last lost years of my life searching for the daughter I wrongfully disowned. I now know where she lives and I have seen her often from afar. I sometimes wait outside her apartment in her Chinatown alley, but…my shame and the fear that she might reject me hover over me like a wrathful dragon and prevent me from making my peace with her. The sands of time are too quickly slipping away from me, and I cannot continue like this much longer. Please! If you can, if you will, find my daughter and give her this."

Chou tugged at a handkerchief in his pocket and pulled it free. Fingers trembling, he untied the four-cornered knot and flattened out the handkerchief. There, amid the folds, sat a large antique gold medallion. Placing it in Kekoa's hand, he closed the boy's fingers around it. "It is a family heirloom, worth little to anyone else, but precious to me. Give it to her." Chou picked up a folded scrap of paper that had fallen from the handkerchief and gave it to Kekoa as well. "This is her name—address too. I know I can count on you to not deny a dying man his last request." He looked deep into Kekoa's eyes and when he found the assent he searched for, offered his most knowing smile. He released Kekoa's hand.

"I will do everything I can to find her. I swear it. Come inside with me," the boy urged. "You can take a shower. I'll give you clean clothes and a pillow. I'll...I'll help you get well."

"Cleanliness and comfort are no longer important to Li Tien Chou. I'm a far cry from the neat, prim university professor, even from my better homeless days, eh? No, K. I will rest now, and we can talk later." He lay back. His eyes fluttered shut.

Kekoa reluctantly left him there. Inside, he sat down on his bed to think. He'd been up since 4 a.m. The day's chores were already done. He set the medallion and scrap of paper on the shelf beside his bed where they could not be forgotten.

His fatigue caught up with him, and he fell asleep, but only to sink into a dream that seemed so real because he and Ol' Chou had actually lived the scene where it took place.

It was the time Kekoa snatched the vegetables out of the river. That night, in their alley they crouched beside the simmering cook pot as it steamed with tempting vapors. A sense of warmth and well-being enfolded them. Abruptly, the scene grew distorted, like the bleeding colors of a scrambled television program. Kekoa felt hot. He watched Chou's face in the light of the coals growing red, then yellow, then...the old man's image faded from light and sight...to nothing. The broth boiled over. Froth spewed from the top of the pot and ran between the cobblestones. Terrified, Kekoa wanted to run, but wouldn't. He wanted to understand, but couldn't.

The boy awoke suddenly, his T-shirt and hair drenched with sweat. Sitting up, he swung his feet to the floor. The nightmare had frightened him. He splashed some cool water on his face and made his way to the alley door again. Fearfully, he opened it. Chou lay where he'd left him, in the heap of cardboard. But not quite the way he'd left him. His red-webbed eyes stared into nothingness. His slack mouth gaped open. A pool of urine had soaked into the cardboard beneath him. Ilio lay close beside his master, with his chin resting at the bend of Ol' Chou's arm, somehow sensing that Ol' Chou had passed from among the living.

Tears flooded the boy's vision. Without thinking why, he picked up the white paper sack and metal measuring cup and carried them inside. Ilio remained with his master.

Feeling sudden panic, Kekoa slipped back to his room and sat down on his bed to figure out what to do next. A wave of self-pity washed over him—one more incredible loss. Everyone important to Kekoa had been taken from him: his mother and father, his grandmother, Uncle John, Leilani. And now Ol' Chou, who had protected him when he'd needed a friend most.

By sheer will, Kekoa forced his thoughts into a plan of action. He grabbed a towel and mopped the sweat off his chest and from under his arms. Changing into a fresh T-shirt, he combed his hair and walked resolutely into the storefront to find Yasuko. She and Mauro were waiting on customers. When Yasuko had finished ringing up her sale, he whispered close to her ear, "I need your help out back."

"I thought you were through for the day," she said.

"I am, but...Yasuko!" he murmured insistently, "I need you to make a phone call for me."

She looked confused. "A phone call?"

"I want you to call an ambulance for me. There's an old homeless guy lying out back in the alley, across the way where the boxes are. I think he's dead."

"Can't you call?"

"No! Because he's dead, the police will want to question me. I want you to say you found him when you took out the trash."

"Then they'll question me."

"Yeah, but you got nothing to hide, yah?"

"Uh..." she said uncertainly. "I guess so. You want me to call now?"

"Maybe you should have a look first. They may want you to describe what you saw."

Following him through the back door, she took one quick look and turned away. "Oooh man!" she said drawing a deep breath. "Now what?"

"Just call 911 and tell them there's a sick old man lying in the alley behind the bakery and give them your name and address."

Yasuko hesitated. "Can't we just forget about it?" she asked. "Somebody'll find him." But the pleading look on Kekoa's face gave her answer enough. She walked slowly back inside and dialed 911 from the phone in the workroom. The police operator told her not to leave the scene until help arrived.

Kekoa hurried into the shop and explained the barest details to Mauro. "I go now, gotta meet Andy down at the rec center. Be back later." Before Mauro could question him, he left.

An ambulance arrived in eleven minutes, followed by a police car. The woman paramedic checked Chou for vital signs and shook her head. The two policemen took pictures and searched the immediate area for clues. When satisfied that it was just another case of a street person meeting a logical end, they signaled the paramedics that the body could be removed. They put Chou into a long black bag as if disposing of so much garbage, and carted him away, a demeaning end, even to a derelict life. The barbershop owner and his only customer stood a few yards away, gawking and soaking up the excitement. Ilio watched from behind them until one of the policemen approached the trio, and then Ilio darted up the alley and around to the front of the store where he saw Kekoa crossing the street. He followed.

While the first policeman questioned the barber, another police officer turned to question Yasuko. "Tell me in your own words what happened, Miss."

Yasuko hovered in the doorway. A glass of water and eleven minutes' wait had helped her. "I came out here to the dumpster with the trash from the shop and saw him lying there like that."

"Like what, Miss?"

"Like with his eyes and mouth open. Poor guy, but ugh, what an awful sight!"

"I understand, Miss. Anybody else see you or him?"

"Not that I know of," she lied.

"Would anybody be feeding him?"

"Don't know. Why?"

"Well, he had crumbs on his chin and a milk mustache."

"Must have been something he found in the dumpster," she improvised quickly.

"Anybody else know he was there?"

"I don't think so. What did he die of?"

The officer merely shrugged. "Thank you, Miss, we'll be in touch." He put away his notepad and returned to the cruiser with his partner.

174

Cry Ohana

Two blocks away, Kekoa crouched in the shadows of the rec center, leaning against the wall that faced the tennis courts. Ilio nudged his leg and Kekoa scratched him behind the ears. "I guess I'm all you got now, fella."

In the scorching noon heat, the tennis courts stood empty. Kekoa had had no plan with Andy. He just knew he had to get away before the police arrived. He'd seen the cruiser and ambulance pull up in front of the bakery, then drive around to the alley. After twenty minutes, the ambulance left, and now, a half-hour later, the police car sped off down Waialae. All clear, Kekoa trotted home with Ilio and left him out front—he didn't believe the Osakas were ready for a dog just yet.

He slipped in the front door, relieved to find no customers there. Yasuko came out from behind the counter, her face somber.

The boy impulsively hugged her. "Thanks for covering for me. How…how did it go?"

"Okay. They accepted everything I said. They got suspicious when they found milk and crumbs on him. Kekoa—did you give him something to eat? Did you know him?"

"Yeah, and I tried to help him." Kekoa knew better than to lie to his closest friend and teacher. He loved her in much the same way he loved Leilani. "I met him when I was on the run. He helped me survive in Chinatown. I just couldn't turn him away."

"You're a brave and true friend, Kekoa Pualoa."

Not brave enough, he thought. Returning to his room, he recalled the time he and Chou had strolled through the Ala Moana mall and sat on the low wall bordering the fish pools filled with koi. "Some live to be a hundred years old," Chou had told him.

Hypnotized, Kekoa had watched the fish: speckled orange and black; pale yellow; gray and white. There were no two alike. They swam oblivious to the attentions of shoppers, lovers, and exuberant children. But the koi had behaved differently for Chou. He lowered his face to the water's surface and spoke in gentle tones. Then he put his hand in the water, and the gathering koi fed from it. Not in the frenzied fashion that accompanied the normal feeding by the mall's fish-keeper, but in a calm, nibbling way that denoted a kindred spirit with this old man. He never revealed what he fed them.

Fed them! That shook Kekoa from his trance and reminded him that *Ilio* needed to be fed, so he placed some leftover scraps and a water

175

bowl out back. The dog was his responsibility now, and he wasn't going to be so neglectful this time around.

* * *

A letter notified Red Murphy of the trustees' meeting scheduled for the following Tuesday. Ever since receiving it, he'd had trouble sleeping. He worried about this meeting, and about Cindy. How far could he trust her? Well, he'd found out how much—or rather, how little—when she told him on the phone that Coland had filched the photos from her dresser drawer. That news had infuriated Red.

"You goddamn ignorant bitch, why didja leave them around where he could find them?"

She had screamed back, "You've screwed up my life enough. Get lost!" and hung up.

He slumped into his LAZ-Y-BOY recliner, too distraught to even turn on the TV. His eyes drooped shut, and his chin fell to his chest. He snored and snorted as he sank into a tormented dream.

They were after him, threatening him. Faces. Familiar and angry faces of men and women he'd victimized. Behind him, the roar of machinery. He turned to look. A giant yellow bulldozer charged toward him, gleefully driven by Kekoa. Suddenly, the front-end loader scooped Red up. Red cried out: "I didn't mean it. It's just good business. Everyone cheats!" The laughing boy swung the bulldozer around and headed down a major thoroughfare. People lined the street, jeering and applauding. Murphy was on exhibit for everyone to see. A cracking, snapping sound pierced the air as the loader rumbled toward a barred enclosure at the end of the street and stopped directly over the open-topped cage. Red hung suspended above the huge iron cage containing a lioness and her tamer, who wielded a snapping whip. Red looked down at the lion tamer and saw he was Coland Benfield-Rice. The loader moved to the DUMP position. Red hung on for dear life. The loader banged on the top of the cage until he fell to the ground inside. Coland began to whip him, and Red saw purple welts appear on his arms and legs. The face of the lioness melted into the face of a woman—Cindy's! She clawed him without mercy. Rivulets of blood surfaced in the slash marks. He tried to climb up the side of the cage, but she continued slashing him, and he fell.

Red awoke, sprawled on the floor with the LAZ-Y-BOY turned on its side on top of him. Pain stabbed his shoulder. His head throbbed.

He listened. Had Wilma heard him fall or cry out? He'd play dumb if she asked about it. Wincing with the pain and feeling like an ass, he struggled out from under the chair and turned it upright. A drink—that's what he needed. From the kitchen cabinet he pulled out a bottle of Country Gentleman bourbon, drawing long and hard on the bottle. The booze sent his aching head swimming. He fell back into the recliner and closed his eyes.

It took some time for his head to stop spinning, but even then his brain functioned less than rationally. Anger replaced dizziness, and the more he recollected, the more he blamed Cindy for his failures. He'd given Coland only one of the incriminating prints. He had kept a single copy in his wallet, assuming the remaining prints and negatives were safe in her hands. "How could that bitch be so stupid? She's ruined everything," he bellowed aloud. No one heard him. Wilma had gone for a walk while he was asleep.

He forced himself upright, tucked in his rumpled shirt, and guzzled a cold drink of water at the kitchen sink. Grabbing his keys from the coffee table, he stormed out the door and slammed it shut behind him. Waiting for the elevator, his temper rose by degrees and stayed at a fever pitch during the twenty-minute drive to Chinatown.

The last wisp of daylight hung impatiently over the deserted alley. He could see that Cindy's rooms were nearly dark, except for a modulating blue-white light dancing from her television set. Red didn't try the door handle. He simply bent his shoulder to the task, and in one lunge powered by the adrenaline of rage, took the flimsy door from its hinges.

He found a surprised and very frightened Cindy sitting cross-legged on her bed, clad only in a filmy, flesh-colored baby-doll top that loosely caressed her luscious breasts. The unexpected sight of her voluptuous body stopped him in his tracks. The woman stirred him still, but only for a moment. Then his rage took possession once more. She tried to get up, but he pulled her to the edge of the bed and began to slap and backhand her mercilessly. He hit her so hard his own hand hurt and that made him more determined than ever to inflict pain.

"Bitch! Whore! Dumb bitch!" he cried.

Cindy, her cheeks puffy and deep red, lay on her side sobbing, her knees drawn up in a fetal position. Red, breathing hard, looked down at her in disdain, ready to inflict more punches. Suddenly, powerful arms grabbed him from behind. Huge hands spun him around to face his assailant. Even if he had seen the punch coming, it was doubtful he could have done anything about it. He slumped to the floor like a spill of half-set Jell-O.

A six-foot-eight island visitor of Cindy's now stood over her with an alarmed look. He had been in the "John's john" when Red broke in the door.

"Help me, please!" she whispered hoarsely. He was hesitant to touch her for fear he would cause her more pain. Instead, he brought a basin of water from the kitchen sink and gently dabbed away the unsightly mixture of blood, tears, and makeup. She let him, wincing with every dab.

"What else can I do for you, Cindy?"

"Take that crazy sonofabitch the hell out of here."

"You sure you're okay? I can stay awhile if you want."

"You've done all you can for me now. I'll be fine. It will take some time to heal." She sounded far more confident than she felt. "Just take him!"

"You want me to go through his pockets?" he asked.

"No. Wait! Let me see his wallet. You can have the cash. I want something else."

"I don't want any cash from this piece o' crap," he said, handing the wallet to Cindy.

She frantically pulled it apart, business cards and plastic falling on the floor, until a weak grin painted itself across her bruised face. She gripped the one remaining photo she'd given to Red. Cindy looked up gratefully and said, "He's all yours, handsome."

Her rescuer easily lifted up the 250-pound Edgar A. Murphy and hoisted him over his left shoulder. With a parting note of triumph, he touched the fingers of his free hand to his lips and blew Cindy the gentlest breeze of a kiss. "I'll take the trash out now," he said. Her champion deposited Red's midsection over the staircase railing while he replaced the broken door in its frame as best he could. He then left quietly with the "trash."

* * *

Red woke up at 5:30 a.m., face down in the grass at Sand Island Beach Park. Every inch of his sore body displayed reddish blotches beginning to turn black and blue. He knew he'd been worked over in a most professional manner—nothing seemed broken, but *auwe*, how he hurt.

Chapter 25
Pain and Perseverence

"IT's IDIOTIC! You'll never change that sadistic alley cat. He'll hurt you again."

Wilma held the phone two inches away from her ear and scowled as she waited for Grammy's ranting to end. She'd heard it all before.

"Haven't you gone through enough?"

"You don't understand, Gram, I'm doing him a favor—a profitable favor at that. I'm gonna make money on it. Besides, it's only temporary, a few weeks at most. Trust me, I'll be fine."

"Whenever you say 'Trust me,' I know I shouldn't. What am I going to do with you, child? You never learn."

"Gotta go now, Gram. Love ya." Wilma hung up and let out a long sigh. She slid into a chair at the kitchen table and looked over Red's notes. John Pualoa's house in Ewa had new owners, a father and son. But she couldn't find any Louis Lynch listed in the phone book. Well, she'd just have to drive out there after supper.

A call to Peke Palaneke at the diner was next, and Wilma geared herself up for the condolence routine. "Hello, Peke. My name is Wilma, Wilma Minnet. I was a business partner of Pop Rodder. I'm sorry for your loss. No, I couldn't come to the funeral, I live in L.A. Just got into Honolulu last night. Yes, we were fond of him, too. Peke, I wonder if Mr. Murphy and I might call on you this afternoon. We'd like to make you a very attractive offer. Three-thirty would be fine, thank you."

Wilma hung up and heard a key turn in the front door. She watched Red let himself into the living room and gingerly ease himself down in a chair opposite her. "You look awful. What the hell happened to you?"

"I feel awful. I got mugged in the park."

"Out on an all-night binge? Hope you had fun," she said. "What park?"

In truth, he couldn't rightly say what had happened to him. Nor would it be wise to bring up the subject of Cindy at all. There had been someone else, someone big in the room, he was sure of that. He remembered waking up in the park with a note stuffed into his hand: "If Sistah Cindy don't get better, your *okole* is chop meat."

Red knew that such a threat to his rear-end wasn't just idle talk. He recognized local vigilante justice when he saw it. He'd never go near Cindy again. That was for sure.

"What were you doing in a park at this hour of the morning, anyway?" Wilma asked.

"I went last night…late…I was sleeping off too much bourbon. Couldn't drive any more." His swollen lips made his speech almost incoherent. "Oh, damn! I hurt like hell all over. The only things that don't hurt are the soles of my feet." Red waited for her to comment, but she had gone to the bathroom to get first-aid supplies. He pulled off his shoes and socks.

She returned and began to strip away his shirt and trousers. It took all her strength to hold him up while he dropped his undershorts. Manipulating him to the shower, no easy trick in itself, she regarded the dozens of black-and-blue marks all over his hairy torso.

"This is more like a ritual mutilation job than a mugging. Are you sure that's what it was?"

"Yeah. He must have been some kind of nut with a vengeance. Damn it! Easy with that," he yelped as she laid the stinging soap to his tortured outer body. His inner body hadn't fared too well from the bourbon, either.

Wilma rinsed and toweled him down with the care ordinarily reserved for a newborn. He slept for hours after that, aided by two aspirins and half a tube of Ben Gay.

He awoke, his whole body still aching and more stiff, to find Wilma standing beside the bed. "What's up?" he asked.

"I called Peke. We have an appointment to see her at 3:30 this afternoon."

"Excellent! I'll put on some clothes. Be with you in twenty minutes. We can stop for a hamburger on the way."

"No need to," she said. "We can grab a bite at her place. It'll soften her up."

"Very clever."

180

Cry Ohana

Moaning, he disappeared into his own room. "How many shares did Pop own?" she called to him.

"Twenty thousand, and he didn't put up any cash for them, either. Pop simply accepted the shares in return for being the front man. He..."

She couldn't hear any more because he had closed the door to the bedroom. Forty minutes later they were in her rental car headed windward toward Waimanalo. Red had slipped back into a sullen mood.

Peke stood at the counter, a sponge in hand as they entered. She motioned them to a booth and hung up a CLOSED sign.

"Can I fix you anything?" she said.

"A couple of burgers and some Diet Cokes would be nice," said Wilma.

"Sure, that's easy."

Peke went behind the counter, opened the freezer section of the fridge, and threw a pair of meat patties on the grill. Steam rising from the splatter produced a great sizzling hiss. She set two Diet Cokes before her visitors, moving quickly and decisively for a woman of her bulk. Back at the grill in a flash with spatula in hand, she flipped and spanked and flipped again. Two split buns joined the cooking patties on the grill for toasting, and before long, the hamburgers appeared at the table, complete with a two-pickle garnish and a handful of Maui potato chips. She slid into the booth next to Red, who squeezed closer to the window. He smiled weakly, trying to hide his aversion to the grease-splattered apron still tied about her waist.

Wilma took her first bite, and with her mouth still full, mumbled, "Mmmm, this is good." She ate in very small bites, continuing to talk. "As you know, Rodminn Realty is a small business used to buy and sell commercial real estate. Horace ran the business for us, and we put up all the cash. In return for his services he was given 20,000 shares of Rodminn stock. We have a very limited supply of cash, you see, and now we're going to have to find someone else to run the business."

Peke's eyes narrowed. "Far's I could tell, Miss Wilma, it's been a whole lotta years since Pop could run any business."

Red nearly gagged on his hamburger.

"Oh," Wilma countered smoothly, "but Pop did run things fine for us."

"If you say so." But Peke's expression revealed that she knew bet-

181

ter.

Wilma pressed on. "Because the firm has had expenses and has thus far shown no profit, each share is worth considerably less than its one dollar par value, probably nearer to fifty cents. However, we are prepared to offer you a full $20,000 for those shares, and believe you me, that's quite a sacrifice for us. We may never make any money, but that is certainly our risk, not yours." Wilma nibbled on her chips, looking for some sign of affirmation from Peke.

Peke didn't understand any of the technical stuff, but her eyes lit up at the sound of $20,000. "I'd like some time to think this over." She tried to hide her excitement.

"Of course. You can take all the time you want, but if you delay more than a day or so, the shares might continue to devalue. That is, there might be nothing at all in the end and then we wouldn't be able to pay you the $20,000."

A hint of fear crossed Peke's face. Wilma's scare tactics were working.

"On the other hand," Wilma continued, "I can have a certified bank check for twenty big ones, payable to you, in your hands by tomorrow. How does that sound?"

"When you put it that way, how can I refuse? What do I have to do to sell the shares to you?"

Red felt better. He broke into the conversation. "Well, young lady, on the reverse side of each 5,000-share certificate there is a place for you to sign your name. That's all you have to do. You get the certified check, and we walk away with the shares all nice and proper."

"I bet there are a lot of things you want to do with that money, right?" Wilma asked.

Peke got more excited than ever as she told them of her plans for renovating Pop's place and expanding the diner. They let her run on and on, encouraging her to the point of no return.

Red stood up to leave. "By the way, Peke, we'll have the office rent check for you tomorrow also. Would the same time tomorrow be good?" Peke nodded eagerly. "Then 3:30 it is."

Red and Wilma drove off together, each feeling pretty confident that he or she alone had cinched the deal.

"How'd I do back there?" Wilma asked.

"Huh?"

"I said how'd I do back there? With Peke, I mean."

"Okay, I guess."

"You know, Red, sometimes I feel like my life is a poorly packed car trunk. Lots of space, but I can't fit my own skills into any of it. I don't know where I belong."

"Well, if it was my life, I'd shove some baggage around and just make space for Red Murphy."

"That's just it. You always make room for Red, but for no one else. It's like I don't exist. You think you did that back there all by yourself? You charmed her right off her feet? Well, Mr. Murphy, let me inform you, you had a little help with Miss Peke."

"Hey, Wilma, cool it. You know there's always a space for you with Red."

"Yeah, when you need something."

"No. I need you all the time, love." Even though his body continued to ache, he leaned over to the driver's seat and planted a loud kiss on her cheek. She turned her face toward him in time for another on the lips before returning her attention to the road ahead. The corners of her mouth curled up in a grudging smile.

Red felt as though he'd made another conquest. He was on a roll, as they say in Vegas. They headed over the Like-Like Highway toward Ewa, arriving at the house that had once belonged to Big John Pualoa just as the burning sun dropped into the ocean.

Cars of every sort cluttered the driveway and the street in front of the house. A young man in his early twenties answered the door.

Wilma apologized for not calling first. "But there was no telephone listed for Louis Lynch."

"I'm Lynch. Who are you?"

"My name is Wilma Minnet and this is Edgar Murphy. We represent a real estate firm that's interested in acquiring rental properties within a few blocks of the ocean. Could you tell us if the place is for sale?"

"Not unless the price is super-right. You see, we, my father and I, just purchased the house for me and my friends from school. There are eleven of us from the university living here this semester. We'd have no reason to move. Sorry."

"Wait!" Red had an idea. "Suppose you didn't have to leave.

Suppose you could go on living here and paying rent? How about a four-year lease? You see, we have a second purpose in acquiring the property. We need the garage space out back for some commercial vehicles. That would not interfere with you living here, would it?"

"Well," said Lou, "I guess it would be a matter of price then. How much for the house and how much for the rent? My father would have to agree, since he signed the loan." The young man led them to a grouping of rattan armchairs in the living room, where they all sat down. Cigarette butts and crushed beer cans littered the coffee table.

Red thought for a moment. "I'll give you $8,000 more than you paid for it and let's say $1,000 a month rent."

"Make that $12,000 and $1,000 a month," Lou countered.

"More like $10,000 and $1,100 a month? I'll assume the closing costs as well."

"Sounds okay, but like I said, I can't agree to anything without my dad."

"How soon can you get in touch with him?"

"Probably not until tomorrow morning. Dad will want to think it over too, so give us a week to respond. Okay?"

"Sounds reasonable. There is one other thing. I will want to renovate the garage out back to hold more vehicles, and it may be a little noisy. Don't you fellows have a spring break or something coming up soon? I could do it then."

"Yes. The week of the twenty-first, all but two of us go home." Lou neglected to mention that he was one of the two.

"Tell you what. I'll pay to put the two of them up at a reasonable hotel. Doesn't that sound fair?"

Lou nodded. "Dad should go along with this. He wasn't happy about tying up so much cash in a beach house for four years. I had to pressure him to make the purchase in the first place."

They stood, and Wilma extended her hand to seal the deal. They shook on it.

Red and Wilma left the Ewa house and drove in silence back to Red's apartment. Although the deals appeared to be going smoothly, his pain and general discomfort continued to grow with the miles they covered. He felt like a pot about to boil over. He needed the Ewa house now. It was the only way to get his hands on John's body without being discovered. *If only that big bastard hadn't gotten so nosy, none of this*

184

would have been necessary. How the hell had Big John found out about me cooking the books? What had possessed him to call in the auditors? So what? I had "borrowed" a few thousand here and there from the business? I intended to pay every penny of it back—eventually. It was all Big John's fault.

* * *

It had been dark for nearly two hours. Leilani's watch indicated 8:50 p.m. Almost time. Leilani, in the seat behind the rear door of the bus, observed her fellow passengers. An elderly Asian man with two shopping bags sat sideways by the front door. His head nodded near the brink of dozing off. A local woman with a whining preschooler sat a few rows back. Two teenage girls chatted three rows in back of the woman. Leilani pulled the stop cord. The air brakes hissed, the doors opened, and she stepped to the curb. The bus engine roared to full power and accelerated once more, leaving her in a cloud of carbon monoxide and uncertainty. She stood in the illumination of the corner street light. She could see nothing beyond the edges of its artificial brightness. And when she stepped away from the curb into the shadows of the sidewalk, she noticed a shopkeeper locking up and walking away down the far side of Waialae. A lone figure stood in the doorway of a bar. The hair on her neck bristled.

She walked slowly up the avenue, encountering no one else. There were storefronts—some dimly lit, others totally dark. She quickened her steps as she passed the darkest doorways. Her eyes strained to see around every corner.

The young tough sprang out of the shadowed recesses. He'd taken her by surprise, blocking her path. Glistening tattoos bulged out of his grubby tank top. He spoke.

"Okay, *sistah*, you wanna see your *bruddah*, Kekoa? Follow me, yah?"

Leilani trailed after him, searching right and left for signs of humanity, a friendly face, anyone who'd help if she needed it. As they passed through a longer stretch between street lighting, the sky seemed blacker—no stars.

"Hey, wait up," she called to him. "You're going too fast."

He turned, but just for an instant. She could barely see his face—just eyes and teeth. He said nothing. A few steps later he turned into an alley and kept going. She stopped—hesitant to leave the main drag, her lifeline. Looking around, she saw only one man with a shopping bag lumbering slowly uphill across the street.

"Where are you taking me?" she yelled after her guide.

"I' see your *bruddah*, yah?"

"But where is he? How far is it?"

"You see 'im soon."

She cautiously started down the alley after him. What else could she do? She'd come this far to find Kekoa, and the guy seemed to know him. Some distance in, she heard a screen door slam and the din of heavy metal music. A few yards farther, the tough opened a small gate in a fence, a broken row of waist-high pickets. He stepped through. A red brick wall ran along a second alley on the other side of the fence—a blank wall without a door or a window. She stepped through the gate and over a crushed cardboard carton. Fence pickets and scattered trash lay on the ground. A queasiness grew in her stomach, but she followed anyway.

He waited for her to catch up with him.

"Here?" she asked doubtfully.

"Here!"

When Leilani stood opposite him, the tough shoved her backward toward the wall. She heard a click. His right arm came up flashing a switchblade. She flinched and tried to run, but he shifted the knife to his left hand, threatening her passage. She tried to move in the other direction, but the knife flew to his right hand once more, barely grazing her cheek. Trapped.

Leilani began to shake. Beads of cold sweat sprouted from her pores. She thought it was blood.

"What do you want from me? I'll scream." She wasn't sure she could.

"You scream, you bleed. Gimme your money, your wallet."

Leilani slid her fanny pack around front to remove her wallet. In one moment of mistrust he slashed the long blade in a threatening arc from left to right in front of her. A full mouth of crooked teeth sneered at her. She froze. He came closer, waving the knife back and forth, feinting, taunting her. He thrust the knife toward her belly, but deliberately short of its mark. Spooked, she hopped backward.

He lunged a second time. Leilani backed against the wall and stumbled over the cardboard carton. Her left hand reached behind her for the rough brick. It kept her from going down altogether. Her right hand curled around an abandoned fence picket leaning against the wall. She watched him withdraw the knife and move in closer to make still another taunting thrust. A flash of perception hit her. He didn't want just her money. He wanted her, too. And there was no Kekoa. A sudden surge of adrenaline rushed through Leilani. She swung the fence picket up under his knife-wielding arm and struck his left elbow. The blow caught his funny bone, and as she followed through, the knife flew up and over the fence.

He stood stunned, holding his elbow. She swung again—not targeting any particular part of his body, but him...him...him! He held up an arm to protect his face and a rusty nail gouged into the flesh of his right forearm. She ripped downward. He screamed. She ripped still harder. In the instant before her next blow, he pulled out the picket with its rusty barb and ran down the alley, away from the avenue, cradling his wounded arm. She found her voice and screamed.

Then she saw the bloodstains on her jeans—his blood. Her whole body shook. Loud footsteps coming from Waialae Avenue caused her to spin about. A massive shadow moved toward her. She raised the picket again in a baseball grip and the footsteps stopped.

"Leilani, it's me!" the figure said.

"Alex!"

She dropped the picket, leapt into Alex's embrace, and began to sob. He held her tightly.

"You should've screamed earlier," he scolded as he led her out of the alley. "I would have gotten here sooner."

"I tried, I couldn't."

"You promised me that you wouldn't have anything to do with him."

"There wasn't any way I couldn't. He knew Kekoa's name and the fact that I was looking for my brother. He sounded so genuine. He was my only clue. I had to follow him."

"I should never have let you do this," Alex said, his voice shaking. "It was too dangerous."

"You couldn't have stopped me. But I'm glad that you followed me anyway."

He took her hand, and they fled to the car.

187

Chapter 26
Kasalan: A Filipino Wedding

KEKOA SQUIRMED and fidgeted, uncomfortable in his new clothes: black leather loafers instead of flip-flopping slippahs, a small-patterned aloha shirt in fashionably faded blues and greens, and sharply creased black chino trousers. The nervous wedding guest got off the bus at Weed Circle just beyond Haleiwa town after riding halfway around the island to the northwest shore. The bus roared away, leaving a billowing cloud of dust and exhaust fumes. The Ballesteros wedding would be the very first in his fourteen years.

He stood alone on the deserted circle. Minutes passed, and he wondered if they'd forgotten him. Then he recognized Enrico's pickup truck swing around the circle and jerk to a stop. Andy slid closer to his brother to make room for his friend.

Enrico parked on the road out front of the Ballesteros home. A chair blocked off the driveway. White wreaths with Styrofoam wedding bells adorned the back of it. Wide red and purple ribbon ran the length of the drive to lead the guests to the backyard.

The Ballesteros house, with its tin roof and wrap-around lanai, stood on concrete blocks. Seven crowded rooms fitted cheerfully into the two-story wood-frame house of single-walled construction. For the occasion, it sported a fresh overcoat of white paint.

Kekoa carried a large box of fancy fruit-filled cookies he'd baked. For his wedding gift, he had painted, glazed, and fired a nine-inch piece of ceramic tile to be used as a trivet. He gave his gifts to Enrico, who carried them into the house.

A stately old Chinese banyan tree dominated the left side of the backyard. Under its sprawling shade, a gray-haired man sang and strummed *kundiman* music on a guitar-like instrument made of bamboo. Within arm's reach lay a ukulele and a set of *ipus*, drums made from bottle gourds.

188

Cry Ohana

While the Ballesteros boys finished their special chores, Kekoa wandered about on his own. He chose a spot close to the guitarist, who winked at him, grateful for an audience.

"*Mabuhay! Mabuhay!*" Kekoa heard Papa Ballesteros greet the guests in a Tagalog dialect. Then the groom and his party arrived. He wore a white shirt with a frilly front, white pants, and white shoes. A red silk sash ran from his right shoulder across his chest to the left hip. The groom's family and friends moved to the arched trellis. Soon guests filled every seat, and their children spread blankets and sat on the grass. A padre and two altar boys in white and gold garb had prepared and sanctified a holy altar area in front of the trellis, creating a chapel among the trees.

Musicians in ankle-length skirts called *patadyong* took their places. Suddenly, the music came alive, powerful and loud. Everyone stood to watch the procession emerging from the back door of the house. Maria, the only bridesmaid, appeared first, a little bird in a frothy pink dress. She walked slowly and demurely, as she had been rehearsed to do.

Then came the *Ninong* and *Niang* sponsors, godparents, and parents. At last Esmeralda stepped out on her father's arm. The bride's beauty awed Kekoa. Esme had Maria's face and sleek black hair crowned in a *haku lei*, a head wreath of small white orchids.

Leading the procession, Maria stole looks to her right and left. Kekoa strained on tiptoe to catch her eye. He waved. For just an instant their eyes met, and Maria's shy smile turned impish with delight.

The guests took their seats again. Kekoa watched the couple exchange rings and vows. Then the priest poured the *Arras*, thirteen silver coins, through the groom's cupped hands, trickling like a waterfall through the bride's open palms to the sacristan's plate below.

Ringing bells heralded the traditional *sanctus* blessings by the priest. Then the marriage couple stood beneath a veil while they were bound together by the *yugal*, a nuptial cord of flowers. The ceremony concluded with the blessing of the enlightenment candles.

The crowd converged on the couple in a rush of kissing and hugging. According to some master plan, the entire yard underwent a transformation. Chairs, benches, and tables were rearranged to accommodate the wedding feast. Some of the men strung a huge blue plastic tarp from tree to tree to form an enormous umbrella of shade for the reception.

"Hi, Kekoa!"

He turned to find Maria before him. Her slight body bobbed with excitement. "I'm so glad you're here. Mama's putting your cookies out. Come on, let's talk!" Her words spilled out so fast that he blushed. He wasn't used to so much attention, and certainly never from such a vision in pink. She led him to a cluster of lawn chairs at the edge of the yard and plopped down, sliding her bare feet out of new white Mary Janes.

"It was beautiful…you look so pretty, Maria," he whispered.

She laughed. "Thank you! Let me tell you about Esmeralda's bridal shower. It was so neat!" Maria explained how the guests brought out rolls of white toilet paper and wrapped it around the bride to simulate a wedding dress, every detail—from bridal veil to long gloves. "We all laughed so hard, all afternoon."

Kekoa listened in puzzled silence. Did all brides have so much fun? Such joking and goofing off held no place in his own life.

Maria jumped up and pulled him by the hand. "Let's go find Andy and eat. You should see the food."

They finally located Andy—with his face squashed into the huge sagging breasts of Auntie Philiamena. Eventually, Auntie found the mercy to let him up for air, fondly patted her nephew on the head, and turned to seek her next prey. Maria ducked behind Andy so she wouldn't be selected.

The kitchen rocked with joyous commotion. The screen door repeatedly squeaked, straining to its limit and slamming as the Ballesteros women rushed food to fill every inch of the tables. Sweet and pungent aromas wafted through the air. Auntie Rosa ladled out *ginataang mongo*—pudding of mung beans, rice, and coconut milk. Auntie Theresa rushed to replace the *maruya*, banana fritters, which kept disappearing quickly.

At one end of the buffet tables stood a card table covered with a white cloth. On it sat a huge glass punchbowl with a lei of orchids surrounding the base. Chattering women approached with small bowls of cut-up mango, papaya, and other fresh fruit and dumped the contents into the nearly overflowing punchbowl.

"Everyone brings fruit salad to a wedding," Maria said. "It's a tradition to sweeten the couple's future."

"C'mon, let's eat," urged Andy.

Kekoa watched Andy and followed his every move. They each took a napkin and rolled it around a fork, knife, and spoon, tucking the rolls into their pockets to keep their hands free while they sampled every delicacy in sight.

"What's this?" Kekoa pointed to a purple pudding covered with coconut flakes.

"It's *ube maja*, made from yams," answered Maria. "But my favorite is *halo-halo*. Have some!" She piled layers of cooked fruits and sweet vegetables topped with shaved ice onto their plates.

The three moved to a picnic table bordering the great circle where guests were dancing. Maria sat down with the boys, but only picked at her food. Kekoa had tried not to overload his plate—so many unusual, luscious tastes.

The music started again, this time romantic and folksy. Toasts came from booming voices all over the yard. The bride and groom kissed after each toast. The music grew louder, the beat throbbing, enticing the couple to enter the circle. Kekoa watched. As family and friends cut in to dance with either the bride or groom, an envelope or a bill of currency was pinned to the bride's dress. Soon they covered her entire gown.

He tried to shrug off a tug at his elbow. Maria stood looking down at him. Her eyes darted between his face and the great circle—she wanted to dance.

His nut-brown face turned a deep shade of purple and he stammered, "I—I don't know how to dance."

"I can teach you."

"Okay, but not here, not now."

Maria understood and instead led him to a rocky knoll at the edge of the property line. They sat side by side on a large slab of lava rock. He talked more easily now—without fear of fumbling through a dance. His stammer disappeared as quickly as it had appeared.

But he didn't have to say much. Maria bubbled like a recycling fountain. She had led the bridal procession! She told Kekoa about the candlelight procession the night before where Padre Armondo and the engaged couple led everyone around the outside of the church twice.

"Sounds very nice," Kekoa said, absently looking over at the newlyweds. He did a double-take as he focused on a woman in a blue dress hugging the bride. A woman with bobbed hair. *Isn't she the same Japanese lady I saw at Mama's grave?*

Maria's voice bubbled on. "Maybe now that Esmeralda's married, they'll notice I've grown up, too. It's always Esme this and Esme

191

that."

He barely heard her. The woman's presence hypnotized him.

Maria could tell that she'd lost his attention. "What or who are you so interested in over there?"

"That woman talking to Esmeralda. Do you know who she is?"

"I've never seen her before," said Maria. "Want me to find out?"

"Oh, no! ...Yeah, maybe, if you can."

"Oh, I can, all right." Maria jumped up.

"But she can't know who's asking. I don't want her to see me, either."

"I can keep a secret, you know," Maria announced. "I'll find out what I can from Esme. But then you have to tell me what this is about. Promise?"

He nodded. It was several minutes before she returned, beaming.

"Well?" he asked.

"Her name is Lori Yamashita. Esme used to work for her in the steno pool. Lori is a paralegal or something. Anyway, they got to be friends. Kekoa, what's this about?"

Kekoa found himself very uncomfortable with the prospect of answering. But Maria soon drew him out and learned the story of his flight from Red Murphy. Slowly, very slowly, he told her everything, including his frustration over not finding his sister.

"But what's this Lori got to do with it?"

He told her about the cemetery and why he hesitated to approach the woman. He had to remain in hiding and didn't know if he could trust her.

When Miss Yamashita turned and faced their direction, Kekoa looked away and began to sweat. Feeling the armpits of his aloha shirt dampen, he wished he'd never come to the wedding. He had to get away, but how?

"Let's take a little walk," Maria said. He nodded. Maybe the Yamashita woman would be gone when they got back. Maria took him by the hand and led him to the road. He recognized the barn behind the Ballesteros property where he and Andy had witnessed the cockfight. He quickened his step. The road curved and narrowed to a trail, gently rising and falling until they were enveloped by a patch of rain forest, green and dark. They stopped to lean over the rail of a footbridge and peer down into a series of cascading pools. Suddenly, Maria kissed him on the cheek. Embarrassed, she ran quickly toward home. He trotted after her.

Enrico met them at the end of the driveway and told them the bride and groom were about to leave. "Best you say your a hui hous now! I'll run you back to the bus stop in about ten minutes."

Kekoa looked down at Maria. "I need to find your parents and thank them." *That woman must've left by now*, he reassured himself. But Lori Yamashita suddenly appeared out of the circle of dancers, calling him by name, hurrying toward him. He had to get away. Whirling around, he plunged through a knot of guests and bolted toward the far side of the yard. Only the row of buffet tables stood in his way. He cut to one end and pivoted around the punchbowl table. But his loafer hooked onto a table leg. He turned and watched in horror as the table tipped and fell. The glorious punchbowl hit the stone walk with an earth-shaking crack and—as if in slow motion—split in two. Fruit flew everywhere. Juice oozed into the ground.

A shriek pierced the air as Auntie Philiamina charged toward him. "Look what you've done, boy! Now the bride and groom will have bad luck. Bad luck, do you hear me? It will follow them always!"

Kekoa sputtered, "I didn't mean to!"

Mama Ballesteros rushed over to Auntie Philiamina and screamed at her. "Don't say that, you vicious old lady. Don't you dare put a curse on my children!"

Kekoa hesitated for one agonizing second. Miss Yamashita stood only a few feet away, frozen in place, clutching her purse. "I'm sorry," he whimpered to Mama, and then he ran. Down the driveway, down the road. Maria's voice called after him, getting fainter and fainter. He ran until his chest ached, until the voices and music faded to nothing. Under the setting sun, he began the five-mile trek to the bus stop.

Just before darkness fell, a pickup truck rumbled behind him. It slowed to a stop and Enrico motioned for him to get in. With head lowered in shame, Kekoa climbed aboard—grateful for the ride, but he just couldn't face the driver.

Enrico elbowed him in the ribs. "Hey, man. It was an accident, yah? It's forgotten already."

But Kekoa wouldn't forget it. Not ever.

Chapter 27
Who's Who—The Morning

LORI STUCK her head into Terumi Fujita's office and chirped "Good morning" with a cheerfulness she didn't feel. She could have saved her breath, the office was empty. Next, she went to Yoshiro Fujita's door to offer him the morning's tea. A sign on the senior partner's doorknob stopped her: MEETING IN PROGRESS, DO NOT DISTURB. She deliberated for a moment, then turned away.

"Ah, there you are, Lori." Terumi appeared in the doorway. "I'd like you to join us in this meeting."

"Of course." With her zipper-edged day book and a legal pad under one arm, she stepped inside. She seated herself at the table, nodded formally to Paul Wong and Coland Benfield-Rice, and then acknowledged the senior Fujita.

"And this is Hal Perry," said Yosh.

She turned to face the client across the table. Two aluminum walking canes lay hooked over the back of the adjacent chair. Her mouth fell open. Confusion flooded her features.

"You!" she said, her voice squeaking with uncertainty. "You're the man at Punchbowl!"

"Yes, I am, Lori, dear."

"Lori, dear? I don't understand." Her jagged tone cut like a serrated knife. "Do I know you, Mr. Perry?"

"A long time ago you knew me," Hal murmured. He did not look directly at her face.

Lori's black eyes narrowed under her finely lined eyebrows. She pushed her chair back, stood up, and walked around the long table, approaching him cautiously. Still he didn't look up. Silence draped the room.

Hal took the canes and used them to push himself up and out of his chair to an awkward standing position. He slowly and purposely

194

turned to face her. "Look beyond my scars, gray hair, and mustache. Who do you see?"

She stared back at him, scrutinizing every feature until she was certain. "Oh, my God," she cried, "it's you! Hank Pualoa! You're alive! But...I would never have recognized you."

Then, without warning, pent-up years of anger pushed her on. "Where on God's earth have you been? Why did you leave those precious children? What kind of a monster are you to have run off like that? How dare you call me dear after all these years? And what's this Hal Perry business?"

The torrent of her own words left her breathless. Blushing, she bowed stiffly to the others, excused herself for the outburst, and returned to her own place at the table.

A shocked Yosh leaned back in his chair and said, "At the risk of stating the obvious, I take it you two know each other."

"Yes, you might say that," Lori cried. "I was maid of honor at his wedding and his late wife's best friend." She turned back to glower at Hank.

Yosh surrendered his place at the head of the table, saying, "I see. Well, that certainly complicates matters, doesn't it? In any event, enough questions, Lori! Hank Pualoa is our client. As Hal Perry, private investigator, he is also our employee. This might seem a bit confusing for you, so I'll ask him to come to the head of the table and enlighten the rest of us." He paused for a moment, adjusted his horn-rimmed glasses, and said, "Lori, I feel I owe you an apology for not filling you in on his assignment with us."

Hank exchanged places with Yosh. His awkwardness in rising to meet Lori had been more emotional than physical. He'd tried to evoke her sympathy—a stupid move. Easing himself into the armchair at the head of the table, he paused to collect his thoughts and began. "Lori called me a monster. I wish to God things were different, but she has a point. I got sent to jail for my crimes—a gut too full of beer my only excuse. I've destroyed my *ohana*, my family, and everything else worthwhile. I am that monster."

Hank stared at the ceiling tiles; a single tear slipped down his cheek. He could not face his accuser. "The *keiki* and their grandmother rejected me—not surprising, I suppose, she was my wife's mother. It seemed to me that I had no choice but to run. I suppose you think I'm making excuses for myself."

Lori nodded vigorously, and Hank winced, the virtual sting no less than a whip's lash. But Hank stumbled on. "Twelve lousy years I've been running—from myself, mostly." He launched into the narrative of his exile.

"Yosh here can tell you, I provided for my kids—their crazy grandmother, too. I sent money to the trust all those years. I sold or transferred everything I owned to start that trust."

"Where did you go on the Mainland?" asked Lori.

"Seattle. I found work there as a heavy equipment operator in construction. As a Teamster in good standing, I had no trouble finding work with a decent paycheck. The construction jobs made a gypsy of me, taking me to Portland and into northern California, then down to L.A. I still drank often and heavily, but never on the job or before going to work. Then..." Hank's hand unconsciously touched the red scar on his neck as he told them of his encounter with Coke-head Joe and the resolve that came afterward. "I took a pledge that day to get off and stay off the booze."

"I say! What did you do then?" Coland asked.

"Well," said Hank, "I decided I needed another fresh start. Couldn't take it anymore, so I bought another plane ticket, this time to Baltimore, Maryland."

"Why Baltimore?" asked Paul.

"It's on the East Coast. Just about as far away as I could get and still be in the continental U.S. It sounds corny to say this, but I still hadn't learned that I couldn't run away from myself."

Hank stopped talking, took a deep breath, and ran callused fingers through his thick hair. Aware that Lori had been staring at his shirt, he glanced down: three buttons open revealed salt-and-pepper chest hair. A spasm of shame shot through him. Shame and something else: vanity. Could she find him attractive? Did he have feelings for her, too?

Hank shrugged off his fleeting thoughts and struggled on with the story of his exile. "Baltimore turned out to be a good choice. The old harbor was being transformed from warehouses and slums into world-class real estate. Plenty of good-paying construction work: office buildings, fancy hotels, condos. One week I even hit the lottery for twenty thousand, enough to start investing—a little real estate and a few good stocks. As the amounts grew, I leased some heavy equipment on my own.

"And I'll have you know I never neglected the trust," he said, his voice rising in self-defense. He coughed and vainly tried to clear his throat.

Lori rose and brought him a silver tray with a pitcher of ice water and glasses on it from the sideboard. Her hand shook as she poured.

He drained a full glass and continued hesitantly. "Ten years later, it took a mean tumble down a flight of stairs to bring me to my senses. It's been a long recovery, and I've got some to go yet. It gave me plenty of time to think—and I swore that, God willing, I'd return to Honolulu and make things right with my family.

"But my kids were gone. Big John had disappeared into thin air and I'd counted on him to look after everyone. To top things off, Grandmother Eme had passed away. I couldn't call Red. I encountered him in Baltimore and he was part of the problem—a big part, but I don't want to go into that right now. It's a long, ugly story. So I called my good friend Yoshiro Fujita.

"Yosh managed to locate Leilani through the trust and the Wong family. I'm very grateful to them for what they're doing for her." Hank looked directly at Paul.

Paul chose that moment to speak. "With all due respect, sir, I find these revelations quite disturbing. Why haven't you tried to contact Leilani yet? Masako and I would be willing to bring the two of you together. Although she's come to love us, she has been in great anguish over the loss of her own family. She's tried hard to hide it, but Numi has quietly let us know. I'm sure Leilani would agree to a reunion with you."

"I wish I could be so sure," Hank said. "I'm not convinced she's forgiven the father who abandoned her." He pressed his lips together and fought back tears. "Or ever will forgive me."

Terumi interrupted. "Allow me to get to the main purpose of this meeting. My father and I have uncovered a gross conflict of interest in our land dealings. Our Japanese client wanted to purchase land for his Ocean Vail development project. This client offered Red Murphy a generous bonus for delivery of all the land parcels as one package. And Murphy accepted his offer without telling me he was one of the trustees of the Pualoa children's trust. When Dad found out about the deal, he was furious. I apologize for the lack of communication between my father and me. Now we have to protect my client and our firm's reputation."

Father and son nodded in agreement before Terumi continued. "In return for clear title to all these parcels, Murphy personally stood to make millions. I became more suspicious when I learned that a firm called Rodminn Realty, and not Murphy, had been buying up the real estate of interest. We needed answers." Everyone nodded.

From the other end of the table Yosh said, "I decided to start checking up on Murphy—without his knowledge, of course. At that point we hired Hank as a private investigator to find out if Murphy had any connection to Rodminn Realty. So we applied for a PI license in the name of Harold 'Hal' Perry."

Hank told them he had followed Murphy fourteen hours a day for nearly five weeks. By day, Red appeared to be a competent business-man, legitimately managing the affairs of Finast Construction Company. After dark he moved in the sleaziest of circles, spending a lot of time in the company of hooker Cindy Chou. "But that in itself isn't worth prosecuting."

At the mention of Cindy's name Coland squirmed in his seat.

Hank pursued his story. "All the parcels, presumably under Murphy's personal control, were traded to Rodminn Realty using cashier's checks. They're like cash, of course, untraceable."

Yosh commented: "Murphy has every legal right to dispose of his own property as he wishes, but it appears he transferred other properties as well." He reached for a small poster lying flat on the table and held it up for everyone to see.

RODMINN REALTY
(Ownership and Control of 20 Parcels)

Edgar Murphy   4 Parcels (Deeded directly to Murphy)
John Pualoa   4 Parcels (Ownership claimed by Murphy)
Hank Pualoa   2 Parcels (Ownership claimed by Murphy)

Pualoa Children 2 Parcels (Keystone lots)
Adjacent Land   8 Parcels (Acquired by Rodminn from local families)

"Hank found that only three shareholders of record exist. Horace Rodder, who passed away some weeks ago, left his shares to a local woman named Peke Palaneke. She seems to be an innocent player in all this. The remaining shares belong to Wilma Minnet and one Edwin Mulrooney, who appear to reside in a postal box at Makiki Station."

"I'm convinced Mulrooney and Murphy are one and the same, but I can't prove it yet," Hank said. "However, I can prove that Wilma Minnet is Murphy's ex-wife." He reached into his briefcase and slapped a pile of documents on the table. "The ex is back in Honolulu, shacking up at Red's place. I ran a police record on her. She's clean. I don't know what part she plays in this scheme. She could even be a patsy." His demeanor had shifted from guilt-ridden supplicant to take-charge investigator. He sat up straighter, his broad back erect.

"Coland," Hank said, "I tailed Murphy to your rendezvous up at Punchbowl and recorded the conversation. The blackmail threat, it's all on tape."

"I was there, I heard it, too," Lori chimed in. "I didn't know the connection then, so I passed the information along to the Wongs and Leilani. I could do no less for Malia." She glanced over at Hank. He smiled back, half-encouraged that she eventually might be an ally instead of an enemy.

"For your information and certainly not for the record," Coland broke in, "the extortion threat has been entirely defused. I've recovered all the damaging material and would like to restore my life to normalcy. I'm ashamed of what transpired, but I am not a criminal. The main thing is that my wife has full knowledge of what happened, and thank God, she's forgiven me. However, I would like to see that black-hearted bounder get his due."

"We'll get to that this afternoon," Yosh said. "Why don't we break for lunch now? I've taken the liberty of sending out."

Terumi began a quiet conversation with Coland while they waited. "I thought Murphy still had one photo in his possession."

Coland did not expect the question and wanted to brush it off, but Terumi's intense gaze left him trapped.

"Ah, yes, Murphy did. Fortunately, Miss Chou recovered the photo. Destroyed it by burning, I should think."

"And you trust her in this matter?" posed Terumi.

Coland blanched. "Do I have a choice?"

"Perhaps not," Terumi said, his face a mask of respect. But he couldn't quite suppress the glint of amusement in his keen gray eyes.

Chapter 28
What's What—The Afternoon

"SO, PAUL, what's Lani like?" An embarrassed Hank bit into his pride to pose the questions he'd been burning all morning to ask. "Is she well? Is she pretty? She's just seventeen now, isn't she? I mean, how's she turning out?" He jabbed his fork into his macaroni salad. "A helluva thing," he muttered, "having to ask a stranger about your own daughter."

Hank's questions caught Paul with a mouthful of sushi. He laid down his wooden chopsticks and finished chewing.

"You have a lovely, healthy daughter," Paul said. "A good student with a fine mind. You can be proud of her. I know we are. She's like one of our own." He pulled a wallet from his back pocket. Shuffling through some photos, he offered one of Leilani and Numi standing side by side in front of the house. "I can still make the arrangements, you know."

"Oh, God," said Hank. He took the photo and studied it. "Soon, but not just yet. Once you let her know I'm back, we'll both need time to adjust to a meeting. I don't think either one of us could stand another rejection right now."

"You may think you need time. But the longer you wait, the more Leilani might wonder what's holding you back. In fact, your reluctance might give her more reasons not to forgive you. That's the way I see it, anyway." Paul waited while Hank poured a cup of green tea from the china pot. "By the way, don't you need those to get around?" He indicated the two canes Hank had left at the table.

"For short distances I can do fine without them."

Following lunch, Hank returned to the front of the room and launched into the toughest aspect of his briefing. "A few weeks ago, purely by chance, I met a youngster around Kekoa's age. He called himself Keith, but wouldn't give me his last name. Keith didn't quite fit the description of Kekoa that I had fixed in my mind. Of course, I

200

didn't have anything to go by, just a baby picture. He was only twenty-months old when I left."

In painstaking detail, Hank recounted each of the incidents that had brought them together. He described the night Red chased the boy down Maunakea Street during Chinese New Year; and the school construction site, where the wrecking ball crushed the hood of the police car containing the boy. As luck would have it, Hank—as P.I. Hal—had just happened to be there both times and had rescued Kekoa.

Yosh could barely conceal his annoyance. "Hank, why haven't you told me this before?"

"What was there to tell? After the wrecking ball disaster I offered to drive him home. He accepted, but in the car the kid clammed up! Wouldn't tell me where he lived. Made me let him off at the corner of University and King." Hank bit his lower lip. "Since then, I've been putting two and two together, some things the boy told me. First, Keith said he had proof that Red Murphy had killed his uncle. Said he actually saw it happen! Second, when I told him I was a private investigator, he wanted me to find his missing sister. Now I realize I've let him slip through my fingers. Damn! I still don't know how to reach him. He does know how to reach me, though. I gave him my Hal Perry business card. Maybe, just maybe he'll contact me. Listen, if Keith is my son, then he witnessed Red murdering Big John, my own brother!"

A shock wave followed his words.

He took a deep breath and glanced around the table before continuing. "Big John was also my partner and best friend. I don't know how Red killed him, or why, or where the body is, but I do believe my son does. I'm assuming that Red knows Kekoa witnessed the murder." Hank slammed his broad hand down on the table. "And now Red is stalking my son with a mind to kill him."

Yosh intervened. "The boy appears to be quite street smart to have evaded Murphy this long. Yet he doesn't seem to think you are the enemy. You've at least established some sort of bond with him."

Terumi asked, "Aren't you presuming a great deal here? How do you know the boy's telling the truth?"

"I don't," Hank admitted. "I'm going on gut feeling. I'm convinced he is my son. Besides, why would Kekoa lie to me, a perfect stranger?"

Lori got up from her chair and slipped into one beside Hank.

She took his hand in her own. "He may call you yet," she said.

Paul rubbed his smooth chin and said, "Maybe that explains why Kekoa got off the bus and ran from Leilani and me on the street the last time we were at this office. He saw Murphy with us."

"Exactly!" said Hank.

"Meanwhile," said Terumi, "it's imperative that we get Murphy off the streets before he gets to Kekoa."

"I agree," said Hank. "But what's our next step?"

Lori responded with a tremor in her voice. "Several weeks ago I dropped by Diamond Head Cemetery with flowers for Malia. Someone was already there, a teenager lying on top of her grave. He was crying. It could have been Kekoa. But when I approached, he ran away. I called to him, but he kept going. He had a bicycle with him. So, it's my guess that he's living somewhere in the vicinity. I suggested to Leilani that she leave a message for him at the grave."

Paul added, "Leilani and Numi went to the grave last week and left a message and telephone number there in a clear plastic envelope. It might be weeks or months before he returns, though."

Hank responded. "Short of cruising the streets of Kahala, Kaimuki, and Diamond Head, there's little that any of us can do. It's unfortunate that none of us have a recent photograph of Kekoa. I suppose that's something only good parents have. If I'd been a good father and been there for him, none of this would have happened."

"That's true. But don't you go maudlin on us now, Hank Pualoa. It won't do Kekoa any good," scolded Lori.

"Damn it, woman! What the hell do you want from me?" Hank flared up. "I'm between a rock and a hard place."

"You could listen to the rest of what I have to say," Lori answered.

"There's more?"

"Yes. I saw the same boy yesterday at a friend's wedding out in Mokuleia." Lori described how he'd panicked and run from her again. "I—"

Yosh interrupted. "You weren't able to find out his name? If he was a wedding guest? Someone in the family could have told you that much."

Lori shook her head. "Esme's off on her honeymoon and her mother refused to tell me his name. She admitted that the boy was her

202

son's friend. He's about the same age as Kekoa, but he avoided me, too. There's a younger sister, Maria. She wasn't talking either. I got the feeling they were protecting Kekoa. It was like a conspiracy."

"Maybe I could talk to them," suggested Hank.

"I think you'd only frighten them," Lori answered. "We'd better wait two weeks for Esme to come home. She's the only one who'd trust me."

"But two weeks might be too late," Hank pleaded.

Yosh said, "I think we must assume the worst: that Murphy already knows where to find Kekoa and is now only waiting for a chance to get at him. We need to move quickly."

Suddenly, the two Fujitas pulled their chairs together and began chatting rapidly in Japanese. Everyone turned to watch them, and they continued until they became aware of the eyes upon them.

Yosh stood and apologized. "My son and I have formulated a plan."

He detailed every aspect of their four-point strategy and scheduled another meeting for the following morning.

As they all stood to leave, Paul placed his arm on Hank's shoulder. "Masako and I have never heard Leilani speak ill of her father. With your permission, I should like to explore her feelings about a possible reunion."

Hank could only nod in agreement.

* * *

Red sat at his desk in the living room, studying documents he had brought home from the office. He leaned back for a moment and heard a sharp creak coming from underneath the swivel chair. It startled him, but his mind returned to the meeting he intended to schedule with Coland Benfield-Rice. Red counted on bluffing the banker into thinking he had yet another print of Coland cavorting in bed with Cindy. He shook his head. How dumb could that broad be to give up all the prints and negatives?

The phone rang, disturbing his reflective mood. "Murphy," he answered. "Yes, Mr. Lynch…You want to arrange a closing for the Ewa house on Wednesday afternoon? Excellent! Oceanic Mortgage Company at three o'clock? I'll be there. See you then."

Red settled back in his chair, but jumped up as he heard a second creeeak! Then cluuunk! The spring had sprung, leaving the swivel chair to flop backward as he barely made it to his feet.

"Damn!" he bellowed. He heard the spring fall to the floor. Dropping to his hands and knees, he started to search for it, when he heard the front door open. Wilma had returned.

She set her purse on the coffee table and grinned when she spotted him. "At last, I've brought you to your knees," she quipped. But when she saw the storm clouds gather on his face, she took a step back.

Red dragged himself to his feet. "No one brings Edgar Murphy to his knees, especially not you," he growled. "Remember that!" He'd already forgotten the broken spring. "How'd it go with Peke?"

"Fine. I got her to sign over the shares and gave her the check." Wilma dropped the envelope on the desk just as the phone rang. She picked up the receiver and handed it to Red. He sat down on a corner of the desk.

"Yeah, Murphy here. Tomorrow? Nine-thirty? Yeah, I'll be there." He hung up.

"Who was that?" she asked.

"Sugarman's Bank," said Red. "There's a trust meeting in the morning."

"Then why are you looking so nervous? You wanted the meeting, didn't you?"

"Yeah," he replied. "But Coland didn't call me. His secretary did. The short notice makes me suspicious that something else is up. Oh, by the way, I settle on the Ewa house on Wednesday."

"Good." Wilma bent over, picked up the stray coil spring from under the desk, and handed it to him. "Is this what you were looking for?"

Red snatched the broken spring from her hand and examined it, wondering if he held a premonition of things to come—things about to come apart.

Chapter 29
Trust in Trustees

TUESDAY MORNING brought a drizzling December rain. Streamlets of water slid down the tall arched windows of First Sugarman's Bank.

After steaming coffee and warm malasadas had been distributed in the boardroom upstairs, the trustees took their seats around the great table. Coland welcomed Terumi and Lori as a support team to provide legal counsel to the trustees.

Red shifted uneasily in his leather armchair. The sudden appearance of outside legal counsel spooked him. Still, he felt that the voting could be controlled. He wiped a few grains of sugar from the corners of his mouth and directed an exaggerated wink in Coland's direction.

"How's that lovely wife of yours?" he asked.

"Er…eh…fine." Coland scowled.

"Good! Let's get to the voting, then. We're all busy people here."

"Not just yet. There's some trustee business that must take precedence."

Coland's words ran a chill through Red.

"First," Coland said, holding up a sheet of paper, "Miss Yamashita has a notarized power of attorney from Hank Pualoa, enabling her to represent his position on trust business. Because it is Hank's revocable trust, we hardly need a vote to accept her as a bona fide trustee." He turned to Lori. "So let's welcome her to the trust."

"Let me see that!" Red snatched the paper out of Coland's hand and read through it several times. "It's dated yesterday!" he exploded. "Hank's alive?" Visibly stunned, Red fell silent and slack-jawed. He could not immediately comprehend the full impact of this tactic, but one thing was starkly plain: his ability to obtain clear title to the entire Pualoa landholdings was now in jeopardy. His done deal was taking a nose-dive.

"Second," said Coland, taking the document back, "because Paul Wong was appointed to represent Hank's interests, he would normally have stepped down in favor of Miss Yamashita. However, due to an unexpected conflict of interest, I'm resigning my position as trustee and selecting Paul to serve in my place. Paul has previously served as trustee, so there can be no question as to his suitability. To be sure, I ask for a show of hands. Exercising my right to choose my successor, there is my hand and yours, Lori. Opposed? No one. It's settled then. The board of trustees now comprises Lori Yamashita, Paul Wong, and Ed Murphy. Paul, would you take over for me now?"

It happened so fast that Red could find no rationale to intercede in the proceedings. He could hardly challenge Coland's conflict of interest without criminally exposing himself. As for the power of attorney, it was Pualoa's notarized signature. Red felt things rapidly slipping away.

Paul introduced the next order of business. "Coland has presented us with sufficient evidence that you, Edgar Murphy, have not only misused your position of trust on this body to further your personal interests, but you have resorted to extortion to achieve that end."

"What?" Red shouted, scrambling to his feet. "This is preposterous. I'll sue the lot of you for defamation of character."

Terumi addressed Red. "It is well within the rights of this body to conduct censure proceedings. True, this is not a court of law. Nor are its findings binding. However, I believe it is in your best personal interest to hear the other trustees out. I can tell you that the evidence they have accumulated will hold up in a court of law. As long as the proceedings are confined to this room, you do not have a case for slander or defamation of character. You can, of course, take the censure findings to a court of law."

Lori reached into her purse and pulled out a small tape recorder. She laid it on the table with the tiny, one-inch speaker facing Red, and pressed the PLAY button.

Red lowered himself back into his chair as he recognized the Punchbowl conversation with Coland. *It's my voice all right,* he thought, *but how did they manage to get that close in the open reaches of Punchbowl?* "Wait! Wait just one damn minute here." Red lunged forward and jabbed his finger down on the STOP button. "This is not evidence," he bellowed with a tremor in his voice. "Anyone can doctor a tape. This is nonsense, a conspiracy to get Red Murphy. Sure as hell ain't admissible in court."

"Please!" Terumi said. "If you will continue to bear with us, we can not only substantiate our case, but we can offer you a deal to protect yourself as well. First, it is our wish to convince you that we *can* have you for lunch, Mr. Murphy. Then we can talk about horse trading lunch for real estate at a fair price. So please hear us out." He re-pressed the PLAY button.

Red sank back into his chair as his beefy face turned the color of raw hamburger.

At the end of the taped segment, Lori turned off the recorder and said, "Three witnesses can verify the accuracy of the tape. I'm one of them. Coland is the second witness. Across the hall is the third. If you wish, I can bring him in at this time." Red shook his head, and Lori continued. "Both this gentleman and I sat on benches adjacent to yours when you spoke the words heard on the tape. He's prepared to testify to that and so am I. And there is more, Mr. Murphy, I assure you."

Lori flipped through a sheaf of documents and began her next assault. "Mr. Perry, our third witness, is a private investigator," she said. "He has been able to establish that you—alias Edwin Mulrooney—are the leading shareholder in Rodminn Realty. We know the late Horace Rodder and your ex-wife, Wilma Minnet, comprise the remaining shareholders. Your circuitous Rodminn Estates offering is enough to prove a conflict-of-interest charge against you. Certainly, it provides sufficient cause to censure you as a trustee."

"I admit nothing. But just as a matter of supposin', what are you offering me? How do I benefit?" His hands shook in his lap.

Terumi replied, "Mr. Murphy, I've drawn up a document for you to review. In return for your resignation from the trust and certain land concessions, we are prepared to give up any and all evidence connected with these extortion and conflict-of-interest charges."

Red leaned forward and took the papers from Terumi. He settled back, rested his elbows on the arms of his chair, and read the document page by page. His steely eyes narrowed. "This price is piracy. It'll be worth far more than current fair market price."

"That is true," Terumi agreed, "but you'll never get that kind of money for it. My client would rather choose an alternate site, and you would have no one else to sell to. No, the price is as fair as you'll ever see."

"And I'll have to relinquish any claim to Hank's and John's par-

207

cels as well?"

"Correct!"

"But I'll take a financial bath under these conditions. I've had operating expenses, too. It's a lose-lose proposition."

"We know exactly what you paid for each parcel, and we know that you'll still turn a modest profit after all is said and done. Without my client's offer you'll sustain a half-million-dollar loss. As thin as you're spread, you won't be able to absorb that kind of shortfall. I think this deal is more than fair, considering the stunts you've pulled. You could hardly reap any profits from a jail cell, could you?"

"How much time do I have to decide?"

"Today, before you leave this room. Is that clear?"

"Yeah! I can hear the train coming already." Red knew he'd been railroaded, but he also knew he'd run out of options. He slowly read the document once more from start to finish. At last he put his signature to it and each of three copies underneath. A shaken man, he removed a folded white handkerchief from his pants pocket and wiped his brow. Terumi took the original and two of the copies, leaving the third copy on the table. Handing Red the tape cartridge from the recorder, he said, "Have a nice day."

The trustees had debated the wisdom of dealing Red too potent a blow and turning him into the proverbial cornered rat. All eyes watched him for some kind of reaction.

Red tried hard to conceal it, but his stomach churned with swallowed pride. The acid taste of unexpected defeat hung in his mouth. He shot bitter looks first at Terumi and then around the room before easing himself out of the chair.

As he rose to leave, Paul confronted him: "Another matter—do you have any knowledge of the whereabouts of Hank's son, Kekoa?"

"No, damn it! Why should I?" Red shot back, his powerful body suddenly on the alert, a predator poised to strike. Then the day's defeat and humiliation overcame him. He sighed deeply and said, "Sorry, I don't." He left the room, dragging his heavy depression with every step.

When Red could be observed leaving the bank from an upstairs boardroom window, Coland opened the door across the hall and beckoned the third witness to join them. Hank Pualoa found the others at the large window, staring down at the figure crossing Merchant Street in a downpour of rain.

"How'd it go, Lori?" Hank asked.

"Fine. We truly broke the man, but I'm sure it's only temporary. I just hope we've stalled him long enough to locate Kekoa and bring him home."

Coland walked over to Paul and put a hand on his shoulder. "This is certainly a festive occasion. The trust should benefit by almost half-a-million dollars."

Paul gave him a polite but stony look and reminded him, "A victory of sorts, but not a total one until Hank finds his son. Why don't we have lunch at the Pagoda Restaurant? I'll call Masako. She and the girls can meet us there. I think they're all free of classes until one o'clock. We can reserve one of those private gazebos that extend over the water."

"Good. Lori, will you join us?"

"I'd love to," she said, proud of her day's work.

Paul looked inquiringly at Hank.

"Thanks, but no," he said. "I think it's too soon for a reunion." Inwardly, he knew it was the fear of his daughter's rejection that held him back. *For sure,* he thought, *after I've found Kekoa.*

Lori turned away so Hank wouldn't see her disappointment.

* * *

The rain finally stopped, and the sun actually bared itself. Red's anger mounted as he inched his car along Richards Street and swung onto King. Somehow, over the past year, lunchtime Honolulu had turned into a third rush hour. At Kapahulu Avenue he turned right.

Whatever humility had been imposed on him in the boardroom now fueled his temper. And Paul, by mentioning Kekoa, had tossed in the additional ingredient of terror. That situation, that problem had now taken on urgent proportions. After bullying his Buick Regal through a crowd of ambling Waikiki tourists, he turned onto the Ala Wai and then into his apartment garage, screeching into his designated space. Bounding out and slamming the car door shut, he stomped into the building and rode the creaking elevator to the eighteenth floor. Still grumbling to himself, he nearly broke the key off in his front door wrestling with the aged lock. He swore with every move.

Murphy did not expect to find Wilma there. She lay on her stomach, topless, in a chaise lounge on the lanai in full view of his foyer. He found her gazing down at the Ala Wai Canal, absorbing the glistening rays for a tan. Hearing the door close, Wilma stood up, lazily stretching her limbs, and came through the sliding glass door to greet him. Her trim milky-white breasts rippled with every purposeful step. The dark nipples stood erect.

Stopped in his tracks, Red simply stared at her. Boiling over with anger and pent-up frustration, he couldn't decide whether to hit her or love her. Instead, he flung himself to his knees, buried his head in her belly, and sobbed—something she had never seen him do before.

Despite her confusion, Wilma dared not ask questions. Helping him to his feet, she led him to the bedroom. His loyal ex-wife undressed him and played with him, slowly, gently, taking nearly an hour before he reached a climax. She literally eased the pain from his body. They had never had gentle sex before, and although he remained the primary recipient, she enjoyed it immensely. He fell into an exhaustive sleep. She returned to her room to shower and dress.

It was the last bit of tenderness they shared. When Red awoke several hours later, all his anger had returned and he wanted—no, needed—to strike out at someone. His ex-wife, the most convenient and vulnerable target, took all the slapping around she could possibly bear. Then she managed a swift, sharp kick to his groin.

He doubled over and fell in a spasm to the floor, looking questioningly up at her. *How could you do that to me?*

For once, his ex-wife openly enjoyed the look of pain on his face. As he struggled to recover, she ducked back into her room and threw her few outfits into her suitcases. She left without a word, to return to California. This time Wilma was quitting for good. None of his slimy deals, no amount of promised cash could make her come back. She had a life to live, a life without Red Murphy.

Chapter 30
A Comeback

AS A SMALL BOY, Edgar Murphy had frequently gotten into trouble, and the memories of those days had never left him....

Whack! The eleven-year-old felt the sting of an angry father's hand against the side of his head. The blow knocked the red-headed lad to the floor. He cowered there, whimpering, an arm raised in anticipation of another back-handed strike.

"Stop being such a sissy!" Ian Murphy had bellowed. "Get up and take your punishment like a man. You gotta be tough. You've sinned. You've brought it on yourself."

Red felt that his harsh father had never tried to reach or understand him. Constant beatings and scornful words burned into the boy's flesh and soul. He soon learned to stash anger, then vindictiveness into his own emotional baggage. Early on, Red vowed that no one would ever hurt him deep down again....

The trustees at the meeting yesterday had come close. It had made him think of his father for the first time in ages. They had gotten a piece of Red Murphy this go-around, but he wouldn't let them get any more. He'd cover his tracks better now, and faster.

Wednesday afternoon, Red parked in the lot behind his bank on Waialae. From there he crossed Koko Head Avenue to the drab storefront office of the Oceanic Mortgage Company, a shlock firm with an expansive name. He was here to meet with the Lynches, the current owners of Big John's Ewa house, and close on the sale of the property to him.

He announced himself to the receptionist, and she motioned him toward a folding chair. No sign of the Lynches yet. Red checked the time—he'd arrived ten minutes early. His chair faced the receptionist, so he entertained himself by studying the plain-Jane *haole*, totally absorbed in her horror magazine, *A Theater of Blood*. She felt the weight of his glare and raised dull eyes to stare right back at him. Embarrassed,

Red asked if any other magazines were available. She shook her head, and kept her eyes fixed on him, as if punishing him for regarding her at all.

His sport coat, over an open-necked shirt, felt heavy in the barely air-conditioned room. He set his briefcase on his lap and flipped the catch. To look busy, his thick fingers rummaged through the papers inside. Within minutes, a fortyish local woman, carrying a briefcase like an armful of groceries, entered from the street. She mumbled something to the receptionist, ignored Red, and disappeared into one of the cubicles.

The two Louis Lynches, father and son, arrived together. They exchanged handshakes with Red, and followed the receptionist to a table beyond the last cubicle. The local woman joined them, introducing herself as Thelma Soloman.

Thelma laid out piles of documents in front of the three men and explained the essentials of a real estate closing. The actual signing took only about ten minutes, and Red walked away with the paperwork for the Ewa house, including a lease agreement. The Lynches had accepted his cashier's check, and Thelma had accepted his personal check for the closing costs. The younger Lynch had reassured Red that the house would be totally empty of students during spring break, the week of the twenty-first through the twenty-eighth.

The done deal put a new lift in Red's gait as he strode down Waialae to his car. At least one thing had gone right today. Between Tenth and Eleventh he nonchalantly glanced into the grounds of the rec center, where a half-dozen youngsters played basketball and shouted at one another. Murphy stopped in his tracks. Kekoa Pualoa had just slam-dunked the ball.

Red told himself, *I'm not gonna blow it this time. I'll follow him and find out where he lives.* Crossing Waialae, Red bought a *Star-Bulletin* out of a newspaper rack and sauntered over to a park bench in the playground on the far side of the rec center. Opening the paper to hide his face, he kept his eyes glued to the basketball court.

The game lasted until a Dodge Ram pickup pulled up to the curb on the Eleventh Street side. Kekoa and a second boy trotted over, and the other boy got in. Before closing the door, he held up the flat of his hand, and Kekoa high-fived him. Red rose from his park bench to watch, wondering if Kekoa would also get into the truck. With relief, he saw him turn away, walk back down Eleventh, and cross over to the *mau-*

ka side of Waialae. Red followed at a safe distance from the *makai* side. Mixing in with other shoppers, Kekoa stopped at a bakery and glanced down the street. Had Kekoa sensed his presence? Apparently not. The boy casually stepped inside.

Red slowed his pace directly across from the Osaka Family Bakery and partially concealed himself in a shoe store doorway. He could see Kekoa through the bakery window talking to a young woman behind the counter. He seemed to be the only customer. A little kid roaring by on his skateboard momentarily distracted Red, and when his eyes returned to the bakery, Kekoa had disappeared altogether. With no better lead, Red decided to wait.

After fifteen fruitless minutes, he entered the Kaimuki Koffee House next to the shoe store and took a window table with a direct view of the bakery. Ordering coffee and a Danish, he paid in advance so he could leave quickly.

Twenty minutes passed. A car pulled up, partially blocking his view. Red slid his chair over and saw the salesgirl from the bakery leave by the front door. He also caught a glimpse of Kekoa hanging a CLOSED sign on the same glass door. A broad grin stole over Red's freckled face. He knew why the Pualoa boy was in the bakery: this is where the boy worked or maybe where he lived. He could pick the best opportunity to get at Kekoa whenever he wanted.

Red suddenly felt both exhilarated and hungry and decided to order a full meal. The puzzled waitress cleared away his pastry plate and brought her only customer his next order, a rare T-bone steak dinner with all the trimmings. The food gave Red a sense of well-being for the first time in months. He figured on having himself a great evening.

* * *

Kekoa went to bed shortly after nine that evening and slept soundly until a torrential rain pelted on the metal roof above the workroom. The storeroom where he slept opened into the workroom with only a fabric curtain to grant him privacy. He found it difficult to fall asleep again— too much noise and so many things going on in his head. While he lay there, he thought he heard a scraping noise at the back door above the pounding rain. Perhaps it was just his mind playing tricks. But when the noise persisted, he decided to investigate. Without turning on the light in the storeroom, he stepped out into the massive workroom lit only by the red STOP lamps of the machinery housed there.

As Kekoa neared the back door the scraping noise seemed to be less desperate, but an animal-like, whining sound joined it from outside. Both sounds ceased as he began unlocking the door. A drenched Ilio stood there with a pitiful pleading look on his face. The dog shivered from the cold downpour. Kekoa searched the alley for the boxes that provided the usual nighttime shelter and saw that the pile had been removed that afternoon. He knew the Osakas wouldn't appreciate a dog inside the bakery, but he couldn't turn down his furry friend. Kekoa brought Ilio inside and commanded the sopping dog to wait by the door while he brought empty clean flour sacks to towel off the water. Halfway through the toweling process, Ilio decided to shake himself dry.

Kekoa arranged a heap of several more empty flour sacks near his bed, and the dog circled and settled contentedly into the nest. The boy hoped that the rain would subside before morning and that he would awaken in time to let Ilio out before Sam came down to work. These very thoughts interfered with his ability to sleep for several more hours, but finally, sheer exhaustion caused him to doze off.

"Kekoa! Kekoa!"

Opening his eyes, Kekoa found Sam standing over his bed, scowling down at him. A fifty-pound bag of rice lay at Sam's feet. One end of the heavy paper container had been gnawed into shreds. A small mound of rice grain littered the floor. Ilio, frightened by Sam's sudden appearance and tone, backed into the farthest corner of the room with his teeth bared. A low-level, motor-boating growl emanated from him. Sam stood his ground.

"Who dog? Where dog come from?" yelled Sam. "Look at mess. This bakery not dog place. Out, out, out. Now!"

A silent Kekoa retrieved the dog from the corner and led him outside via the workroom's back door. The rain had stopped, so Ilio accepted his expulsion with a minimum of resistance. Sam stood waiting for his explanation when the boy returned to the storeroom.

"Sorry, Sam, I'll clean it up and pay for the rice bag outta my pay. Okay, Sam?"

"Who dog? Why dog inside?" asked Sam in a weary voice, with only a touch of anger remaining.

"It's my dog, Sam. I've been taking care of him on and off as long as I've been working for you. I've never taken him inside before—it was just that awful rainstorm last night—he was so miserable, I couldn't turn

214

him down. It won't happen again. I promise!"

Sam stood in a wide stance with his arms folded across his chest. "You make plan for your dog live elsewhere. *Nei?* Health Department close us down if dog here."

Kekoa was in no position to argue. Sam left to start the morning work. *Maybe Andy guys will take him,* he thought while he pulled on the day's clothes. Ilio would have plenty of room to roam out at their place. Plenty of company, too. Andy likes Ilio and Mama's home all day.

Later that afternoon, after listening to Kekoa's proposal, an excited Andy convinced his father that the dog would be a great addition to their family. Ilio was coaxed into the cab of their pickup between Andy and his father for the ride to Mokuleia. In a matter of days, the Black Lab ingratiated himself into the entire family, especially with Mama, who wanted to put some meat on his bones. She spoke to the dog in her native tongue all day long, and Ilio had the freedom to roam both house and grounds at will. He'd never had it so good.

* * *

A vile taste filling Red's mouth awakened him to semi-darkness. The poison-green hands on the bedside clock read 5 a.m. His head pounded like a dribbled basketball. Sore eyes scanned the walls of the unfamiliar surroundings. A tiny light shone from the partially opened bathroom door—a lighthouse to his faltering ship, tossing, pitching on waves of nausea as he staggered toward the door. After retching his gut, he felt only minimally better.

Red stared in disgust at the puffy kisser in the mirror above the sink as he supported himself on both hands. He stank. The room stank. Three days of mindless drinking had brought him to this state. One steak dinner hadn't been able to obliterate his humiliation by the trustees. He had wanted to forget everything. At his lowest point, he'd craved a woman. He bit his lower lip when he recalled what he'd done to Willie. How triumphantly she'd kicked him in the balls and marched out the door. He wanted to cry and almost did.

It occurred to him once more that he was in a strange apartment. *Whose?* he wondered. He washed, wiped himself clean, and threw the towel on the floor. Who had he come home with? He edged closer to the bundle of bedding. A ghostly beam from the streetlight escaped around the drawn shade and crossed her face as she slept. Red cringed at the sight the snoring creature and tiptoed away to search for his clothes. He found them on the floor, a trail from the bed straight through the living room, right up to the front door. Dressing quickly, he let himself out.

Stepping onto the broad lanai, Red viewed his surroundings. The creature's apartment was one of four in a stately old home situated near the top of Wilhelmina Rise Drive, a narrow two-way street that dropped steeply—almost a thousand feet—to Waialae Avenue at the bottom in only five blocks. He sat down on the steps for several minutes until his innards returned to a tolerable state. But where the hell was his own car? That babe must've brought him to the house in hers. Oh, yeah, he'd met her at the Full Moon Saloon in Waikiki. His car remained in the parking stall at home.

As the nausea subsided, Red scanned the half-dozen nearby houses built into the hills. Most were substantial and each one was surrounded in greenery. Illuminated by the streetlight, a gleaming white Mercedes caught his eye. The car sat in the driveway of a large contemporary stucco house three stories high with a lanai on each level and a blue tiled roof. Not only did the car look familiar, the vanity plate told him why. The letters spelled F-U-J-I-T-A.

Red walked across the deserted street to the driveway. The big house was dark. Nobody was likely to come out at this hour. He didn't really have a plan. A few deep scratches on the driver's side might make a nice point. He tried the door. Unlocked! More possibilities. He reached under the dash and yanked on the hood release. The heavy mass of steel popped up a few inches until it rested on the safety hook. Softly closing the door, he stole to the front of the car and raised the hood. The well-oiled hinges didn't squeak. He looked for something under the hood, anything he could tamper with. He knew he didn't have much time. His fingers fiddled with the hood release mechanism.

Then the idea struck him. With brute strength, he bent the hood's safety retaining hook so that it barely engaged its home notch. Then he stretched the hood release catch spring over its stationary stud and removed the spring. Searching for some greenery that would substitute for rope, he saw a low wall next door covered with thick, sturdy vines that he decided would serve nicely. He ripped a long length of vine off the wall, doubled it over, and looped it through a hole in the catch. Next, he fed it through the front grillwork, enabling him to manipulate the pivoting catch from outside. Slowly, he lowered the hood while he slid the freely moving catch in place to temporarily hold the hood in place. Pleased with his efforts, he tossed the spring into the bushes and started back down the steep slope to Waialae, where he caught a bus home.

* * *

Three hours later, at 8:30, Terumi Fujita climbed into his Mercedes, clicked his shoulder harness and seat belt into place, and backed out of the driveway. His mind was already on the office as he shifted into DRIVE. The car accelerated down the bumpy incline until it bounced across the first intersection. The sudden jarring caused the catch mechanism to release the hood to the safety position, where it bounced unnoticed.

Going forty miles an hour, Terumi tapped the brake, but not quite enough. At the second intersection, the hood's retaining hook rattled out of its notch. The hood sprang upright, a looming mass of steel that blocked his vision. The hood smashed against the windshield, streaking it with tiny green crystalline cracks. Terumi literally stood on the foot brake. Blindly angling the Mercedes to the right, he slammed into the side of a car parked along the curb. He'd narrowly avoided a head-on collision.

The vibrations and secondary impact sent his body forward and back, forward and back—but only by a few inches. The seat belt mechanism held.

The clangorous racket breached the early morning quiet. Heads popped out of windows and doorways. Badly shaken, Terumi pulled on the emergency brake, climbed out, and surveyed the damage. His car had driven a huge wedge in the left rear quarter-panel of a Honda Accord. Terumi walked around the front of his beautiful new Mercedes. The hood lay flattened against the windshield, making the powerful engine look obscenely exposed. He examined the hood release mechanism with the scrutiny of a lawyer discovering evidence. He saw immediately that the hook had been forcibly bent out of alignment, the spring was missing, and in its place lay an odd residue of twisted vines. Terumi didn't have to be a mechanic to see what had happened here. This was no accident. Now he was a target. They had driven a greedy man to desperate, vindictive measures. He knew that proving it would be another thing.

217

Chapter 31
Fearful Encounter

CLACK-TUM, tum-tum-clack, clack-ta-tum. The rhythmic beat emanated from a *kupuna* sitting under an ohia lehua tree. Waist-length gray hair and deep creases in wizened skin acknowledged her eighty-plus years. A lei made of green ti leaves hung from her neck to her lap. In her left hand she grasped a great hollow gourd by its midsection. This *ipu* emitted deep rich tones through the small opening at the top, as she finger-thumped and palm-slapped the side and bottom for the musical tone she sought. Gazing skyward, she continued her chant about a mountain on the neighbor island of Kauai:

> "Kau li lua i ke anu Wai'ale'ale
> He maka halalo ka lehua makanoe
> Wai'ale'ale stands haughty and cold
> Her lehua bloom, fog-soaked, droops pensive…"

Alex and Leilani stopped to listen. On the first of May, a Lei Day Saturday, they'd come to Kapiolani Park to peruse the island crafts and music. Alex didn't care much for crafts, but Leilani did, and he counted any day with her a gift. He adjusted the two rolled-up tatami mats under his arm and glanced at her affectionately. How striking she looked in her brown and white tapa-print playsuit, her necklace of polished black kukui nuts gleaming in the morning sun.

Alex casually reached up to pluck a red lehua from the branch above them, but before he could reach the hair-like blossom, the chanting stopped abruptly.

"*Kapu!*" a throaty voice barked. "Forbidden!" He hastily lowered his hand and looked over at the old *kupuna*.

"You pick the blossom, you make it rain tears in the mountains." She turned and scolded Leilani. "You *kamaaina*—you know bettah."

218

Leilani smiled sheepishly back at the woman and told Alex the ancient legend. "The goddess Pele chose for herself a handsome mortal paramour. But he was in love with a mortal beauty. The jealous Pele ordered the man to abandon his true love. He refused. Well, Pele was so infuriated that she turned him into a beautiful ohia tree."

Alex grinned. "Beautiful, maybe, but still a tree. That Pele, she's a real tough broad."

"Shhh," Leilani giggled, "don't let her hear you. Anyway, his brokenhearted girlfriend cried continually and finally sought the help of a sorcerer. Unfortunately, the sorcerer couldn't restore her man to life. Instead, he turned the girl into lehua blossoms, the next best thing. So whenever anyone plucks a blossom, she cries again, causing it to rain in the mountains." Leilani sighed. "Isn't that touching?" She tilted her head toward him in an afterthought. "And you know what? It's really rare to find an ohia down here at sea level. They mostly grow in the mountains. So you'd better not disturb it."

Properly chastised now by two females, Alex took Leilani's hand as they walked under a majestic banyan tree. Its brown shaggy roots extended earthward from sprawling branches to penetrate the ground some distance from the trunk. Appearing as the bars of a cage, these wandering roots entwined space, captured time, and claimed new territory like a benevolent army.

As they strolled, Leilani could sense Alex getting more and more introspective. "A penny for your thoughts, Alex Wong," she teased.

"I think they're worth a lot more than that."

"They are, but I want you back from la-la land, where you've been for the last ten minutes."

"I'm sorry. I've got something on my mind. Something my dad and I discussed at breakfast yesterday."

"Does it concern us?" she asked.

"Us maybe, but you in particular. Let's find a place to sit."

At the edge of the park, far from the crowds, they found just the right shade, under an umbrella-shaped monkeypod, and spread out their mats.

"What did Dad tell you about the meeting on Tuesday?" asked Alex.

"He said that Red abused our trust and blackmailed Mr. Benfield-Rice. I understand they censured him and kicked him off the board of trustees. Your dad and that nice Lori are now the trustees," Leilani said.

"Is that all Dad told you?"

"Well, he did mention that our land parcels would bring a great deal of money into the trust. Alex, is that why you're concerned?"

"No, sweetheart. It's not about money."

"Then what, dear? Please don't torture me like this."

"Suppose your father were to reappear. What would you think of that?"

She shrugged. "I don't know. I don't really have any feelings for him. I used to hate him because my grandmother told me to. Then I hated him because he deserted us. I assumed he didn't love us."

Alex fingered the collar on his blue polo shirt and chose his words carefully. "It's hardly likely that the man who initiated and generously maintained your trust did so because he didn't love you. It's also not likely that an uncaring father would return—cross a continent and an ocean—when he found his former partner messing around with his children's welfare. Does that sound like he doesn't care about you?"

Leilani stiffened and turned to face him. The impact of the word return had suddenly sunk in. "He's back? He's here in Honolulu?"

Alex cupped her face in his hands. With one thumb stroke, he brushed a rolling tear from her cheek, and then held her close until their lips met in a kiss. The kiss seemed to calm her. He spoke softly. "Your father told Dad that he left because he'd inflicted so much pain and harm on his family."

"Paul spoke with my father? Where?"

"He's been at the trust meetings for two days and—"

Leilani interrupted. "And no one has said a word to me? Why the secrecy?"

"Dad couldn't be certain how you'd react. We didn't want you to be hurt."

"Why is everyone always trying to protect and shelter me? I'm seventeen! A grown woman now with a mature brain and feelings."

He slid his hands around her upper right arm, massaging, kneading it, enjoying its soft ripeness. His warm touches reassured her. In response, she gently pressed her lips to the side of his neck. He reacted with a delighted body quiver.

"Does my father really want to find me and Kekoa?"

"Yes. Very much. Dad says he's a nice man, Leilani. What's more important, though, is whether you want to see him. Do you?"

"I don't know. What do you think?"

"Hey, kid, you can't lay that one on me. It's your decision to make." And then Alex relented. "Yeah, I think you should. Besides, you've got nothing to lose by just meeting him. You can always back away from a relationship afterward if it doesn't work out. He is your father, in any case."

"I feel stupid having to ask this question, but how in the world do we meet—get together, that is?" she asked.

"There are choices. You could meet on neutral ground, some-where for lunch, say. Or maybe on home ground—he could come to our house."

"Would you be there?" Head bent, Leilani played with her necklace, spinning the kukui nuts in trembling hands. "At the house, I mean."

"Yes, if you want me to be there. Mom, Dad, and Numi will all be there, if you want them to be."

Leilani looked up. "I'd like them close by in the house, but I'd want you there in the room with me. Can you arrange it that way?"

"Of course." He stroked her cheek. "And very soon."

* * *

Pungent aromas from the Wong kitchen meant company com-ing. Alex and his dad had been at a loss as to how to arrange a comfort-able, or at least non-threatening meeting between Leilani and her father. Masako came up with the solution. She suggested they invite Hank to one of her grilled salmon and pan-fried noodle dinners. Hank accepted.

Masako had skipped her English Department meeting after school and rushed home, bringing the girls with her to help cook. But Leilani's hands shook as she opened the bags of vegetables, sending a flurry of snow peas and shiitake mushrooms to the floor. She was gently banished from the kitchen. In the living room, Alex tried to calm her.

* * *

Paul left to pick up Hank at his furnished apartment on Lunalilo Street. To Paul's surprise, Lori answered the door. They exchanged a brief greeting, and then Paul looked past her to see Hank sitting on the couch in an old T-shirt and rumpled shorts.

"What's the matter, Hank?" Paul asked, stepping into the living room. Hank didn't answer.

221

Lori answered for him. "He's just plain scared, chickening out. He can't forgive himself, so how does he expect his children to forgive him? That's why he's not even dressed yet. I called him an hour ago to invite him to supper myself, and he broke down and cried on the phone."

Paul nodded in sympathy. "I'm here to bring him to our house for dinner. If you would like to come also, you are most welcome."

"Thank you, Mr. Wong, but no. This is their night, a most important reunion, not one to be shared. Thank you, I will take a rain check if I may. But it's Hank we need to get there."

"Now there's two of you ganging up on me. Don't I have a say in this?" Hank protested.

"Frankly, no! You may be willing to lose a wonderful daughter, but you'll have to deal with me first," Lori answered. "I'm not going to let those children be without the father they need and deserve."

"You don't have to be so damn pushy," Hank retorted.

"I should walk out of here and let you ruin your own life? Is that what you really want? Haven't you done enough of that already?"

Hank bent his gray head and pressed his mouth against his clenched right fist. His bicep bulged with tension, making him look like a shabby version of Rodin's *The Thinker*.

Lori hastened into the bedroom. Paul heard dresser drawers open and shut, the closet door slam. She reappeared and stood squarely before Hank, hands on her hips.

"I've laid out fresh clothes for you, Mister. Now get in there! Shower, shave, and get dressed or I'm going to do it for you." Hank picked up his canes and took his leave of them, closing the bedroom door behind him.

Paul could no longer conceal his astonishment. "I can't believe you would take this much interest in our affairs," he said.

Under the fringe of black bangs, Lori's face grew somber. "Mr. Wong, I'm afraid I wasn't totally honest with you and Leilani that day at the museum. Hank was more than the husband of my best friend. The three of us grew up together." A faint blush crept up her high cheekbones. "Before he married Malia, he was my friend, too, a very special friend. I would have married him if he had asked me, but he never did. Neither of them ever had any inkling of my love for him. Malia and I remained best friends, and I watched their children grow, until the accident. But afterward, Eme was so overprotective of them. She seemed to be sending me a message that I wasn't welcome. So, yes, I do have a stake in this."

She turned and yelled through the closed bedroom door, "How-zit going?"

"I'm coming! I'm coming! Keep your shirt on," Hank shouted back.

Her explanation seemed to satisfy Paul. He took a step closer to her. "Lori, won't you reconsider dinner with us? You might be able to furnish just the courage he needs tonight. Besides, the rest of the Wong family will need to give them their privacy to get reacquainted anyhow."

"If you really think I wouldn't be intruding." She surveyed her outfit, a flowered print blouse tucked into dark slacks. "But I'm hardly dressed for a dinner party."

"You're dressed very appropriately. After all, it is a family dinner. You would honor and grace our table."

"You are more than gracious, Mr. Wong. I do accept. However, I have my own car. I can bring Hank along with me when he's ready, if you like."

"Good, then it's settled. I'll run along now."

Paul left. A minute later, a neatly dressed Hank emerged from the bedroom. The slightly too-long tufts of gray at his temples gave him a certain dignity. Hank felt Lori's eyes upon him and enjoyed the sensation.

Realizing she'd been caught in the act of giving him the once-over, Lori reached up and straightened the collar on his aloha shirt, although it had needed no adjustment.

To break the spell, he spread the cane handles away from his waist, and said, "Tah-dah!"

* * *

Leilani paced the Wong living room like a tawny jungle cat. Curling her hair behind one ear, she continually smoothed her aqua sleeveless dress as she moved. Her composure decayed by the minute.

"Relax!" Alex told her, but he might as well have saved his breath.

She heard the family car pull up in front of the house. Her feet carried her cautiously to the window. She saw Paul come away from the car alone.

"I knew it!" she cried. "I knew he wouldn't come. I knew he didn't want me. He doesn't need a daughter. He doesn't love me. That's why he left in the first place."

Alex had a difficult time wrapping his arms around his bundle of despair. He felt helpless to console her.

As Paul came through the front door, he immediately perceived the situation. He had to shout at her to break the frenzy. "Leilani! Leilani! Listen to me. Your father's still coming. He's scared, too. Lori Yamashita is bringing him in a few minutes."

Leilani stopped flailing and broke into quiet sobs, burying her head in Alex's shoulder.

Hearing all the commotion from the kitchen, Masako burst into the living room to take Leilani from Alex's arms. "There, there," she said. "We can't have you meeting your father like this, can we?" She led Leilani up the stairs to the master bathroom.

Paul called to his wife, "We have another guest for dinner—Lori Yamashita. I'll explain when you come down."

"Fine. Set another place for her."

Walking into the dining room, Paul saw that Numi had already set the extra place. She smiled at her father, and he simply had to hug her for it.

Moments after Masako returned to her kitchen, Leilani started down the stairs. The doorbell rang, and she stopped midway. In the hall below her, Paul was leading Lori and Hank toward the living room. But Hank just happened to look up at his daughter. He stood transfixed, for he saw the image of a young Malia and found her breathtaking. Leilani was so much more beautiful than her picture, the one Paul had shown him.

Leilani came down one step, then another, and stopped. She felt immobile as she sized up the stranger below. The stunned man she saw did not fit the threatening, dangerous image her grandmother had drilled into her. She descended the remaining steps and timidly held out her right hand. Hank took the warm hand and held it firmly, but the distancing gesture deeply disappointed him. His eyes watered, and he managed to smile. "Hi, Leilani," he said, forcing the words from his constricted throat.

"Hi. I…I'm glad you came," Leilani said in a soft voice. I've always wanted to know what you were like." She maintained her composure completely. She had made up her mind not to shed another tear.

Hank coughed and recovered his voice once more. "Dearest Leilani, I'm so sorry for all those missing years, so very sorry."

"I'm sorry, too." She spoke the words without a glimmer of emotion, took his arm, and led him to a chair in the living room.

The rest of the family came in to greet them, and minutes later, Masako announced dinner. "Please come to the table. Lori, Mr. Pualoa, you're over here by Numi and me."

Lori helped Hank to his chair and then took the canes to lean them against the buffet. The conversation stumbled awkwardly all through the meal, but everyone tried. Everyone, that is, except Leilani. She couldn't stop staring at her father. Hank pretended not to notice as he understood completely. He could hardly take his eyes away from her either. *My daughter wants an explanation for my past behavior,* he thought, *and, by God, she shall have one. She certainly deserves one.*

When the last morsel of chocolate-haupia pie had reaped its final accolade, Hank drew upon the courage of a contented guest and clinked his water glass lightly with his dessert fork. He spoke determinedly and slowly, fearing his courage would fade otherwise.

"I thank everyone here, especially the entire Wong family, for welcoming me into their home and for being so kind...Lori and Paul for seeing that I got here...Mrs. Wong and Numi for that lovely dinner. And last but not least, you, my dearest Leilani, for your willingness to see me at all." Hank coughed again and cleared his throat. "Thank God for that. I only wish Kekoa was here with us, too. I suppose you're wondering why the father of two small and beautiful children would choose to disappear for over thirteen years. I'd like to..."

Paul interrupted him, "Perhaps it would be better for just you and Leilani and maybe Alex to continue this conversation?"

Hank thought for a moment and said, "No, this is easier for me, and the time is right. Although it is Leilani I want to tell, you all deserve to hear whatever answers I can offer."

"The dishes can wait," Masako told Numi.

Hank began again. "You must understand how much I loved Leilani's mother. Malia and I were heaven and earth to each other. When you children came, we were blessed beyond belief. Although Malia's mother and I got off to a rocky start, you children brought us together to make one big happy family."

Hank told them his story—how it had been beforehand, the excessive drinking, the accident, Malia's death, Eme's vengeance.

"I was responsible for the death of the love of my life, the mother of my children." Hank bowed his head, bit his curled lower lip, and turned his teary face from side to side. "I accept the full blame. If there were any way to change what happened—if there were any way I could have given my life for hers I would have done it. What I did was criminal.

"Needless to say, I served a horrible six months in Halawa prison. Throughout the trial and afterward, your grandmother refused to let me see you. If it had been just you and Kekoa, we would have found a way to be together. I had two choices. I could seek legal proceedings to get custody of you, or I could leave you with Eme. I chose the latter because you had already become a family again, and I couldn't bring myself to tear you apart one more time. Besides, Big John lived next door and I knew my brother would protect you."

Leilani sat upright against the back of the dining room chair, her mind attentive, her hands gripping the seat under her to keep her body from squirming. Her father was really speaking to her. She wanted to capture every word and test it for belief and sincerity. She needed to see through the somber expression he wore. She wanted to know if a real father, her father, existed there. She wasn't even sure of her own feelings, let alone his.

"But why did you leave Honolulu?" Alex asked. "Where did you go?"

"I felt responsible for the death of the love of my life—my children's mother." Hank looked down and shook his head. "My own family held me in contempt, my so-called friends passed judgment on me, and my own self-esteem couldn't get any lower. I felt I had to get away, at least for the time being. If there had been any hope of reconciliation, I never would have gone at all. At the time I remember thinking that I wasn't running from anything so much as I was looking for some thing or some place to have a normal life again."

His eyes never left Leilani's face as he told them about his Mainland travels, and how he had eventually wound up in Baltimore and stayed for eleven years. He attributed his financial successes there to heavy equipment leasing, some real estate ventures, a few good moves in the stock market—and starting his own company as a construction contractor. "I sobered up…"

Leilani's dark eyes burned into him with a look of skepticism.

Hank understood. "Believe it or not, my dear daughter, I did. I stayed sober for years," he said. "And I felt like I was finally getting my life together. But…a little over a year ago, something happened…"

Chapter 32
Before the Fall
Baltimore, Fourteen Months Earlier

HANK ANGLED his Dodge pickup into a parking space at the east Baltimore strip mall and hurried inside Mail Services Plus. Standing before the sea of postal boxes, he turned a flat steel key in number 384 and retrieved the day's catch: the usual pleas from charities, lures for platinum credit cards, and a large white envelope edged in green. The envelope bore the logo of the First Sugarman's Bank in Honolulu. It was what he'd been waiting for. Without opening the statement, he returned to the truck and headed for his Calvert Street apartment.

Bounding up the white marble steps, he unlocked the door in the foyer and took the first flight of stairs two at a time; then, heaving and huffing, trudged up the last flight. That was the problem with these old Baltimore brownstones. Long on charm, short on elevators.

Dropping into a chair at his kitchenette table, he slit the envelope open with a steak knife and spread out the pages. His index finger followed the columns of figures down the first sheet, then to the others and back again. A deep scowl crossed his face. He and his two partners had agreed, in writing, that they would put his one-third share of the profits from the Finast Construction business into the kids' trust. That had not happened—not for the last three months, as far as he could see. At least the money orders he'd been sending from Baltimore had been credited.

Hank swung his arm wildly, knocked over an innocent kitchen chair, and left it crippled and forgotten. He felt so frustrated and so out of touch. Until now, isolation had been his choice, twelve years of intentional solitude. But a copy of *Honolulu Magazine* in a dentist's office had stirred his curiosity and sparked his resolve to reconnect with home. He phoned his brother at the Ewa house first. An operator answered, telling him the number was not in service. Directory As-

228

sistance had no new number for John Pualoa, not even an unlisted one. All logic told Hank he should call his lawyer. After all, Yosh had established the children's trust for him in the first place. But something impelled Hank to cut to the chase. He'd call Red Murphy first and demand an explanation.

Thumbing through his small leather address book, Hank grimly noted how few names he'd actually entered into it. What an antisocial jerk he'd become. Pulling the rotary phone on the table closer to him, his finger spun the 808 area code and number.

"Finast Construction," a bass voice growled.

"Red? That you?"

A thin silence. "Yeah, who's this?"

"Hey, you red-headed bastard, it's a ghost from the past."

Another silence, a long one. Then a jovial tone, almost too jovial, Hank thought.

"Pualoa? Hey, Hank, where the hell are ya?"

"Baltimore, Red. I'm working here."

"Well, I'll be damned. How many years has it been now? When are ya coming back to Hawaii?"

"Not just yet, Red, not yet. But I'm calling for a specific reason." Hank tried not to let his anxiety show as he complained about the bank statements, the missing payments to the trust.

"Hey, look, man," Red answered, his voice sugary. "Our expenses, they're sky-high. The Japanese have come in and bought out the real estate market. Our raw materials, they cost three times what they did when you left. Sure, we're a little behind on the trust payments. But, let's face it, you're not holding up your end of the business here either. These are tough times."

Hank chose not to get into a sparring match over that. He had precious little to say in his defense. "What about Big John, Red? I haven't been able to reach him."

"Well, man, things have changed around your old place. The kids' grandmother died. Big John...believe it or not, he took off. Took Kekoa with him. Sold the house."

"What the hell are you talking about? John wouldn't do anything like that. And where's Leilani?"

"Look, I didn't believe it either. I feel just as bad about it as you do," the sugary voice continued. "But you'll be glad to know I've taken care of Leilani. Put her with a nice family in Manoa. The Wongs—they're both teachers at Oahu Preparatory Academy. She's going to Oahu Prep, too. Let me remind you, Hank, that tuition's no small piece of change. I take care of it every month."

Hank stumbled through a few more sentences. "As soon as Big John gets back, have him call me." He gave Red his number.

"Sure, Hank, no problem. And don't worry about the trust payments. The economy's supposed to start heating up again, and we'll get back on top of things. Great to hear from you."

Hank felt like slamming the phone down, but instead placed the receiver into the cradle with excess deliberation. Murphy seemed to have all the answers, fitted neatly together like a jigsaw puzzle. But the piece that didn't fit was the news that Big John had up and left. And taken Kekoa with him? Separating brother and sister? Impossible.

Hank had been careful to keep Big John informed of his post office box addresses over the years. But John hadn't responded. No, something didn't smell right.

* * *

Two weeks later. The October sky vibrated an electric blue over the urban renewal of Baltimore's Inner Harbor. The sun's five o'clock rays cast a mosaic of amber and russet on the trees of Federal Hill across the water. Up close, these same rays created skyward pillars in the dust. Brick, mortar, and building rubble lay scattered in random heaps around the demolition site. The sounds of machinery abounded, and ordinarily, Hank Pualoa would have been content. But he'd been troubled ever since talking to Red.

Hank sat in the control cab of his construction crane, in full command of boom and ball. His arms and the levers moved in unison. His high-top work shoes drove the clutch pedals in and out in perfect coordination. The ball hit, cracking mortar and tumbling brick, sending an immense cloud of dust and debris surging skyward.

One thunderous boom, then another. Finally, a crash of bricks as the stubborn south wall of the old Osborne Building surrendered. Most of the original demolition had been accomplished by expertly placed explosives. But now the job was left for the wrecking ball to take down the remaining sections—the final clearing of land for the next prize piece in the downtown Baltimore skyline: a luxury condo apartment building.

When the last of the dust had settled, he pulled off the red and white kerchief protecting his face and took a deep breath. The door folded away, and he swung his frame out of the cab. The foreman's flag in its trailer mount signaled the end of the day's work. Hank felt a surge of pride in his crew. Running his own company sure as hell beat working for someone else. And he was good at it. He waved the foreman clear and hoisted a length of safety cable. The two men secured the ball to the near end of the boom. As they secured the last bolt into the U-buckle, the foreman turned to him: "Care to hoist a few before heading home to the little woman?"

"Thanks, but not tonight. Besides, there's nothing to drink to and no one to go home to," Hank said. The foreman shrugged and headed for his VW. Hank zipped up his windbreaker and picked his way across the uneven rubble. As he unlocked his apartment deadbolt, he hardly expected to find the lights on in his living room. Nor did he anticipate someone lounging in his easy chair.

"Hey, old buddy, surprise!"

Hank stopped dead just inside the door.

"How the hell did you get in here?"

Red Murphy grinned. "That's what I love about you, Pualoa. So hospitable. But, hey—your landlady's a real peach. A little sweet talk goes a long way."

Hank's large hands trembled as he hung his jacket on a hook in the front hall closet. His mind clicked off a bunch of alternatives. Be friendly? Hostile? He decided to play it cool and cut the surly attitude. This was his business partner, after all. And they went back a long way.

He and Murphy had met in the mid-Fifties as Seabees in the U.S. Navy. Right off, they'd struck up a tight friendship. They had a lot in common: both twenty years old and green, both from Hawaii, both toughened up from construction jobs that started part-time in high school. Their stint as Seabees taught them specialized skills as they built roads, schools, orphanages, and public utilities in underdeveloped countries. But when it came time to re-up, they elected to return home and set up their own construction firm in Honolulu.

"So...," Hank said, "what brings you to Baltimore, Red?"

"Hey, I felt kinda bad for you when we talked on the phone. Thought maybe I'd cheer you up a little. Maybe get you to come on home."

Hank took in his partner's relaxed pose and fancier dress than he'd

231

remembered: a new-looking tweed sport coat, Ralph Lauren polo shirt, and tooled leather boots. "Six thousand miles to cheer me up? That's pretty decent of you." *Not like you at all,* he thought to himself.

"How about we go out and hoist a few, pal?"

"I don't drink any more, Red."

"That so? How long's it been?"

"Ten years now."

"I'm impressed. Can I at least buy you dinner? How about some of those famous Maryland crab cakes I've heard so much about?"

A little after seven, they followed the hostess at Donlevy's Crab House up to the second floor. Hungry customers had already filled up all the space downstairs. Even on a week night, the place jumped with raucous conversation and laughter.

Their chairs scraped the gray plank floor as Hank and Red pulled them up to the table. At the table next to theirs, a waiter covered the bare wood surface with white butcher paper and piled it high with steamed hard crabs and wooden mallets.

A chubby waitress with a wide smile and large bosom approached. "What'll it be, folks?"

"A pitcher of Miller on tap," Red said.

Hank scowled. "Iced tea for me."

They ordered clam chowder and platters of Maryland crab cakes with fries. Service was slow, but none of the other diners seemed to mind. At Donlevy's you made a night of it.

"Tell me again what's going on with Big John and the kids," Hank said, trying not to sound too tense. "It was kinda hard to digest all that over the phone."

Red savored a few spoonfuls of soup before responding. "Just what I told you…" He said it all again, with a few more details thrown in: the price Big John got for his house; where he thought John might have gone with Kekoa. "The Big Island, I would guess. Maybe Hilo-side."

Hank felt depressed. No matter how many questions he asked about Big John and his kids, the details came out either sparse or sounding contrived.

Red got more and more cheerful. Through a mouthful of cheese biscuit, he said, "I've been doing the best I can to keep the business running. Hired another stone mason, and a welder and steel worker. We're getting a few of the bigger jobs now."

"Like?"

"A couple of school renovations. Plus a new little strip mall on Dillingham." He took a long swig on his second mug of beer.

Hank tried to focus his eyes on the walls covered with trophy marlins and swordfish. But the pitcher of beer beckoned. The golden liquid gleamed wickedly in the low lamplight. He gulped the last of his watery iced tea.

The effect was not lost on Red. "Hey, old buddy, it'll all come together, everything's gonna be fine. How about one beer, just to help you lighten up?" Without waiting for an answer, he poured Hank's empty glass full. Hank didn't protest. He stared moodily at it, and after long hesitation, picked it up.

Red raised his mug. "Here's to better days, pal."

It didn't take long. By the second beer, despite a full stomach, Hank's head began to feel light. A second pitcher left him with a buzz. Around ten o'clock the crowd had thinned. He and Red traded jokes, reminisced about their Navy days, and the waitress left them their check. The pitcher of beer stood empty again, nothing but a few dribbles of foam sticking to the sides. By now they were the only diners left upstairs. Hank tried to pull his wallet out, but his fingers had trouble unbuttoning his left hip pocket.

"Not to worry, man, dinner's on me, remember?" Red said. He handed the waitress a fifty plus a $10 tip.

"Thank you, sir," she said brightly, and disappeared downstairs.

They rose to leave. That is, Hank tried to. His head floated like a balloon on a string. The room swirled, refusing to stand still. He grabbed the edge of the table to steady himself on two rubbery knees.

"Allow me, old buddy," Red said. His powerful hairy hands gripped Hank under the armpits, lifting and steering him to the top of the staircase. "Easy does it, you're doing fine."

Red scanned both the room and the staircase. No one in sight. Boisterous chatter and clattering plates floated up from the ground floor dining room. Now was the time. Red leaned Hank forward past the point of no return and let go.

Hank teetered for a moment. Then his legs caved under him. He tumbled and crashed, step over step. His arms flailed to grab the handrail. But gravity defied his best effort. As he hit bottom, his head cracked against a large ceramic pot housing an ersatz ficus tree and thudded to the floor.

Red followed him down the stairs, stepped over the sprawled body, and knelt down. A stream of blood trickled from under Hank's head, making a zigzag pattern in the grain of the wood floor. Hank emitted two short gasps and then seemed to stop breathing.

But was he dead? Red grabbed a handful of Hank's thick salt-and-pepper hair. He meant to raise the head up and drop it to the floor with a finishing slam. But he heard footsteps, probably a busboy coming to clear the tables upstairs. Red released his grip, stood quickly, and slipped out the restaurant's lounge-side door.

Chapter 33
Fortune and Forgiveness

SHOCKED SILENCE echoed through the Wong family dining room. Hank had momentarily halted his story, but having so captivated their attention, he felt bound to continue. He unraveled the rest in a dry, unemotional voice, stopping only to gulp a full glass of water.

"The busboy at Donlevy's discovered me, and the restaurant manager called 911. The fact that I'd been drinking probably saved my life because my body wasn't tensed when I landed, which would've caused even more broken bones. On the other hand, if I hadn't been drinking I wouldn't have fallen in the first place. Yeah, I hit bottom all right, in more ways than one.

"As for Red, by the time the paramedics arrived, he was nowhere in sight. Most likely, he got out of there fast, grabbed a cab, and headed straight for the airport. He left me for dead, but I was only unconscious. Only, I say." Hank gave a hoarse laugh. "I remained unconscious for nearly a week. In fact, the doctors at Mercy Hospital thought I wouldn't make it at all. I had severe head injuries, a broken collarbone, and multiple fractures of both legs. They kept me four months. When they finally released me, I still had three months of physical therapy to go through, five days a week."

"What about your construction company during all that time?" Paul asked.

"Fortunately, I'd hired a great crew, all reliable men, and a conscientious foreman. They stayed loyal to me and finished the condo job and met all our other contract obligations. Then, just before I left, I heard that a much larger firm was looking to buy mine out. I probably could have done better, but at that point expediency became more important."

Leilani leaned forward and spoke with great agitation, her dark eyes flashing. "But Daddy! Why didn't you have Red Murphy arrested?"

235

Hank could hardly believe his ears. She had called him "Daddy." It took him a moment to recover. "I wish I could've, dear, but I couldn't prove it. Nobody saw him push me."

Hank explained that his survival and recovery made him more determined than ever to find his family. "So I returned to Honolulu just as soon as I could get around on these," he said, fingering the canes. "My first order of business was to tail Red and find out what he was really up to."

"You mean I wasn't your first order of business? Or Kekoa either?"

Leilani burst out in gasps, a volcano ready to erupt.

"But Leilani...sweetheart, Yosh reassured me that you were living here with the Wongs and doing wonderfully. I'm a coward. I'd been so afraid you'd reject me that—so help me, God—I wasn't sure how to approach you."

Leilani shrank back in her chair. An accusing pout lingered on her full lips. "But why were you following Red?" she persisted. "You just said you couldn't prove he pushed you."

"Please let me explain a little more," Hank said. "For some time now I've suspected that he's been dealing in shady business practices in our partnership. And I've uncovered some irregularities in the trust I set up for you kids. I wasn't sure how to go about investigating all this without Red finding out. Yosh suggested that I could open a few more doors if I assumed the identity of a licensed private investigator working for the Fujita law firm. So I became Harold Perry, P.I. I think it's been convincing enough. I've aged a helluva lot these last months, and the injuries have altered my looks. With Big John gone and having no clue where to look for Kekoa, I've devoted myself full-time just trying to nail Murphy."

"What's Kekoa got to do with Uncle John's disappearance?" Leilani broke in.

Hank stole a glance at Leilani, trying to calculate how much bad news she could absorb. "When Red paid me his surprise visit in Baltimore, he told me that Eme had died and that, afterward, Big John sold his house, left Oahu, and took Kekoa with him."

Leilani nearly jumped out of her chair. "That's a lie! Uncle John disappeared long before *Tutu* passed away. And what's this about Kekoa? You know where my brother is?"

"Well, yes and no. Several times now, in the process of tailing Red, I've encountered a boy who calls himself Keith. Paul showed me a beautiful picture of you and Numi. But I have no idea what Kekoa looks like after so many years. I'm almost certain Keith is Kekoa, but I've failed to gain his trust or learn where he lives. I'm only hoping he'll find us."

"There's something else, Leilani," Paul interjected.

Hank took his cue. "Dear," he said almost in a whisper, knowing there was no gentle way to break this news. "Uncle John didn't just disappear. He was murdered—we're quite certain by Murphy. Kekoa may have witnessed the murder. Red probably knows this. It looks like he's been stalking Kekoa ever since to silence him."

"Oh, my God!" Leilani slumped and buried her face in her arms. "So that's what happened to poor Uncle John," she murmured. It was several minutes before she could raise her head again.

Hank leaned forward and looked deep into his daughter's eyes. "Leilani, I promise you, we will find Kekoa and we will get Red." He stopped talking. The story had exhausted him emotionally and physically. And then he asked—pleaded, "May I spend a few minutes alone with my daughter?"

Alex looked at Leilani, and she nodded. When Lori and the Wongs moved out to the lanai to enjoy the cool evening trades, Hank began speaking in hushed tones.

"I would give a thousand lifetimes to have your mother here now. I can't tell you how much you look like her. You're every bit as lovely as she. Oh, how I loved you guys. How I love you now. Is there no place in your heart for me? Can you forgive me? Haven't we both been punished enough?"

Leilani said nothing. Thinking he had been rejected, Hank reached for his canes and tried to pull himself to his feet. He rose unsteadily.

Leilani had every intention of making her father earn his way back into her affections, but she could hold out no longer. She reached out for him, and he almost fell into her arms where they sobbed together, she squeezing him around the shoulders and he stroking her long hair.

Raising her head, she looked him squarely in the eye and said: "I want to love you, Daddy. But it's going to take me some time. I really don't have the right to forgive you, but if my forgiveness is what you

237

need, I'll try. I'm already trying hard, Daddy."

"Thank you, my dear daughter. That's enough for me."

Alex peeked in the living room window from the lanai and motioned his mother to his side to see the reconciliation. He viewed it as a sign for everyone to return and celebrate the reunion of father and daughter.

Chapter 34
The House at Ewa

Upstairs, in the smallest bedroom of Big John's former house in Ewa, rumpled sheets hid two passionate college students. Louis Lynch, Jr. and his girlfriend, Abby, were wrapped in the ecstasy of their newfound love. Nobody outside heard their noisy mutual climax. Quite the reverse. A tractor's backup beep-beep jarred them from their cozy afterglow, and the crunch of loose gravel grinding beneath the wheels of a flatbed truck broke their mood entirely. Lou sprang to the window and watched the truck back down the full length of the driveway, vibrating the entire house as it went.

Lou and Abby raced for the bathroom. They had planned to leave the house much earlier that day, before Mr. Murphy and his crew arrived. Lou had promised the new landlord they'd vacate the house during spring break. They showered and dressed as quickly as they could, using only single words and grunts to talk about the challenge facing them: how to get out of the house without being seen. Abby pulled up the bedclothes, covering the rumples with the chenille spread. Lou threw their overnight bags up onto the bed. They tossed in the rest of their things just as they heard the diesel engine of a backhoe reversing itself off the flatbed.

They had worked out a plan for spring break. They'd store their stuff in a locker at the university during the day and come back to the house at night. Mr. Murphy would never know they were there at all. They hugged once more and slipped out the front door, where Lou caught sight of a yellow cardboard notice stapled to a stanchion supporting the lanai. The document was a building permit for 800 square feet of garage to house at least three vehicles; and 1,200 square feet of office space. The permit also contained a commercial zoning variance. Lou raised an eyebrow and whistled softly. They hustled to his car, which they'd deliberately parked half a block away, and drove off.

* * *

Behind the Ewa house, Red maneuvered the powerful diesel backhoe, blade first, into the tool shed, unaware of the two lovers who had just stolen away. He waved to the driver of the flatbed truck as it eased out of the yard and roared off down the street. The lowered blade began to crunch the compressed mixture of dirt and clay that had served as the floor of the old tool shed. Red knew the concrete block walls and corrugated tin roof would be needed for the expanded garage, so he took care not to disturb the concrete footings that supported the foundation. He was especially careful along the wall adjacent to the sidewalk.

This morning, Red had to clear away the dirt floor to make room for washed gravel and to eventually pour a heavy concrete slab over the top. Tomorrow the carpenters would come and frame in the three overhead garage doors. The actual doors would be installed on Wednesday. He planned to complete the digging on Thursday and finish his more delicate personal business here Thursday night.

Red used the front of the big blade to scrape each layer of dirt and clay free of the hard-packed floor. He'd planned the excavation carefully. A casual observer wouldn't be able to tell that, inside the shed, the depth at the wall next to the sidewalk was four feet deep instead of the eighteen inches elsewhere inside. To ensure that even his crew wouldn't notice the difference in depth, he placed three sheets of plywood over the deep end. He also parked his pickup in front of the doorway at that end for the rest of the daylight hours.

A tired but satisfied Red returned to his apartment that night. The unpleasant meeting in Fujita's office a few days earlier seemed to be just an annoying memory now. He had managed to survive the Rodminn Estates escapade with only a minimal loss and he did have other irons in the fire. He still had connections in the right places downtown, too. He'd had no trouble getting the variance on the Ewa office and garage once he explained that the building would be for low-traffic business use and no large equipment would be stored there.

* * *

Lou and Abby returned to their love nest each night, managing to conceal their presence. On the third evening, as they lay on the bed chatting, they heard the crunch of gravel. They scrambled to the window. In the bright moonlight, a familiar pickup backed all the way down the long driveway and parked in front of the new garage.

240

"That's weird," Lou whispered. "No lights."

For the first time, they noticed doors on the garage. The middle door opened—apparently by remote control. The pickup backed partially into the middle bay, and the door lowered to the top of the truck bed. The driver, a burly man, got out and pulled four very large nylon duffle bags from the truck bed. He then attached a small portable spotlight to the garage door frame, turned it on, and adjusted it to shine inside the garage. During those few enlightened seconds, Lou recognized the driver from their real estate dealings. That same Mr. Murphy disappeared inside the garage.

Abby and Lou crouched at the window, motionless. Scraping and digging noises reached their ears—the sounds of a shovel and pick in gravel, then hammering. They moved the settee to the window to watch, but their efforts went unrewarded. They remained there until the digging and hammering sounds stopped.

* * *

Inside the garage, Red rolled out two drop cloths, nine-by-twelve rectangles of heavy-gauge clear plastic, one over the other. Making a careful calculation of where Big John's body lay, he began to pick away at an area just below the sidewalk wall. A faint stench wafted up. He was getting close. Murphy donned a gauze industrial pollution mask from one of the bags and kept on working. Before long, rotted traces of denim jeans fabric sprouted up through the red clay like new pineapple shoots. At the sight of the jeans his breathing grew heavier.

Sections of the wall began crumbling. He used four-by-four posts to shore up both sides of the work area. A flat plywood board between the posts helped to support the footing below the wall. He'd prepared well for these eventualities.

Red decided to start from the top. But before he could clear a two-foot section, a large area below the shoring collapsed, leaving the shoring, the footings, and the wall still intact. The collapse came as a surprise, but it turned out to be a welcome one, reducing his task considerably. He used a rake and broom to clear debris from the drop cloths. But nothing could have prepared him for what he saw next.

He stood face to face—no, bone to bone—with the man he had murdered. Was it even John? The flesh remained, but the face and body had shriveled and darkened to the color of bitter chocolate. The huge strong man had been dehydrated to a third of his former weight. But two years underground—the moist hard clay and hot tropical climate had kept the body from decomposing completely. The maggots couldn't do their job efficiently and eat away his huge, robust business partner. The shrunken and brittle corpse lay within shreds of rotting jeans and fragments of a once white T-shirt. But the bashed-in head, more or less intact, with its full crop of hair seemed to take on a force of its own. Its black, vacant eyes stared up at him. The full set of teeth formed a sinister smile.

Red swore nonstop for a full minute, the only way he knew to mask his fear. The hairs on the back of his freckled neck bristled, his burly chest heaved. The hard breathing restored him to his senses. A leer crept over his lips as he thought, *Moving a lighter corpse is a helluva lot easier than wrestling a 300-pound body.* "Thanks for making it easy for me, old buddy," he growled aloud.

Fishing around in one of the duffel bags, he pulled out three heavy duty trash can liners and propped them on the floor, wide open. With the flat blade of a pick-axe, Red reduced his former partner and sometime friend into manageable pieces. Afterward, he raked the pieces into three fairly equal piles. He did it in such a matter-of-fact way that he looked like any homeowner raking leaves. Red Murphy shoveled the remains of Big John Pualoa into the three trash bags, twisted the top of each bag, and secured it shut with a yellow plastic twister seal. Each trash bag fit easily into its own duffle bag. Now he had to get rid of the drop cloth. Shaking it out, he folded it tightly and flattened it out until it also could fit into one of the bags. And finally, he stuffed all three duffels into the stainless steel tool locker that sat transversely in the pickup bed, just behind the cab. Slowly, gently, he closed the lid and secured it with a padlock.

Red knew he couldn't finish the cleanup until later in the day. The backhoe would be needed to move the earth back into place. His final task right now was to clean up the burial spot.

At the water spigot next to the house, he halted and listened. His eyes were drawn to an upstairs window and he had the strangest feeling he was being watched. He took a few minutes to walk around the entire yard and out toward the front of the house, but saw nothing and no one. He dismissed his suspicion as a case of nerves.

Operating by moonlight, Red dumped two five-gallon bottles of bleach into a large garbage can, added water from the garden hose, and hauled it into the garage. With a large empty Maxwell House coffee can, he splashed the strong antiseptic mixture into the entire area that he had dug out; then poured the remainder into the actual hole left by the body itself. "That'll do it," he said aloud.

Changing into a pair of street shoes, he used the garden hose to douse the muck from his tools and mud-spattered boondockers. Red raised the garage door with its remote so that he could pull the pickup out of the middle bay, and then lowered it again. Headlights off, he drove out of the driveway slowly to minimize the noise. But this night was far from over for him.

* * *

At 2 a.m., the wind-up alarm clock on the dresser ticked away the seconds of silence in the room Leilani and Numi shared. Leilani tossed on her bed. Her thick hair hung damply from perspiration, and her cotton teddy stuck to her glistening body. She kicked the covers down to her feet and felt a gentle trade wind's breeze across her face and breasts. Not all her discomfort could be blamed on the heat. How could she sleep with so much going on in her life?

Leilani had a real father again, but she couldn't imagine just how her life would be changed by their reunion. She liked him immensely and felt pity for all that he had been put through. But only pity? No! Their new relationship involved a good deal more, with lots to grow on. But she couldn't imagine moving in with him either. After all, he was still pretty much a stranger. She would remain with the Wongs, at least until after graduation. They had agreed to this. In the fall, she'd go away to college. The University of California at Berkeley had already accepted her. The thought of being on the Mainland, more than two thousand miles away from Alex—it might be too far. Would their love survive?

She took the foam pillow from beneath her head and wrapped both arms around it, squeezing firmly. The breeze slipped through the blinds once more to run a chill up her spine. In defense, she rolled to her side, placing the pillow close to the wall, and her conscious thoughts turned slowly to dreams. She knew Alex slept on the other side of this very wall. Would he miss her if she went away? Would he be there when she came home?

Chapter 35
An Offering to the Goddess Pele

JUST AFTER 9:30 p.m. Murphy's pickup sped along Nimitz Highway toward the airport. Red intentionally avoided the ramp for the elevated access road to the modern airport complex. The pickup contin- ued along beneath the massive concrete freeway structure. At the third traffic light he turned onto Lagoon Drive, which led to the original Honolulu passenger terminal. Now, with the new international and in- ter-island air terminals, only express freight, charter, and private flights used the old facilities.

As he approached Keehi Lagoon, silhouettes of wrecked and abandoned sea craft, backlit by moonlight, penetrated the silvery lagoon surface. By day—any man's eyesore, pure blight. But at this late hour— any boy's vision of mystery and adventures.

Stopping short of the high chain-link fence, Red beeped his horn and got out of the pickup to await rent-a-cop security. The guard drove to the gate in a jeep, and recognizing Red's familiar face, he unlocked and swung open the gate to the private aircraft parking enclosure. The guard knew him because of the number of inter-island jaunts Murphy had been flying in recent weeks. Red had filed successive flight plans to each of the outer islands in their turn. That afternoon he'd filed one for Hilo on the Big Island of Hawaii. He intended to continue the random pattern of deceptive destinations in the weeks to come. Then there'd be nothing distinctive about this night's flight.

Red edged the pickup toward the two-seater Cessna 150 parked on the near end of the tarmac. Aging but well-kept, it meant more to him than any human being. Unlocking the tool chest in the pickup bed, he removed the three gym bags and tossed them casually on the pad in front of the cockpit while he unlocked the passenger side door. He set the bags inside, one propped on the passenger seat, the other two squeezed into the space on the floor.

Cry Ohana

Flight preparations entailed the release of the tie-downs holding the wings and tail. When he removed the wheel chocks, he kicked the tires to prove sufficient air pressure. Next he walked slowly around the plane, checking it for obvious faults. He could not afford an accident, tonight of all nights. Having successfully completed the external checks, he climbed aboard and fastened himself securely into the pilot's seat.

He began another series of flight checks before starting the engine and continued throughout the warm-up process. Using the radio to request access to the taxi paths and runways, the Cessna pulled away from the assigned tether pad. When the necessary clearances emanated from the speaker, the revving propeller thrust the small Cessna forward, and after a short length of runway, another thrust lofted it airborne.

Red loved to fly alone. To him it represented a cleansing, a sense of freedom only a pilot or a deep sea diver could know. The hour-and twenty-minute southeasterly flight would take him just beyond the Big Island—toward the Hawaiian Trench, one of the few truly deep places in the world's oceans. He'd just pick his spot and push the bags from the plane. Then he would come about and put into Hilo's airport without anyone noticing the slight detour.

Forty minutes into the flight, a dark thought hit him. "Damn!" he said aloud. After all that planning he'd forgotten to bring anything heavy enough to weight down the bags. He couldn't have them washing up on a beach somewhere, could he? He checked his watch—too late to return to Oahu for the cinder blocks and chains in the pickup's bed. He let out a bellowing stream of expletives, then paused. He would now launch into plan B, almost as good as plan A. Red altered the Cessna's course slightly, for a direct approach to Hilo International Airport on the east coast of the Big Island. The plane landed thirty minutes later and taxied up to the transit parking pad assigned by the control tower.

Red secured the plane. At the Budget rental counter he picked up car keys and paperwork for a white Mercury Bearcat. The three gym bags and his personal overnighter, which he usually kept in the plane, easily fit into the trunk.

A lonely road led up the 4,000 feet to Volcanoes National Park. Although the air remained clear at sea level, a vog had settled over the higher elevations. Kilauea and Mauna Loa were both active volcanoes these days, so the presence of fog, smoke, and volcanic ash actually proved the norm.

The Mercury pulled into the parking lot of Volcano House. The desk clerk handed Red the key to 213 in return for his credit card information, and he found his way to the room without a bit of trouble. In fact, he'd spent the night with Cindy next door in 215 only two months before. He missed Cindy, but he missed Wilma even more. Why, he asked himself, did he always mess up with the great women in his life?

He tossed the overnighter onto the folding luggage rack, fell back on the bed, and tried to relax. Despite his show of bravado at the Ewa burial site, his skin still crawled from his ghoulish chores. Even a fifteen-minute shower didn't wash away his jitters. With the bath towel wrapped around him, he tried the bed once more. He flipped on the television remote, but the reception proved bad and the programming even worse.

He opted for a walk outside instead. Maybe the air, even vog, would do him good, so he pulled on his olive-green jumpsuit over a clean pair of briefs and remembered to take along a flashlight. The duffle bags remained in the trunk of the Mercury, waiting the several hours he needed before completing this night's work. He wanted no accidental intrusions.

In the lounge, a combo worked the crowd with Hawaiian songs, some mournful, some seductive, accompanied by the plucking of ukulele and guitar. He longed to kill the next few hours in there with a tall cool one, but decided the less he was seen, the safer. The lounge would close at 12:30, and he'd wait another hour for good measure; by then most guests would be in bed. However, there'd be nothing wrong with him scouting out a good secluded route for later.

At the north end of the parking lot Red found a service road used by the park rangers. The road dwindled and deteriorated into a narrow path as he walked on. He followed it to the string of steam vents that surrounded the gigantic Halemaumau crater. Seeking a particular vent, he came across a cul-de-sac near the Crater Rim Road with a few wooden benches and room enough for several cars to park. A sign stating the park rules included an after-dark warning. *I'd better take care on that one*, he thought. A night chill, an icy shudder raced through him until he discovered a rocky shelf exhaling hot steam curls. The warmed air smelled like rotten eggs, emanating from a rich sulfur content. The rising steam glistened in the moonlight. Red had heard that Pele, the fire goddess, was supposed to live in the crater, and although he didn't usually buy into that nonsense, he had to acknowledge a fearful presence. Up close, her passionate breath smothered him. He imagined this is what a walk through hell would be like.

Striding a few more yards, he finally located the gaping vent that he and Cindy had encountered on their recent trip together. *Would she remember his comment? Naw! Look at the way that dumb broad had screwed everything else up.*

Red gazed at the lava rock lips worn smooth over time. Wet and voluptuous, they awaited his offering. He noted with satisfaction that the opening between the parted lips would be more than adequate for his task. On his hands and knees, Red crept as close to the edge of the vent as he dared and lowered his flashlight six inches down the mouth before turning it on. The beam barely illuminated a sloping ledge about six feet below that led to a large crevice at one side. His offerings could easily pass down through that crevice to hellish depths beyond. Just as the scalding steam nearly overpowered him, he withdrew from the edge, dousing the flashlight before its beam breached the surface.

A large rock, over three pounds, became a test of depth and concealment. Releasing it over the vent, he heard several loud claps and clicks as the rock fell, careening from level to level. Not bothering to count the number of lesser noises that followed, Red grew confident that he'd found the right place. As a final precaution, he looked about for a loose branch to use as a pry in case one of the gym bags got hung up on the top ledge. Across the road he found an eight-foot branch in a pile of cleared brush and broke off the smaller pieces that protruded from it. He left it lying beside the vent opening.

Satisfied with his advance research and planning, Red returned to the parking lot and the rental car. He'd spent nearly two hours scouting for the right vent. Back at the inn, he saw only a few rooms still lit. He killed the next couple of hours lying on his bed, dozing, still wearing his dusty boots. Then abruptly, he sat up. Primed and ready, he stole outside once more.

Guided by moonlight, Red drove slowly back toward and as close as he could get to the selected vent. He retrieved the duffles from the rental car trunk and lugged them the rest of the way. He carefully selected several good-sized lava rocks from the nearby area and shoved them into the bottom of each duffle bag to stabilize its drop. He congratulated himself on preparing well this time—especially by choosing duffle bags of slippery nylon fabric.

Now it was time. He poised the first duffle bag over the wider part of the vent, holding it with the heavy end down, so it would not rotate as it fell. Releasing his grip, the duffle fell, but a quick dull thud told him it hadn't fallen far. He peered down the hole in alarm and flicked on his flashlight. Somehow the bag had wedged in the narrower part of the hole.

Grabbing the long branch he'd set aside earlier, he poked at the bottom of the duffle, dislodging it and sending it tumbling to a deeper destiny. He counted at least two ricochets a few seconds apart. The second duffle seemed to fall freely. The third passed the first ledge. He listened intently, then peered down through the eerie beam of the flashlight, but he still could not tell how much farther it had fallen. Feeling the sting of panic now, he dropped a succession of stones, large and small, hoping to dislodge the duffle if it were stuck too close to the surface. But he still couldn't determine its fate.

"Damn!" He kicked a hunk of crumbling lava. Finding nothing more that he could do, Red drove back to the inn in a fit of frustrated rage.

After a sleepless night, he returned to the site at 8 a.m. To his dismay, two sunbathers lay on the rocks that lipped the edge of his personal vent. They had towels beneath them and additional towels rolled up under their heads. He kept his distance and sat down on a wood bench at the end of the cul-de-sac. With growing irritation and anxiety, he regarded their brief attire, especially the man's bikini swim suit. *There ought to be a law against dressing like that in public,* Red thought, but then smiled wryly. *Who the hell am I to be wanting more laws?*

His wait ended a quarter of an hour later when a U.S. Park Ranger vehicle pulled into the cul-de-sac and chased the sunbathers away. Red sat there until he was sure that everyone had moved out of sight before he ventured any closer to the vent. A nylon climbing rope lay over one edge of the hole. The other end had been secured around the post supporting the guard rail. It must have belonged to the young sun worshipers. They probably planned to play daredevil and climb down into the vent for a bit of a steam bath. *Idiots,* he thought, *you can scald yourself to death that way.* He untied the rope and tossed it over the edge.

Cry Ohana

Now for his real mission here. He searched the vent opening for any traces of the gym bags, but found nothing. The wet, slick vent walls were probably the reason the couple had abandoned their climbing attempt. He decided that if the kids had seen anything unusual inside the vent, they'd have abandoned their adventure sooner.

Red's mood shifted into manic high gear, and his burly chest swelled with macho satisfaction as he climbed into the car. The murder could truly be put behind him now. Checking out at Volcano House, he drove to the airport and dropped off the car. The morning sun found his Cessna 150 airborne once again.

* * *

"Ker-runch!" The sound of a vehicle on gravel came from outside their window.

"Oh, no!" Lou cried. He bounded out of bed and leaped to the window. "It's him!"

Abby gasped, jumped up, and joined him. Together they huddled naked in the curtained shadows of the solitary bedroom window. Lou left the window first and began dressing—pulling on one khaki trouser leg, off-balance, staggering, pulling on the second, nearly falling in his hurry.

Abby dressed quickly, too. For a moment or two they considered spending the day hiding out in the house, but the incessant "beep-beep-ing" of the backhoe's reversing signal changed their minds. They easily stole out the front door, hurried down the block to the car, and drove off toward Waimea Beach Park.

While the backhoe's diesel engine warmed up, Red opened all three garage doors. He pushed a portion of the dirt and old gravel back into the four-foot-deep hole and raised the shoring to the new level, repeating the process until the entire shed was leveled at eighteen inches below the block line. He used water from the garden hose to settle the mixture into a hard-packed surface. With the job done, he pulled his pickup around to the street and entered the house to relax and wait for the truck bringing a fresh load of gravel.

Upon setting foot in the living room, he stopped. He had never expected that his student tenants would be tidy, but even the downstairs hadn't been picked up. He hurried into the kitchen. Ugh! A garbage stench wafted up from the sink. It smelled like Li'l Abner's Skonk Works. Throwing open the kitchen windows, he pulled a bottle of Clorox from

249

under the sink and poured it down the drain. The refrigerator was empty except for half a loaf of molding bread and two jars, one of peanut butter and the other of guava jelly. The door held three cans of soda and two cans of beer. He threw out the green bread and helped himself to a beer.

Red climbed the stairs slowly, sipping his beer while pondering the lived-in smell. Louis Lynch, Jr. was supposed to have been out of the house a week ago, home on spring break. Scanning the five bedrooms and two baths, Red scowled. Not one of the eleven beds had been made. He saw laundry strewn all over the place. The odor seemed strongest in the room at the back of the house, the one with the queen-size bed. Perfume or eau-de-whatever lingered and permeated the room.

Were kids living here during their spring break? The question, and any impact it might have, was dislodged when he heard the gravel truck enter the driveway. Red hurried down the stairs and out the door with the single thought of directing the driver into his dumping positions.

For two hours Red and the driver distributed the freshly washed gravel into a uniform depth of six inches that would become the foundation for the concrete floor. Almost light-headed, Red paid off the driver with an extra five, and headed back to his trailer office to order the concrete truck and cement-finishing laborers for Monday morning.

Chapter 36
An Appetite for Answers

SPIRALING THE Ford Escort in tight upward turns, Paul Wong found a parking place on the third garage level of Ward Warehouse. The Old Spaghetti Factory occupied a prominent corner on the second floor of this fashionable waterside mall.

Paul held the leaded glass door open for Masako and Numi. The three Wongs found the rest of their party sitting in the foyer on oversized Victorian velvet chairs and sofas. Alex stood to kiss his mother. "It'll be a ten-minute wait. They'll call us," he said.

Paul regarded Hank Pualoa. "I see you're down to one cane now. You're making great progress."

"Thanks, Paul. I've been going for whirlpool and exercise therapy several times a week. It'll be a great day when I can toss this one, too."

Lori squeezed his arm and that gave him pleasure. His reunion with Leilani had made him a much happier man. Although she chose to continue living with the Wongs, the two of them actually invented reasons to see each other often. Leilani and Lori had come into his life in a big way.

The hostess stepped out from a carved wood and brass kiosk. "Wong, party of seven." Their table was ready.

She led them to the largest room, featuring an immense stained glass window in the shape of daisy petals bursting with golden and crimson light from the late afternoon sun. Amid heavy Victorian sideboards and chandeliers, they slid onto padded benches backed by polished brass headboards and footboards that had once adorned some handsome bedstead. Hank sat on an extra chair at one end.

The lively dinner hubbub comprised a dozen or so languages. And abruptly, without warning, it dissipated entirely. At an extended table behind the Wongs, more than thirty locals sat singing. The low, sweet chorus of voices commanded the attention of every diner in the

251

ꟍ the waitresses stopped to hear *The Lord's Prayer*, sung in

E ko makou Makua i loko o ka lani;
E hoa no ia kou Inoa.
E hiki mai kou aupuni;
E malama 'ia kou makemake ma ka honua nei.
E like me 'ia i malama 'ia ma ka lani la.
E ha'awi mai ia makou i keia la i 'aina makou no neia la.
E kala mai ho 'i ia makou, i ka makou lawe hala 'ana
Me makou e kala nei i ka po'e i lawe hala i ka makou.
Mai ho'oku'u 'oe ia makou i ka ho'owalewale 'ia mai.
E ho'opakele no na'e 'ia makou i ka 'ino.

No ka mea,
No ke aupuni,
A me ka mana,
A me ka ho'onani 'ia a mau loa aku.

'Amene, 'Amene.

Festively wrapped presents lay all along the table. Seated in the place of honor was the family matriarch, a regal, silver-haired woman in a *muumuu*. She wore more than ten leis around her neck.

"It's her eightieth birthday," the approaching waitress told the Wongs. "Isn't it wonderful?"

When their orders had been taken, Masako turned to Hank. "I've just heard from a newspaper friend of mine that Red Murphy recently repurchased your brother's house. Paid a lot more than it's worth, I'm told."

The news hit Hank like a belly punch, but he pretended nonchalance. "Oh, yeah?"

Masako pressed on. "Do you think it has anything to do with your brother's disappearance?"

"I wouldn't know, Masako. I...uh..." The arrival of their salads and warm loaves of sourdough bread saved him from trying to justify his ignorance. He pushed back his chair and excused himself for a trip upstairs to the men's room. Managing on the single cane, he climbed the wide mahogany staircase. Leaning against the handrail, his eyes idly surveyed the bar and lounge.

A lone figure occupied a booth at the rear. Hank recognized the tattoo on the freckled left forearm even before he saw the face of the red-haired man who sat eating there. This man with a large Seabees' bumble-bee tattoo had to be Red Murphy. Hank began working his way toward the booth. He had no great desire to confront Red right now, but felt drawn to him anyway. Moving still closer, he hadn't the least idea what to say to him when he got there.

Red sensed someone approaching and glanced up. His mouth gaped open, looking comically wounded as it dripped red with marinara sauce. His poise and a lone strand of spaghetti slipped to his plate. Red swallowed hard and used his smeared napkin to wipe his mouth and chin.

"Mind if I sit down for a minute?" Hank asked.

"What for? We don't have a friggin' thing to talk about." Red reached for his glass of Lambrusco and sipped, marking time. Peering at Hank over the top of the glass, he set it down and blurted out, "Have you come to extract another pound of flesh? You got at least ten pounds at the meeting last week. It was you in the other room upstairs in the bank, wasn't it?"

Hank nodded. "But if you want to talk about pounds of flesh, let's set the record straight. You didn't mind leaving me for dead at Don-levy's in Baltimore, did you, old buddy?"

Red's teeth ripped into a hunk of sourdough bread and he chomped for several moments before responding. "You got it all wrong. The manager came over right away. Said he'd already called 911. Hey, it's not my fault you can't hold your liquor. Besides, I had a plane to catch."

The two men glared at one another, each looking for some indi-cation in the other's eyes. Red's sips of wine had turned into long swigs.

Hank placed the cane across his lap and re-ignited the conversa-tion. "I understand you bought Big John's old house back. I asked myself, why would Red want to do that after selling it off in the first place? Of course, I also know you paid more than market value for it. I thought that was kind of strange."

Hank didn't have to wait long for Red's reaction. A gulp of wine sprayed forth from his lips, leaving an irregular pattern of red spots across the table. He began to cough.

"Easy, my friend, easy does it," Hank whispered, pleased with himself.

"Bull crap, git off this my friend crap," Red sputtered. "I had good reasons for buying the place back. We needed more space for our equipment. I checked out warehouse rentals on the island, but the costs were out of sight. Big John's place has the double lot behind it, and it's deeded with the house. Plus, there's the big shed. That's why. And now you can stop with the third degree."

"Sure, man, but I have one last question for you. I don't buy that garbage you fed me about Big John moving off-island and taking Kekoa with him. No way would he do that. Where the hell is he?"

Red leaned forward. "Just what do you think I know, you sly bastard?"

Hank knew that he had shaken Red. "I'm just soliciting your help. After all, we're still partners. And we were friends once. Why shouldn't I come to you?"

"I can think of a lot of reasons. What do you want from me? I don't know anything. Can I help it if Big John turned out to be an irresponsible sonofabitch?" Red pounded his left fist down on the table. "Get out of my sight, you crippled bastard, you!"

Hank slid out of the booth, but stopped beside the table. Leaning over, he dipped his right forefinger into Red's wine glass, swirled it around, then sucked at it with his lips in an insulting gesture. "Have a nice day," he said.

Maneuvering over to the bar, Hank ordered a glass of Alka-Selzer. "Take it to that booth over there," he told the bartender, pointing to Red. "The gentleman has just received some terrible news."

Halfway down the stairs, Hank heard, "Damn your friggin' hide!" resound from the lounge. Hank smiled. *Shaka*, right on! Red's last drink had arrived.

He rejoined the others and, with great gusto, dug into his pasta, Italian sausage, and meatballs. He didn't mention his confrontation with Red Murphy. That pleasure was all his.

* * *

Sam Osaka left the bakery shortly after nine the next morning. Nothing unusual about that, except that he refused to tell anyone where he was going. Just before noon he suddenly reappeared at the back door with a broad grin across his face. He'd been shopping and had left a large cardboard box from Sears just outside the door.

"Kekoa! Come quick!" he called. "There's a present for you."

Kekoa opened the box and gave Sam a big hug, sending a red flush over Sam's sallow complexion. A new bike! But his happiness turned to dismay when he saw the words, "Some assembly required." He sat down on the floor to study the instructions. An undaunted Sam directed the meticulous assault on the bicycle parts. An hour later, Kekoa rolled his brand-new bike to the corner of his room where the old one stood. He'd gotten a lot of good use out of the old bike, especially making local deliveries in the neighborhood.

"Why, Sam? Why a new bike now?"

Sam could hardly be called a demonstrative man, but the time and place had come, so he put his arm around Kekoa's shoulder and drew him close.

"You are son I not have. You bring great happiness to Mauro and me, more than I can say. You work very hard, and you care deep for us. I weep for heavy sadness you bear, and wish we lighten you. You keep all locked up in heart, but we respect your wish."

"Oh, Sam! You and Mauro gave me a real home and work when I had nothin'. You gave me all that love when I needed it most. I don't remember my father, but if I could pick one out now, it'd be you."

"Kekoa, my son, you much wiser than anyone we know of such small years. Someday, when we gone, bakery be yours. Till then, we got each other." He put his hand on Kekoa's head and stroked the mop of dark hair.

"But what about Yasuko?"

"She benefit other ways. College, some properties, and much money. No worry about dear, dutiful Yasuko. Whole family see she prosper."

Kekoa walked back to the new bike to take it outside for a spin. He looked at the old one with its dents, rust, and jury-rigging. It was an old friend not to be dismissed lightly. He hesitated a moment. "What about this old bike? What'll I do with it now?"

"You decide, Kekoa."

"I don't think my friend Andy's got a bike. Okay if I give it to him?"

"I think excellent choice. Yes, most excellent choice, indeed!"

* * *

Lori closed the door to Hank's apartment and followed him into the living room. "I really can't stay long. Tomorrow's a work day."

Hank sat down on the deeply cushioned couch and beckoned her to sit beside him. She shook her head. Instead, she bent over and tried to kiss him lightly on the cheek, but he purposely turned and guided her lips to his own. Lori didn't resist—she returned his kiss warmly, and when it came time for their lips to part, hers hung there a little longer. He pulled her gently down on the couch beside him, and they embraced for the first time. They closed their eyes and felt the presence of one another for lingering minutes.

"Mmmm! I've wanted to do that for a good long time," whispered Lori in short, panting breaths.

"But I've only been back a few months."

"I don't mean since you returned. I've loved you since we were kids, even before Malia. But for some reason, you preferred her to me."

"Lori, I…I never knew, not the slightest inkling. There were no signs."

"There were some, my dear, but you had eyes only for our Malia. I loved you both too much to come between you. You still have the power to stir some of my old feelings for you. After the accident, I tried to hate you, but once you came back…"

He didn't let her finish. "I did like you first, but your brother told me your parents wouldn't let you date anyone who wasn't Japanese. Wasn't that true?"

"I think I would have dated you anyway. That is, if you had actually asked me instead of my brother Buddy."

Hank laughed, "Now you tell me." They kissed again, and his fingers toyed with the top button on her two-piece dress. He made no attempt to undo it. "Somehow, I know these feelings I have for you are not new either. Perhaps it's just time for them to resurface."

She reached under his hand to release the top and second buttons. His fingers roamed freely for a few moments, and then they kissed long and tenderly.

He clumsily undid the third button. "Will you spend the night with me?"

She allowed his hand to slip under her bra and embrace her softness there. Her hand slid over his and squeezed. She sighed and her small firm breast rose from beneath to fill his hand.

"Will you stay the night with me?" he asked again.

"Tonight I can't. Auntie Mariko's medicine is in the car. I have to take it to her. I'm truly sorry." The spell was broken.

"You've got a whole list of excuses memorized," he said ruefully.

She stood up and re-buttoned her dress. "Please, my dear, don't stop asking. I will spend many nights with you. As many as you wish, but not tonight. No, don't get up." She bent over to kiss him again, and he buried his head in her breasts. His arms encircled her waist.

"Goodnight, dear." Lori turned, and with a great tangle of emotions, left Hank on the couch. "Goodnight, my dear," she repeated with even more tenderness. And she was gone.

Chapter 37
A Test of Friendship

SOMEONE was following him. Red had noticed the faded blue Chevy earlier in the week. It had stuck to him like a flea on a dog's back. And yesterday the same Chevy had appeared again—once too often to be pure coincidence. He'd tried a few evasive maneuvers, and when the Chevy clung too close, he knew he'd grown a tail for sure. It had to be a professional, as he could never catch a glimpse of the driver's face. About all he could put together was a probable male, a Padres baseball cap, sunglasses, and an aloha shirt. He wondered how many days he'd been followed unknowingly. Then it hit him—the Chevy belonged to Hank Pualoa.

The very thought chilled Red, driving him to redouble his caution. He hadn't been near the bakery in two weeks, but he had frequented the area on a regular basis for weeks before that. Now that he knew where his prey nested, he could choose his opportunity. First, however, he had to lose his own tail.

Early Friday afternoon he drove his Buick into the underground parking garage of a county office building on King Street. He parked quickly on the second level down and ran to the rail to see if the Chevy had followed him. It had. In about ten seconds it would appear on his parking level. Red dashed to the enclosed stairwell at the front of the building. He walked up three flights and emerged on the first office level. He did a lot of business in this building and knew the layout. At the washroom door of a private suite, he punched in a familiar keypad combination and ducked inside. Half an hour later, he poked his head out and checked the hall. Finding it deserted, he walked to the rear stairwell and descended to the second garage level, where he peeked through the small wire mesh window in the fire door. Just as he expected, the blue Chevy lurked there with its faceless driver.

Red took the stairs up to the lobby and walked out the rear

258

door to an alley that led to Young Street, one block beyond the building. Seizing the moment to outwit his tail, he flagged down a taxi and gave the Ewa house address to the driver. He'd fetch his car later this evening.

Forty minutes later, he walked into the Ewa house's backyard and unlocked one of the new overhead doors in the renovated garage. Passing up the newer red truck, he selected the old Ford pickup. As he was about to climb in, an idea struck him. He removed a large empty plastic tub from a shelf and set it down on the new concrete floor. He tore a hole in a bag of Sackrete mix, scooped up half a shovelful, and tossed it into the tub. Adding a little water from the hose at the side of the house, he sloshed the mix about, then smeared it over the front and rear license plates of the pickup. He hosed out the tub and dumped the remaining mix on the ground next to the garage. When the Sackrete film began to thicken on the license plates, he backed out of the driveway and closed the door again. He drove away from Ewa thinking himself pretty clever.

Exiting the H-1 freeway at Koko Head Avenue, Red turned onto Waialae and parked down the block from the Kaimuki Koffee House. He took his usual seat by the window across the street from the bakery and ordered supper. He didn't expect Kekoa to show himself for at least another half hour.

No other diners had shown up this early. Once the waitress had placed his order, she sauntered back to his table for their usual friendly chat.

"Hi, Lucille," he said, eyeing her name tag. This was the first time he'd called her by name.

Scarlet lips and large teeth flashed a smile. But as hard as he tried to look at her face, his eyes kept dropping to her copious cleavage, which just refused to stay tucked into the deep V-neck of her uniform. Lucille chatted nonstop. Her throaty voice invited him to cling to her every word, but his eyes adhered to her breasts like fuzz to peaches.

Red had every intention of pursuing this woman, but right now he needed to keep a watchful eye on the bakery. Good-naturedly, she sensed his preoccupation and left to check on his order.

Lucille returned to the table with a large plate of Korean-style barbecued ribs, white rice, and canned green beans. He dove in with the manners of a dedicated carnivore. With his mouth full, he motioned for her to sit down across from him. His dinner knife accidentally fell to the floor, and as he bent over to pick it up, he failed to notice Kekoa leaving the bakery.

* * *

At the rec center, Andy sat on his basketball, lost in his own daydreams. He felt a hand on his shoulder. Without looking up he said, "About time you got here. My dad's gonna pick me up in forty-five minutes."

"I know," Kekoa said. "Forget about shooting baskets tonight. I got somethin' to show you back at my place."

Andy fell in behind Kekoa, and the two of them crossed over and strolled up the street into the bakery. Andy followed his friend through the shop to the rear door, where two bikes leaned against the inside wall.

"Hey, man!" Andy said, gaping at the bright blue and silver frame with thin racing wheels. "That yours? No way."

"Kiss mine, dude. Sam and Mauro just gave it to me." Kekoa grabbed the narrow black leather seat and ram's horn handlebar and rolled the bike away from the wall, so his friend could see it better.

Andy ran his hand over the short front fender, the brake cable, and gear shift. "A ten-speed, racing bars an' all. You sure as hell stepped in it and went t' heaven, dude."

Kekoa hesitated. "Andy?"

"Yeah?"

"I know my old bike sucks. It needs a bunch of work, but it still gets you there. You kin have it if you want it."

Andy approached the old bike as if seeing it for the first time. The solid red paint was bubbled with under-rust and dulled with age, but he envisioned it as though it already had a fresh paint job.

"Want it? You kidding? Sure. Thanks! I'll never forget this, brud-dah." He gratefully punched Kekoa's upper arm.

"You wanna try 'em out?" Kekoa offered, but before Andy could answer, they heard a familiar toot: Mr. Ballesteros bearing down on his horn out front. They leaned the bikes back against the rear wall and rushed through the shop to the curb.

Kekoa blurted out: "Would it be okay if Andy slept over? Tomorrow's Saturday. We want to go bike riding together tonight and tomorrow."

After some discussion, Papa smiled. "Okay, son. Behave yourself. I'll pick you up here at five tomorrow afternoon."

"Right on! Thanks, Dad."

The boys didn't wait for Mr. Ballesteros to drive off before bounding through the front door to the bakery, very nearly bowling Mauro off her feet.

Mauro chuckled as she followed the boys to the rear door and held it for them while they walked the bikes into the alley.

Kekoa turned toward her. "Andy's spending the night with me. I guess I should've asked you first, but is it okay?"

Mauro nodded her approval. She watched as they mounted, rode down the alley, and disappeared from sight. "You be careful!" she called.

After a few blocks of dodging rush-hour buses and cars on Waialae, the boys turned into Palolo Valley to escape the traffic.

* * *

As Red licked his last rib clean, he spied Kekoa and another boy emerging from the bakery. They hustled over to the pickup parked at the curb, its driver leaning over to open the passenger door. Red was surprised when no one got in; the friend usually left about five. Now, suddenly, it pulled away, and both boys went back inside.

Lucille took orders from an elderly couple in a booth, the only other customers in the place. She returned to Red with a cup of coffee for each of them, resumed her seat across the table, and smiled brightly. But he kept staring out the window.

Red spilled the last drops of his coffee down his chin when he caught sight of Kekoa and friend—riding their bikes right past the restaurant window! He wiped his chin and stood.

"Gotta go now. Sorry!" He pulled a $20 bill from his pocket. "The change is yours."

Lucille's face fell in a combination of surprise and disappointment.

Outside, Red opened his pickup truck door and stood on the running board, searching for any sign of the boys. Looking left, he spotted them turning onto Tenth Avenue. He cursed when the truck door slammed shut on the instep of his left foot. He pushed it open again and a passing car had to swerve to avoid hitting it.

"Get a grip, idiot," he scolded himself.

Rosemary and Larry Mild

After three tries, his engine sputtered to life, then very nearly coughed to its death as he executed a hurried U-turn. He took a right onto Tenth, but saw no sign of the boys. He picked up speed. At the fourth corner he spotted them. A sense of exhilaration surged through him, and he slowed down to observe them from a distance. Just past Palolo Elementary School they veered right onto Waiomao and started up the hill. Red followed, and about halfway to the next intersection, he saw the boys dismount their bikes and push them up the steep incline. Up, Red figured, so they could coast all the way back down on the left side of the road and see the oncoming cars.

He noted the lack of activity on the street. Strange for six o'clock at night. No car traffic. And, oddly enough, no homeowners tending their little gardens. He had to act now—and fast.

He accelerated slightly and rode past the boys. At the Lamaku Place intersection, he made a U-turn and again pressed the pedal closer to the floor. Now he was driving straight toward the boys, who were pushing their bikes up the incline side by side. Kekoa was on the open street side.

How convenient, Red thought. Adrenaline surged through him. Sweat poured onto his forehead like drizzle on a windshield. He bit his lower lip until he could taste blood.

He gathered speed and took precise aim at Kekoa, who appeared totally unaware of the danger ahead. But Andy instantly perceived what looked like a runaway truck. In a heroic split second, he dropped his bike, yanked Kekoa away from the new bike, and shoved him to safety behind a parked car. In rescuing his friend, Andy tripped over the new bike and fell, helpless and sprawling, into the road.

Kekoa lay huddled against the bumper of a parked car. He heard the loud thud as the pickup struck Andy's slender body. Metal crunched as the two bikes collapsed under the weight of the truck. For a brief moment in the dusk, Kekoa saw the truck speed down Waiomao toward Tenth Avenue. Kekoa's shoulder hurt. His knee was cut, scratched, and bleeding where his jeans were torn. But so what? None of it mattered now.

He staggered to the spot where Andy's mangled body had come to rest. "Andy!" he screamed. "Don't be dead!" No response. Kekoa looked up at the silent houses across the street and began to howl. "Help! Help! He's hurt. Somebody please help."

262

Cry Ohana

An Asian woman appeared in a doorway. "I'll call 911!" she cried out and disappeared inside the house.

Kekoa laid his head across Andy's chest. His own body shook with anguish, and he lay there until the ambulance arrived only minutes later. The woman came down from her house and tried to pull Kekoa to his feet, but he violently shook his head and clung to Andy's still form.

Kekoa crawled away only when the paramedics knelt down. They checked his friend's vital signs and inserted an I-V in his forearm. Fearing for broken bones, they very carefully slid Andy onto a board and then onto a gurney to immobilize him. Lifting it into the ambulance, they closed the door behind them. It roared away, siren blaring.

Streetlights blinked on as full darkness fell. A crowd began to gather. The neighbors stared in silence, arms crossed over chests, shaking their heads in sympathy. Kekoa didn't notice the police car with its blue light flashing until the ambulance had pulled away. The woman who had dialed 911 spoke excitedly to the uniformed cop. Then she pointed directly at Kekoa. "That's him," he heard her say.

Kekoa began to shake. His knees wobbled. Fear had never been a stranger, but now he realized something even stronger—shock. The same shock he had felt listening to the murder of Uncle Big John.

"Hey, son, I want to talk to you."

The policeman's deep voice sent a second tremor through the boy. Somehow Kekoa found his legs and began to run up the hill. At the intersection, he veered left and charged downhill on Lamaku Place.

"Wait!" the cop called. "I want to help you. You haven't done anything wrong!"

Kekoa wasn't sure why he ran from the officer. Maybe because he'd done it so often it had become a conditioned reflex. He just wanted to get away and think things out. He heard the thudding of rubber soles on stone-filled tar as the cop began chasing him.

The boy ran, half stumbling and scrambling, down the bumpy hill. At the bottom, the grade flattened, and when he looked ahead, he saw the road's end—a concrete block wall. The sprinting feet behind him grew louder. What now? Was he trapped? The tiny cul-de-sac was illuminated by a combination of streetlight and fresh moonlight. The block wall wrapped around to his right. No escape there. On his left, he found a carport stuffed to the ceiling with trash—squashed beer cans, filthy mat-

263

tresses, and a rusting cement mixer. But just to the right of the carport, he discovered a driveway and darted down it. To his surprise, it soon forked. The right fork led up to a house, a massive modern structure, well-lit inside. No, he didn't want to meet up with nosy people right now. And the cop would find him easily. Kekoa chose the left fork, a path that dipped steeply. Amid a thicket of dense underbrush, the path ended at a running stream.

He took one last look up the driveway he'd just fled. The officer stood at the top, at least 150 feet above, with his hands on his knees, bending forward trying to catch his breath. Kekoa knew the cop wouldn't follow. He also knew that he could make better time downstream than the cop could make going back up the road. He needed to stay hidden and keep moving along the stream—parallel to the road, but far enough to get past the crash scene and see the cop drive away.

In almost total darkness, Kekoa felt his way from rock to rock beside the stream. Exhausted, he plodded through tangled grasses. His arms flailed as he swatted at huge swarms of mosquitoes. The bleeding of his knee had slowed as far as he could tell. It still hurt. Aching all over and splattered with mud, he rested for a moment. A large flat rock gave him a place to sit and wash his wounds in the clear mountain stream runoff that snaked its way into the city's storm drain system.

Kekoa cupped his hands to splash water on his face. The dank coolness drained the suffocating fear from his mind. For the first time since Uncle John's death, he felt entirely devoid of fear. Intense rage had taken its place. He picked up a good-sized stone and boldly flung it as hard as he could through the concrete culvert ahead of him. He heard the loud, sharp crack as it struck, and the shattering of glass as it fell on some broken bottles along the ground.

High above, an outside light came on in a house at the top of a terraced yard. "Who's there?" a voice barked. "Who's there?"

Kekoa saw a moving flashlight beam and darted into the covered culvert to hide. He knew no one would take the trouble to search the dark stream bed, not without benefit of full daylight. Waiting in the ankle-deep stream, he felt cold and wet and miserable.

Just as he thought things couldn't get any worse, alien noises stole into his brain: sounds of squealing, squeaking, and the splashing of tiny feet at the other end of the culvert. Rats! He wanted to throw up, but swallowed hard to hold everything down. The sounds grew louder and bolder as the rats padded toward him.

Chapter 38
Getting Away

TWO VIOLENT thuds shook the Ford, leading Red to believe he had struck both boys. At twenty-five miles an hour, he should have succeeded in killing at least one of them. He'd aimed at Kekoa and thought he'd flattened him. But Red knew that fear had sabotaged his concentration—the fear that someone might have seen him deliberately run over two innocent boys. The shadowy twilight hadn't helped either. He wished he'd had a cleaner shot at Kekoa. Maybe he should have planned it better. Too late now.

A swift retreat became Red's only option. He floored the accelerator and the elderly vehicle protested with congestive coughing and heel dragging all the way to the freeway entrance at Eleventh and Harding. Once his foot relented, the jerking motion subsided and the pickup moved west toward Pearl City. Red remembered a gas station with an automatic car wash. Soon the clog of rush hour slowed traffic to under ten miles an hour. Agitation boiled and his head swelled with pain. Finally, he came to the Pearl City exit. As the car wash came into view, Red let out a long sigh of relief.

Three vehicles waited in line, all pretty grungy. The wait and wash took almost an hour. The old Ford shed several coats of construction grime during the sanitizing. Holding a large rag, Red dallied in the bright lights of the parking lot. Under the pretense of drying down the finish, he checked for any telltale damage. There was none that he could see. Both headlamps were protected by a welded mesh of iron re-bar. As he had suspected, the two oak planks that served as a front bumper had taken the brunt of the impact. With a flashlight in his left hand, he ran the rag in his right hand along the planks, inspecting them for traces of blood, paint, or fabric—using the lightest touch to avoid raising splinters. The surface felt suspiciously rough, so he removed the bolts holding the planks in place. Flipping the planks to the reverse side, he rebolted them. Red threw the crescent wrench into the toolbox and stepped back to examine his work.

Although the truck had come clean, it retained a certain dull-gray, oxidized finish. Could this finish be used to identify it? No way. Too many others like it on the island. Still…A number of dripping oil cans in the recycling bin at the gas station fence inspired an idea. He poured a little motor oil on his rag and began to rub it all over the paintwork. A minimal effort raised a shiny black surface wherever rubbed. In less than twenty minutes, the old Ford truck looked newer and blacker than it had in years.

Satisfied with the new look, Red drove back toward Honolulu in the lighter inbound traffic and exited at School Street, his company's current renovation site. He left the truck in a visible place, next to the construction trailer, and started the eighteen-block walk back to the office building where he'd left his Buick early that afternoon. The long walk and fresh air turned out to be therapeutic, rebuilding his shaken confidence with each step.

As Murphy approached the building where the Buick was parked, he noticed the crowd breaking from the movie theater across the street. *Sister Act* was playing, a movie he'd seen and liked just a week earlier. He stopped to observe the people leaving, particularly an elderly man pulling a handkerchief from his pocket. A pair of theater stubs dropped out of the man's pocket and landed on the curb. Red kept watching as the man continued down the street with his female companion. Red bent over and picked them up. *You never know when you might need an alibi,* he thought, as he slid them into his shirt pocket.

He didn't expect to find the blue Chevy in the garage, and of course, it had left hours earlier. Red received a date-and-time-stamped receipt as he paid to exit. He drove back to his apartment, reliving the day in his mind's eye and wondering if he had missed any detail. Even if he hadn't killed Kekoa, the kid would be too scared to cross him now.

Red entered his apartment and kicked the door shut. Tossing the keys on the coffee table, he whiffed his own sweaty stench. I need a shower—but the hell with that, I need a drink more, he thought. He headed for the liquor cabinet in the kitchen.

Tilting the bottle shakily, he poured nearly six ounces of bourbon over four ice cubes. It tasted cool in his mouth and went warmer as it slid deeper. He refilled before moving away from the cabinet. Glass in one hand, bottle in the other, he leaned against the door jamb to his bedroom. The room sorely lacked warmth, so Red went to the room where Wilma had slept.

He set his drink and bottle down on the ring-stained nightstand and stretched out on the bed. He hadn't changed the bedding since she left. The sweet smell of Wilma's perfume lingered on her pillow, along with strands of dyed golden hair. The more Red inhaled, the more he missed her. Tears surfaced and self-pity reigned: for a Wilma lost...and possibly some remorse for the day's deed—but only because of his fear that he might have been seen. In either case, the bottle of cheap bourbon did its job. He fell, zonked, into an uneasy sleep.

* * *

In the darkness down at the stream bed, quick tiny feet ventured closer, bolder. Kekoa crouched and tugged vigorously at a thick piece of wire mesh screen that blocked the opposite end of the culvert. Just as he had hoped, the loud metallic clatter caused the rats to back away. Kekoa knew they were still there; he could hear them squealing, continually moving. Mostly ignoring him, they splashed in the shallow running water at the high end of the culvert. After again rattling the wire mesh screen, Kekoa broke it loose and held it up as a shield between him and the bolder romping rodents.

A half-hour passed while he hid, trembling, in the culvert. The outside light from the house above the stream bed had finally been turned off. In the darkness, a drizzle came and went. The drops trickled off the trees and tangled shrubs.

Gathering up all his strength, Kekoa bounded out onto the bank of the stream bed again. He traced the path of the storm drain system for several blocks before emerging to street level. Thankfully, no police cars were in sight. He thought it best to avoid Tenth Avenue, so he followed Ninth back to Waialae, trudging the mile slowly. The night drizzled again and then turned into a rain forest downpour.

The boy's young, wiry body ached with nagging exhaustion. Then anger and depression returned. Arriving at the rear door to the bakery, he dropped to his knees while fumbling for his keys, keys that should have been in his pocket, but weren't. He must have lost them. His soaking body shivered as he leaned his face against the door and pounded on it with open palms.

The pounding brought Sam from his bed. "It one a.m. Who

there?" Sam stood at the door in his nightshirt listening for an answer, but the only sounds he heard were a desperate sobbing. Something familiar in the sobs moved him to open the door. Kekoa's body slid to the floor in front of him.

"Mauro! Mauro! Come now, it Kekoa. He hurt and bleeding." Sam pulled him through the doorway, cradled him in his arms, and carried him to the bed in the storeroom. Mauro came as quickly as her feet would allow. Together, they stripped the clammy, ragged clothes from his shaking frame and wrapped him in dry towels and blankets.

His limbs went rigid as Mauro cleaned his scrapes with peroxide and covered them with bandages where she could. He continued to shake, and Mauro, sitting on the edge of his bed, took Kekoa's head to her breasts to comfort him. Her arms went around him and held him close as she rocked back and forth. She hummed a lullaby from somewhere in her Kobe past. The soothing Japanese words of her youth were no longer known to her, but she rocked and hummed them all the same with the instincts of the mother she ached to be. Some time went by before the shaking stopped and Kekoa went limp. He slept, and Mauro and Sam stayed with him through the night.

Kekoa awoke to find them leaning over him. He smiled weakly. Sam spoke first. "You want to tell what happen?" Kekoa didn't know how to answer.

"Where Andy? Where the bikes? What happen?" This time Sam's questions elicited a grim look from Kekoa.

Mauro wrapped her arms around him. "Take time and tell what happen."

Without picking up his head, Kekoa said, "He tried to kill me... again."

"Who try kill you? Andy?" Sam asked.

"No! Not Andy! He's hurt bad, maybe dead. I didn't see him move after."

"After what? Where Andy now?"

"In Queen's Hospital, I think. The ambulance took him away." Suddenly, Kekoa sat up and pulled his legs up under him. Mauro padded upstairs to get him some hot green tea.

"Sam," Kekoa cried. "I gotta call Andy's family and tell 'em what happened."

"Just what happen?" Sam tried once more.

269

"A pickup truck tried to run over both of us—on purpose. I'm sure of that. In Palolo, over on Waiomao. I got lucky. Just scratches and bruises. Poor Andy got hit and bumped a long way. He was slammed onto the street. I don't know how bad he's hurt. I gotta call his folks before... Maybe it's too late already." Kekoa opened a dresser drawer and started to pull on some fresh clothes. The lingering soreness forced him to groan with every move.

Kekoa dragged himself from the makeshift bedroom to the front of the bakery and sat down beside the wall phone next to the display case. He dialed as Mauro came down the stairs with his tea. A single sip slid down while he waited. The phone rang endlessly at the other end of the line. Finally, Andy's father answered.

"It's Kekoa, Mr. Ballesteros." His voice choked. "Andy's hurt. He was hit by a truck when we were riding our bikes...I don't know. Queen's Hospital, I think...I don't know how bad. Maybe real bad. Please help him...Okay?"

Kekoa reached up and replaced the handset in its cradle. It rattled about before settling in place. Sam and Mauro stood in front of him, expecting more of an explanation, and when it wasn't forthcoming, they helped him upstairs to their apartment.

As they sat down at the dinette table in the center of the small, scrubbed-white kitchen, Sam decided to try again. "Why you think it not accident?"

Kekoa struggled to begin his difficult story. "When I came here, you asked why I was alone. I didn't tell you the whole truth. My real name is Kekoa Pualoa. It's true my mother and grandmother died, and my father ran away when I still wore diapers. But I've got a grown-up sister somewhere in Honolulu. Her name is Leilani. I just can't find her. I've been trying for over two years now."

"You still not answer question. Why you think it no accident?" Sam repeated.

"I'm coming to that now. I got separated from my sister when I ran away. I saw a man murder my Uncle Big John at our house in Ewa. He knows I saw him, and he wants to kill me, too, because I was his only witness. He's tried a couple of times already, but I always got away before. This time he got Andy instead."

"You know this man?" Sam's voice rose excitedly.

"Yeah! He was my father's business partner, Red Murphy."

270

Cry Ohana

"Why you no go tell police?" Mauro asked.

"I'm scared of him and what he'll do to my sister."

"What you think we do now, young man?" Sam asked. "I say we 'cause it now family problem—your family."

Kekoa looked deep into Sam's determined eyes and then at Mauro. She nodded in complete agreement.

Anger punctuated Kekoa's response for the first time since he had come home. "He's not gonna get away with it. He better not. I wanna go tell the cops, but first I gotta go to the hospital and see Andy. I wonder…" Kekoa pulled out his wallet, still damp from his ordeal. He searched each of its compartments, stopped, and held up a business card. "Here!"

"What? What that?" Mauro and Sam asked in unison.

Kekoa fingered the card with its bent corners. "I know a private detective. He says he wants to help me."

"Can you trust him?" Sam asked.

"I think so. He saved my life once. No, maybe twice. He's after Murphy, too—for somethin' else. I think I'll call him from the hospital later in the morning. I don't know if he likes waking up this early."

"Would you like us go with you?"

Kekoa shook his head. "No, Sam. You stay here and open the bakery as usual, and I'll call you if I need help."

Mauro began thumbing through the phone book. She found the number she sought and dialed it on the kitchen phone. Sam and Kekoa listened, curious. "Hello? Queen Medic' Center? Info'mation, please? Please, you give info'mation 'bout fourteen-year-old boy named Andy Ballesteros? I spell: B-A-L-L-E-S-T-E-R-O-S …You don't? He hurt. Teen-boy from hit-and-run over Waiomao in Palolo. You say he not identify yet?…Police wan' talk with me?…We jus' call parents, and they come hospital now. I sure parents answer all question…No, I just neighbor… No! I not witness scene. I not there…Please, you tell me how bad? We come by soon in morning. Thank you very much."

Mauro hung up and turned to Kekoa. "You not go there. Five ayem too early morning. He not good—she say critical. Also say no allow visitors. Intense care patient. Why you no go back bed and get more sleep? I wake you at seven and we go over together."

"I can't sleep. Not with Andy hurt so bad. Besides, I want to help Sam with the morning baking."

271

Sam put his arm around Kekoa. "You no condition do work," he said. "Go downstair and wait for me, I put on my work clothes. You watch, I work."

Kekoa trotted downstairs determined to help anyway, and spent the next ten minutes getting out ingredients. Sam joined him and they worked side by side until the first trays went into the ovens. By the time they reached the kitchen, Mauro had their breakfast on the table.

"There's one other thing I didn't tell you." Kekoa started. "Because I don't want t' be found, I haven't gone to school for over two years now."

Mauro looked shocked. "School books in your room, where they from?"

"The books are Yasuko's—old school books and library ones, too. She knows the whole story and she tutors me all the time. I don't go to school so Murphy can't find me. Besides, no school would take me without grades and records."

"You poor dear." Mauro leaned over and hugged him from behind his chair. "You much too young, carry big beast by self."

"Mauro," Kekoa said, "Andy... He won't die, will he?"

Chapter 39
Anxiety and Anger

THE WHITE stretch-limo taxi slithered to a halt on the Punch-bowl Street side of Queen's Medical Center. Mauro counted out the fare, plus a $2 tip. With her hand on Kekoa's shoulder, she ushered him through the door.

The receptionist informed them that Andrew Ballesteros had been taken to Intensive Care Unit Three. "Immediate family can wait in the ICU waiting room. No visitors, ma'am," she ordered.

Mauro thought this over and brazenly announced, "We wait with family, *nei*?"

Seeing the determined look on her face, the receptionist directed them to the ICU.

Mauro and Kekoa neared the glass door with its sheer white curtains. Kekoa took a deep breath and was about to push the door open when he stopped short. His hands turned cold, his mouth went dry, and all the determination oozed out of his body. There stood Andy's parents talking to a uniformed policeman. But Mauro's hand on his back firmly urged him forward, so he pushed the door open. And he saw that it wasn't the tall, thin *haole* cop who'd chased him the night before. This cop's blue shirt covered huge shoulders and a barrel chest.

As they entered the waiting room, the conversation halted. Hesitantly, Kekoa approached Mama Ballesteros. Would she even want to see him? But when he stood close enough, she reached out and bear-hugged him. The tears running down her cheeks mingled with his own. Papa patted his head.

"Is Andy gonna be okay?" Kekoa whispered.

Papa's emotion-choked words came out in a mix of Tagalog and pidgin. The worried father shook his head. "Mehbe not so good."

Andy was still listed as critical. The doctors hadn't finished reading X-rays and analyzing test results. Kekoa introduced Mauro as his mother, and although he did it for convenience, Mauro smiled faintly in complete approval and lowered her head in a gesture conveying sensitivity toward the distraught couple. During the introductions, Kekoa's eyes dwelled for a moment on the police officer, who waited patiently.

"I'm Officer Fred Haiakane." It sounded like Hi-yah-kah-nay.

Mauro dipped her head once more in polite acknowledgment. Turning back to Andy's parents, the officer said, "We've still got a lot of details to clear up, folks."

Papa pointed to Kekoa. "He my boy's best friend. He gonna tell you."

Mama continued to cry, her fingers fidgeting with the clasp on her purse .

"You were there?" Officer Haiakane asked.

"Yeah," answered Kekoa.

"Please!" the officer said, pointing to one of two corner chairs.

Kekoa cautiously sat down, and the officer squeezed his own large frame into a chair diagonally across from the boy. Papa and Mama seated themselves on a vinyl couch to listen. Balancing a clipboard on his knee, the officer wrote the names and addresses of everyone there, and then turned to Kekoa.

"You can call me Officer Fred, son. Tell me all about it. You were there? At the scene of the accident?"

"Yeah, but it wasn't any accident," Kekoa said heatedly.

His words caught everyone but Mauro by surprise. Even Mama stopped her sobbing to be sure she had heard him correctly.

"Just what do you mean by that, son?" The officer's eyes peered out through his wire-rimmed glasses. While he waited for an answer, he ran the eraser end of his pencil through his bushy black mustache.

Kekoa jammed both hands down onto his knees and then gripped the front edge of his shorts with fists. It bought him time while gathering in his thoughts. "Just what I said. It wasn't an accident. Red tried to run me over. But Andy saved me. He pulled me away from my bike and shoved me behind a car, and… and… and he got hit instead. He saved my life! Andy's in there hurt. I should be the one. That's supposed to be me!"

"Whoa!" the officer interrupted. "Why would anyone want to run you over? Who is this Red? Did he drive the car that struck your friend? Did you actually see him?"

"Yeah, I did. I saw Red Murphy driving the truck that hit Andy. When Andy pushed me out of the way, I landed with my back against the trunk of a parked car, and just as the driver passed us, I saw his rotten red face. I'm never, never gonna forget that face. Never! He's been after me for two years now."

"Why, son? Why is that?" Officer Fred's voice turned gentle.

Kekoa hesitated. He cast a sidelong glance at Mauro as if he needed her approval.

"Go on! Tell!" she urged.

"I saw Red Murphy murder my Uncle Big John over two years ago, and he knows I saw him. He's been after me ever since." Anger leapt into his words, lifting his voice to a falsetto pitch "He's tried to kill me other times, too. At least three times before!"

"You say his name is Red Murphy, M-U-R-P-H-Y? Does he have a first name besides Red?"

"Yeah, Ed. Edgar, I think."

Officer Fred wrote quickly, and then looked up. "Where can we find this man? Do you know his address? Either where he lives or where he works?"

"No, sir. But he was business partners with my father and Uncle Big John. The firm's called Finast Construction Company. That's Finast with an a not an e. It's local in Honolulu. They've got trailers and da kine all over the place."

Officer Fred asked, "Why haven't you gone to the police before this?"

"I wanted to, but I couldn't."

Kekoa's voice trailed off. His throat felt tight and his breath caught. After more than two years of suppressing the truth, it took his greatest effort to articulate it. The whole story gushed out. In rapid-fire bursts, Kekoa told all that he had pent up inside for so long.

"Slow down, son." The officer struggled to get every detail written down on his clipboard pad. "Is there anyone who can corroborate your story?"

"What does that mean, sir?"

"Someone who can verify, uh, confirm your story."

"Yeah. Yeah! Some of it, anyway."

But before he could continue, a doctor in operating room greens entered the room. "Mr. and Mrs. Ballesteros?" They both struggled to their feet. "I'm Dr. Diem. Your son came through the operation with flying colors. He's in the ICU recovery room now. You'll be able to see him in about forty-five minutes. He does have a concussion, though. There's a small hematoma in the back of the head that we're watching very carefully. We'll know more about that when he comes out of the anesthesia."

"Anything else?" Papa asked in a quivering voice.

"Yes, some broken bones," Dr. Diem said. "Dr. Reilly has set two compound fractures below the left knee, a simple fracture just above the right ankle, and a simple fracture to the radius in his right arm. Your boy got lucky, believe it or not, in being hit by the vehicle but not actually run over by it. However, he will be in considerable discomfort for at least a month."

Mama needed to know the bottom line. "Will my Andy be able to walk again, Doctor?" Mama looked pleadingly at this mortal-god who seemed to hold the life of her son in his hands.

"The bones will mend fine. He'll be in walking casts for many months, but then he should be able to walk normally. We're still hoping that the head injury is minimal. I'll get back to you just as soon as we have more news." He left the room as quickly as he had arrived.

Officer Fred stood and faced Kekoa. "I want to make a phone call. I'd like someone from Homicide to hear your story." He walked to a row of pay phones just outside the ICU waiting room.

"I have a call to make, too." Kekoa followed him into the hall. Clutching Hal's business card in one hand, he dropped two coins in the slot and dialed the top number on it. Hank's answering machine picked up on the fifth ring. In frustration Kekoa started to hang up, but he decided to leave a message instead.

"Mr. Perry? Hal? It's Keith."

"Don't hang up. I'm here," Hank interrupted the machine. He'd been eating breakfast and screening messages from the table. "Glad you called, Keith, what's up?"

"Uh, that's not my real name, Hal. Kekoa Pualoa—that's my real name. Yeah, I made Keith up. Hey… please! This is real important. I need your help. Red Murphy tried to kill me again and he injured my friend Andy really bad instead." While he awaited an answer, Kekoa heard Hank emit a deep gasping breath at the other end of the line.

276

"Good God! Are you alright?" asked Hank in a very concerned voice.

"Yeah, but Andy's in the hospital."

"Kekoa! Where are you, son? I'll come get you."

"Queen's Medical Center in the ICU waiting room. I'm talking to a cop here. I'm telling him the whole story."

"What's the telephone number there?"

"It's 512-6127, but it's a pay phone, Hal."

"Wait for me. I'll be there just as soon as I can. Stall the police. I'm bringing my lawyer with me. Stall them and don't say anything more until we get there. We'll make a formal statement then. Okay?"

"Yeah—I guess. Hal? I'll, uh, try to."

"Good, then! Bye!"

Kekoa held onto the handset for a moment longer while he waited for Officer Fred to finish his call. They returned to the ICU waiting room together. Kekoa held the door for the officer.

"Thanks, son. Lieutenant Mahaila will be here in an hour." He pronounced it Mah-hi-lah. "Would you mind waiting until she gets here?"

"She?" Kekoa sat down next to Papa, who stared off into nowhere. Mama dozed lightly on his shoulder.

"Yes, she. Gert Mahaila is a homicide detective and a good one. The lieutenant wants me to hold off on the questioning until she gets here. Look, I'm heading down to the cafeteria for coffee. Anybody want anything?" Silence. He shrugged and left.

Kekoa curled up on the couch beside Mauro and laid his head in her lap. He slept for nearly an hour, awaking with a stiff neck and a severe headache. Mauro found Advil in her purse and took him into the hall for water. He swallowed the pills with a sour face and a stream of warmish water from the drinking fountain.

They encountered Hank and Terumi Fujita coming down the corridor. Seeing his son once again, Hank found himself at a loss of words. He still wasn't ready to reveal his true identity. The emotional meeting brought tears to his eyes. On the other hand, Kekoa found new strength and became angry and excited all over again. "Mr. Perry! Hal! He tried to kill us. Can't you stop him? Can't you make the police go after Red?"

"Easy there, son. Calm down." Hank finally managed to say. He placed both his hands on Kekoa's shoulders. "How would you like some good news first?"

"What kind of good news?" Kekoa tilted his head to one side, trying to figure out what could be more important than stopping Red Murphy.

"You once asked me if I could find your sister for you. Well, I've found her. You'll get to see her just as soon as we're through here."

Kekoa's eyes lit up. He stared in disbelief for several moments while he digested the news and then he couldn't be stopped. "You found Lani? But how?"

"It's a long story."

"You're the greatest, Mr. Perry." An attempt to hug Hank nearly toppled the man from his cane. Kekoa, embarrassed that he'd reacted like a little kid, said, "Uh, sorry. She's okay, isn't she?"

"Better than okay. She's fine. You'll see, later."

Hank gripped Kekoa by the shoulders and guided him and Mauro to the now empty waiting room. Mama and Papa Ballesteros weren't there, and Kekoa became immediately concerned.

"Maybe they're in the room with Andy," Hank suggested.

Ten minutes later Andy's parents reentered the waiting room, anxious to share their good news with Kekoa.

"Andy woke up and asked for us. He's gonna be okay, thank God."

Papa blurted out. "They threw us out after ten minutes—he needs rest, they say. But he's gonna be like new again." He put his arm around Mama and squeezed. "They don't expect any changes, and Andy's gonna be sleeping anyway. The doctor told us to go home and come back tonight."

"Mr. and Mrs. Ballesteros, this is Hal Perry. He's gonna help us get the guy that did this to Andy. He's gonna put Murphy in jail where he belongs."

Papa nodded and shook Hank's hand. Fresh tears welled in his eyes as he and Mama left for home through the big glass doors.

Kekoa turned back to Hank after the door closed. "I'm sorry I lied to you, Mr. Perry, but I didn't know whether I could trust you."

"I have some things to confess to you, Kekoa," Hank began. He had every intention of telling all, but he hesitated and said, "Mr. Fujita here works for your father."

"My father? I don't know my father. He ran away a long time ago.

He could even be dead. And if he ain't, maybe he doesn't want me. I don't care anyway. I don't know him. I don't want to know him."

Terumi looked over at Hank's deflated slack-jawed expression and intervened for him. "Your father is very much alive. He does care about you and your sister. He's been sending money for many years for your support and education."

"Money? Yeah, sure," said Kekoa. "How come I've never seen none of it?"

"It's in a bank, held in trust for you. Your father was a broken and devastated man when he left you. He's deeply regretted leaving. However..." Terumi abruptly changed his manner from compassionate to businesslike. "I would like to hear your story before you tell it to the police. What have you told them so far?"

"I told the cop..."

As Kekoa spoke, the door to the waiting room swung open and Officer Fred entered with a short, handsome woman in a brown floral aloha shirt. He introduced her as Detective Lieutenant Gertrude Mahaila. The lieutenant appeared to be athletic, with broad shoulders and strong arms. A police badge was clipped to her shirt pocket, and a pager hung on the belt of her black slacks. She threw her jacket across one of the chairs.

Detective Mahaila addressed Kekoa in a somewhat masculine voice. "I understand you're the young man who witnessed a hit-and-run. And a murder as well?"

"Yes, sir, I mean yes, ma'am."

"Lieutenant," Terumi said as he produced his business card, "I represent the boy's father."

Gert looked puzzled. "I thought the boy's mother was here." She eyed Mauro, seated next to Kekoa.

Terumi replied, "The boy's mother has been dead since he was eighteen months old. I'm not sure of Mrs. Osaka's relationship to the boy."

"Maybe I help," Mauro responded. "Kekoa live with our family more than two years now. He family. He help my Sam in bakery, and we pay him allowance. He come to our door hungry—no home, and we give him food and bed. We not ask questions. He now our son, only child. We all love."

"Are you his legal guardian as well?" Gert asked while writing notes in her own spiral flip pad.

"I not know legal," said a confused Mauro. She wished Sam were here.

"Since his father has not given up that right, may we presume that he is still the boy's guardian?" Terumi said. "I'd like to make a suggestion. The boy is a willing witness and will tell you all he knows about the hit-and-run. And certainly, a two-year-old murder won't get any staler in the next few hours. Why don't we all reconvene at my office after lunch? I can assure you the boy's father will be present then."

Gert said nothing. She tucked the spiral pad in her pants pocket and simultaneously pulled out a small red ball, which she grasped in her fist. Everyone watched her squeeze and release, squeeze and release, her biceps flexing in rhythm.

Terumi repeated his offer to host the afternoon meeting. Gert started to agree, but just then her pager beeped. She pulled it off her belt to see the calling number, and then politely asked everyone to please wait while she phoned in.

Kekoa waited for the door to close behind her before he asked, "You said my father would be there this afternoon. Will I get to meet him?" Kekoa surprised himself with this question. He still felt almost unbearable hostility toward his father, but now it had melted into an anxious curiosity.

Terumi replied: "Yes, Kekoa, yes, this afternoon at my office." Then he addressed Mauro. "You are very welcome to join us and your husband as well."

"You most thoughtful. I talk with him soon I go home."

Kekoa looked up and searched Hank's face for another answer. "Are the cops gonna arrest Red now, or do I hafta go on hiding from him?"

Hank patted him on the back. "I can't make any promises for the police, but I'll sure do my best to protect you until he is behind bars."

Lieutenant Mahaila sprang into the room and held the door behind her. "There's been a multiple shooting down at the docks. I'm afraid our meeting will have to be postponed until Monday morning. Can you handle that, Counselor?"

"I believe we can," said Terumi. "Then Monday morning it is. Would 9:30 be suitable?"

"Fine," said Gert, throwing her jacket over her shoulder. "Maybe you should be there as well, Officer Haiakane. I think both our cases could benefit from it."

Officer Fred grabbed his clipboard and scampered after her, an oversized puppy trying to keep pace. "Sorry, folks! I'll keep you informed of the investigation as it progresses."

Terumi left the room and made a hasty call to Lori back at the office. Upon returning, he said, "Kekoa, how would you like to meet your father right now back at my office?"

"Hey! Yeah... sure... okay, I guess. But I'd much rather see Leilani." Kekoa's face couldn't mask either his agitation or confusion.

Terumi looked over at Hank and murmured, "Lori will drive over to the Wongs and get Leilani."

Mauro addressed Kekoa. "This very important meeting for you. Sam and I wait 'nother day meet family, *nei?* I take taxi home now."

"Are you sure, Mauro? You'll always be my family. You and Sam. I won't leave you."

Mauro leaned forward and kissed his cheek, and with her forefinger, wiped away the tiny tear she encountered there.

Another day—as hopeful as it sounded—remained a complete and frightening unknown for the two of them.

Chapter 40
Officer and Friend of the Court

KEKOA HUDDLED in a corner of the back seat as the air-conditioned Mercedes whisked him through the streets of Honolulu. *What do I call this stranger who's supposed to be my father? What if he doesn't like me or me him? Worse yet, maybe I'll lose Sam and Mauro.* At a red light he fought the terrible impulse to bolt from the car and run. *That's one thing I'm good at,* he thought grimly. The only thing that stopped him was the prospect of a reunion with Leilani at Terumi's office. He folded his arms across his chest, a shield against the unknown.

Kekoa studied the back of Terumi's perfectly combed gray head, wondering if he could trust this man in the expensive suit. With his polished manners, he seemed almost too smooth and too confident. But still, Kekoa found him likable.

Terumi drove straight to his office building and into a personal parking space on the fourth garage level. They entered the express elevator. The sudden upward motion caught Kekoa so unaware that he reached for the brass railing.

The elevator's stainless steel doors slid open. Kekoa stepped into the room first and halted abruptly on the rich carpet. He'd never seen such a place. Burnished wood and glass abounded with startling brightness as sunshine touched everywhere.

He walked up to the large reception desk and gawked at the woman seated there. "You! You're the lady from the cemetery! With the flowers for my mother's grave. And at Esme's wedding!"

Lori rose. "Yes, Kekoa, I am. I was your mother's best friend. My name is Lori Yamashita." She started to reach out to hug him, but refrained—it would only embarrass him.

Kekoa looked her over carefully and immediately warmed to this lady with the generous smile. The sparkle in her dark eyes exuded

282

sincerity. The mere mention of his mother sent a comforting sensation through him.

"You really were her best friend?"

"Oh, yes. All the way back to grade school. I'm still a good friend to your father."

My father, he repeated to himself. The sinking, shivering feeling returned. He looked about the room once more, wondering where his father could be. Even Mr. Fujita seemed to have disappeared. Funny, Kekoa hadn't seen him leave.

"Your father's in there," Lori said, indicating the large oak door in the middle of the wall. "He's waiting for you." She ushered Kekoa through the door and shut it behind him, leaving him seemingly alone. At first he saw no one in the room. A surge of anxiety and panic seized him.

A familiar voice said: "I'm over here, Kekoa, at the end of the table."

"Huh? Mr. Perry?"

The tall upholstered chairs on one side of the table had partially hidden Hank from the boy's view. A deathly silence prevailed as Kekoa approached.

Hank laid his cane on the table, gripped the back of the chair next to him, and rose to his feet. He held out his arms in a humble, welcoming gesture.

Kekoa's pace quickened, but then he stopped short, only a few steps away.

"Hal! Mr. Perry! Where's my father?" Then the powerful reality sank in. "You? You're my real father? How? I don't get it."

"Yes, son. And I promise to be a real father from now on if only you'll let me." Hank again extended his arms.

Kekoa's body went rigid. He woodenly offered his hand to be shaken instead. A disappointed Hank shook hands with his son.

Kekoa withdrew his hand quickly, as though the physical contact had been a mistake. Anger and desperation hung on his face. "Why?" he whispered.

"Why what?"

"How could you leave Lani and me and run away? We needed you. We needed to be a family. How could you? Didn't you love us? Didn't you even like us? Did you kill my mother? *Tutu* said you did."

Hank looked his son squarely in the eyes. "I didn't kill your mother—at least not deliberately. It wasn't like that. But she did die because of me. There's a difference. It was a terrible accident. I was drunk and I wrecked the car with all of you in it."

Kekoa stood unmoving and silent before his father. Now only a few inches shorter than Hank, the boy felt a stubborn resistance. Out of years of loneliness and despair, rage overtook him, and he swung his right arm with a clenched fist—a fast right hook. It came close—within inches of his father's chin. But Hank's sharp reflexes allowed him to sidestep the blow even though his motion caused him to stumble backward into the table.

Immediately, Hank realized that, unless he did something drastic, he could lose the boy forever. He awkwardly fell to his knees, sobbing and hugging his son about the waist. "I love you and Lani! Always have. Please forgive me. I hope someday I can make you understand. Sometimes it's even hard for me to understand."

"Please get up," Kekoa urged in a rasping voice. His chest rose and fell as he panted with the shock of what he had just done. But fire gleamed in his eyes. He felt revulsion at his father's whining and didn't want to yield just yet to the impact of his father's anguish—or his own.

Hank struggled to get off his knees, but the effort was too much for him. Kekoa helped him to his feet. Without another word, they sat down in adjacent chairs at the table. While the opportunity for reconciliation seeped away in an ebbing tide, father and son stared at one another, each fearful of making the next wrong move.

But Kekoa wanted answers and he wanted them now. "I liked you better as Hal Perry. Why have you been hiding from me? Where have you been all this time? Why did you stay away so long? Didn't you think we needed a father?"

Several minutes passed while Hank found his voice. "I know it must seem that way to you. It's not true. As if losing your mother wasn't terrible enough, I went to prison for that—six months for what I did. *Tutu* Eme poisoned both of you against me, wouldn't let me come near you. I suppose I could have tried legal means to get you back once I got out, but I figured you needed her more than you needed me. That's why I took off for the Mainland."

"So…Dad…While I was living in the streets, you were living it up on the Mainland?"

The sarcasm hurt. "Not exactly, son." For the next hour, Hank meticulously related the saga of his life during the last twelve years. Then he told Kekoa the kicker: how Red had tried to kill him in Baltimore and then left him for dead.

"I spent all those painful months recuperating in the hospital afterward. I came as soon as I was able. When I finally got here, you and Leilani had disappeared. Of course, I never stopped looking for you."

Kekoa's voice softened. "But you did find me. You saved my life—twice. I owe you that much."

Hank forced a smile. "I saved someone by the name of Keith with no last name. I had no idea you were my son. You were only twenty months old the last time I saw you—a chubby-faced toddler then. I had nothing to go by."

"When did you figure it out?" Kekoa asked.

"Remember the school construction site? When Red tried to crush you in the police car with the hook and ball? I gave you a ride. After you got out at the corner of King and University, two things hit me."

"What things?"

"You told me about Red killing your uncle, and then you asked if I could find your sister. The details were just too much to be a coincidence. I'm here now, if you'll have me." He stretched out his sinewy arm and rested it on the table.

The boy seemed to be making a mental calculation. Then, as he fought back tears, he inched his hand over his father's and squeezed it tentatively. They urgently searched each other's eyes for signs of greater meaning, deeper feelings.

A knock at the door disturbed the echoing quiet of the conference room. Father and son broke their mutual gaze and turned toward the door. It opened slowly, cautiously. Leilani's face peeked around the edge. Kekoa sprang up. His chair toppled backward as he sprinted past the long table to the front of the room. Then he and Leilani leapt into each other's arms and swung round and round, laughing and giggling and crying with happiness as they spun. Hank looked on with a newfound respect for his children. Still embracing, they danced down the aisle of conference chairs until they came to Hank. Leilani grabbed Kekoa's hand as she bent to kiss and hug her father.

"Hi, Daddy! Isn't it wonderful? Kekoa's gotten so tall and so handsome. Oh, I love you guys so much." She hugged them both at once.

Kekoa, seeing the genuine affection between Leilani and his father, recovered his voice long enough to ask, "Are we going to be a family again?"

"I sure hope so," Hank managed to reply as the three of them embraced once more.

Brother and sister turned and faced each other. "Where have you been?" they asked, almost in unison. They laughed at that. Leilani told her story first, describing her life with the Wongs and school. She threw in a few words about her relationship with Alex, but just a few.

Before she could finish, another knock was heard. This time Masako Wong, Lori, and the two Fujitas entered the room. They left the door open.

Terumi began to speak even before he sat down. "I am terribly sorry to disturb such a momentous reunion, but we all have a great deal of work to do before Monday morning. You'll have plenty of time later to get to know one another. I must say that I am very happy for all of you. I intend to act as an officer and friend of the court to assemble evidence against Edgar Murphy and put him away for life. I just got off the phone with Lieutenant Mahaila's office and the District Attorney's office. Each has confirmed their interest in my performing this public service."

"Remember, Kekoa is a witness to Murphy's crimes," added Hank. "His very life is still in jeopardy."

"I agree, our top priority is to protect Kekoa."

Terumi turned to the boy. "Kekoa, we need to know exactly what happened to you and Andy on Friday night. The whole story in your own words, please."

"Yes, sir!" Kekoa responded. He retold every painful detail of his story.

They all shuddered as he described the rats in the culvert.

Occasionally, Terumi interrupted: "Can you give me a more precise description of the pickup truck? Where exactly were you when the truck passed? Do you ever remember seeing the truck before? Why did you run after the paramedics came?"

Kekoa responded to each question in turn—elaborating, leaving little doubt that he was the perfect eyewitness.

"I'm hoping your identification of Murphy was by actual recognition and not just an assumption."

"Oh, man! I mean, sir, I know the guy!"

"Good. But… Kekoa, do you think Andy could identify Murphy as well?"

"I haven't been allowed to speak to Andy since that night."

"I see. Perhaps," Terumi suggested, "you and I might attempt to get a statement from him tomorrow. If he's well enough, of course. Now, if you could describe for us some of the other attempts on your life. And Hank, since you were involved in these other episodes, I should like statements from you, too."

The stories, questions, and answers continued laboriously into the late afternoon, when the younger Fujita finally stood and suggested: "Why don't we call it a day and let the rest of you get acquainted. Let's reconvene tomorrow morning, say, nine o'clock in this room. I think that's about all we can digest for today."

As Masako rose from the table, she invited everyone back to the Wong house for supper. The two Fujitas declined, saying they needed to stay in the office and map out a working strategy.

"I want to come," Kekoa said, "but I need to check with Sam and Mauro first. They're my family, too."

"Why don't you invite them to join us for dessert at eight?" Masako asked. "My husband will pick them up. I believe we all have a lot of catching up to do."

Kekoa nodded. Leilani squeezed his upper arm with both hands. "I'm so thrilled. I can't wait for you to meet Alex."

Hank observed their excitement with pride and wondered how he could keep his family safe. Would Red be brazen enough to make another attempt?

287

Chapter 41
Diversions and Cover-ups

LUCILLE RAN a stiff brush through her raven hair and paused to inspect herself in the mirror. She tilted her head slightly, tucking into place a strand here and a wisp there. After waiting tables on the early shift, she'd gone to the ladies' room to change into street clothes. She had a date tonight. She undid the top two buttons of her polyester blouse and smiled at her reflection before turning around to squeeze through the door of the tiny washroom.

The groaning air conditioner played to an almost empty restaurant. In the pre-supper hour lull, Red Murphy sat at his usual window-side table with both hands wrapped around a coffee cup. "Do they have to keep this place so friggin' cold?" he muttered. Two toothpicks, topped with red and yellow cellophane frills, marked the only remains of his BLT. He'd thought it best to maintain his routine of eating an early supper here every evening so as not to arouse suspicion.

No sign of the boy. The time had come and gone when Kekoa usually appeared across the street. Red seemed to be staring out the window at the bakery, but in truth his mind's eye stayed fixed on the previous evening. He needed to know how much damage he had done.

He spread open the *Star-Bulletin*, folded back the page of police beat items, scanned and scanned again. Nothing. And nothing in this morning's *Advertiser*, either. Have I gotten rid of the boy for good? He reflected. *Was Kekoa only slightly injured? Maybe scaring him was enough. Maybe there's plenty of time to try again.*

Dating Lucille had been an added stroke of genius, he decided. Reaching into his shirt pocket, he smirked slightly, feeling the two theater stubs he'd put there. Now his first priority would be to build them into an alibi for last night. With any luck Lucille would help him do that. He stood to welcome her with all the gusto he could muster. She thrilled to the extra attention and chuckled at his wonderful exaggerations.

"Where to, my friend?" she asked.

"I thought we'd try an early movie, a late dinner, and a little leisurely night music," he responded.

She giggled, something that came naturally to her. "Oooh, that sounds sooo romantic."

"How does *Sister Act* sound to you? I've been dying to see it." He wanted to remove any doubt that the selection was even debatable. He needn't have bothered. He could've chosen a Disney movie for all she cared. He held the rear door of the restaurant for her and gestured flamboyantly in Sir Walter Raleigh fashion. She passed through the door and descended the steps to the parking lot in a queenly manner, giggling all the way. Red looked at his wristwatch. "Perfect timing, same as last night," he mumbled to himself.

"What's that you said?"

"I said that we have perfect timing for the movie. It should be a great night."

* * *

Masako drove the reunited siblings to the Wong home. In the back seat of the Honda Civic, Kekoa gripped his sister's hand tightly. He was pleased that Sam and Mauro would join them later in the evening. With the exception of Leilani, everyone else there would be essentially a stranger to him.

"I missed you," Leilani said, squeezing her baby brother's hand just a little bit harder. "I've wanted to ask you all kinds of questions this afternoon. I think everyone wants to know where you've been, so I won't ask you now. But why haven't you tried to get in touch with me?"

Kekoa took a moment before answering. Perhaps Yasuko's coaching had something to do with it. Neither a dropped consonant nor any sign of pidgin lingered in his speech while he addressed his sister. Then again, Leilani had always inspired the best in him.

"Oh, Lani," he began, "I tried for days—then weeks, but Red always hung around, and I got so scared. He almost caught me twice, but I got away. I watched you from a distance for awhile, and then I needed to get farther away and hide from him. I thought if I gave him enough time, he would forget about me. I waited nearly a year before trying again. And when I did, *Tutu* Eme had died. The house was sold, and you had moved away. Nobody there knew where. Later I tried looking for you at different high schools." He leaned against her as the car turned a corner. "Lani?"

"Yes?"

"How did *Tutu* Eme die?"

"The doctor said emphysema, all that smoking, I guess. She had a weak heart, too. That terrible night—she coughed and retched and then nothing. I could hear her from the other room. She kept me awake for hours. Not only that night, but for two weeks beforehand. When I went to her room and saw the bloody mess she'd made from the coughing, I called the doctor right away, and he sent the paramedics. But they arrived too late. She was already dead." Leilani paused, choking back the painful memory. She didn't want to cry; she'd done enough of that. Curling her hair around one index finger, she gazed out the window. "*Tutu* Eme kept up her hopes of finding you right to the end."

"Thanks, Lani. I never knew that."

The Honda pulled to the curb. To Kekoa, the white clapboard house in Manoa looked huge, with its square pillars and wrap-around lanai. Certainly it appeared finer than any he'd ever lived in.

Masako turned around to face them. "Welcome to the Wong home," she said.

Paul and Numi waited in the living room and rushed to introduce themselves. Paul shook Kekoa's hand. But Numi hugged him.

"Lani is like a sister to me, so I hope you will become my brother," she said.

"Oh, Numi, isn't it wonderful?" Leilani wrapped both arms around Kekoa from behind. "He's back. I'm so happy I could cry."

"Well, don't cry on my account." Alex came through the front door and entered the living room.

"Don't flatter yourself, Alex," Leilani teased back.

Alex stopped to give Leilani a hug. "And who is this?" he asked. "What's going on?"

"It's Kekoa, Leilani's brother," Numi piped up. "He's returned from two years of hiding."

"Hi, Kekoa. I'm Alex Wong, Numi's brother." Alex extended his hand and Kekoa cautiously accepted it. "Welcome home. Leilani worried like crazy over you. Would it be too forward of me to ask where and why you were hiding?"

"Leave him be, please," Masako said firmly. "He's been answering questions all day and needs some peace and quiet." She then ordered both girls to the kitchen to help her. Before Leilani left the room, Alex gathered her into his arms and gave her a tender kiss on the lips. It caught Kekoa by surprise and filled him with strange emotions: protectiveness, concern, and a tinge of jealousy. But when he saw them look happily into each other's eyes, he mellowed quickly.

"Dinner's ready," Masako called from the dining room.

Miso soup, fried tofu, and white rice accompanied a stir fry of chicken and vegetables. No bread, Kekoa noticed—a few of his home-baked taro rolls would've been nice. The blue and white china with its Oriental scenes impressed him, but the lively conversation impressed him even more. He decided that meals with the Wong family were magnificent dining room events that lasted decidedly longer than the simple, quiet meals in the Osaka kitchen. But it all made him a bit uneasy, too.

Masako and Leilani had just cleared away the dishes when the doorbell rang. Numi jumped up and raced to the door.

"Ladylike, please!" Masako reminded her. Numi opened the door to Lori and Hank and the two Osakas.

Kekoa stared in wonderment at his adoptive parents. Sam looked so different, so formal in a black suit and tie, even if the cut spoke the style of another era. Mauro appeared elegant in a long dress with black and white cranes, a narrower, straighter Japanese version of the Hawaiian muumuu. They both smiled shyly back at him.

The chatting continued over dessert until Hank finally turned to Kekoa. "We're all very anxious to hear your story, from beginning to end, but since you'll have to tell it in detail tomorrow, I won't ask you for it now."

Kekoa nodded eagerly—and with some relief.

"The hour is getting late, and the boy must get some rest," Masako said. "Tomorrow will be an exhausting day. Kekoa, you are more than welcome to spend the night if you wish. We do have an empty guest room upstairs."

Though strongly tempted, Kekoa replied, "No, thank you. In the morning the baking's gotta get done. I have responsibilities now."

For the first time that evening Sam spoke more than just a few words. "Tomorrow Sam bake, like all time before Kekoa come. You always big help, strong, too, but I can do alone. Maybe soon, maybe longer, something change all that, and I can accept this. You bring happy

291

spirits of young into Osaka home, love too. This old man ver' grateful, but you free like bird to go to new nest."

A lump caught in Kekoa's throat. When he found his voice, he said, "I'll come home with you tonight and help you bake in the morning as usual. It's still my home and my work, isn't it?"

"Ah, yes, my son!"

Mauro rose, moved to Kekoa's chair, and kissed the top of his head. "You our family still, only now must share with real family. You make education. It most important."

Leilani burst in: "Sam and Mauro are right, Kekoa. You have to go to school. Other than that, you're free to make any choices you want. We love you, and we want what's best for you."

An impish grin curled Kekoa's mouth. "Hey, Lani, big sister, bossy as ever, right?"

She had to laugh. "Look, little brother, I've missed out on almost three years of bossing you around and I need the practice."

"Perhaps I can get Kekoa enrolled in Oahu Prep," Masako suggested.

Kekoa's eyes grew wide with alarm. "They'd never accept me, a fancy school like that."

"We'll see," Mauro said. "Paul and I both teach there. First, we'll get you some catch-up tutoring."

Kekoa had a sudden feeling of panic. "Can I have a few days to think about it? Everything is happening so fast, I don't know what to do." He wanted to go home now, but he couldn't be sure what that meant any more. He hugged his sister, and Hank put his arms about the two of them. They said their goodnights, and Lori drove Kekoa and the Osakas back to the bakery.

* * *

At two o'clock on Sunday morning, Red and Lucille stood in front of her door. She lived in an apartment building across from Kapiolani Community College at the opposite end of Kaimuki. Lucille handed him her keys. Although the gesture amounted to an invitation for Red, he returned them to her after unlocking the door and surprised her by saying, "I'll see you tonight. We can do another movie. He lingered for a few minutes to give her a long goodbye kiss.

"But I don't get off work until ten tonight."

"I'll come in a little later to eat, and then we'll do the 10:15

show," he insisted. He planned to rush her with a lot of movies, night clubs, and attention in the next few weeks, so that she would willingly back up any alibi he needed.

"I'd love it," she whispered as she planted another kiss on his lips. At the same time a pout expressed her disappointment—he didn't want to come in.

"Say, Lucille, do you ever get a few days off?" he asked on a whim.

"Mondays. Isn't that enough?"

"Can you get Tuesday off, too? I know this sounds kinda wild—pretty last minute. But I thought maybe we could fly over to Maui tonight after the movie and spend a couple of days there."

This got her attention. "I'm sure I can get one of the girls to work my shift for me. It sounds so exciting." She frowned. "But are there any flights that late?"

"The last commercial flight is at 9:30, but in my Cessna, we can come and go when we are ready. I want to fly to the stars with you, baby."

"You're kidding. Your very own plane?"

"You bet, baby!"

He'd scored so many points with that revelation that she simply melted when he took her in his arms and pressed his lips on hers. She gasped for breath and felt her knees wobble.

His strong arms held her firmly for a few seconds longer while he looked deep into her eyes. "Until tonight, my sweet."

"Until tonight," she repeated. He spun about and quickly walked away. She closed the door behind her and leaned on it. "Wow!" she whispered.

Chapter 42
Home Is Where the *Slippahs* Are Parked

"MR. PERRY? HAL? Hank? Uh, Dad?" Kekoa jammed both hands into the pockets of his khaki shorts. "I never know what to call you."

"Whatever you're comfortable with—although I do like the sound of Dad."

It was Sunday morning, and they were weaving through church traffic on the way to the Fujita office.

"Dad," Kekoa tried it out. "Dad, then. What do you think I should do now?"

"What do you mean *do*?" Hank's hands tightened on the steering wheel as he kept his eyes front.

"Do I hafta go live with you or Leilani, or can I stay with Sam and Mauro?"

"You know, my boy, there are many people who don't even have one of those choices. You understand that, of course. You've lived in the streets. Our custom says you leave your shoes or *slippahs* at the door of the house when you enter. I'd like to believe I could be at home anywhere I leave my *slippahs*. As your father and legal guardian, I might be required to approve of your choice, but ultimately, I think you've earned the right to choose for yourself. I believe you already know what you want. Don't you?"

"Yeah! Stay with Sam and Mauro where I'm really needed."

"It may be your wisest decision. But if you stay with them, what would you want to do with your life, son?"

"Be a master baker like Sam. I'm getting good at it. I like being around the smell of the ovens, and I sure like the feeling of being needed. Sam's getting older, and someday I'll take over for him. You wouldn't believe how much he's teaching me. In the meantime, I can go to school during the day after the baking's done. Everyone wants me

294

to go to that private school. I don't think I'd fit in there. Besides, Lani won't be there next semester. She'll be going off to college. Would it be okay with you if I went to Kaimuki High instead? That's where Andy goes."

"I don't see why you couldn't."

"Great! Uh, Dad?"

"Yes?

"How'd you get from construction into detective work?"

"Well, it's kinda tough handling crutches and canes on a construction site, don't you think?"

"Yeah, but that's not gonna be forever."

"Hey, son, you know what? You're right, it isn't forever."

Still unsatisfied, Kekoa had to ask. "But why a private eye? Why Hal Perry?"

"Yosh suggested a P.I. license might open some doors in my search for you. And I needed to go undercover with another name to pursue Red. Yosh's firm has more work for me. Not that I need it. I've got enough put away to support my whole family, at least for the time being." Hank's weathered face broke into a broad grin. "My whole family. God, it feels good to say that!"

As he pulled into the office building garage on Kapiolani, he added, "But what I'm really thinking of doing is taking over Finast Construction again—as soon as we put Murphy away. There won't be anybody else to run it, and I'd hate to see it go under. Besides, it's what I do best."

Pressing the elevator button, Kekoa brought up another subject that had haunted him for weeks. "Dad, could you find one more person for me?"

Hank looked puzzled. He shrugged his shoulders and said, "Sure. At least, I could try to find him."

"Her," Kekoa corrected. "He's a her."

"Who's a her?" Hank asked.

"She's the only daughter of a close friend of mine. I have her name and address on a piece of paper at home. I'm supposed to give her a locket and a message from him."

"Why doesn't your friend give it to her himself?"

"Ol' Chou's dead," Kekoa replied curtly. He slid his hands deeper into his pockets. "He asked me to do this as his last request. He was very sick and so weak. He'd been homeless and living in the streets for years. You see, he took care of me when I had nowhere else to go. I did try the address, but the lady downstairs said she'd moved away. Couldn't you please find her for me?"

"Bring me the name and all you know about her, and I'll see what I can do. Okay?" Hank extended his open palm for a low five, and the boy responded with an energetic downward slap.

The elevator doors opened into the law firm. In the partners' conference room, Terumi passed out legal questionnaires called interrogatories for each of them to fill out. He started the tape recorder rolling, and for the next two hours, Hank and Kekoa answered every question on the list. Terumi handed the cassette to a stenographer to transcribe. Kekoa and Hank remained in the office to sign the copies intended for Lieutenant Mahaila.

Left alone with his father, Kekoa asked: "So when are you and Lori getting married?"

Hank paled at the blunt question and pressed his lips together to prevent the wrong words from escaping. Psychologically, he felt as if he were teetering on the edge of a cliff, about to plunge into a subject that spelled nothing but tragedy. During all these years, he'd stubbornly avoided any female companionship. But sitting at this conference room table, he heard the underlying desperation in his son's words: Kekoa's yearning—childish and almost frantic—to be part of a genuine, complete family.

Hank knew he'd better be honest. "I haven't asked her. It's such a radical step, we need to spend time getting to know each other. Frankly, after all these years alone, I'm having a helluva time visualizing myself as a husband."

"Bullshit, Dad! You'd make a great husband, especially now that you don't drink any more."

The remark stunned and wounded Hank momentarily. He studied the boy's earnest face. No malice there, just the bluntness of youth, yet so much wisdom for his fifteen years, he concluded. "I don't know if Lori'd have me. She's the first woman I've looked at seriously since your beautiful mother died."

"I know she will."

Hank continued, "We'll see. Maybe when I get rid of this last cane." He tapped its rubber tip lightly on the carpet.

"I like her a lot, and I know she loves you."

Hank broke into a broad smile. "You think she does?"

"Oh, yeah, I can see it in her face. You better do it, Dad, before some other guy snaps her up first."

Now his father laughed out loud—something he hadn't had much reason to do in a long time. "Well, okay, maybe you've convinced me. Actually, that's another reason for me to go back to the construction business. What woman wants to put up with a P.I.'s irregular working hours, waiting for my *slippahs* to appear at the door with hers? Besides, I'm a helluva lot better builder than I am a snooper."

He and Kekoa laughed. As they waited for the lawyers to return to the conference room, Kekoa said, "There's something…"

The hesitation caused Hank to anticipate something foreboding. "What, Kekoa?"

"Would you spend the afternoon with me? There are two things I'd like us to do together."

"Just what did you have in mind?"

"Well, first, can you come with me and meet my friend Andy at the hospital? Mr. Fujita and I are going there to get his statement."

"Of course."

The door opened and Terumi and Lori entered the conference room with the typed statements for them to sign. He told them that as soon as they took Andy's deposition at the hospital, they were free until the following morning.

Fifteen minutes later Terumi, Hank and Kekoa walked down the ICU corridor of Queen's Medical Center. As they approached Andy's room, a doctor was just leaving. Terumi quickened his step and presented his business card. "Excuse me, Doctor. Is the boy up to answering a few questions about his ordeal? We'd like to get the culprit behind bars as soon as possible."

"In that case, yes. But please keep your visit short."

Kekoa entered the room alone. He found Andy pulling on a trapeze bar and stretching his neck with difficulty, trying to see around the edge of the curtain that separated his half of the room. "Hey, *bruddah!*" Kekoa said.

"Hey, yourself!" Andy tried to sound cheerful, but he winced with the slightest move. "Are you okay?"

"Yeah, man." Kekoa gazed at the confusing array of pulleys,

weights, and ropes between Andy's casts and the scaffolding above him. He forced himself to sound upbeat. "Look at all this stuff. It's like having your own workout room."

"I'm sorry about the bikes."

"Don't worry about that. I'll get another one. Mauro says the insurance might pay for most of it. And maybe we can get one for you, too." Several minutes of silence passed between them and finally Kekoa broke it. "You know it wasn't an accident, don't you? That guy in the truck was trying to hit me. I'm supposed to be the one in the hospital, maybe even dead, not you."

Andy looked shocked. "Who? Why?"

Barely stopping to take a breath, Kekoa poured out the whole truth. Andy devoured every word. Finally, Kekoa told him, "There's some good news, too. I've found my sister and my father. He's here in the hall, and I want you to meet him. And, uh, Andy, there's someone else—our lawyer. He wants to ask you some questions about what you saw and heard Friday night."

From the door, Kekoa summoned Hank and Terumi. After the introductions and a few minutes of pleasantries, Andy decided that he liked Kekoa's father real well, but he wasn't too sure about this Fujita guy.

Terumi placed a tape recorder on the nightstand and hit the RECORD button. "Andy, tell me in your own words what happened last Friday." Andy recounted the details that he could remember.

"Can you identify the make, type, year, and color of the vehicle that hit you? Anything?" Terumi asked.

"Well, sir, it was an old pickup, a Ford, I think, maybe a '66 like my father's truck. I think it had been a darker gray or blue once, but the paint was in real bad shape. The last thing I remember is the two big boards on the bumper coming at me. I guess I blacked out then."

"Two big boards. That's unusual. Could you see who was driving well enough to identify him?"

"I...I guess so."

Terumi opened his briefcase and pulled out four glossy eight-by-ten photos; they were among Hank's surveillance shots of Red. "Could any of these be the man?"

Andy stared hard at one in particular, the telephoto close-up of Red behind the steering wheel of his Buick. A heavy silence filled the room.

Suddenly, he became agitated. He pulled himself up a little higher on the trapeze bar to get another look in the light, and stared again, one by one, at the four photos. Then abruptly he released his grip and fell back on the pillows. "I think it's him. It could be. But I'm not sure. It was getting dark." He looked mournfully at Terumi. "I'm sorry, sir."

"That's perfectly okay, my boy," Terumi said gently. "The fact that you recognized the wood bumpers will be a big help to us."

But Andy could not calm down. He felt that he had failed them. His exertion had caused more pain than anyone had expected. He began to sob.

A sense of helplessness and guilt flooded Kekoa. His best friend's misery was all his fault. He rushed to the bed and squeezed Andy's shoulders to console him, but he had no chance to do more.

"That's it! You'll have to leave now." A nurse burst into the room, exercising her iron authority. Embarrassed, they all waved their goodbyes and promised to be back soon.

Once outside, Terumi headed back to work. Hank turned to Kekoa. "Son, back at the office you said there were two things you wanted us to do today."

The boy nodded, pleased that his father had listened to him so closely. "Dad, I want to go to the cemetery. We can pick up Leilani on the way. We need to visit Mom."

* * *

Lucille had never been in a small plane before. This was only the second time she had ever been in any airplane. During takeoff, she maintained a fearful grip on her seat's vinyl armrests. She closed her eyes to the runway lights slipping past them faster and faster and then too fast as Red suddenly pulled away from the ground. He banked to the right and continued to climb, eventually leveling the aircraft.

Lucille opened her eyes to the now steady motion. She gasped in amazement. The whole city of Honolulu lay to their left. Lights flowed like lava from the populated land rises into the bright pool of the densely lit city below. Long, dark voids separated the flows from the adjacent valleys. These voids were the shear cliffs too steep or rugged to build on.

Soon the whole sky blackened, except for glittering moonlight on the dark green sea. Whitecaps, whipped like meringue, broke above the ocean's lime pie. Scant starlight danced behind veils of clouds.

Red intended this to be the most romantic night of Lucille's thirty-one years. It had begun three hours earlier when he picked her up at the restaurant. In the car, he kissed her firmly yet gently, letting her know she had a serious lover here. She'd melted in his arms like butter in a hot frying pan. And when he knew she wanted more, he'd broken away politely and started the car.

Now, tucked into the two-seater Cessna, Red felt her eyes on him. She radiated with affection. He knew he had her charmed and eating out of his hand. Then she rested her head on his shoulder. The thought of spending three days with her on Maui made him tingle with anticipation.

"That's Molokai down there on the left," Red told her. "We'll go there sometime. And there's Lanai off to the right." She raised her head long enough to see patches of twinkling lights below on either side of the plane. When she tried to put her head down again, he told her, "Sweetie, you'll have to sit up now. I'm beginning my descent into Kahului Airport."

She straightened up, and all her fears returned. "Aren't you coming down too fast? What if you miss the runway?" Squeezing her eyes shut, she again clutched the armrests with a steel grasp. They felt the great bump of the plane's first touch-down, and then more tire rumblings as the engine roared loudly to brake their landing speed. When the plane had come to a complete stop, Red leaned over and brushed his lips against her cheek. She came alive again. He assisted her down from the cabin, and she helped him secure the four tie-downs for the Cessna's wings.

Red pulled their bags from the plane and carried them to the rental car waiting in the lot. Steering the Chevy Nova out of the airport, he turned south onto Route 30 through the central plains. The highway curved west, hugging the coast, then north through the town of Lahaina, where a whaling industry had once flourished. In the darkness, Lucille succumbed to the intensity of the day and dozed off. The car sped up the Kaanapali coastline of resort hotels towards Kahana, a long stretch of oceanside condominiums: some modest structures, others towering high rises.

They pulled into a parking lot, and Lucille awoke with a start. She stared at the modest stucco three-story building. "I thought we were going to a resort hotel." Disappointment tugged at her voice.

Red took the bags from the trunk. "This is much more exclusive and private," he told her. "Don't worry, you'll love it."

She wouldn't be convinced of that until they entered their unit on the top floor. He dropped the bags just inside the door and flicked on the lights.

Kicking off her shoes, she ran through the elegant rooms, surveying the white furniture upholstered in pastels, the azure-blue carpeting, a modern kitchen, and a dining room with a chandelier made of shells. She flung open the sliding glass doors to a spacious lanai and stepped out. Coconut palms surrounded it, creating a cove of complete privacy. Ocean waves could be heard lapping at the rocky shoreline below.

She returned to him, locked her arms around his neck, and buried her head in his chest. Then she kissed him on the tip of his nose.

"Give me a minute to put on something more daring."

Actually, he wanted to rip off her street clothes and take her right on the spot. But Red restrained himself and let her go. When she closed the bedroom door, he stepped out onto the lanai, took off his aloha shirt, and laid it across the back of a large rattan sofa. His hand pushed into the plump cushion to test its softness, and then he moved to the railing and leaned on it thoughtfully while he waited.

Red didn't hear her coming into the living room, but sensed her presence. He turned and saw much more than he had expected as she stood still, watching him. Lucille's filmy nightgown hung softly about her body. She stood in front of a lamp that backlit a lovely sight, so clear that he knew at once that she wore neither bra nor panties. The low-cut, close-fitting bodice uplifted her luscious melon breasts and provocative pointed nipples. She stood there waiting for him to take her in. He wanted so much to approach her immediately, but the tantalizing view caused him to linger a bit longer.

When his growing hardness begged louder than the feast of sight, he slipped through the glass door to get at her. His eyes never left her body as he swept her into his arms and carried her back outside to the double lounge chair. This was their first time together. They joined in slow, exploratory lovemaking, gently at first, and then more fiercely as their forms melded.

When they'd delighted each other enough, a serene mood slipped over them. She lay with her head on his chest, running fingers through the thick, rough hairs.

He looked from the soft form cuddled beside him out to the ocean, where an artistic moon carved silhouettes from two neighbor islands. A gentle breeze blew across the lanai. The warmth and exhaustion they shared that night enveloped them with a sense of deep commitment: she to him and Red to his purpose.

Chapter 43
Deposition and Denial

"SOUNDS LIKE we're dealing with one desperate SOB. I'm afraid Murphy won't stop until he gets the boy or we get him."

"Exactly why we're here, Lieutenant," Terumi responded.

Detective Lieutenant Gert Mahaila and Sergeant Fred Haiakane had arrived at the Fujita law suite shortly before nine, and the Monday morning meeting had gone as expected. Seeing that the endless repetitions disturbed Kekoa, an observant and sympathetic Gert wrapped it up.

"If you think of anything else, don't hesitate to call me." She passed out her business cards. "Thank you all."

Both officers left to pursue their own investigations. In the parking garage, they agreed to share information but to keep it confidential until the DA felt they had built an airtight case.

Half an hour later, Fred queried the Motor Vehicle and Licensing Division and quickly confirmed that Finast Construction did own two pickups: a '75 green Dodge Ram and a black '66 Ford 4x4. Murphy personally owned a red '80 Ford 4x4 and a red and white '74 Buick Regal sedan. Even though none of the vehicle colors on file fit the description the two boys had given, Fred decided to try his luck at the Finast Construction yard, just off Nimitz Highway.

The company's office trailer stood in the middle of a large lot enclosed by a high chain-link fence. Construction equipment and building materials occupied much of the surrounding yard. The tailgate of a Dodge Ram pickup stuck out on the far side of the trailer. While it bore no obvious signs of damage, the body had been poorly repainted a pathetic pea green. The truck bed contained a clutter of displaced wooden cabinets and broken lengths of quarter-round moldings with bent nails protruding from them.

Fred didn't see a wooden bumper or any sign of one ever having been attached. Just as he began to photograph the truck for the record, a booming voice startled him from behind. "Kin I hel' you, brah?"

Fred wheeled around to face a large Hawaiian with a ponytail. "Yes, sir! You sure can." Fred displayed his badge and offered a cursory explanation—"investigating a hit-and-run." Satisfied, the worker informed him that the second pickup could be found at a renovation site on School Street, just off the Pali access road.

"Tha' piece a junk's been there for days. It's nothin' li' this Dodge at all."

"Thanks, you've been a big help."

"Ho' they get the bastar'."

"Me too," Fred said as he drove off.

Fred's arrival at the renovation site went unnoticed for the most part. A crane moved back and forth loading roofing materials to the top of the school gymnasium. The din of machinery droned over the site, and the sharp odor of steaming hot tar assaulted his nostrils.

He located a Ford pickup parked next to a three-ton stake truck full of lumber, but its black paint gleamed in the sunlight. On closer inspection, the officer noted tiny patches of a lighter, grayer color seeping through the shiny paint, giving it the look of spots missed during polishing. And this truck had a pair of makeshift bumper boards! In fact, the entire pickup fit the descriptions in both boys' depositions. He examined the bumper boards and grille work, but found no trace of blood. Next, he took a series of photographs. Satisfied that he'd found the right vehicle, Fred drove back to his office without hearing the foreman yell to him from the crane cab.

* * *

Over on Maui, Lucille basked in the time of her life. Red gave generously, and his bedazzled waitress attended to him, filling his plate with all the affection she could serve. Red ate up every morsel of it. Their sessions of intense lovemaking proved arduously pleasant for both of them.

It was early Tuesday morning, and Red had told her they would leave in the late afternoon, so she could be at work that evening for her dinner shift. The sun worshippers at the condo pool hadn't shown up yet, so the entire place belonged to Red and Lucille. They relaxed on adjacent lounge chairs under the shade of an umbrella, with Red sitting up and Lucille stretched out sensually on her belly. She reached over and rested her hand affectionately on the inside of his foreleg. He wore his dark glasses and seemed to be scanning the *Honolulu Advertiser* for something.

"Find what you're looking for?"

"Nope," he grunted. He'd been searching for an item on the hit-and-run since Saturday morning, but the papers had printed nothing. He didn't understand. Why would the police withhold the information? Maybe he had somehow missed it. He folded the paper and set it beneath the chair, then rolled over and slapped her on her ample backside. "Last one in the water's a rotten egg, babe."

He dove into the pool at the deep end. Lucille cautiously lowered herself down the deep-end ladder and slipped into the water. Red caught her in his arms and towed her to mid-pool.

When they could both stand easily, Lucille faced him and whispered, "I love you, Mr. Murphy."

Red kissed her long and hard as they embraced. When they parted to take a much-needed breath of air, she said, "There's nothing I wouldn't do for you, Red."

Red gazed into her eyes with his most earnest expression and found a marionette willing to be manipulated. Creating confusion about the day of their first movie date might not be necessary after all.

"Would you, could you possibly love me enough to tell a very small lie for me?"

Although she flashed him a puzzled look, Lucille nodded her assent.

Red lowered his eyes apologetically. "I got involved in a small accident last Friday when I left you. I don't know why, but I left the scene and drove off before anyone saw me. I'm actually ashamed, but I can't turn myself in. I committed a crime and I could go to jail for it."

"Did anyone get hurt?"

"No, I don't think so. Not bad, anyway. I believe he's a teenager. A broken leg at the most. I can't find anything about it in the papers, so I don't know for sure. I'm assuming he was taken to a hospital. When I find out which one, I'll send an envelope with $5,000 in it for his medical bills, plus a little extra for the boy."

"That's decent of you. Did anyone see you or your car?"

"No, I'm sure nobody did. Besides, that night I drove a company pickup, an old wreck that's really hard to identify. There are so many pickups on the island."

She didn't say a word, but sealed her private pact with the devil by pulling Red's lips to her own. The passionate kiss let him know he had much more than an alibi. He would tell her about the movie tickets on the way home. They slid beneath the water's surface to fondle each other briefly.

At four o'clock the Cessna took off for Honolulu. Red drove her straight to work and offered to pick her up afterward. She shook her head.

"I'm beat. Let's make it tomorrow. I'll bum a ride home with the cashier."

Without argument, Red headed for his apartment. As he pulled into his parking space, headlamps from the car parked opposite him suddenly burst alive. Two men in street clothes approached. The shorter of the two flashed a badge and an ID.

"Honolulu Police! We'd like to ask you a few questions."

Red wanted to run, but something told him he'd better stand his ground.

"Are you Edgar Murphy?" the other officer asked, showing his badge.

"Yeah. What's this all about?" Red blurted out. Then he thought better about being so abrupt. "Sorry, officers, but you took me by complete surprise."

"The lieutenant wants to ask you a few questions down at the station. Would you please accompany us? I'm sure we can straighten everything out in a hurry."

"Am I under arrest? Do I need a lawyer?"

"No, sir, you're not under arrest. Our instructions are to bring you in for questioning. Once you're at the station you are, of course, at liberty to call your lawyer. Shall we?"

Red threw his weekender bag in his car trunk, and slammed down the lid. They ushered him into the back seat of an unmarked police car. He noticed that the car's rear doors lacked the usual push-pull lock handles; it would be impossible for him to run now. In spite of his every effort to question the two officers in the front seats, he couldn't get more than "Yes, sir!" or "No, sir!" out of them. He wondered how much they knew, or for that matter, how much anyone knew.

At the station the officers led him into a windowless interrogation room, furnished with only a simple table and wooden chairs. A fluorescent fixture hung from the ceiling via chains, casting a ghostly glare. One of the four tubes had worn to the stage of continual flickering.

An officer indicated the chair facing the door. Red declined an offer of coffee or water, and the two detectives left him, saying, "The lieutenant will be with you in a moment."

Red looked around the room, but the only thing that caught his eye was a framed photo of a precinct basketball team on the longer wall. The flickering fluorescent tube unnerved him. He wondered if they'd left him alone to brew in his own kettle for awhile. If that's the case, it's working, he thought. He heard the door rattle and expected it to open immediately. Instead, several stomach-churning moments passed before Red saw the knob turn and the door swing open. He didn't expect to see a woman. She was not particularly attractive and definitely not his type, he decided. The self-assured, tough way she carried herself—probably into the martial arts. But he did find something interesting and cool about her presence.

She took a chair across from him and dropped a pile of file folders on the table. "Hello, Mr. Murphy. I'm Lieutenant Mahaila, and I'd like to ask you a few questions. May I have your cooperation?"

"I suppose so. Yeah, sure, why not?"

"Mr. Murphy, can you tell me where you were last Friday evening, say, between six and eight o'clock?"

"Let's see. Friday…six and eight. I'm not sure, but I think we were at the movies at that time." Red decided not to blab his alibi out all at once. He would make her drag it out of him. He would have more credibility that way.

Gert never took her eyes from him. "We? Who are we?"

"My girlfriend, Lucille Kioni. Saaay, why do I need an alibi? Am I under arrest? I wanna know what this is all about."

Gert's apparent friendliness slipped from her face. "We're investigating a hit-and-run, and depending on your answers, I will decide whether to charge you or not."

"I think I'd better call my lawyer."

Gert stood and gathered up her folders. "That might be a wise decision, Mr. Murphy, very wise. I'll get you a phone." Returning a few minutes later, she handed him a portable phone and an Oahu directory

307

and left the room. "I'll be back in fifteen minutes. The law guarantees you absolute privacy."

Red thumbed through the phone book until he came to B.E. Bailey, Esq., Atty. at Law. He dialed the number, but to his dismay, reached an after-hours answering service. After leaving a message for Mr. Bailey to contact him at the Beretania police headquarters, he yelled to the operator, "Tell him it's urgent, damn it!" Red barely restrained himself from slamming down the receiver. When he tried to dial a second number, he couldn't obtain a dial tone. He complained to Gert when she returned.

"You're entitled to only one completed phone call," she said. "Let's get back to where you were Friday evening between six and eight."

Red felt a knot of fear growing in his gut and tried to steady his voice. "Look here, Lieutenant, I'm not saying another word without my lawyer."

"Your choice, Mr. Murphy. We can arrange for you to see a bail bondsman if you like."

"Then I am under arrest?"

"Yes. For your involvement in a hit-and-run accident and leaving the scene." She read him his Miranda rights.

Red quickly mulled over his options. Unless Bailey got back to him immediately to arrange bail, he'd be spending the night in the lockup. Reluctantly, he decided to arrange his own bail and went, with the bondsman, before the night court magistrate. Bailey's return call came in after Red had already left the precinct.

He took a cab home, feeling desolate and far less confident than the Red Murphy of just a few hours earlier. Once again he'd lost control of his own fate, a feeling he just couldn't tolerate.

Chapter 44
Battling Beetle Bailey

BERTRUM Esterhaus Bailey sat in his Matterhorn Building office, listening to the playback of incoming phone messages. He completely filled the red leather swivel chair, custom-made for his immense body.

Thirty years ago and 150 pounds lighter, he'd served his country in Korea, where his Army buddies had instantly issued him the nickname "Beetle" after the popular cartoon G.I. The name had stuck the rest of his life. In truth, he rather enjoyed playing the inept goldbricker; it served to disarm adversaries. Never having married, Beetle Bailey gave over his entire life to building the best criminal practice in the islands.

He jotted down a few notes with each new phone voice coming from the machine. Edgar Murphy? The name required some recall. He inched the chair around like a tank turret until it faced the windows and the regiment of cabinets beneath them. Pushing off with marching feet, he rolled the chair along the plastic floor mat until it halted in front of the "M" drawer, where he pulled out a file folder marked MURPHY, E.

His stubby fingers flipped through the pages until the summary comments, dated six years earlier, jumped out at him: "Failure to perform contract and misappropriation of funds, resulting in fine and settlement."

A loud thud of books dropping onto a desk in the outer office announced the arrival of his receptionist. "Aloha, Mr. B. I stopped by the library and got the books you asked for."

"Thank you, Rosie. I know you don't do coffee, but would you bring us both a cup, anyway? I want to get started on a couple of new cases and I need your help."

Rosie came in with two steaming mugs and set them down on coasters beside the desk blotter. "What's up, Mr. B.?"

"I'd like you to get in touch with the Beretania Station police and find out what charges are being filed against a Mr. Edgar Murphy. Also, let me know who the arresting officer is. If Murphy's still behind bars, let's see if bail has been set, and if it's reasonable, make some arrangements to free him. And, Rosie, make an appointment with him to see me this afternoon." He took a long slurp of his coffee and winced at its biting temperature. "And get me all you can about the man and his business."

* * *

Red's eyes popped open in his darkened bedroom. What had awakened him? He listened, but only street sounds broke the thick silence. He closed his eyes to shut out a motorcycle's roar. Then he heard it again—unmistakable this time, a knock at his door. He fumbled for the lamp switch, dragged his feet off the bed, and pulled on his plaid boxer shorts. Stomping barefoot down the hall, he flung open the front door.

Damn! he thought. Why didn't I look through the peephole first? A young uniformed policewoman with blond braids stood there. Before he could recover any false modesty, she presented him with two envelopes.

"Have a nice day," she chirped, and did an about-face.

He stared after her. When she reached the elevator, she turned and grinned slyly at his protruding plaid bulge.

His befuddled self would have stood there even longer, but the ringing telephone jarred him back to awareness. He kicked the door shut and made it to the phone on the fifth ring. "Yeah! This is him. Bailey's office, 1:30 this afternoon. I'll be there."

Red set the phone down and studied the two envelopes clutched in his left hand. He quickly tore the end off the first one and shook out the contents: the copy of a court order to confiscate the old Ford truck. That woke him up in a hurry.

He stared at the second envelope, afraid of what it might contain. He slit it open slowly, hoping the delay would soften the blow. It didn't. The contents revealed the copy of another court order, this one to dig on the Ewa property. He realized that the Pualoa boy had gone on the offensive. There weren't enough curse words to fit the occasion.

In the kitchen Red grabbed a bottle of Jim Beam from the cabinet over the sink. Empty! He hurled it into the trash basket, took down a second bottle, and poured a stiff drink of Old Grand-Dad into a dirty glass sitting on the counter. In one slow, steady draining he finished it off. He started to pour a second stiff one, but settled for a good deal less this round; he needed a clear head for his meeting with Bailey.

Red took the half-inch of whiskey to the sliding door of the lanai and laid his head against the glass, looking up in time to see a rainbow disappear into its own mist. He felt terrible.

* * *

Kekoa's heart pounded as he climbed out of the police car. Gert and Fred followed him into the backyard with a pickax, a sixteen-pound sledgehammer, and a garden spade. Hank came out last, lightly leaning on one cane. After a few steps, he turned around, tossed the cane into the back seat of the cruiser, and plodded after the others.

Gert, in jeans and a Honolulu Marathon Finisher's T-shirt, walked around to the front door and rang the bell. No one answered. Just as she was about to give up, a gangly young man with a homely face came to the door.

"Lieutenant Mahaila, Honolulu Police." Gert flashed her badge. "Mr. Louis Lynch, Jr.?"

Young Lynch nodded, looking scared.

"You live here?"

"Yes," he said.

Gert handed him the court order for digging on the premises. Lynch wanted to protest, but simply didn't know how to accomplish that.

A buxom young woman appeared behind him. "What's wrong, honey?"

"It's some legal paper allowing the police to dig in the back-yard. I don't think it concerns us." Lou tried to sound both flippant and reassuring.

"Excuse me," Gert interrupted. "May I come in for a moment?" Without waiting for an answer, she stepped into the living room. Her nostrils flared as she detected the smell of garbage. She asked, "Have you seen anything unusual happening around here lately? Anything at all?"

"Not really," Lou answered. "I'm just the tenant. But...now that you mention it, we did see Mr. Murphy, the owner. We saw him working real late one night in the garage."

"What's so unusual about that?"

311

"Well, he drove into the driveway without headlights. At first I didn't recognize him, but then I saw it was Mr. Murphy."

"I thought you said his headlights were out."

"They were, but he clipped some kind of lamp onto the top of the garage door—must've been battery operated—and when he turned it on, we saw who it was. And then he pulled the nose of the pickup into the open garage door and turned on his headlights."

"How do you know all this? Where were you at the time?"

"Looking out the rear bedroom window. I'll show you," Lou offered. Gert and Abby followed him upstairs.

"Whew!" Gert said as the odors of mildew and stale sex assaulted her. "You kids hiding dead animals in this house?"

Abby flushed with embarrassment and Lou answered. "No, sorry, we're a little behind in our cleaning, with school and all."

Gert walked over to the window and looked out, assessing just how much of a view the young couple had. "Did you see anything else that night?"

"We couldn't actually see anything," Lou said, "but we heard him using a pick and shovel for hours. That's what it sounded like, anyway. We thought this was a little strange, digging by hand, when he had that machine out there."

"What machine was that?"

"A small bulldozer or backhoe. I'm not exactly sure."

"What night was this?"

"Wednesday, the week of spring break."

"Did Mr. Murphy come back any other time at night?"

Abby thought hard. "We did hear him back the gray pickup out last Friday—say, four or five in the afternoon."

"Gray? How can you be sure it was him?" Gert asked.

"I saw him get out and pull down the new garage door," Abby recalled. "He must have forgotten the remote."

"I see. And what did he do then?"

They looked at each other sheepishly. Lou tried to answer. "Um, we're not sure. We were, uh, busy."

Gert glanced at the rumpled sheets and suppressed a grin. "Well, I certainly thank the both of you." She closed her little notebook and hurried down the stairs.

Outside, she joined the threesome in the backyard and placed her arm around Kekoa's shoulders. "Well, young man, where do we start?"

Kekoa's body tensed, and he jammed his hands in his pockets as he surveyed the site. "It's so different now, ma'am. They've changed the whole backyard. The shed's brand-new—it's a first-class garage now. But it would be over here." He led them around to the side of the shed and stopped under the corrugated roof overhang. Counting the number of sidewalk squares from the front of the shed, Kekoa halted at the spot where Red had dug before the walkway was poured.

"Here!" he pointed.

Gert removed a red rubber ball from one of her jeans pockets and began squeezing impatiently. She nodded to Fred. He took the first hearty swing with the pick, but it merely bounced off the concrete like a toy. Hank handed him the sledge. Eight or ten swings later a few minor cracks and a chipped surface appeared, but no sign of any major crumbling could be seen. When Fred stopped to rest, Gert shoved the ball back in her pocket and took the sledge from him. Her years of weight-lift workouts always paid off at times like this. With rippling biceps, she swung the sixteen pounds easily and mauled the surface until a major fault arose.

Backing away, she motioned to the two men to use the pick and shovel as pries to lift, flip over, and drag away the three flat chunks of walkway cement. With the shovel, Fred probed the exposed gravel, sand, and dirt.

"Hold it!" Gert said, pointing to the shallow hole. Something shiny flashed in the sunlight. She stooped down and, with the tweezers from her evidence kit, lifted the object out. It appeared to be the broken end of a watchband. She shook it carefully until more of the band, and the watch itself, emerged from the clinging dirt. The stenciling brush from her kit carefully eased away the remaining debris without disturbing any fingerprints it might hold.

Before slipping the watch into an evidence bag, Gert turned it over and read the inscription aloud for everyone to hear: "John Pualoa, Big in Body, Mind, and Heart."

Hank spun away. His broad back shook as he wept. The red scar on his neck throbbed.

No one spoke or moved. The pained seconds turned into minutes before Hank recovered enough to tell them: "That was the watch I gave my brother for his fortieth birthday."

It was all too much for Kekoa. He ran to the back of the yard and scrambled up the trunk of the mango tree—the same tree he'd hidden in the night of the murder. He wedged his wiry body into the cradle formed by two major branches.

Hank started toward the tree, but stopped abruptly, realizing he needed to respect his son's desire to be alone.

Gert, Fred, and Hank resumed their digging. At a depth of about three feet, a strange odor hit the air.

"Smells like decomposition," Gert said.

"I don't think so," Hank countered, "more like acid."

Not wanting to take any chances, the lieutenant brought three surgical masks from the police cruiser. A few moldy scraps of dungaree material appeared. Gert carefully tucked them into an evidence bag.

They took turns digging for another hour and two feet deeper without uncovering anything of significance. They agreed to give it up only when the dirt turned to blackish clay, porous lava rock, and lime deposits. Obviously, the ground had not been disturbed before at this depth and would hardly qualify as Big John's current burial site.

Disappointment and a sense of failure settled thickly over them. In a low voice so Kekoa couldn't hear, Gert said, "I think there are three possibilities. One, Kekoa is mistaken about the exact location. Two, the body has been removed to another location. Three, we're the victims of a young boy's overactive mind."

Fred shrugged his shoulders. Hank leaned on the shovel and said, "I can't believe that. What about all the threats to Kekoa's life?"

"We have only his word for that."

An agitated Hank replied. "You have my word, too, and Andy's deposition. Plus the injuries to both boys."

"Yes," she agreed. "Besides, we do have your brother's watch and the clothing scraps. That's just too much of a coincidence. And don't forget the contaminated soil. That smacks of an intentional, calculated effort to cover up a crime scene. You realize I have to consider all possibilities, even the remotest." She walked to the edge of the house and turned on the hose to a trickle. She rinsed her hands and face, then sipped from the end of the hose. The men followed suit.

Kekoa slowly climbed down from his tree perch. As he approached them, Hank hobbled forward, gathered his son in his arms, and held him tight.

Gravel crunched in the driveway. A cream-colored Cadillac Seville pulled up. Red Murphy stormed out of the passenger seat, bellowing. "What's the meaning of this? Why are you destroying my property?" And then he saw Kekoa standing beside Hank, clutching his father's arm. "You! You little bastard, you."

They heard the voice of the driver in low, angry tones. "Murphy, you'd better get back in the car if you want me to represent you," Beetle Bailey growled. Then he called to Gert in a friendlier voice. "Oh, Lieutenant? May I have a few words with you?" He made no attempt to get out of the car. Gert approached the driver's side.

"Yes, sir. And you are?" She looked curiously at this huge man stuffed into the Cadillac. His seat was positioned as far back as it would go, and yet the steering wheel made a deep impression in his midsection.

Beetle handed her his card. "Please excuse me for not getting out. It's somewhat difficult for me. Ma'am, can you explain the court order to dig on my client's property? Is this something to do with the hit-and-run charges lodged against my client?"

"The court order," Gert replied, "has to do with the disappearance of one John Pualoa, who has been missing for over two years. We have some new information leading us to believe that he is or was buried on this property. And no, we are not charging your client at this time. Oh, the property will be restored to its original condition—just as soon as a forensic team goes over the dig."

"I see. You realize, of course, my client did not own this property until recently."

"Yes, sir. Nevertheless, he had access to it beforehand. But please advise him that this is an official crime scene and will be marked as such before we leave. No one is permitted to cross the yellow tape barriers that we erect." Gert eyed him sternly. "By the way, I'd like to see the two of you in my office at, say, 9:30 tomorrow morning, for questioning. As I'm sure Mr. Murphy has informed you, he is under arrest on the charge of a hit-and-run."

"Yes, ma'am. Thank you! And please have a good day." Using only the rear view mirror instead of turning around, Bailey shied the Cadillac slowly out of the driveway like a wounded beast.

While Fred installed the crime scene barrier tapes and Hank collected the tools, Gert re-questioned Kekoa. The boy stuck to his story: Murphy had killed his uncle, he had been in the shed when the murder occurred, had heard the whole thing, and this was the location.

Finally, she told them they were finished with the Ewa house for now, but they would have to come up with a lot more than this before Murphy could be charged with murder. "Fred, I hope your lab boys are having better luck."

* * *

The lab boys had indeed fared better. They'd gone over the confiscated pickup with a fine-tooth comb and made several discoveries. One technician eagerly explained to Fred that a shiny finish to an otherwise neglected paint job seemed highly unlikely, especially in the construction business. "These guys either take immaculate care of their vehicles or they neglect them altogether. On this old Ford truck, a thin veneer of SAE 30-weight motor oil has been rubbed over the entire surface."

The wooden bumper boards initially revealed no sign of bloodstains. But the rusty bolts securing the boards to the metal chassis bore signs of bare metal and rust stripping on their threads. On a hunch, the technicians removed the boards and flipped them to the reverse side. The hunch paid off: several bloodstains were detected, and the lab was typing the blood now.

The hit-and-run case was slowly coming together. Eyewitness depositions placed Murphy at the scene. Fred now knew the vehicle's identity, assuming that the blood type on the bumper matched that of at least one of the kids. But Fred needed Gert's help to prove attempted murder. They needed a motive. And if Gert could find Big John Pualoa's body, they would not only be able to prove attempted murder, but murder itself.

* * *

Red followed Beetle into the lawyer's office and watched the man waddle past his secretary's desk until he reached his massive chair. Bailey sank into the depths of padded leather, forcing air to escape from it like a depleting balloon. A look of pure bliss crossed his face. And then it dissolved as he conjured up his professional bearing.

"If you ever cross me again the way you did today, you can find yourself a new attorney. I expect to do all the talking in legal matters. You say nothing except what I tell you to say, and only when and where I tell you to say it. Is that clear?"

"But…"

"Is that clear?"

"Yeah."

"Now that we've got that straight, let's get down to cases. You engaged me to advise and defend you on the criminal charge of hit-and-run. Was that all you had in mind, or did you want murder charges added to that? I don't know why yet, but I have a strong feeling that the two sets of charges are inseparable. Am I right?"

"I...uh...I..." The question took Red completely off guard.

Beetle reassured him. "The lawyer-client relationship is privileged, strictly confidential, and anything you say will go no further. That relationship extends to my staff as well. Should you not want to discuss the possibility of a murder charge, I will continue to represent you solely on the hit-and-run charge. Now, what's it to be?"

Red was silent for several minutes before muttering, "Both charges, I guess."

"Suppose you begin by telling me if you're guilty or not. But let me warn you, I'll know if you're lying."

"Damn it, man, do I have to admit it?" Red slouched into the chair opposite the lawyer.

"Not really. In any case, I think I already have the answer. With that in mind, let's get the hit-and-run thing out of the way first. Suppose you tell me about it instead of dancing around like you did earlier today."

Red cocked his head and tried to size up the man. He wondered how much he actually had to reveal. The lawyer stared back at him, unblinking. Red buried his humiliation and slowly told Beetle what he wanted him to know. He included the alibis, but not the fact that they had been concocted.

Beetle stared at Red for a long moment and then exclaimed, "So it was attempted murder after all?"

Red squirmed in his chair. "I don't have to answer that either, do I?"

"No, you don't, but you'd better not be holding back anything else from me if you want me to get your ass out of this sling." Beetle tapped his pen on the desk. "How many attempts have you made on young Pualoa's life, or was this hit-and-run the only time?"

Red told him about the crane at the construction site. "Hell," Red protested, "that one could've been an accident."

Beetle suppressed his feeling of disgust. "Now," he said, "we're

317

going to go over everything you know about John Pualoa's death. Tell me in your own words."

Again, Red knew better than to disobey Beetle's order, so he poured out everything he thought to be pertinent.

"Was Pualoa's body ever in that hole?" Beetle asked.

"How the hell should I know?"

Beetle cleared his throat loudly.

"Well, maybe," Red corrected.

"Where is the body now?"

Red's sulking demeanor turned bold. "That's something you don't need to know."

The answer didn't surprise Beetle. "Meet me here at nine tomorrow morning," he said. "We'll go in to see Lieutenant Mahaila together. And remember: I tell you what to say and when to say it. Agreed?"

Chapter 45
Allies and Alibis

BEETLE BAILEY struggled up the steep steps to the main police station on Beretania Street. Perspiration boiled from his round face. He dabbed and wiped with his handkerchief to little avail. Checking in at the reception desk, the duty sergeant handed him and Murphy visitor passes. He also gave them directions to the second floor conference room.

The day before, Beetle had obtained a copy of the hit-and-run report from the traffic division. He and Red had gone over it thoroughly before preparing Red's statement for the police. The statement contained a perfect alibi. Murphy had been at a movie with a girlfriend at the time of the incident.

In the conference room, they found Gert mulling over a pile of paperwork. On spotting lawyer and client, she hastily closed her manila folder and slipped it into a brown accordion file. She stood to greet them as if they were old friends. Although this disturbed Red and put him at an uncomfortable disadvantage, Beetle accepted the gesture warmly.

"Why, thank you," he said as Gert pulled a double-seater bench to the table especially for him.

Beetle spread open his calfskin briefcase and slid out a single sheet of paper. "Before we begin, my client has prepared a statement."

Gert read it through. When she had finished, she asked, "How might I get in touch with this Miss Kioni?" Red wrote down her home address and telephone number. Gert asked, "And is there anyone else who can establish your whereabouts at that time?"

"Well, there's that detective who's been following me. He saw me park in the garage," Red offered, after getting the nod from Beetle.

"One of our detectives? Why would he be following you?"

"No, no, no. It's that private shamus. I think his name is Perry."

319

"Oh. Harold Perry?" she asked.

"Yeah, that's him."

"So why's he following you?"

"I don't know. Why don'tcha ask him?" Red snickered.

Gert ignored the question and continued. "Anyone else see you?"

"Not that I know of, but I do have these." He held out a parking receipt and two theater stubs to *Sister Act.*

Gert accepted the three chits and examined the times and dates carefully. Disappointment struck her: the times fit perfectly, giving Murphy all the alibi he needed to queer a quick conviction.

"Mr. Murphy, suppose I told you that we have absolutely established that one of your pickup trucks was the instrument of the hit-and-run casualties in this case?"

"Lieutenant!" Beetle broke in. "If I may point out, my client doesn't own any pickup trucks. They belong to the Finast Construction Company, and most of the employees have unrestricted access to them."

"That's not true, Counselor. Motor Vehicles says he owns a red '80 Ford 4x4, in addition to his personal sedan, a '74 Buick, I believe."

Beetle turned to Red, who reluctantly nodded. Beetle scowled. "Sorry, ma'am, he does own an '80 pickup. Was that the vehicle involved?"

Gert enjoyed putting the two of them on the defensive. "Nope, the one involved was a company pickup."

Red leaned over and whispered something in Beetle's ear. Beetle nodded, and Red spoke up. "None of the company trucks require keys anymore."

"Oh?" she questioned.

"They all have toggle switches—anyone can drive them."

"I see." Gert looked down at her notepad before asking the next question. "Why would anyone want to cover an oxidized paint job with motor oil?"

Following a brief private exchange between lawyer and client, Red said, "It was a mishap. One of the men must have spilled oil on the hood. When I saw it there I tried to wipe it off with a rag. It looked so good that I continued over the rest of the truck."

"And when did you do this?" Gert asked.

"Several weeks ago at least. Well before that Friday, anyway," Red shot back without first checking with Beetle. "I had the car in the shop on Tuesday, so I borrowed the truck from the Ewa garage and left it on site."

Gert scowled. Pulling a notarized sheet of paper out of her accordion file, she handed it across the table to Beetle. "This is a corroborated eyewitness deposition placing your client at the accident scene."

Beetle mulled it over, then held several low-level exchanges with his client. "Lieutenant," the lawyer intoned, "this document strikes me as a hysterical and unreliable teenage reaction to a most unpleasant experience. He describes the windshield as dirty and cracked. Then how could he have seen who was driving? And there couldn't have been too much light at that time of day. It was dusk. Most certainly, it's a case of mistaken identity."

"Yeah!" Red snarled. "How're you gonna believe that *hanabata* kid?"

"Runny-nosed kid or not," Gert retorted, turning to Beetle, "the boy knows your client very well and has had a frequent connection to him in the past. His father and your client are business partners. Kekoa identified Mr. Murphy even before seeing a photograph of him. He claims that the hit-and-run was premeditated, and therefore it could be construed as a case of attempted murder. According to him, one of many attempts."

"Lieutenant," Beetle persisted, shifting his great bulk for emphasis, "I don't think you honestly believe you have enough to make the charge stick on the hit-and-run, let alone attempted murder. Otherwise, you'd be revoking bail. Are you intending to do that now?"

Gert's voice lost a fraction of its confidence. "I'm planning to consult with the District Attorney's office right now. Would you like to ask Mr. Murphy if he's amenable to some sort of plea at this point?"

Beetle smiled. "You're dreaming, Lieutenant. I believe my client to be innocent altogether."

Gert excused herself and left the room. As soon as the door closed, Beetle turned to Red and admonished him for not revealing that he previously knew one of the boys. "Is there anything else I should know or are you trying to dig your hole even deeper?"

In about twenty minutes a sour-faced Gert reentered. Looking straight at Beetle, she said, "The Assistant DA has decided to retain the charge of hit-and-run, at least for the time being. We may add other

321

charges later." Addressing Red, she announced, "Since your bail is posted, you're free to go—anywhere on Oahu, that is."

Red smirked with satisfaction as the two men left.

* * *

"Hey, Gert! Howzit?" Nate Wasserman, a local crime beat reporter, stuck his head in the door. "Boy, you sure look down."

"Oh, hi, Nate, howzit yourself?"

"Great! What's this about a court order to dig in Ewa? Wasn't that your name on the request?" Nate asked.

Gert thought for a moment and then decided it couldn't hurt to advertise a bit, so she told Nate as much as she knew for certain. Nate's "Police Beat" byline carried the piece in the morning paper:

* * *

The five prostitutes, all in classic pants suits, could have passed for

> Following an anonymous tip in an unsolved missing persons case, police have dug in a backyard in Ewa looking for the body of John Pualoa.
>
> The yard behind his home of thirteen years at 4110 Iliili Street became the site of an intensive search for his remains. Evidence found at the digging site suggests that it once held a body, but it could not be determined whose body had been removed.
>
> The present owner of the Ewa property, Edgar Murphy, could not be reached for comment. Mr. Murphy is currently being questioned in connection with another police matter, a hit-and-run incident in Palolo Valley.

five secretaries. They sat cozily in a booth at the Sunrise Restaurant, chatting over the buffet lunch. Cindy Chou felt elated to be here. Her face had finally healed from Red Murphy's beating. The nasty cuts and purple bruises had faded into near nothingness, and she was once again enjoying weekly outings with her friends. Today they celebrated her recovery.

"Anyone up for a movie this afternoon?" Cindy asked.

A chorus of voices agreed, but no one knew what was playing. Volunteering to buy the morning paper out of the wire basket at the counter, Cindy returned and dropped the paper on the table. The women immediately pulled it into disarray to find the movie listings. Cindy idly picked up the front section and flipped through it. A brief article on the third page caught her eye. She gasped, and her mood suddenly turned somber.

"What's wrong, Cindy?" one of her friends asked. "You look awful."

"Thanks a lot. No, really, I'm fine," Cindy insisted, but clearly she wasn't. "Sorry, girls. You all go to the movie without me, there're some things I've gotta do. In fact, I should be running along now." Cindy removed a $5 bill and two singles from her wallet and tossed them in the middle of the table. "There, that should do it." She blew a kiss to each of them and, within seconds, disappeared into the lunchtime crowd.

* * *

Beetle had insisted that Red bring Lucille to his office. He wanted to coach her before Lieutenant Mahaila got hold of her. He relaxed in his chair, sipping on a tall glass of seltzer over ice.

On the intercom, Rosie's voice announced, "They're here."

"Send them in, by all means."

Red steered Lucille into the room, pleased to have Beetle see him with his pretty dark-haired girlfriend. Still, Red couldn't help but notice that her long-sleeved, high-necked dress seemed at odds with her prominent breasts, fire-engine lipstick, and matching nails.

"Ah, Miss Kioni, Mr. Murphy! How nice to see you. Please have a seat. Can we get you anything?"

"No, sir," Lucille managed to murmur with more than a hint of fear in her voice. Rosie entered the room with her steno pad and took a seat near the door.

"Now, Miss Kioni, suppose you tell me what happened that night."

Lucille explained how they had met at the restaurant where she worked and how Red had been a regular there. She often sat at the table with him when things were slow. They had become fast friends over a period of several weeks. "That particular night was our first actual date," she said coquettishly, "and we decided to see a flick. We went dancing afterward and stopped for a bite to eat before going home."

What was the plot of the movie? Who was in it? Where did you go dancing? What restaurant afterward? Beetle questioned her until he satisfied himself that she must either be telling the truth or Red had coached her extremely well.

"You should know, Miss Kioni, that the prosecutor will try very hard to disprove your story and shake you up. There's nothing to be afraid of, though, as long as you're telling the truth."

Lucille flinched at the word "truth."

"The prosecutors may even threaten you with perjury and punishment," Beetle warned, "but you have nothing to fear as long as you stick to your story." She looked over at Red. He formed an exaggerated kiss on his lips and blew it silently at her. Beetle turned to Rosie. "Let's see what we have so far."

Rosie left the room to type up Lucille's deposition, and Beetle busied himself at his desk. Red chatted with Lucille in whispers for the next thirty minutes until Rosie returned with a draft copy. Beetle penciled a number of changes concerning order, tone, and pertinence. He handed it to Lucille. "Is this the formal statement you wish to make?"

As she read, the waitress's lacquered nails tapped a frenetic drumbeat on the desk. When she finally reached the end of the two pages, she scanned the last lines over and over, hardly seeing the words. Then she stared off into the distance.

"Miss Kioni?"

She smiled weakly. "Yes, sir. That's it, all right."

Red rose from his chair to put his arm around her. In a whisper he reminded her that he was footing the kid's medical bills. *Ain't love wonderful*, he thought. He had no doubts she'd do much better in court.

Rosie returned with several copies of the final deposition. Beetle watched Lucille sign them. Beetle's secretary then signed as a witness, and put her notary seal to each document.

Rosie waited until they had left and remarked, "I don't think either one of them is telling the truth."

"I don't pay you to have opinions," Beetle snapped.

* * *

Kekoa finished the last of the Saturday baking at 10 a.m. He hung up his apron, pulled off his mesh baker's cap, and laid it on the sink while he washed his hands. When he looked in the mirror, he saw Mauro standing behind him.

"You have visitor in shop."

"Who is it?"

"Surprise! You see," she teased.

Alex and Leilani stood before a glass case, almost visibly drooling over the lilikoi cakes.

"Kekoa, we came to take you away for the day," Leilani said. "Dad and Lori are waiting for us in the car." He and his sister hugged, and when they parted, Alex began to laugh.

"What?" she asked.

"Your cheek and Kekoa's eyebrows, they're full of flour." He ran his finger down her cheek and showed her the white tip.

Kekoa and his sister went to wash up. Afterward, he changed into a fresh T-shirt and shorts and gave Mauro a big hug on the way out the door.

"I finished my morning work. Tell Sam I'll help him with the new supplies when I get back."

Mauro nodded. "Now go have fun."

As soon as everyone got settled in the car, Hank spoke to Kekoa. "I want you to have a look at yesterday's morning paper." The *Advertiser* had been folded back to Nate Wasserman's "Police Beat."

"Am I the anonymous tip?" Kekoa asked. Hank assured him that he was.

Lori asked: "And where would you like to go today? We have a full tank of gas and a packed picnic lunch. "

Kekoa spoke up, his voice tense. "Do you think maybe we could stop and see Andy? I know it's pretty far away. But he came home from the hospital yesterday, and I feel I owe it to him."

Hank agreed. "That is, if Lori doesn't mind driving."

"Of course not," she replied. "Maybe Andy can join us for our picnic." She knew the way to Mokuleia only too well. She'd had a good laugh over the disaster at Andy's sister's wedding. How Kekoa had spotted Lori and run away—but not before he'd broken the fruit-filled punch bowl. In the comforting presence of his dad, his sister, and Lori, even Kekoa was able to crack a smile over the memory. Somehow that accident didn't seem so momentous now.

Hank was still thinking about the "Police Beat" article and turned to face the back seat. "Leilani, just how did you discover that Uncle John was missing?"

The question came so bluntly that Leilani gulped before answering.

"Well, the day after Kekoa ran away, *Tutu* sent me over to invite Uncle John to supper, and I couldn't find him either." She paused, pulling her thick chestnut hair behind her right ear. Her voice grew agitated. "I found both his front and back doors unlocked and two days of newspapers lying on the lanai. I ran back to get *Tutu*. We went over the entire house; nothing appeared to be missing. *Tutu* called a few of his friends. They knew nothing. Then we called the police, but all they did was ask questions and look around a bit."

"Didn't the police make any attempt to link the two missing family members? Didn't they even consider that it was too much of a coincidence?"

"Are you kidding, Dad?" Leilani's voice rose, then subsided just as quickly as she throttled her anger. "I admit they couldn't have made a connection at that point. We hadn't reported Kekoa missing yet, because *Tutu* felt certain he would come home again when he got good and ready. The next week, when we did call the police about Kekoa, they didn't even raise the possibility of a connection between the two. The whole investigation was totally pathetic! But *Tutu* really should have called them the day after he ran away, because he'd never done that before. It just wasn't like him."

"It's okay, Leilani. I didn't mean to upset you." Hank fell silent. He still had a lot to learn about being a dad.

They drove for over an hour before pulling into the Ballesteros backyard. From the driveway Kekoa saw Maria pushing her brother in his wheelchair toward the shade of the monkeypod.

Maria looked up to see Kekoa get out of the car and wave. She applied the wheelchair brakes and broke into a jog toward him. She leaped at him and threw her arms around his neck. A tail-wagging Ilio stood patiently by her side, waiting his own turn.

"Boy, am I glad to see you," she said. "Maybe you can knock some sense into his head."

"Whose head? What's wrong?" Kekoa asked as he scratched Ilio behind the ears.

In a choked voice Maria whispered, "Andy doesn't wanna leave the wheelchair. He's afraid of falling. He says the pain is too much and the pills make him sick. Things are bad. Real bad."

Hank stood by the side of the car, observing. Meanwhile, Andy had turned his wheelchair to face the other direction. Hank sensed, even from the driveway, that something was wrong. He approached, catching the end of Maria's frantic whisper:

"He can walk, but he won't, not even with his crutches."

"Can I be of some help here?" Hank asked.

The screen door behind them squeaked open, and Andy's parents emerged from the house. Hank reached out to shake Papa's hand. Papa grabbed it like a drowning man catching a lifeline. "Andy's not so good," he murmured.

It had been four weeks since the hit-and-run. Andy, although small in stature, was strong and had healed substantially. The orthopedist had fitted him with walking casts for both legs. The physical therapists at Queen's had worked with him for three weeks, helping him build up his strength and acclimating him to walk in the casts. He'd done well in the hospital, but he'd taken a bit of a fall on his first day home.

When Maria finally released her grip on Kekoa, he trotted over to the wheelchair, calling out, "Hey, *bruddah!*" He tried to give Andy a high five. But his friend responded with a limp show of fingers.

"What's wrong, Andy, you were doing so great!"

Andy slumped in the wheelchair as if he were cemented to it. He shook his head. "That was in the hospital. Here, it's so hard. I fall all the time—it hurts. It stinks, man. "

A shocked Kekoa stood helpless, not knowing what to say or do. He released the brakes and wheeled Andy toward the others.

A grim-faced Mama mumbled, "My Andy, he won't even try to walk."

Alex, Leilani, and Lori hung back near the car, not wanting to interfere. But Andy had spun an emotionally charged atmosphere that hovered over them like the eye of a hurricane. Only Hank knew what to do. He moved toward the wheelchair.

"Hey, Andy," he said.

"Hey." Andy eyed Hank suspiciously.

"Why don't you and I have a little talk, son?"

"I guess so, if you want."

Hank turned his head back to Mama and Papa. "Mr. and Mrs. Ballesteros, your son and I have a great deal in common. I had a nasty accident back in Baltimore. I was in the hospital for four months and I know what it's like—it's real tough. Maybe I can help him."

Mama and Papa looked hesitant, but Hank pretended not to notice. "We've brought a picnic lunch. The whole drive out here, we were hoping your family would join us. Why don't you all get things started while Andy and I talk?"

Mama nodded. "Let him, Papa. Besides, we've already got *Huli Huli* chickens on the grill."

Papa shrugged his okay. "I'll put another couple on."

Hank called to his family at the car. "Bring the stuff out!" Then he grabbed Andy's crutches leaning against the lanai railing, propped them horizontally on the handles of the wheelchair, and propelled Andy toward the back of the yard, out of earshot. Sitting down on a wooden bench along the fence, he waited. Andy shot him a sullen look.

No one could hear what Hank said to him, nor the boy's replies. Half an hour passed. Then Andy grasped the arms of the wheelchair and raised himself up. Hank slid a crutch under each of the boy's armpits.

"Hey, guys, look!" Kekoa whispered.

Andy stood, wobbling slightly, but upright. With Hank's strong arm to encourage rather than actually hold him, Andy steadied himself with the crutches and took several steps. Everyone held their breath as Andy and Hank manipulated the uneven terrain.

Kekoa could contain himself no longer. "Hey, man, way to go!" he shouted.

"How 'bout that?" his pal answered with a broad smile.

Papa went to fetch the wheelchair. With the painful spell broken, Maria leaped up to hug Andy, almost toppling him over. Everyone laughed.

"Easy does it, kids," Hank said, grinning.

Mama smothered Andy with a fat kiss on his cheek. "Do you need to sit down now?"

"Well, maybe," Andy admitted, "but not in that lousy wheelchair. Not ever again in that thing." He cautiously lowered himself onto one of the long benches at the picnic table and joked, "Hey, can't anyone get anything to eat around here?"

"Wise-ass kid," Papa said, his face glowing with pleasure.

The two families chatted as if they'd known each other forever. When the talk lapsed, they scarfed down smoked turkey, ham, and chicken grilled in teriyaki sauce. There were sides of macaroni salad and Maui chips as well. Mama presented two macadamia nut pies, and after one bite, Kekoa asked her for the recipe to take back to Sam. Mama bowed, a diva taking a curtain call.

Afterward, Hank gathered the Ballesteros family together and said, "If you need me, I'm here to help. Andy, it's going to take time, so don't get discouraged. You're on your way, son. No doubt about it." He also played a bit of the stern father. "I hear the doctor wants you to continue physical therapy. Do it!" Andy smiled and held two thumbs up.

When the west end darkness overtook them, they exchanged their reluctant alohas and parted.

On the drive home, Hank said, "Do you know what Papa Ballesteros told me? When he went to pay the hospital bill, he found that someone had already paid it. That's not all. A nurse brought him an envelope—no return address—with fifty $100 bills in it. Think of it, an anonymous gift of $5,000! Papa even wondered if we had something to do with it. I told him no, but it's got me wondering. Could it be Red?"

Lori retorted, "Red Murphy hasn't got that kind of conscience. He'd steal from his own mother."

"He wasn't always that way," Hank said, sinking into deep thoughts of the past.

Chapter 46
Pele's Gift

LIEUTENANT Gert Mahaila leafed through the forensics report of the Ewa dig. It confirmed that the site had held human remains, perhaps as recently as thirty days ago. The few blood and fiber samples were so tainted that analysis had been worthless. The lab technicians attributed the tainting damage to either a dilute solution of hydrochloric acid or, more likely, to a commercial laundry bleach. With the hole covered over, the forensics team had remained at the property long enough to monitor a concrete delivery, hired to replace the damaged sidewalk.

After studying the report, Gert called Louis Lynch and requested a second interview with him and Abby for later that morning.

The interview took place in the living room of the Ewa house. Seated in a smelly overstuffed chair, Gert decided to pursue a long shot. "Did you ever see anything unusual stored in the shed?"

Lou shook his head. "But I do remember some pickup trucks," he said. "I haven't seen them here lately, though."

After some discussion, he and Abby agreed that the owner had driven the old gray Ford away around four o'clock Friday afternoon, the same day, it turned out, as the hit-and-run. Abby remembered the date and time because they had gone to a party that night. Gert then showed them photographs of both the confiscated truck and Red Murphy, and got a positive ID on both. Placing Red in the truck that night punched a major hole in his alibi.

* * *

Gert often lapsed into serious body sprawl while studying her case notes. Today, with her wooden swivel chair tipped back, she rested her feet on the opened bottom desk drawer. The ringing phone broke her concentration. "Homicide, Lieutenant Mahaila," she barked. "What? You say I'm looking in the wrong place for the body of John Pualoa?" The lieutenant swung her feet to the floor and stiffened to military attention. "Where is it then?... Say, who is this, anyway? You say 'a friend'? What's your name? How do I get in touch with you?...Gertie? Hey, I haven't been called Gertie since high school. Your voice sounds awfully familiar....No! Please don't hang up. Tell me who you are. I can protect you. Can we meet somewhere? How do I know this isn't just a crank call or wild goose chase? We need to talk."

And then it came to Gert. "Wait a minute! Only two of my girlfriends called me Gertie. We need to talk, Cindy Chou. I know it's you. Please don't hang up. Let me buy you a cup of coffee...Great! How about the Columbia Inn—two blocks from the King Street split on Kapiolani. Give me half an hour. Don't disappoint me now."

Gert arrived at the restaurant a few minutes early and chose a booth along the celebrity photo wall.

"Hi, Gertie."

Gert wheeled around.

"I parked in back. Came in the rear door."

The policewoman's eyes scanned her high school friend from head to toe: the sleek black hair, the trim figure in a smart pants suit. Gert glanced down at her own short, muscular body and black oxfords.

Cindy Chou slid hesitantly into the booth. She set her purse on the table and kept her delicate fingers tightly wrapped around it as if she planned to depart within seconds. The two women remained silent, each trying to read the other's expression. Finding nothing revealing there, Gert reached out and touched Cindy's hand. Only then did two melting smiles emerge to break the ice. Gert motioned to the waitress, who responded with two coffees.

"Why haven't you kept in touch?" Gert asked.

"Do you really want to know?" Cindy replied. "After graduation I couldn't find a job. I tried for months, but without skills, experience, or connections, no one wanted me for anything but the menial jobs."

"But you seemed so bright in school. Your grades must have been better than mine. And your family could afford the UH tuition."

"I know, I know, but...You sure you want to hear this? It's not pretty."

Gert nodded. "Between friends."

"My father kicked me out of the house. Called me a tramp when he found out I was sleeping with my boyfriend. So I had no money for college or training. Right after that, the boy dumped me, just when I needed him most. I was too proud to go back home. It would've meant admitting to my father that he'd been right. I suppose you can guess where I wound up next. But you're a police officer. I'm not going to spell it out."

Gert tried to reassure her. "I'm in Homicide, girl—nothing to do with Vice. You don't have to worry about me. However, I am concerned that one bad dude will get away with murder unless you help me nail him."

Cindy eased her white-knuckled grip on her purse and set it on the bench beside her. After taking a sip of black coffee, she said. "There was nothing else left for me, so I turned to the streets and became a successful working woman. My father disowned me, and my mother didn't dare cross him. Fortunately, I've done so well that I haven't used the streets in years. I have a regular clientele of very generous gentlemen and a nice apartment."

"That includes one Red Murphy, I assume."

"Yes, how did you know about him?" Cindy asked.

"As you well know, he's a person of interest in the Pualoa murder case, and I can only guess that he's the reason you called. Tell me about him."

"Red was one of my regulars. He used to pay for whole weekends at a time, very generous, and quite a lover. He even wanted me to be his full-time woman. Offered to set me up in a Waikiki apartment. But he has a temper with a very short fuse. He beat me up badly several months ago. I'd like to see him get what's coming to him."

"Talk to me, Cindy. On the phone you said you think you know where John Pualoa's body is buried. It might just be the break I need in this case."

Cindy's dark eyes glittered at the thought of revenge. "Red took me to the Big Island for a fabulous weekend. We stayed at Volcano House. While we were out walking on the lava fields one evening, we came to a bunch of steam vents. Red became very intrigued with them, almost obsessed, and over one in particular, he made a strange comment."

"What kind of comment?"

"He said something like, 'What a great place to dispose of a body!' That really creeped me out, Gert, and I told him so. He just laughed and said he was kidding. But when I saw the article in the *Advertiser*, I knew you were looking for the man's body. Red might have hidden it there. With the beating he gave me, I'm ready to throw him to the wolves."

"Cindy, do you really believe he's capable of murder?"

"All you gotta see is his temper to know that. He's one crazy man, capable of anything."

"I believe you're right, Cindy, but I still need your help. The Big Island has hundreds of steam vents, and unless you're willing to come there with me, I'm going to have a tough time convincing my boss to launch a general search. If you come along and help us zero in on the specific search area, I think we can swing it. We'll even pay your expenses." She looked Cindy straight in the eye and then smiled. "No, we can't cover your business losses for your time spent over there." Both women laughed, a little less nervously now.

Cindy leaned forward, her stance urgent. "If you put him away, it'll be worth it. That is, if you can guarantee my safety in the meantime."

Gert drained the last of the coffee from her cup. "You know we'll try our damnedest." She left three dollars on the table. "Then it's settled. Pack a few things for overnight, and I'll book us on the six o'clock *Mahalo* flight."

* * *

Later that afternoon, as Gert flipped the last dog-eared page of her notebook, she discovered Officer Fred and Hank standing before her desk.

"What brings the two of you here?" she asked.

"I thought you wanted to see me about something," Hank said with a perplexed look on his face. "I got the message on my answering machine about an hour ago."

"Oh, yeah. The night of the hit-and-run, were you following Murphy?"

"Sure. But I lost him in a garage on King Street. He went into the office building next door, across from the theater, and never came out. I saw him take the elevator to the second floor, but when I got up there, he'd already disappeared."

"Was he alone or was there a young woman with him?"

"He was alone."

"Are you absolutely sure?"

"Absolutely."

333

"Could he have gone to the movie across the street that night?"

"I doubt it. At least, not while I was there. I would have seen him go in. I waited an hour and-a-half for him to come out and then I gave up. Why, Lieutenant? What does it mean?"

"Let me make a couple of phone calls and I think I can explain what happened that night." The first two calls wound up as dead ends, but a call to the Sida Taxi company dispatcher paid off. "A fare was taken to the Ewa address," Gert said. "The fare was picked up on Young Street, and the times match perfectly."

Fred began to reconstruct that fateful night. "Murphy drove the pickup truck from Ewa to the hit-and-run scene and then to the School Street construction site. He must have walked back to his car afterward. By the way, Gert, we just got through talking to Murphy's foreman. After we caught him in a lie trying to cover for his boss, he admitted that the pickup truck appeared at the School Street site that night. He was positive, because he had made deliveries to the site that afternoon and the next morning. Someone left the truck there that night."

Gert thought this one over. "Murphy couldn't have gone straight to the School Street site. He had to stop somewhere to wash and oil down the truck."

"Yeah. And reverse the bumper boards," Fred added.

"That could have been done later," Gert corrected. "Fred, maybe you'd better start checking out car washes around town. Oh, before I forget, we may have another break in the case. We have a witness who overheard Murphy talk about stashing a body in one of the steam vents on the Big Island. We're heading over there late this afternoon to see if there's anything to it."

Hank looked aghast. "Murphy's pretty devious, but I'm kinda skeptical that he'd go that far. How reliable is this witness that you're willing to take off on such lean hope?"

"Very reliable."

"Not his ex-wife, Wilma, is it?" Hank tried again.

"No, just an embittered girlfriend he beat up once too often."

"You mean Cindy Chou?"

"How in hell did you know that name?" gasped Gert.

"You forget, I've been following Murphy for many moons now. There's not much I don't know about him. You should have seen her face after that beating. Her eye was black and swelled out to here."

Hank gestured with the tips of his fingers. "She's a good kid, though. She once helped us break open a blackmail plot. One of Murphy's, I might add. That may have been the reason for the beating. By the way…" He reached into his pocket and pulled out a small scrap of paper that Kekoa had given him. "I have reason to believe that Kekoa knew Cindy's father. Ask her if her father was ever known as Ol' Chou."

"Ol' Chou. I will. I also promised her police protection, so I would appreciate you both keeping all of this under your hat for now."

"Sure, Lieutenant," said Hank. "And good luck on the fishing trip."

Fred left, but Hank lingered at Gert's desk. "Lieutenant, you might want to question the ex. I know she's spent some time in Honolulu during the last two months."

"It's an idea," Gert said, "but he's got a new girlfriend now. She's the one supplying his alibi."

* * *

Red staggered into his kitchen, still wiping sleep from his bleary eyes. He wore a pair of boxer shorts yanked so high above his waist as to make himself indecent.

Lucille sat at the kitchenette table with her legs drawn up and her bare feet perched on the chair. An oversized T-shirt stretched across her knees, not quite covering her rounded bottom. A day-old newspaper was spread across the table. The automatic coffeepot gurgled and belched away on the counter.

Lucille watched Red drag himself about the room looking for a mug. "Your own apartment, and you can never find anything in the cupboards on the first try," she commented.

It had been a late night to start with, and they had shared a lengthy 2 a.m. lovemaking feast. She watched him with a curious look. He gave her a dutiful peck on the cheek as he reached for the pot, which had not yet stopped perking. When he received no response from her, he sensed a newly established distancing between them.

"What's wrong now? Got your damn period or something?"

"No…I don't know. Suppose you tell me what this is all about." Lucille spun the open paper in his direction so he could read it. Red flopped down in the adjacent chair and for the first time read the "Police Beat" item about the investigation at the Ewa house.

"Son-of-a-bitch," he said under his breath. When he finished reading, he looked at her and said, "I didn't know you read this part of the paper."

"Is that all you can say? It so happens I don't just read the funnies, Red." Her sarcasm could have cut a loaf of bread. "I ask you again, what's this all about? Did you kill somebody?"

"Of course not. I don't know anything about this. I didn't even own the place when it happened."

"Did you know the man…Big John Pualoa?"

"Yeah. He was my partner. But I didn't kill him or bury him there, either." He leaned over to kiss her and reassure her. She slammed her feet to the floor, and the chair screeched as it skidded backward on the vinyl tile.

Red's anger rose like steam within him and receded as fast as it came. It might have been her too-short T-shirt, or the realization that he needed her to testify. "Come on, baby, what's wrong? I told you I didn't do anything like that."

She let him kiss her. "Let me fix you some eggs," she said. From the refrigerator she removed the half-empty egg carton and proceeded to fry three, easy-over. While they spittered and splattered, her fussing over him soothed his savagery. When she put the plate of eggs and rice in front of him, he grabbed her about the legs and pulled her to him. She hugged him quickly and planted a big kiss on his forehead. He relaxed his grip long enough for her to slip away.

She grinned at him. "I'll clean up later. Gotta get dressed now. Got the early shift today." She ducked into the bathroom while he ate.

He glanced up from reading the paper when she emerged, fully dressed. Lucille blew a kiss to him at the apartment door. He motioned for her to come closer, but she answered with a few bars of "Tonight, tonight" and slipped smoothly through the door, out of Murphy's reach, and out of his life.

Chapter 47
Snake Eyes and Craps

AN ALMOST palpable tension inhibited any real conversation between Cindy and Gert on the flight to the Big Island. Landing in Hilo at seven-thirty that evening, they settled into modest hotel rooms.

First thing the next morning they checked out an old brown Pontiac from the police inter-island motor pool. The car's air conditioning didn't work, so they drove the thirty miles to Volcanoes National Park with the windows wide open. The air streaming in blew hot and damp at the lower elevations, then cool and dry as the car lumbered up 4,000 feet to the park. At one point along forest-lined Route 11, they drove straight through a small rain cloud.

Flashing her badge at the park's gatehouse, Gert drove to the park police headquarters and waited on the tarmac lot. Minutes later, an unmarked white panel truck pulled up next to them.

"I think these are our people now," said Gert. "Hi," she called as she climbed out. "I'm Lieutenant Mahaila, Honolulu Police. We're supposed to meet a police surveillance team here."

They held out their official identification warrants and climbed down from the truck. "That's us, ma'am. I'm Sergeant Beau Dressler, and this is my technician, Officer Eddie Wailee." With his shoulder-length blond hair and deeply tanned face, Beau fit his name. He took out a map of the park and laid it on the hood of their Pontiac. "So, where do you want us to set up first?"

Gert introduced her companion as Ms. Chou, a material witness in the case. Cindy, in khaki pants and cotton shirt, waited anxiously beside the car. She stepped forward and tried to orient herself on the map, moving her finger in a small circle over the area where she thought the vents were. Shaking her head, she said, "I'll have to get much closer before I can be any more specific."

"Why don't you ride with us?" Beau offered.

He motioned for Eddie to get in back. Beau swung the truck onto Crater Rim Drive, in the direction of the lava fields most heavily populated with cave-like steam vents.

The dormant crater of Halemaumau, legendary home of the goddess Pele, loomed large in the background. Sulfur smoke mixed with steam billowed and curled toward the sky. They parked in a cul-de-sac beside several clustered vents. Some of these had safety railings around gaping holes that exuded white clouds of sulfur vapor.

Cindy stepped out and looked around the area for several minutes before she decided that one of the vents looked more familiar than the others. She tried to visualize all the steps she and Red had taken during their walk more than two months earlier.

"There!" Cindy pointed. "I think that's the one where he said it."

Beau drove off-road to the spot, and the officers removed three sizable steel containers from the truck. The first housed a power supply, which Eddie plugged into the side of the panel truck. He stretched out a set of cables from the power supply to a fourth container, which had been slid to the rear of the truck next to the doors. Removing the protective cover, he turned this unit on its side to reveal a monitor/screen and a panel of complex controls.

"Hey, that looks like a very complicated television set," Cindy commented.

"That's just what it is," said Beau as he restarted the truck's engine and set the manual throttle to rev at a high idle speed. We're going to have us a little peek at what's down there."

At the rear of the truck, Eddie threw some switches and manipulated several controls before yelling to Beau, "Up and running. Let's unpack the rest of the cables."

The men walked over to the unopened containers and unpacked two thirty-foot lengths of cable. The flexible armor covering resembled BX cable used in older household wiring, only these cables were much thicker in diameter and lighter in weight. While Beau spread out the cables, Eddie coupled the two lengths together and attached one end to the control and monitor unit at the rear of the truck.

"Hey, how far down are you guys planning to go?" asked Gert. "Do you really need all that cable?"

"These vents are deep and tricky," Beau answered. "You never know what you're going to run into." He turned to Eddie. "Wanna get the camera?"

Eddie retrieved a felt-lined case from the glove box and removed the miniature camera probe. The business end looked like a pair of round white eyes attached to a long, thin, flexible tube. He connected the probe to the free end of the cable and stretched the remainder out in a straight line.

Eddie moved back to the rear of the truck and sat on a folding chair in front of the control panel while Beau held onto the camera end. All of a sudden, the cable seemed to come alive like a snake ready to hiss and strike. It stiffened as individual sections began to rotate and bend to Eddie's commands. A bright, sharply focused beam emerged from one "eye" at the end of the tube, allowing the probe's other eye, a camera lens, to see. He stood up and proudly introduced his prodigy, Snake Eyes.

Beau dragged Snake Eyes to the first vent and lowered the probe into the vent opening. While the two men communicated via headsets, Eddie manipulated Snake Eyes to search each of three main caverns in this particular vent. The snake squirmed and stretched. It entered and retreated from each nook and cranny, whining and winding its way as it went.

At first, the two women were drawn to the monitor, anxious to be the first to make a discovery. But their untrained eyes couldn't distinguish anything meaningful. Their tension mounting, they retreated to a grassy knoll out of the direct sun. Seeing the visible distress on Cindy's face, Gert drew her into conversation.

"Did you ever try to make contact with your family after you moved out?" They settled cross-legged on the grass away from the men.

"Yes," Cindy answered. "A little over a year after I'd left. I heard that my mother had died, and I wanted to see my father again. He wouldn't let me in the house. He told me he didn't have a daughter any more, that she had shamed herself out of his life. He turned me away at the door."

Gert shook her head. "Did you try to write?"

"I would have—if I thought he'd have read a letter from me. But I'm sure he would have torn it up on sight. I didn't give up. I kept track of him through one of my regulars, a fellow professor and friend of his at the university. I almost felt guilty charging the guy, because I spent most of our time together questioning him. But he said he enjoyed the conversation—it helped to put him more at ease." Cindy lowered her wide-brimmed straw hat over her brow and rubbed the morning chill from her arms before continuing.

"Through my client," she said, "I found out my father had started hitting the bottle heavily and had begun to miss classes. After several unheeded warnings, the university dismissed him. Luckily, they let him keep his pension and some other benefits. You can imagine my surprise when I learned that my father had taken to the streets of Chinatown as one of the homeless; an alcoholic, drinking away his pension checks. He'd lost face—humiliated among his beloved peers."

"But Cindy, you live and work in Chinatown. Didn't you ever run across him there?"

"Well, there were a few times when I saw a pitiful old man who looked something like my father. Whenever I tried to approach him, he'd hurry away and disappear—far too quickly for me to make contact with him." Cindy swallowed hard. "I thought I didn't care, but I still do. Really I do." She fought back the tears, tears she'd vowed never to shed.

Something clicked in Gert's mind, and she played out her intuition. "Was your father ever called Ol' Chou?"

Cindy looked shocked. "Yes! His students used to call him that behind his back. My father always knew about it. But how did you know? Why do you ask?"

"When we get back to Oahu, I want you to meet a young friend of his from the streets."

"I assumed my father would be dead by now. He'd be nearly eighty. You mean my father is still alive?"

"No. No, I'm afraid not. If it is the same Ol' Chou, he passed away several months ago in the arms of his teenage friend. I think this friend has a message for you."

With nothing more to say, the women fell silent and shifted their attention to the experts at work. The men spent about forty minutes more before deciding there was nothing to retrieve at that location.

Eddie approached the knoll and informed the women that they were moving to examine the next vent. This location required them to pull the truck up much farther off the road. He and Beau again put Snake Eyes to work. The sun beat mercilessly down on the black lava until it gleamed. Wavy lines of heat floated skyward.

Cindy's anxiety rose as another hour slipped by. All this manpower and equipment because of her. Had she made a mistake in the location?

Suddenly, Eddie shouted, "Craps! There's something down there. Maybe two, maybe three bundles. There's a good deal of resilience, so it's not rock." The light-emitting tube had a built-in pressure sensor.

Eddie made a few adjustments in contrast and brightness before pushing a small round button on the panel. A printed picture comprising multiple shades of gray slowly emerged from a slot at the bottom of the control panel screen. He handed the printout to Gert. With a heightened sense of excitement, she studied it for several minutes. But then she shook her head. The image contained a myriad of shadow shades—far too little definition for her to comprehend.

"What do we do now?" she asked.

"We try to retrieve whatever's down there," Beau said.

Meanwhile, Eddie had lowered a long, narrow ladder down into the vent and secured the top to the panel truck with wire rope.

Several cars braked to rubberneck the off-road scene. As the tourists climbed out of their vehicles to approach and watch, Gert shouldered responsibility for crowd control. "Stay behind the guard rail, please. It's for your own safety," she replied to their repeated questions. One young woman in cargo pants and hiking boots attempted to duck under the guard rail for a closer look. Gert sighed. There's always one. In a firm voice, she warned, "Stay back, please, this is a police investigation." The disappointed thrill-seekers got back in their cars and drove away.

When Gert turned back to the vent, she saw that Beau had donned a thermal safety suit zipped up to his neck. A helmet covered his blond locks, a clear visor shielded his face, and the apron secured around his waist contained multiple pockets filled with small tools. He descended the ladder out of her sight.

From the bottom of the ladder, Beau jumped two feet to the nearest floor. At this level, the vent took a right angle turn for several feet and then dropped another four feet to the next landing, where the objects they'd seen on the monitor lay. Beau then jammed a tubular flare into a crack in the vent wall and ignited it for additional light in the murky atmosphere. Here he noticed that a section of the wall had recently broken away and dropped to some greater depth.

The two men stayed in closed-circuit, two-way communication.

Eddie sent down a second bag of tools in a lightweight net with a thin line attached to the four corners. Beau took out the tools and extended two telescoping rods with hooks on their ends to their full six-foot length. Holding opposite ends of the net with the hooked rods, he leaned over the edge and spread the net on the same landing as the objects.

Beau recognized the objects as canvas or nylon duffles. He hooked them easily and transferred them to the waiting net. With two of the objects already in the net, he tried to reach the third and last one, which lay much farther away. As soon as he touched it, it slid deeper. He kept trying. On the fourth try, it didn't stop sliding. From the succession of thudding sounds, he determined that it had fallen into a deep abyss, perhaps fifty or more feet below. He swore, knowing they had no equipment to work at that depth.

Beau gathered in the slack from above and below, tugging on the line above, so that Eddie would close the net carefully around its catch and slowly raise it to the surface. Beau attached a small nylon line from his waist kit to the bottom of the net as it passed him; he used it to help guide the objects to the surface. He waited for the net to be lowered for a second trip. This time he packed up all the tools, including the collapsed rods, and sent them to the surface. He then jumped for the highest rung he could reach and climbed up the ladder hand-over-hand.

Beau was impatient to get out of the heavy, hot thermal suit. Peeling the gloves off first, he clawed at the helmet snaps with clumsy fingers. Eddie came to his aid and released the remaining snaps. It took several more minutes to peel the suit off his sweat-drenched shirt and shorts. Beau excused himself and climbed into the rear of the panel truck. A few minutes later, he reappeared in fresh khaki shorts and a clean T-shirt.

"Feel better?" Gert asked.

"You bet—always come prepared."

Eddie, meanwhile, had maneuvered the two retrieved duffle bags onto separate black plastic drop cloths on the ground. It was obvious to him that they were gym bags. He donned a surgical mask and Latex gloves in order to play it safe. Beyond the sulfur dioxide given off by the vents around them, there was hardly any other detectable odor. But there was no need to take chances.

Gert drew close, her right hand clutching and squeezing her red ball.

Cry Ohana

Eddie unzipped the first duffle bag, exposing a dark green trash can liner. He undid a twister tie at the top of it and slowly spread it open.

Gert's heart did a double beat. There lay a mass of mutilated remains covered with reddish dirt and decomposed debris. Eddie looked up at her for instructions. She nodded for him to proceed. Eddie didn't want to disturb anything for the lab boys, so he quickly closed this bag, wrapped it carefully in the thick-gauged drop cloth, and sealed it with tape.

Gert hovered next to him as he turned his attention to the second duffle. Its zipper had been damaged, so Eddie took a surgical knife and cut alongside the zipper. This bag also contained a sealed plastic trash bag. He undid the yellow twister tie and cautiously spread the bag open.

Cindy shrank back, but Gert—looking hard and long—gasped. She threw back her head, raised her clenched fists, and shouted, "Yes!"

There lay a shriveled brown head: a complete, though bashed-in head and a full set of teeth. The larger of the two wounds ran from the forehead down to the nose cavity. A second fissure was apparent just above the left ear. The teeth showed signs of extensive dental work. Forensics would be able to establish a positive ID from the dental records, if from nothing else. The lieutenant, Beau, and Eddie stood for several moments, somberly regarding the remains.

"Great work, boys, a really fine job!" Gert announced. Wheeling about, she strode over to a quite shaken Cindy, who stood leaning on the guard rail for support. Gert placed her hands on Cindy's shoulders. "Hey, Ms. Chou, bravo! We owe the success of this mission to you."

The four of them shook hands all around.

Eddie packed the second bag as carefully as the first and laid both in a fiberglass container. When he had finished, he told Gert, "The container will be on the next plane to Honolulu, maybe on the same plane with you. It'll go straight to Forensics."

"Excellent," she replied.

Beau and Eddie repacked the panel truck and drove back to Park Police headquarters. They dropped the women off at their car. The four of them gabbed for a few minutes, again congratulating each other. Shortly afterward, the panel truck followed Gert and Cindy to the airport, then turned off at the freight entrance.

While waiting for their plane, Gert made a phone call to Hank on Oahu. By the time she returned to Cindy, they could see Beau and Eddie supervising the loading of the fiberglass container into the plane's cargo hold. At one point, Beau turned around to face the passenger gate and waved to faces he could not see but knew were there.

* * *

On the flight back to Oahu, the two women sat side by side without speaking. Not because of tension, but because of a release from it. They had to consciously restrain their buoyant, triumphant moods. Before boarding, Gert had warned Cindy that the mission to the Big Island was classified, absolutely secret for now, not to be discussed with anyone.

Hank and Kekoa met them at the gate in Honolulu. The four made their way to the serve-yourself airport restaurant and found a secluded corner table where they could talk freely. Following introductions, Cindy addressed Kekoa. "I understand that you knew my father."

"Yes, ma'am, I did. He looked after me and took care of me when we both lived in the streets. He was a very smart and kind man. He taught me how to survive. I never could understand why he chose to be down and out. He seemed to know a lot about everything. Some of the homeless guys even called him a philosopher."

"Yes," Cindy said. "He was a smart man in so many ways. And so…" She couldn't finish the sentence. "Did he ever mention me at all?"

Kekoa looked straight into her teary eyes. "Yes, often, but not always by name. He once told me that he had made a great mistake many years before when he disowned his daughter. He said he made another mistake when he turned her away again a year later. He talked of you with great affection, especially when he felt depressed." Kekoa lowered his eyes and fiddled with his fork as he gathered his recollections.

"He repeated one particular saying a lot of times. I'm not sure I've got it word for word. It went something like this: 'There's no sin so great that…a child of one's own flesh and blood isn't worth any amount of pain to keep close and hold dear.' It may be some kind of poem. I hope I got it right. He wanted to live his life over again to tell you that he forgave you and loved you."

"Were you there when he died?" Cindy asked.

"Yes, but I'm not sure whether he had come looking for me or if it was by accident. I found him dying in the alley behind the bakery where I live and work now. I hope the police gave him a decent burial. Before he died, he gave me your name on this slip of paper and this medallion. He told me to be sure to give it to you if I ever found you." Kekoa passed the medallion across the table to Cindy.

She turned it over several times, but remained visibly puzzled. "This belonged to my mother. She wore it around her neck on a chain. She never left the house without it. She had a long pretty neck. She was so quiet, so kind—and so dutiful a wife to him." Cindy paused. "Better than he deserved." She dabbed at her eyes with a tissue. "I don't understand. Why this? Why now?"

"Does it open?" Hank asked.

"Not that I know of. I've never seen it open. I always thought of it as something sentimental from my grandmother in Sandouping, China. Until now, I never realized that it's made of gold and actually very pretty. Oh, God, Gertie, I loved that poor old woman so much, and I didn't know how to tell her."

Gert took the medallion from her, shook it, and began to examine the edges when she heard a faint click.

"Here! There's a catch."

The large medallion snapped opened wide, like a locket. Gert returned it to Cindy. A small flat key fell into her hand—the key to a safe deposit box. Fitted into the left side of the medallion was a picture of Cindy's parents. Tucked neatly in the right side was a tiny scrap of paper cut in a circle with scribbled handwriting: Central Asian Bank, Box #6-62130-5545. She turned the scrap of paper over and found more handwriting: "My Cindy, My Dearest."

Cindy stood and walked around the table to where Kekoa sat. "I want to hug one incredible young man. If he doesn't mind," she added.

"Yes, ma'am! I mean…no, ma'am."

Cindy burst out laughing. "Call me Cindy. Please!"

Her hearty hug defused his fear. He'd been so scared of actually meeting Ol' Chou's daughter. "Okay, Cindy," he grinned.

Chapter 48
Condemnation

THE LONG GREEN box lay on the small counter in front of Cindy and Gert. The numbered key from Ol' Chou's medallion had brought them to the Central Asian Bank. They were squeezed into two straight-backed chairs in the cramped privacy room next to the vault. Cindy's fingers were poised to open the box. Gaining access to it had taken some doing. Even with Gert's connections, the estate probate panel had dallied almost two weeks before issuing the necessary access order. Eventually, Cindy was named Chou's only rightful survivor and heir.

Running her trembling fingers along the cold steel, Cindy lifted the cover. A tan business envelope lay on top. She unsealed it and pulled out two sheets of yellowing stationery. At first she scanned the neatly scripted lines in silence. Then she chose to read the letter aloud.

My dear dear Cindy,
I should never have thought the day would come when I must ask your humble forgiveness. That day has come, but I cannot reach you to tell you that what I have done was wrong. You are and always will be my daughter. It is I, not you, who is so full of shame. I turned you out of my life because of my own self-righteousness.
You merely followed your heart and not your head. You are more than flesh and blood of my loins, you are the proof of my having ever lived. All that I was denied in my life was to be yours. I wanted to be the instrument of your success.
All love left me when your mother passed away and you were not there. I began to realize there was nothing you could do that was so bad, so terrible as to warrant my disowning you. I found that I was punishing myself, denying this poor soul the endless joys and perquisites of fatherhood.
Although your mother never disobeyed my wishes, we drifted apart because of my anger. Perhaps losing you even hastened her untimely demise. You need never have to forgive her, for the guilt was never hers. It was always mine. She died lonely, having loved you most dearly. . . .

Cindy's voice faltered as the tears flowed down her cheeks.

"Want me to finish reading?" asked Gert.

"No, I'll do it."

I cannot make excuses for the mess that I have made of my life. The demon in the bottle has taken hold of my whole being. I guess it's always been there, but once, long ago, I had the strength to resist. At this moment I am sober of body and mind. It is a rare occasion, and I must take advantage of my last noble resolve while it endures. I realize there is little I can do to make up for the pain I have caused you, but please, please let me try in some small way.

First, I know that if I do not set aside my savings, pension, and retirement accounts, they will become another bottle to consume. I have placed these in an irrevocable trust in your name. I know you will use this trust wisely. Second, the medallion belonged to your mother, along with some other jewelry that you will find at the bottom of this box. It's yours. Third, go on with your life, knowing that you have the utmost love and support of both your parents in any path that you choose.

Your most humble father,

Li Tien Chou

As Cindy finished, she broke into a loud choking sob. The tears flowed so spontaneously and strangely that she found herself frightened by them. She turned to Gert, and the two women hugged for a long time.

"I don't know if I can forgive him. I want to. I need to," Cindy murmured. "It's all I have left now."

"Maybe just time will help," Gert said as she checked her watch. "Speaking of time, we have thirty-five minutes to get back to the courthouse."

* * *

The grand jury convened on a Tuesday, a week after the Forensics people completed their meticulous analysis. They had identified Big John Pualoa's remains from his dental work. The grand jury testimony by Kekoa, Cindy, and Hank had built a strong case against Murphy. Testimony from the younger Lynch and his girlfriend tore gaping holes in Red's alibi. A subpoena for Lucille Kioni went unanswered. But Red's ex-wife, Wilma Minnet, had shown up as a surprise voluntary witness. Grammy accompanied her for moral support.

Today there would be a hearing to read the grand jury findings.

* * *

Red Murphy's bail had been revoked two weeks ago, the day Big John's remains were found. Beetle Bailey had argued before the judge with all the appropriate phrases: "Mr. Murphy's ties to the community" and "a complex business to run." But the judge still denied bail. Today, lawyer and client anxiously awaited the grand jury's disposition. Things had not gone well for Red. A mountain of evidence had been presented against him. To make matters worse, his alibi now held about as much water as a sieve.

Red shifted restlessly on the wooden bench in his holding cell and occasionally rose to check the clock in the corridor. It was already past noon, and he wondered when they'd come and take him upstairs. For the third time in two weeks, he had been taken from his cell at the county jail and brought to one of the courthouse holding cells. Beetle had Rosie bring fresh clothes from Red's apartment each day. This afternoon, on Beetle's advice, he wore his gray slacks, a white shirt, navy jacket, and tie for the grand jury proceedings.

The holding cell was a considerable improvement over the accommodations at the jail. There, despite air conditioning and dehumidifiers chugging away, the cells could not be freed of their inevitable dampness and stale gymnasium-like smell. It crept into his bones, and the taste of steel sat on his teeth.

Down the hall from the holding cell, a buzzer sounded, followed by a loud click as the security office door opened. Steve Obana, a sullen guard just beginning his shift, stepped out and approached the property cage attendant across the corridor with his usual sarcastic greeting.

"Finish another comic book yet, Kurt?"

"Stuff it, man!"

"They're calling for the prisoner now," Steve announced.

Kurt pressed the lock release to the cell block, allowing Steve to pass through to Red's cell at the end of the corridor.

Red hadn't seen a guard since before lunch, just that evil-eyed video camera staring down at him from outside the cell. The other cells were empty, and that was fine with him. He wasn't in any mood to talk story.

It was two in the afternoon when the guard finally came for him. The air crackled with mutual dislike. Steve regarded Red as a wise guy who needed to be prodded. Just for effect, he liked slamming his nightstick down on the steel bars, a table, a chair, or anything else in sight. It got Red's attention in a hurry.

But Red was never long on fear of any individual. He sensed that Steve had a sadistic streak; he could act civilly, but seemed more comfortable playing the bully. At odds with his mean temperament was his too-tight uniform, which made him appear fat and sloppy. The shirt buttons pulled pleadingly at their threads.

Red's main apprehension lay ahead of him. The grand jury proceedings had gone badly, but just how badly he couldn't imagine.

Steve shoved and prodded him down the corridor past the property cage to the key-operated elevator that serviced the courtrooms above. Red saw locked doors along the basement corridor, but had no knowledge of where they went. He knew he'd been brought in through the door at the far end. The elevator opened and carried the two men to the floor above.

The elevator stopped and Steve pushed him roughly into a very short hall. The door to Courtroom One appeared on the right; Courtroom Two on the left.

As soon as Red entered Courtroom Two, he felt the accusing weight of everyone's eyes. Steve gripped his upper arm with unnecessary force and guided him across the black and white marble floor to the defense table. Beetle motioned for Red to sit next to him. In the wooden armchair, Red cranked his head and shoulders to the left until he could see most of the visitors' gallery situated behind the railing.

Red's eyes landed on the third row and a shudder went through his brawny body. Between a Japanese couple he saw the instrument of his downfall: the brat kid. In the second row, just in front of Kekoa, sat the elder Fujita, his secretary, and Hank Pualoa. As Red scanned the center aisle, he saw Cindy Chou in the same row as that bitch Homicide lieutenant and that cop from Traffic. In disbelief, his stare locked onto Wilma's. How could she, too, have turned on him? And he thought he saw Paul Wong and Leilani.

The judge's gavel struck. As Red turned to face front, he noticed Terumi Fujita take his seat next to the Assistant District Attorney at the prosecutor's table.

"That dirty double-dealing bastard," he said half-aloud.

"Shhhhhh!" exclaimed Beetle. "The judge is ready."

Judge Virginia Hironaka had snow-white hair and rimless glasses. She looked petite seated in the tall leather chair behind the massive koa dais, flanked by the federal and state flags. "Will the defendant please rise?"

Beetle struggled to his feet to stand beside Red. Judge Hironaka read the indictment slowly, first outlining and then detailing every aspect of each count. Red stood rigid, fear mounting as he listened to the detailed condemnation. Excited murmurs rippled through the gallery.

Seated again, Red looked pleadingly at Beetle, who merely shook his head and whispered, "We'll make them prove every word of it, but we'll need a lot of help as well."

"What can we do now?" Red demanded. Beetle merely shrugged as the courtroom quieted and they heard the judge's voice.

"Sufficient evidence has been presented for the grand jury to return a unanimous decision to bind the prisoner over for trial by a jury of his peers. The trial is to be scheduled at the earliest possible date." The sound of the gavel rocked the courtroom. "Are there any motions at this time?"

"Bail, Your Honor?" Beetle tried again.

"Bail denied!"

Beetle attempted several other motions. Each one was denied. Judge Hironaka's gavel came down a final time. "Court is adjourned." She rose and exited through the door leading to her chambers.

As a sneering Steve stood to take him away, Red turned to his lawyer.

Beetle replied, "There's nothing I can do for you here and now. You must go back to jail while I work on your case."

Steve guided the prisoner to the same key-operated elevator, and they descended to the lockup area in the basement. This time they made a stop at the property cage. Kurt handed Red an iridescent orange jumpsuit with the letter P stenciled on the front and back in white. Steve then escorted Red back to his cell, left the cell door open, and instructed him to change into the jumpsuit and slippers.

"Don't try anything, Murphy, I'm waiting right outside the cell. You're headed for the jail compound until trial time."

A few minutes later, a humiliated Red Murphy emerged from his cell in the jump suit. At the property cage, the upper half of the door stood open. A wide counter was affixed to the top of the door's lower half. Red handed his pile of folded street clothes across the counter to

Kurt.

While Kurt was making out a receipt for the clothes, Red's wary gaze swept over the property room. He noticed a basket, well out of his reach, containing individual sets of handcuffs and keys in clear plastic envelopes. Steve ordered him to stand on a white line about two feet in front of the window and lean forward with his forearms on the counter. Kurt, inside the cage, placed a set of handcuffs on Red's wrists while Steve body-searched him once more from head to toe. Kurt laid the handcuff key on the counter for Steve to pick up when he was through with his search.

Kurt then turned his back to place Red's street clothes in a bin along the wall. And in that brief moment, Red noticed a second, similar key wedged as a bookmark in the log book in front of him. A light bulb lit up his brain. It was only a flash of an idea, one that required deftness and timing, but he had no intention of going back to jail.

"You can stand up now," the guard said.

With his elbows still resting on the counter and his wrists cuffed, Red managed to slide the flat key out of the log book. Suddenly, he appeared to trip over his size 13 shoes. "Aaah!" he bellowed. As he faked his loss of balance, he stumbled toward the right edge of the counter—long enough to palm the real handcuff key and replace it with the key from the log book.

"Hey, dog meat, ya had a bunch of beers or somethin'? Get a hold of yourself!" Steve growled. But neither he nor Kurt saw the sleight-of-hand.

"Hey, dog meat, hear what I said? Stand up straight."

"You think that's easy, with these goddamn things on?" Red snapped.

Steve reached around Red's bulk and picked up from the counter what he believed to be the key to Red's handcuffs.

Kurt, impatient to get back to his comic book, didn't miss the key from his log book.

The buzzer sounded across the hall and ended with the usual loud click that released the security office door. An officer came out and said, "I'll move the car to the prisoner transport door. I'll knock twice when I'm ready for you to open. Okay?"

"Yeah," said Steve. "I'm just waiting for the paperwork now." They stood there until Kurt handed Steve a large brown envelope with black stripes across it. Kurt sat down and picked up his comic book, while Steve gave Red a major jab with his nightstick to push-start him down the corridor. Red shuffled along and deliberately stumbled a second time. With his hands cuffed in front of him and that pushy bastard of a guard walking behind him, Red had only a few precious seconds to work on the handcuff lock with the key he'd palmed.

At the end of the corridor they waited for the transport officer to knock. By this time, Red had freed his wrists from the cuffs. Now they were no longer a restraint—but a weapon.

Steve moved in front of Red and fiddled with his own set of courthouse keys, anticipating the signal of two knocks. Red made his move. He started low and swung the cuffs up at the back of Steve's head. As the dazed guard turned to face his prisoner, Red swung the cuffs again, this time smashing the guard on the left side of his forehead. The bully Steve melted like a pat of butter and puddled to the floor. Red kicked him in the head for good measure.

Dragging Steve behind a vending machine, out of peripheral view of both Kurt and the surveillance cameras, Red ripped open his prison jumpsuit and peeled it off. So far so good. But getting the uniform off the guard's pudgy body took longer than he expected. Buttons, shoes, belt, and the equipment attached to the belt—all of it slowed him down. He yanked off the shirt and pants, struggled into them, and discovered they didn't fit too badly. He took a moment to survey himself. Yeah, he'd pass. He couldn't put on the shoes, though; they were about two sizes too small.

Red threw a final glance at the unconscious guard, a heap of blubber in his underwear. Next he retrieved Steve's keys and removed his gun from its holster. With the gun tucked into his own belt, Red selected a likely key and reached to insert it in the outside door lock. Two loud thumps on the door startled him: the other uniformed officer was outside knocking, ready to transport him. Red had to avoid a confrontation at all costs. The property room officer had gone to the rear of the cage, so he'd take his chances upstairs. Forcing himself to stride down the corridor at a normal pace, Red fiddled with the guard's keys and located the tubular one for the elevator. He stepped in, rode up to the first floor, and entered the now-deserted Courtroom Two. Tearing around the gallery railing and jury box, he pushed through the bronze doors at the rear.

Cry Ohana

The moment he entered the main corridor, a voice shouted: "Freeze! Stop right where you are!"

Chapter 49
Freedom's Price

MINUTES EARLIER, Hank Puola stepped through the court-house doors into the afternoon sunlight. As he walked along the portico, a voice behind him called out, "Oh, Dr. Friend? We meet again."

Hank spun about and found himself facing Grammy Minnet in her motorized wheelchair.

"Aren't you the university professor who interviewed me in L.A.?" she asked.

Hank had a feeling she already knew the answer. "It's Hank Pua-loa, Grammy," he confessed.

"Yes, yes, I know," she answered. "Wilma explained who you were."

"I'm sorry for the subterfuge, but I didn't think you'd give me the information any other way. It seemed so necessary at the time."

"I really do understand, Mr. Pualoa. If I didn't, I wouldn't be here. Edgar had to be stopped. But Wilma turned out to be such a wimp. I had to browbeat my own granddaughter into coming here to testify. She wouldn't have come here without me, you know."

"And where is Wilma now?" he asked.

"She's gone to get the rental car. I just found myself a mite bit of shade out here while I wait for her." Grammy looked up at him with a winsome smile.

"We're sure glad you came. If you wouldn't mind my return-ing a favor..." Hank leaned over and planted an affectionate kiss on her cheek.

"Oh, my," she exclaimed, blushing. "I don't get too many of those anymore."

"Bless you, Grammy." He winked at her and walked down the steps to his family.

* * *

354

Cry Ohana

"Freeze!"

Red had just burst into the main corridor from Courtroom Two. He wheeled toward the harsh voice.

"I said, Freeze! Keep your hands where I can see them."

It was the transport officer who'd been denied access to the basement door. He had outraced Red to the main corridor by using a side entrance. Forty feet from Red, the officer trained a 9-mm weapon directly at him. Two hands gripped the gun at arm's length for a clean shot.

Red froze. Steve's borrowed baggy trousers began to slip down over his right hip from the weight of the stolen gun stuck in his waistband. The weapon was close to his right hand. He pondered his chances of getting off the first shot.

Suddenly, one of the bronze outer doors swung open, and a couple in their mid-twenties burst in—holding hands and unaware that they had stepped directly into the line of fire. The young man spotted the guard's uniform on Red and eagerly approached him.

"Officer, we're looking for the marriage license bureau."

"Of course, sir," Red replied in his most amiable voice. He pointed in the direction of the transport officer, then ducked behind the couple.

As they blithely started toward the other end of the corridor, the young woman saw the transport officer's gun aimed straight at her. She attempted to scream, but could only manage a whimper. Her protective fiancé moved in front of her. The officer lowered his weapon and motioned frantically for them to move aside. They froze instead.

Taking advantage of this bit of luck, Red palmed his stolen gun, yanked up the loose trousers, and dashed out the bronze door. Outside, he hid behind one of six massive white columns that decorated the courthouse facade. From there he assessed his options. Five marble steps and a handicap ramp on the right led to the patio surrounding a fountain. He saw individuals who had attended his hearing still milling about the patio.

Red hesitated, realizing that many of the courtroom crowd could easily identify him. Glancing down at the stolen gun in his hand, he knew it was his only ticket to freedom. He patted his trouser pockets and found that he had both Steve's wallet and change. Now, if he could only make it to the street and a few blocks more to a cab.

Red's breath shortened. His chest tightened. Caution made him decide on the handicap ramp—fewer people there. He pulled the cop's peaked cap down to cover his hair, tucked in his chin, and edged toward the ramp. One step away from it, the sound of a whirring motor rose behind him. He started to turn, but Grammy's speeding wheelchair slammed into the back of his thighs. Impact drove him forward. He landed at the bottom of the ramp, arms spread-eagled. The gun jarred loose and slid out of reach. His cap flew off, revealing bushy red hair.

"You evil, sadistic, woman-beating son-of-a-bitch," Grammy screamed. Momentum had carried her chair down the ramp, but she managed to brake before running into Red a second time.

Red heard her raspy voice, but paid no attention to the words. The gun! He had to get to the gun! The escapee scrambled to his feet and raced toward the weapon.

Now the crowd paid attention.

Kekoa saw him first and yelled, "It's Red! He's loose!"

"He's got a guard's uniform on!" cried another voice.

Hank, taking two long strides, dove toward the gun and landed on his stomach. He reached out and gripped the gun's barrel. But Red, already on his feet, stomped down on his ex-partner's fingers. The intense pain of crunched knuckles forced Hank to let go. Red stooped over and picked up the gun, brandishing it in an arc over his head. Frightened onlookers screamed and scattered.

A shot ricocheted off the courthouse stonework just behind Red. It came from the transport officer, who hadn't given up his pursuit. Red fired back, and the officer crumpled to the steps. He lay motionless. A hush of fear blanketed the crowd.

Red looked around for a hostage. He saw Gert move forward with her service revolver drawn. But Cindy Chou, trying to duck for cover at the fountain, stumbled into Gert's line of fire.

Red grabbed Cindy from behind and maneuvered her between him and the charging police lieutenant. He put the gun barrel to the nape of Cindy's neck. Wrapping his free arm around her waist, he pulled her toward him while backing away in the direction of the street.

Gert saw Red's eyes fixed on her weapon. "Put the gun down," she commanded. "You're only making matters worse. Give it up! For God's sake, man, give it up!"

"Even God can't help me now, bitch," Red roared. "What's one more murder to a killer like me, eh? You throw your own gun down. I'll kill 'er if you don't."

Cindy moaned and her eyes rolled upward, but she didn't faint. At first she refused to walk, but Red pushed the gun deeper and harder into her neck, and she became pliable. He dragged her across the sidewalk to the curb. Cars whizzed by. He watched the street out of the corner of his eye.

Hank rubbed his throbbing fingers and pulled himself to his feet, ducking behind the large stone fountain and its spray for cover. Choosing his moment, he hunched his shoulders, bent his lanky frame forward, and crept through the terrified crowd to crouch behind a Chinese fan palm in a huge stone pot only a few feet from Red. Hank hadn't the slightest idea of what he should do next. He could only wait for an opportunity to do something.

A late-model white sedan pulled curbside. The driver hopped out and left the motor running. Wilma Minnet darted around the back of the car and started up the walk. She'd come for Grammy, oblivious to the commotion on the patio.

"Willy," Red called to her. "Get back to the car. I need your help. I'm sorry about everything. I'll make it all up to you."

Wilma spun around. A look of horror crossed her face. "Not on your life, you brutal bastard," she screamed. "You've beaten on me for the last time, Edgar Murphy. I hope you go straight to hell!"

Red tightened his grip around Cindy's chest. Still holding her as a shield, he pointed the gun at Wilma.

"Nooo!" panicked Gert as she lunged forward.

Red trained the gun clumsily at Gert and fired. The loud retort echoed in the enclosed stonework of the U-shaped building. The shot went wild. He fired again. The shoulder of Gert's white blouse bloomed red. The bullet's momentum spun her to the right and dropped her to her knees. She fell forward, helpless to return fire. Her revolver slid from her hand and came to rest a few feet away.

Red's steely eyes searched for Wilma, but she had disappeared. He yanked Cindy toward the driver's side of the sedan. Opening the door with his free hand, he tried to push her inside. Forced to keep his eyes on the crowd, his attention to his hostage momentarily flagged.

Without warning, Cindy stiffened against his shove. She gathered up every last ounce of courage, and with all her amassed adrenaline, stomped down on Red's instep with her three-inch spiked heel. This high-fashion weapon penetrated the soft prison shoe and lodged firmly in the flesh between bone and muscle. The spiked heel tore free from Cindy's shoe. Red howled and wrenched away with her heel still impaled in his foot. In a reflex reaction to the pain, Murphy released a bullet wildly into nowhere. He staggered backward.

Taking courage from wounding Red, Cindy dove into the driver's seat of Wilma's car and flung herself toward the passenger side door. She reached for the handle and yanked hard. The passenger door flew open. She was about to slide out to escape when she heard a sinister click and Red's bass voice:

"You're dead meat!" He pointed the gun through the driver's side window directly at her.

Hank took advantage of Red's distraction with Cindy and crept up behind him. With both fists, he slammed Red's head down on the car roof, spun him around, and threw an uppercut straight at his jaw. Murphy groaned. His arms dropped to his side. He staggered backward, absorbing the blow, and then charged at Hank with renewed vengeance. Hank took a dangerous chance. He grabbed the forearm propelling the gun leveled at him and spun Red against the car. The car door banged shut. Hank repeatedly slammed the gun hand, knuckles down, on the door handle until the 9-mm clattered to the street. Hank beat his opponent about the face with a series of punishing blows, driving Red to his knees.

Hank thought he had won. But Red, shaking off the latest attack, spied the gun lying in the road and tried to pick it up just as Hank managed to get his hand on it. The two men wrestled for control of it across the car's hood, rolled over the grillwork, and dropped to the pavement.

The impact to Hank's back was too much. His grip on the gun slackened, and Red wielded the weapon to pistol-whip his ex-partner. Hank's hands deflected most of the blows, but exhaustion soon took its toll.

Suddenly, a wiry young body appeared out of the crowd. "Get off him! You hit my father once more and I'll kill you." Kekoa had commandeered Gert's loose gun to come to his father's aid. Gert had already released the safety, but the boy didn't know about that. He knelt on the sidewalk, sighted his prey at point blank range, and steadied the police special with both hands.

Red held the stolen gun on Hank as he rose to his feet. Keeping it on his target, he reached down with his free hand and, wincing with pain, pulled the spike heel from his foot. As he slowly straightened up, he trained the gun away from Hank and toward Kekoa.

Kekoa fired first. The bullet to the abdomen lifted Red off his feet, throwing him backward. Red's eyes grew to owl size and blood filled his cheeks to a chipmunk shape. He staggered again—backward into the path of an oncoming city bus. The massive machine, with its colorful "TheBus" logo, plowed him off his feet. Shrill, crunching brakes replaced the engine's roar.

The thudding collision threw Red fifteen feet, rolling him for another six feet until the back of his head struck the curb. His eyes stared strangely upward. Into nothingness. Into death.

Near the courthouse fountain, Gert lay bleeding with her head on Terumi's lap. He held a clean handkerchief tightly to her wounded shoulder. Yosh knelt down beside her. He took the radio from her belt, depressed the mike button, and held it up close for Gert.

"Lieutenant Mahaila here. Emergency! Firefight at criminal courthouse…Officers down."

"Backup and emergency medics responding," the speaker crackled back.

Behind them, on the courthouse steps, a young man came out of the crowd and covered the dead transport officer's body with his suit jacket.

Grammy's wheelchair sat at the bottom of the handicap ramp. Her eyes were shut, and blood trickled down her arm. Red's random shot had found her. Grammy's silver-white head lay limp to one side, a grimace distorting her withered face.

Wilma, accepting the worst, knelt and buried her face in Grammy's lap. She wept in sorrow and gratitude. Then Wilma felt a hand slowly stroking her hair and she looked up. Grammy's head had straightened, and there was a bit of a smile on her face. She was trying to say something, and Wilma put her ear closer to Grammy's lips.

"Take more than a mere bullet to kill this tough old broad," she said. "It's nothing, dear. Just a flesh wound."

Sure enough, when Wilma pulled the blanket away and pulled Grammy's blouse up, she could see that the bullet had grazed her, hardly breaking the skin at all. The bleeding had already slowed. The two women embraced while they waited for assistance.

Curbside, in front of the parked rental car, Hank sat in the street. Red's gun barrel had left a gash over his right eye and several red welts on his left cheek. Bolts of fire streamed down his bruised back, and his knuckles hurt. None of this mattered. He locked his arms around Kekoa in a tight embrace. Hank felt the boy's pain worse than his own as his son's body heaved with sobs.

"I killed him, Dad. I had to. I didn't want to lose you again. But Dad...I killed a human being!"

Hank kissed his son's forehead and squeezed him harder. "I owe my life to you, son. You did a brave thing. He would have killed us both. Yes, you killed him, but it needed to be done. A human being? He hasn't been human for years. You killed a monster back there."

Lori and Leilani knelt on either side of them. Leilani reached for her brother and bear-hugged his trembling body.

"I'm proud of you, little brother."

Lori tenderly helped Hank to his feet, scolding him for his heroics.

He stopped her. "I didn't go through all this trouble to bring the family together again just to have it all slip away. No, ma'am! Besides, I'm hoping some day you're going to be a Pualoa, too."

She couldn't argue with that.

It began to rain. At first just a sprinkle, then a downpour. The gutter lining the street filled rapidly with rain water. It ran right through the shallow red pools where Red's body lay, toward the storm drain a few feet away. It ran red to pink to pale, and soon it ran clear, a purification of sorts.

As abruptly as the rain had begun, it stopped. Sunlight burst through the clouds, and a fresh rainbow reached out across the mountains.

* * *

One week later, the Pualoa family laid Big John's remains to rest beside the graves of Malia and Eme, where he would now be at peace. The next day, the family assembled at Magic Island with a cluster of friends. They walked up the path that circled the lagoon to stand on the high wall overlooking the ocean. The world around them went about its business. Surfers caught waves. A loaded container ship headed for

360

Cry Ohana

Molokai. High school kids paddled their outriggers. But those gathered on the wall had their own precious mission. Today Hank led them in a memorial service for Big John—big in body, mind, and heart.

END

Also by Rosemary & Larry

The Dan and Rivka Sherman Mystery Series (#1)

Death Goes Postal—Rare 15th-century type-setting artifacts journey through time, leaving a horrifying imprint in their wake. Dan and Rivka risk life and limb to locate the treasures and un-mask the murderer. Not quite what they expected when they bought The Olde Victorian Bookstore.

Available on Amazon.com, Kindle, and Nook.

The Paco and Molly Mystery Series

Locks and Cream Cheese—In scandal-ridden Black Rain Corners, a Chesapeake Bay mansion harbors locked rooms and deadly secrets. A wily detective and a gourmet cook tackle the case.

Hot Grudge Sunday—Bank robbers and conspirators derail the sleuths' blissful honeymoon at the Grand Canyon. Can our sleuths nail the suspects after they themselves become targets?

Boston Scream Pie—A teenage girl's nightmare triggers a sinister tale of twins, two warring families, and a blonde bombshell who hates being called "Mom."

Available on Amazon.com, Kindle, and Nook.

Also by Rosemary

Miriam's World and Mine—Miriam
Luby Wolfe, a junior at Syracuse U., spent
her fall semester in London exploring her
talents: singing, dancing, acting, and writing. But she never made it home. A terrorist
bomb destroyed her plane over Lockerbie,
Scotland. Learn about Miriam, the Pan Am
families, the bombers, and the political fall-
out.

***Love! Laugh! Panic! Life with My
Mother***—Don't we all have mixed emotions about our mothers? But how many of
us have a mother like Rosemary's—multi-
talented, yet super-tough to live with? Luby
Pollack was a widely published journalist
and popular book author, both heroine and
villain to her ornery daughter.

Available on Amazon.com, Kindle, and Nook.

Photograph by Craig Herndon

Rosemary and Larry Mild coauthor mysteries and thrillers. Their latest wickedly entertaining short stories appear in new anthologies: *Mystery in Paradise: 13 Tales of Suspense* and *Chesapeake Crimes: Homicidal Holidays*. Their eight "soft-boiled detective" short stories have appeared on line in *Mysterical-E*. The Milds recently waved goodbye to Severna Park, Maryland, and moved to Honolulu, Hawaii, where they cherish time with their children and grandchildren.

E-mail the Milds at: <u>roselarry@magicile.com</u>

Visit them at: <u>www.magicile.com</u>

CPSIA information can be obtained
at www.ICGtesting.com
Printed in the USA
FSOW01n0324021117
40473FS